C. J. Cooke is an acclaimed award-winning poet, novelist and academic with numerous other publications under the name of Carolyn Jess-Cooke. Born in Belfast, she has a PhD in Literature from Queen's University, Belfast, and is currently Lecturer in Creative Writing at the University of Glasgow, where she researches creative writing interventions for mental health. *I Know My Name* was C. J. Cooke's first psychological drama, and was inspired by her creative work in mental health. It is being published in several other languages, and a TV adaptation is in development. She lives by the sea with her family.

You can discover more about the author at carolynjesscooke.com

Twitter: @CJessCooke

THE BLAME GAME

Helen and Michael Pengilly are on a dream holiday in Central America with their children, Reuben and Saskia. But a sinister stranger is watching them — and on their way to the airport, a horrific accident devastates the family, leaving Saskia fighting for her life. Terrified as she recovers in hospital, Helen's memory is dragged back to a decades-old tragedy, while other pieces of the fugitive life she and Michael have lived for so long start to fall into place. A slashed car tyre. The night Helen was followed home in Kent. Silent phone calls at 3 a.m. Two bouts of severe food poisoning. To protect their family, Helen and Michael both said they would forget what happened. But there's someone who will stop at nothing to make them remember . . .

Books by C. J. Cooke
Published by Ulverscroft:

I KNOW MY NAME

C. J. COOKE

THE BLAME GAME

Complete and Unabridged

CHARNWOOD
Leicester

First published in Great Britain in 2019 by
HarperCollins*Publishers*
London

First Charnwood Edition
published 2020
by arrangement with
HarperCollins*Publishers*
London

A catalogue record for this book is available from the British Library.

ISBN 978–1–4448–4386–6

Published by
F. A. Thorpe (Publishing)
Anstey, Leicestershire

Set by Words & Graphics Ltd.
Anstey, Leicestershire
Printed and bound in Great Britain by
T. J. International Ltd., Padstow, Cornwall

This book is printed on acid-free paper

for Willow

But I know human nature, my friend, and I tell you that, suddenly confronted with the possibility of being tried for murder, the most innocent person will lose his head and do the most absurd things.

Agatha Christie, *Murder on the Orient Express*

K. Haden
Haden, Morris & Laurence Law Practice
4 Martin Place
London, EN9 1AS

25th June 2006

Michael King
101 Oxford Lane
Cardiff
CF10 1FY

Sir,
We write again regarding the death of Luke Aucoin. The time to meet about this tragedy is long overdue. Please do not delay in writing to us at the above address to arrange a meeting.

Sincerely,
K. Haden

K. Haden
Haden, Morris & Laurence Law Practice
4 Martin Place
London, EN9 1AS

25th June 2010

Michael King
101 Oxford Lane
Cardiff
CF10 1FY

Sir,
We write again on behalf of our clients regarding the death of Luke Aucoin. We request that you contact us immediately to avoid further consequences.

Sincerely,
K. Haden

28th January 2017

MURDERER

PART ONE

1

Helen

30th August 2017

I think I might be dead.

The scene in front of me looks like sea fret creeping over wasteland, closing in like a fist. A smell, too — sewage and sweat. There's a flickering light, like someone bringing a torch towards the mist, and it grows so bright that I realise it's my eyelids beginning to creak open, like two slabs of concrete breaking apart. *Wake up*! I shout in my head. *Wake up!*

Painful brightness. I can make out a ceiling with yellow stains and broken plasterboard, and a ceiling fan that spins limply. I try to lift my head. It takes enormous effort just to raise it an inch, as though an anvil is strapped to it. Where am I? My denim shorts and T-shirt are torn and caked in mud. I'm on a bed wearing one sandal. My other foot is twice its normal size, the blue nail polish that Saskia applied to my toes peeking through dried blood. I wiggle my toes, then my fingers.

I can feel my limbs. Good.

A nurse is busy replacing something at the foot of the bed. A urine drainage bag. A sharp tug at my side alerts me to the fact that the bag belongs to me.

'Excuse me?' I say. My voice is hoarse, no more than a croak.

The foreign chatter elsewhere in the room makes me think that the nurse might not speak English.

'Sorry, but . . . ? Excuse me? Can you tell me why I'm here?'

Even now, when I've no clue where I am or why, I'm apologising. Michael always said I apologise too much. I apologised all the way through both labours for screaming the place down.

A man arrives and consults with the nurse, both of them giving me worried looks as I try to sit up. He's a doctor in plain clothes: a black polo shirt and jeans, a stethoscope and lanyard announcing his purpose. To my left is a window with a ripped insect net, and for some reason I want to go to it. I need to find something, or someone. 'You must be careful,' the doctor warns me in a thick Belizean accent. 'Your head is very damaged.'

I reach a hand to my head and feel the padding of a dressing on my left temple. The skin around my left eye feels swollen and sore to the touch. I remember now. I remember what I was searching for.

'Do you know where my children are?' I ask him, the realisation that they're nowhere to be seen making my heartbeat start to gallop.

The room lists like we're rolling on high seas. The doctor insists that I lie down but I'm

8

nauseous with fear. *Where are Saskia and Reuben? Why aren't they here?*

'This is you?' The doctor holds a shape in front of me. My passport. I stare at it through tears. My face stares back blankly and my name is there. Helen Rachel Pengilly.

'Yes. Look, I have two children, a son and daughter. Where are they?'

The doctor gives the nurse another deep look instead of answering me. *Please don't say they're dead, I beg you. Don't say it.*

I begin to hyperventilate, my heart clanging like an alarm in my ears. And right as blackness reaches up to claim me, a sharp odour tugs me back into the room. Smelling salts. A cup of water materialises in front of me. The water's got bits of dirt in it. Someone tells me to drink, and I do, because instinct tells me that perhaps if I obey they'll tell me Saskia and Reuben are alive. *Give me arsenic, a pint of oil. I'll drink it. Just say they're OK.*

Another nurse brings a rickety wheelchair. She and the doctor help me off the bed and manoeuvre the drip-stand as I lower, my muscles trembling, on to the roasting hot seat-pad. Then we squeak through the ward towards a narrow, dimly lit corridor.

2

Helen

16th August 2017

It's paradise here. Picture a narrow curve of white sand that arcs into the twinkling Caribbean. Six beach huts stood on stilts at a comfortable distance from one another along the strip, each with its own patch of ivory sand and acidic-blue ocean. No one around for about twenty miles, with the exception of the other two groups of people staying in the beach huts. A group of five from Mexico — I can't tell if they're family or just friends; their English is minimal and my Spanish is limited to 'hello and 'thanks' — and at the very far end, the McAdam family from Alabama. Michael was suspicious of them at first when the husband asked a lot of questions about us, and I felt that familiar sting of panic, voices arguing in my head. 'We'll keep to ourselves,' Michael announced cheerily as we made our way back to our hut, but I knew what he meant, and for one horrible afternoon I was wrenched back over two decades, into another century and another skin.

I make coffee and clear away the bowls left on the kitchen table. Saskia and Reuben are playing on the beach outside, their laughter drifting through the warm air. I pull two boxes of pills marked Cilest and Citalopram from my handbag and pop one of each out of the blister packs, knocking them back with a chug of water at the sink. Usually a glimpse of sunlight is enough to turn me into a lobster but my reflection shows I've caught my first actual tan in I don't know how long, a deep bronze that knocks years off my face. Bright golden streaks have started to flash amongst my natural blonde, concealing the grey strands that have started to show. The sadness in my eyes, though — that's always there.

We've been running for twenty-two years and I'm tired. I want to stop, lay down roots. It's not in my make-up to live a peripatetic existence but we've had eight different addresses in Scotland, England, Wales, and even Northern Ireland. We tried to move to Australia but in the end it was too difficult to get visas. We don't vote, don't have social media accounts. Most of the time, we're as normal as any other family. We're content. Four years ago we made the huge decision not to rent any more and bought our first home, a pretty cottage in Northumberland. We have a dog and a guinea pig and Saskia and Reuben are thriving at their schools. But every now and then, I'm reminded of Luke. My first love. Especially at moments like this, when I'm happy and I remember I have no right to be.

Luke is dead because of me.

I'm putting on my sarong when Saskia comes screaming into the beach hut.

'Mum, you *have* to come and see,' she shouts,

both hands splayed in front of her like a mime navigating invisible glass. When I don't move she wraps her hands around my arm and yanks me with surprising force to my feet.

'Starfish!' she yells, skipping down the steps to the beach. 'Careful,' Michael says as we kneel on the sand to inspect them. A dozen orange starfish, bigger than Michael's hand, studded with intricate patterns. He scoops one up, but instead of staying flat it begins to squirm.

Saskia bounces on the balls of her feet and points at something in the water. '*Look!* Right there!' Reuben and I get to our feet and look out at the silky jade-green water. About twenty feet ahead is a pod of dolphins arcing through the waves, sunlight bouncing off their silvery backs. We all gasp. None of us have ever seen a dolphin in real life.

Saskia is weepy with excitement. 'I *have* to go swim with them, Mum! Please, please, *please*!'

'Here,' Michael says, squatting in front of her. 'Climb on.'

She jumps on his back and Michael quickly wades out to them while I hold my breath. *Michael is capable, a strong swimmer.* Dolphins are amazing creatures but the water is deep and there are endless dangers out there.

They'll be fine, don't spoil it.

I can't watch. I busy myself by helping Reuben with his sand sculpture until Michael and Saskia emerge from the waves laughing and the dolphins have moved further down the bay.

We've been here two weeks, and by 'here' I mean the coast of Belize. Our original plan was to spend the school holidays travelling around Mexico. At Mexico City we joined a tour bus to the Yucatán via some jaw-dropping (and knee-wrecking) sights, such as the pyramids at the City of the Gods, where Reuben delighted in telling Saskia about mass human sacrifices. We saw the soaring white peak of the Popocatépetl volcano, the Temple of Inscriptions at Palenque, the pretty pastel-coloured streets of Campeche, and finally Cancún.

Reuben has adapted to the foreign setting more easily than I expected. The tour group was mostly older couples, so the bus was quiet and the air conditioning during long journeys helped to keep him comfortable. We had a problem at first with the lack of pizza — which is all he will eat — but we learned to improvise with tortillas laid flat and covered with salsa and cheese.

We went to Mexico for Reuben's benefit. At least, that's what we told everyone, including each other. Reuben did a stunning Year 9 project on the Mayans, involving a handcrafted scale model Mayan temple and a 3D digital sketch that he projected on to black card surrounding the temple. We'd no idea he was capable of something like that and Michael said we should reward him. A trip to the real Chichén Itzá seemed the perfect way to do this, and as we'd not had a proper family holiday in a long time we figured a bit of a splurge was well overdue. But I also sensed that Michael was on edge, eager to run again. We've lived in Northumberland for four years now. Far longer than any other place.

When we arrived at Chichén Itzá Reuben sat in the tour bus for a long time, his face turned to the grey pyramid visible through the trees. Michael, Saskia and I all held our breaths, wondering whether he was going to start screaming or banging his head off the window.

'Should I do the feet thing?' Michael asked me nervously. The 'feet thing' is how we calm Reuben when he gets really worked up. I discovered it by accident when he was just a baby, and it grew out of the nights that I bathed him and then laid him on his mat to dry his little body. He'd lift his feet up towards my lips and I'd grab his ankles and blurt on the soles of his feet. It tickled him, made him laugh. As he got older and more sensitive to sound and chaos we tried everything to calm him. One night, when he'd worn himself out from screaming and lay down in bed on top of my legs, I ran my fingers up and down his shins. He started to calm down, then lifted his bare feet to my lips. I blurted them. He stopped crying altogether.

Ever since then, we do 'the feet thing' when he seems to be building up to a paroxysm — kissing a teenager's smelly size tens and stroking his hairy shins somehow doesn't have the same appeal as when he was a baby, but whatever works.

'I think he's OK,' I told Michael, studying Reuben, reading the air around him. The trick is to approach him as you might approach a wild horse. No questions, no fuss — even when he strips naked in public places. We'd somehow convinced him to wear shorts in Mexico and he

14

complied (we made sure to buy blue shorts), but he was still ignoring Michael at that point. I tried to tell myself that this was progress. After the thing between Michael and Josh's dad, Reuben had gone ballistic, crying, screaming, smashing up his bedroom. I managed to get him to stop being so violent, but he withdrew and wouldn't speak. Instead, he took to writing 'Dad' on his iPad and then vigorously crossing it out, signalling that Michael was dead to him.

At Chichén Itzá, though, I hoped that we could put everything behind us. Reuben looked from me to the pyramid — El Castillo — as though he couldn't quite believe it was real; that he was here. I glanced at Michael, signalling that now was his chance to make amends. He turned around in the driver's seat and grinned at Reuben.

'We're *here*, son. We're actually at *Chichén Itzá*.'

Reuben kept his head turned away. Definitely not a sign that he wanted his feet to be stroked.

'Do you want to climb to the top with me, Reuben?' Michael asked gently.

He reached out to take Reuben's hand, but Reuben sprang up from his seat and raced up the bus aisle, his long limbs moving in fast strides towards the clearing.

'I'll go,' I said, and I reached down for my bag and followed after. Once I caught up with him I put my arm around his waist. We fell into step. He's already six foot, even though he's only fourteen. I wish he wasn't so tall. It would make the sight of him clambering on to my knee for a

15

cuddle or breaking down in tears when we're out in public far less likely to draw stares.

'You OK, sweetheart?'

He nodded but kept his head down. I handed him his iPad and followed at a comfortable distance while he raced off and began to film the site. We spent the day with the rest of the tour group exploring, giving Reuben hourly count-downs, as promised, so that he could anticipate leaving and manage his feelings of sadness a little better. Even so, when we got back into the bus at dusk I saw that his lip was trembling, and my heart broke for him.

We headed to the hotel at Cancún, and that's where things started to go wrong. It was just too busy. Reuben's noise-cancelling headphones usually keep him calm but the crowds and heat were overwhelming for him. Saskia and I were worn out by the searing temperatures and squabbling couples amongst our tour group too, and the guide seemed intent on traipsing around tourist-tat stalls instead of taking us to more ancient ruins. At one point Saskia lost her teddy, Jack-Jack, in a market and we had to spend an entire day trawling through souvenirs to find it. She's had Jack-Jack since birth — a gift from my sister, Jeannie — and wouldn't be consoled until we found him.

Luckily, we did, but we were all agreed — noise and crowds weren't for us. So Michael went online and changed our booking to a small resort in Belize, within driving distance of a Mayan site even bigger than Chichén Itzá. Reuben was elated. We hired a car, broke free of

16

the tour group and drove to this place.

I go back inside and pull laundry out of the washing machine, then take it out to the side garden to hang on the line. Michael comes into the garden, soaking wet from his swim. He's in the best shape of his life, his arms broad and sculpted from deadlifts, his legs strong and muscular from cycling most nights to counter long days at the bookshop. His deep tan suits him, though I'm not sure about the beard he's grown. He likes to say he's 'an auld git' (he's forty-one) but to me, he's never looked better.

'Where's Saskia?' I say, looking past him at the tide that has begun to creep up the beach, devouring Reuben's sand sculpture.

He slicks his dark wet hair off his face. 'Oh, I just left her to swim on her own.'

'You *what?*' I take a step forward and scan the part of the beach further to the left. In a moment, Sas comes into view, wrapping a strand of seaweed around her waist to make a mermaid tutu.

'Honestly, Helen,' Michael says, grinning. 'You think I'd leave her to swim out in open water on her own?'

I slap his arm lightly for winding me up. 'I wouldn't put anything past you.'

'Ouch,' he says, flinching at my slap. 'Oh, I found something in this shed here. Come have a look.'

He steps towards the plastic bunker that I'd assumed was the cistern and flings open the doors to reveal a storage cupboard chock-full of beach boards, wet suits, snorkels, windsurfing sails, inflatables, rockpool nets, and surfboards. He takes out a rolled up piece of thick cotton and inspects it.

'Doesn't look very waterproof. What do you think it's for?'

We unravel it, each taking an end, until it's clear that it's a hammock. Michael nods at the palm trees behind me and suggests I tie one end to the fattest trunk while he fastens the other to a tree about eight foot in the opposite direction. Both trunks conveniently have metal hooks where other guests have secured the hammock.

'Climb in,' he says once we've set it up. I shake my head. I worry that I'm too heavy for it. I haven't weighed myself in almost a year but last time I did — under protest — I was thirteen stone, an unfortunate side effect of long-term antidepressant use. I'm five foot nine so can carry it, but most of the weight has settled around my waist.

'This is the life,' Michael says, climbing into the hammock. Then, when he spots me tidying up the storage cupboard: 'Helen. Get. In.'

The hammock stretches as I lie beside him, almost touching the ground, but it holds.

'See?' Michael says, slipping an arm under my neck and holding me close to his wet skin. For a moment there is nothing but the rustle of palm trees and Saskia's singing on the back of the wind. I try to resist sitting up to check she's OK and that Reuben is still on his iPad on the deck.

'That's better,' Michael says, kissing the top of my head. He has his hands clasped around me and I can feel his chest rise and fall with breaths that grow gradually slower and deeper. How long has it been since we lay like this? It feels nice.

'Maybe we should move out here,' he says.

'Definitely.'

'Serious. You could home-school the kids.'

'Mmmm, way to sell it to me. And what would *you* do? Build a book shack?'

'Not a bad idea. I could be our designated hunter-gatherer. I reckon I'd make a good Caribbean Bear Grylls. I've got the beard for it, now.'

'Bear Grylls doesn't have a beard, idiot.'

'Robinson Crusoe, then.'

I stroke the side of his foot with my toe. 'I wish we could.'

'Why can't we?'

'Blimey, if we'd the money, I'd move out here in a shot.'

'Cheaper to live out here than England. We could make money by taking tourists out on boat trips.'

'Stop winding me up,' I say.

'I'm not winding you up . . . '

'Neither of us speak a word of Spanish, Michael.'

'*Buenos días. Adiós, per favor.* See? Practically fluent.'

'You wally.'

'Anyway, they speak Kriol here.'

'We don't speak that either . . . '

'Belize is a British colony. We probably wouldn't even need a visa.'

'What about our house? And, you know, *my job?*'

'You're always whinging about how much you hate teaching.'

I feel a bit hurt by this. I enjoy teaching and I care deeply about my pupils . . . but no, this was not my dream. I sort of fell into it, and once I realised that the hours suited family life it was a no-brainer. I could argue that Michael's book shop is the same — not his dream, but a reasonable attempt at fulfilment that pays the bills and fits around our children's lifestyles.

'A holiday is one thing, living here is another,' I say, and I remind him of the conversation we had with the tour operator about Central America. *Got to be careful out there. Lots of dangers in the rainforest. Jaguars, snakes, pumas aplenty.*

'What do you think I'm here for?' he says. 'I'm your protector.'

I roll my eyes. 'I'd like to see you try and walk away from your bookshop. Even if it is burnt to a crisp.'

The words are out before I've a chance to haul them back into my mouth and lock them into the box of unmentionable things. *The bookshop.* We've not spoken about it the whole time we've been on holiday. Not a single mention of the fire that gutted Michael's beautiful bookshop which he has single-handedly built up from scratch to become one of the best independents in the region. A three-storey Mecca for bookworms, the jewel of our town, now in ruins: black, cooked. For one awful moment I'm wrenched back into that night when we saw the flames dancing high into the night sky.

The phone woke us in the middle of the night. It was Mr Dickinson who owned the pet store a few shops along. He'd spotted smoke from the street, then drove down to check his own shop. He said he was about to call the fire brigade, but he wanted to let us know, too. We raced down there, both of us betting on a manageable fire, one that we could tackle ourselves with a couple of fire extinguishers that Michael had tossed into the boot of the car. When we arrived, smoke was already curling out from beneath the front door, orange flames dancing in the first-floor windows. Michael started to unlock the front door but I grabbed his arm.

'Don't go in,' I said. He ignored me and pushed open the door, determined to damp down the flames. I watched, helpless, as he ran inside with the fire extinguishers and took to the stairs. Thick black smoke was funnelling down the stairs and beating across the ground floor, and I could hear the crackling sounds of the fire upstairs destroying the new café, chewing up the beautiful sofas and coffee tables that had only recently been installed. Sirens of fire engines screamed in the distance. I covered my mouth with my hand and tried not to breathe in the smoke, but with every second that went by it seemed to grow thicker, and my lungs ached for fresh air. I couldn't call out to Michael. He was still on the first floor, and to my horror I could see flames at the top of the stairs.

Just when I thought I would have to go up there to drag Michael out he appeared, an armful of books pressed to his chest, struggling *to breathe. He stumbled down the stairs, dropping the books and falling into my arms.*

The shop was destroyed, our livelihood anni-hilated. Some kind stranger set up a JustGiving fund and within a few weeks we had raised eleven thousand pounds. Possibly enough money to recoup some stock, pay some creditors. But there's the mortgage, the loss of income . . . The insurance company are still determining the cause of the fire.

The mood has dipped. I try to think of something to say that will swing it back again to the blissed-out vibe we'd enjoyed here since our arrival. It strikes me why we've avoided talking about the fire out here: the contrast between this heavenly place and drab, icicled Northumber-land make it feel as though we've stepped into another realm. There are no reminders here. But silence doesn't lie. We both know we have to go back and face it all.

'I should have installed CCTV,' he says in a low voice. 'Everyone said to do it and I got lazy.'

'There's no guarantee that cameras would have picked up anything,' I say, recalling how we sat in shock at the fire station, covered head to toe in black soot like two Victorian chimney sweeps. The deputy station chief educated us brusquely about the many causes of accidental blazes: sunlight bouncing off a mirror and hitting newspaper reduced a sixteenth century Scottish castle to embers. Hair straighteners left too close to a notebook on a teenager's dressing table took out a row of houses. Our fire could have been down to a faulty storage heater or a loose wire.

'They'd have caught who started the fire,' Michael cuts in, swinging his legs over the side of the hammock to sit upright. I reach forward and stroke his back.

I recall with a shudder the police calling both of us in for separate interviews. They asked whether someone had a grudge against us. If we had upset a customer or laid off an employee. Just weeks before I'd persuaded Michael to sack one of our part-timers, Matilda. *She doesn't do anything,* I protested. *You're barely paying yourself a salary as it is. The bookshop isn't a charity for lazy eighteen-year-olds who sit around all day reading Tolkien.*

Michael pointed out that she was Arnold's daughter, and Arnold had been the first to help him out when he set up the shop, but I won in the end. Matilda was sketchy about her whereabouts at the time of the fire — her parents confirmed she'd been out of the house, and it turned out she'd been with a boy. But for a horrible few days it seemed that perhaps Matilda could have been responsible for the blaze.

'We never ruled out arson,' Michael says when I remind him that Matilda was found to be innocent. 'Until the investigation closes, every possibility is on the table.'

'Maybe it was a group of kids messing around,' I say to his back. I desperately want him to lie back down with me, to recapture the idyllic mood.

'We both know kids didn't start that fire, Helen,' Michael snaps, getting out of the hammock.

'Michael?'

I'm taken aback by the sharpness of his tone. As I watch him head back into the hut I sense he's exhausted, worn thin by worry. But I wish we could discuss this. Every time we start to talk about something that cuts deep he just walks away.

3

Michael

28th August 2017

We've got a mutiny on our hands right now.

'*Pleeease* can we stay here, Dad?' Saskia howls in the kitchen as I make breakfast. This morning our butler (yes, an actual butler — I feel like a Kardashian) dropped off our food parcel, containing waffles (round, so we can tell Reuben they're pizzas), maple syrup, coconuts, dragon fruit, freshly baked bread, eggs, salad, blueberry pancakes, pineapple, the most mouth-watering bacon I've ever tasted in my entire life, and a bottle of wine.

'I'm sorry, my love,' I say, hugging Sas to my side as I heat the waffles on the hob. She smells of sunlight and the ocean. 'I'm afraid we can't change our flight. We've got today and tomorrow and then we have to head off to Mexico City to fly home.'

'But Daa-aad, I don't *want* to go home. Jack-Jack doesn't want to go, either.'

'Hmmm,' I say, tipping waffles on to a plate. 'So, nobody wants to go home? What do you suggest we do then?'

She does the same thing as Helen when she

thinks. Screws up her nose like there's a bad smell. Face just her like mother's, too. Same twinkling blue eyes that show every emotion and absorb every last detail. Same dimple in her left cheek and buttery curls to her shoulders.

'Can't we just buy a house here?'

'You'd miss everyone, I think. So would Jack-Jack.'

She gives a dramatic sigh, seven going on seventeen. 'Like *who*, exactly?'

'Well, Amber and Holly would miss you. And I bet Oreo can't wait to see you . . . '

'But *they* could come *here* . . . '

'What about your ballet recital?' I ask. She has no answer to that and I know she's excited for it. I set her plate of waffles on the coffee table and squat down to face as her as she begins to do a couple of ballet moves.

'To tell you the truth, my love, I don't want to go home either.'

She widens her eyes. 'You don't?'

I press my lips together, shake my head. 'But don't tell Mummy.'

'Is it because you don't like flying?'

'Nope.'

'Is it because you love this house and the sea and you'd like to live here?'

'Exactly. I like spending my days on the beach instead of having to go to work. I'd like to do it for ever. Wouldn't you?'

She nods eagerly, her face all lit up with hope. I wish I could give her everything. I wish I could make the world as perfect as she deserves it to be.

'Here, come and help me put all this food away.'

She does a little ballet twirl across the floor, arms crooked like she's holding an invisible beach ball between them, and looks into the box of food that I'm unloading.

'Bacon?' she says, holding up the packet like it's a dead rat.

'Not for you, love. Reuben and I will enjoy that.'

'Bacon isn't even nice, Daddy,' Saskia says. She's decided to become vegetarian, like Helen, so all I've heard about for the last three months is how meat is Satan. 'I tried some once and it tasted not very nice. Plus, it's from pigs and they're more smarter than dogs and you wouldn't eat *our* dog, would you?'

'Hmmm. You know, if he tasted like bacon, I'd consider it.'

'Daddy!'

I lean over and give her a kiss. She still kisses me on the lips, a quick peck with a big 'mwah' at the end, just as she did as a baby. When the day comes that she tells me she's too old to kiss me anymore I think my heart will break.

'Do the thing,' she says when I plop one of the blueberry pancakes into a pan on the stove. 'Do the flip, Dad. Do it!'

I wait until the pan is nice and hot before planting my feet wide, gripping the pan handle tightly and tossing the pancake as high as I can. It flips into the air, smacks the ceiling, then lands splat in the pan.

'You did it, Dad!' she squeals, high-fiving me.

27

'Five points for Gryffindor!'

Reuben comes in through the front door, his dark hair and shorts dripping wet. I'm careful to be calm around him. No eye contact. I'm still in his bad books. He dumps a plastic bucket on the floor.

'We can't go home,' he announces flatly.

'Daddy pancaked the ceiling,' Saskia says.

'Five points for Gryffindor,' Reuben says, deadpan. 'Look what I found.'

Saskia peers into his bucket and squeals. I tell her to shush, she'll upset Reuben, but his focus is on the baby turtle, its head no bigger than the tip of my thumb, its shell covered in zigzag patterns. It sweeps its flippers back and forth as though it wants to swim.

'We should take it back to the water,' I say as Saskia plucks it out of the bucket and cuddles it to her chest. 'His mum must be looking for him.'

'Like *Finding Nemo?*' Saskia says.

'That was a clown fish,' Reuben replies.

'Dude,' I say, imitating the turtles in *Finding Nemo*. 'What up, squirt?'

Reuben falls silent, and I freeze, expecting one of two reactions: he'll either storm out of the room or he'll slug me across the face. Reuben isn't often violent but when he is it's ugly, given that he has the strength and height of an adult. He looks like he's thinking really hard about something. Maybe he's trying to control his anger.

'Righteous!' he says suddenly, a big grin lighting up his face.

'Curl away, my son,' I say, suddenly glad that I

watched *Finding Nemo* ten million times.

I raise my eyebrows at Helen who is standing there with her eyes like saucers and her jaw on the ground, stunned that Reuben has actually spoken to me. He's deeply forgiving, full of love, but I could hardly expect him to react any other way after what happened at Josh's birthday party.

I was only trying to protect him. That's my job. My whole reason for existing.

★ ★ ★

I wake to find Helen sitting at the end of the bed wrapped in a yellow towel. She's on the other side of the mosquito curtain but I can make out her gold hair, braided down her back, the web of the Celtic tattoo on her shoulder just visible in the dim light. I sit up quickly, amazed that I actually slept, and she tells me to relax, it's OK, but I'm covered in sweat and my heart is racing. I was dreaming. Bright images pitch and mulch in my head like a soup. When Helen comes into focus I see her face is filled with worry.

'Are you alright?' she says. 'Bad dreams again?'

I push my fingertips into my eyes, trying to blot out the disturbing images in my head. For years, the same dream. A door made of fire. I'm standing in front of it with the knowledge that I have to open it, because on the other side is paradise, a land of pure, endless happiness. Sometimes I'm alone. Sometimes I'm with Helen and the kids, and I have to take them through the door, but I worry about them

29

getting hurt. I always wake in a sweat. Sleeping pills washed it away and now it's back, as vivid as ever.

'I went for a swim,' she whispers. I take her hand, wondering what's wrong. She looks shaken.

'You OK?'

'I saw something weird. It was probably nothing. I don't know.'

'You saw something weird where? Out in the water?'

She nods and holds a finger to her lips, urging me to keep my voice down. 'In the beach hut next to ours. They had a telescope just like the one we have in the living room.'

A telescope? Ah yes, I remember. The scope on the tripod we moved into a corner so the kids wouldn't knock it over. We presumed it was for spotting sharks and rays in the water outside.

'And?'

'It was pointed at our hut.'

'What was?'

'The telescope.' She gives a shudder. 'It was creepy . . . '

'But . . . didn't the butler say all the other huts were empty as of yesterday?'

She bites her lip. 'That's the other thing. When I looked in the window of one of the rooms the bed was unmade. There were clothes on the floor. It looked like someone was staying there.'

'Maybe one of the groups stayed on? Or a late booking?'

'But why would they point the telescope at our beach hut?' She looks on the verge of tears now, terrified. 'It felt like someone was watching us.'

I tell her I'll check it out myself. But if I'm honest this has me worried. The fire at the bookshop was no accident, I know that, but I can't say too much about it to Helen. We were being watched at home, before we left. I saw a guy watching the shop right before the fire. Same car outside every day for a week, and then he followed me home. Couldn't say anything about this to the police, of course. They'd ask questions. *Why would someone be watching you?* It was the reason I pushed for us to go abroad for an extended holiday, to buy some time to think.

I can't change what happened to Luke. I can't stop them from hunting our family. But I can definitely work out a way to protect us.

* * *

I don't go back to sleep. Nothing unusual about that, though tonight I'm wired, all my senses on high alert. I've learned to manage on about four hours a night, with the occasional catnap during the day to keep me going. Four nights a week I'll set my alarm for 3am and get up to work out. Arms and abs on Mondays and Thursdays, a ten-mile run on Tuesdays and Fridays. Then I read, answer work emails, maybe tidy the house or go for a walk. We live near a beautiful tow path in England and at sunrise you see all kinds of wildlife: otters, foxes, hedgehogs. I've tried to persuade the kids to come out with me but they're not morning people.

Here, though, the wildlife is something else. We're about a mile from the rainforest but even so, I spot a monkey in one of the trees at the side of our hut. He helps himself to the coconuts, then spies a half-empty packet of crisps left out by one of the kids on the decking. I film it all on my mobile. He's right in front of me, so close I can touch him. Completely unafraid. I set down my can of Coke to reach out and stroke him. Amazingly, he lets me, then reaches out and snatches my Coke before running off. Little git.

I put my hands in my pockets and take a walk up the bank to the road that links all the beach huts. The family from Alabama are gone, and good riddance. Too many questions about where we were from, why we were here. One of the kids screwed up her face at Reuben and said loudly, 'Why are you so *weird?*' Yeah, so she's only a kid but the parents didn't correct her, didn't tell her gently not to be rude. They just laughed.

The road is clear of cars, meaning that there aren't any guests in the huts. So why would Helen have seen clothes in one of the bedrooms? There's nothing but rainforest for about twenty miles. Someone could have been dropped off at one of the huts, or the guests could have gone out for the day. Holiday season's virtually over, though. That's what Kyle said.

I walk on the sand, my eyes adjusting to the darkness. The moon is bright tonight, a long causeway of silver light tossed over a slate of ocean. I walk carefully around the hut and when I glance into the living room window I make out the shape of the telescope pointed not at the sea but towards our hut, just like Helen said. It could just be pointed at the north end of the bay, though. Hard to tell. The dolphins like that end of the bay so it's feasible that they were watching the pod . . . The other windows are at the back of the hut, too dark to make out what's inside. No lights on. The palm trees sway in the breeze and the sea sweeps forward and back, exhaling. No movement, no sign of anyone around.

After ten minutes or so I turn back.

★   ★   ★

The butler comes just after dawn. Helen and the kids are still sound asleep, so I press a finger to my lips as he passes over the food box for today.

'I found pizza,' he whispers. 'For your son. I can't promise that it won't taste different but at least it's the next best thing.'

'That's kind of you.' I find a $10 note in my pocket and slip it to him. 'Reuben will be thrilled.'

He grins, pockets the cash, then turns to leave, but I set down the box quickly and skip after him.

'I don't suppose you can tell me if someone has checked into that hut?' I say, nodding at the one next to ours.

He thinks, shakes his head. 'Just you and one other family staying for now.'

'Another family? Which hut are they staying at?'

He turns and points down the bay. 'The very last hut, right on the edge of the strand. Has there been some trouble?'

'No, no. No trouble. Thanks anyway.'

★ ★ ★

Around eight I find Helen in the bathroom plaiting her hair and present her with breakfast on a tray and a kiss. Then I wake the kids. 'Get dressed,' I tell them. 'It's our sea safari today.'

'Sea safari?' Sas asks, her hair sticking out like she's rammed her finger in a socket. She leaps out of bed and pulls off her nightie. 'You'll need to bring your poncho,' I tell her.

'Is it going to rain?'

'No, but the dolphins might splash water over the boat. You know, when they jump through the water?'

She gives a squeal and wraps her arms around my waist.

'*Sooo* excited, Daddy!'

The ride out to sea takes an hour on a twenty-foot sailing boat. I tell Reuben and Saskia to stay in the cabin downstairs where they can sit comfortably and eat snacks, though I have to promise that I'll shout the second I spot anything with a fin.

After half an hour Helen comes out to join me. She rubs my back and lays her head against my shoulder.

'You were up again all night, weren't you?' she says with a sigh.

'No.'

'Don't lie . . . '

'I just thought I heard something, that's all.'

34

She leans back, maps my face with a look of concern. 'You don't have to worry about us, you know. I shouldn't have said anything about the telescope. I was probably just being paranoid after . . . '

She trails off.

'After what?'

She looks down. When she meets my gaze again there's hardness in her eyes. And something else. Frustration.

'I need to ask something,' she says, folding her arms. 'And I need you *for once* not to avoid the question.'

'OK.'

She takes a deep breath, readies herself. 'The day you attacked Josh's dad . . . '

'I didn't attack him,' I start to say. 'It was a disagreement . . . '

She raises a hand, signalling that I'm to shut up. 'When you attacked him, you said you were looking out for Reuben. I still don't know what you meant by that.'

I don't want to talk about this. I look around, searching for an exit, a distraction. Unless I'm prepared to swim back to land there's nowhere for me to go. We're at least fifteen miles from land and even I'm not that strong.

'I was protecting him,' I say at last.

'Protecting him from what, exactly?'

'Look, the birthday party wasn't at a climbing centre,' I say, anxious to close this up once and for all. 'Josh's dad was taking the boys climbing up the Simonside Hills . . . '

'And?'

I'm starting to feel angry. What has *this* got to do with what happened at the birthday party? 'And I could see Reuben was nervous about it. Look, I told you. It was wrong of Josh's father to . . .'

'To what?'

I look up, catch her eyes. She's challenging me.

'To . . . to put Reuben in a position where he had to choose between his friend and feeling safe.'

She screws up her face. 'But why . . .'

' . . . and trust me, I did everything to stop it from becoming a scene. You weren't there. Reuben was freaking out, I could see it in his eyes. And the guy kept talking over him. Even made him start to gear up.'

I see her wince.

'Josh's dad wasn't taking no for an answer. OK, so maybe slugging him was a bit over the mark but I did what I had to . . .'

She lifts her eyes to mine, an eyebrow cocked. 'A little over the mark? You knocked him unconscious.'

'It was an unlucky punch,' I say, and I can feel a hot ripple of fire in my stomach. I try to swallow it down but it's insistent. 'I've said I'm sorry. What more do you want?'

She looks hurt, which wasn't my intention, so I reach out and put my hand on hers.

We stand together in mutually wounded silence. We want the same thing, but we go about it in completely different ways. I'm the head of the home, the bad cop. Helen's still pissed off

36

because it's meant Reuben losing his one and only friend, Josh. Nice lad. Like Reuben, Josh is autistic. We've waited years for Reuben to make friends. Years without a single birthday party invitation or play date. Finally, he goes out and gets a pal and I wreck it all by busting his dad's face.

But I did what I had to do. And everything has a price, doesn't it?

And then, there they are, about ten feet from the boat. Whales, as long as buses. Helen spots them and runs to the cabin to alert the kids. By the time they emerge the captain has cut the engine. Sas squeals and jumps up and down at the sight of them while Reuben claps his hands and shouts 'Magic!' The captain tells me in concerned tones that humpbacks out here, especially at this time of year, is a bad sign. They could be sick or dying. Of course I don't mention any of this to the kids. We are close enough to see the barnacles studding their backs, long white lines etched along their bellies, their mouths scissoring the water. A way out to sea another whale bursts out of the water, landing with a huge splash and the peace sign of his tail as he dives below.

'Look how happy they are, Dad!' Saskia shouts, and I agree with her, because sometimes love means telling lies.

★ ★ ★

'Michael. Michael! Wake up!'
'What? What's wrong?'

I sit upright, my head buzzing. I can't believe I fell asleep. The window squares off a lapis lazuli sky speckled with a million stars and a silvery moon. Helen is out of bed, bending over me as I pull back the sheet.

'I think someone's outside,' she says. 'I heard footsteps in the back garden and when I went to . . . '

I'm already up on my feet, pulling on a pair of shorts.

'I thought it was an animal, at first,' Helen says. 'But I saw a man.'

'How sure are you?'

She bites her lip. 'Pretty sure.'

'Stay here,' I whisper quickly. 'Keep everything locked behind me.'

In the kitchen I search quickly for something weapon-like — a baseball bat, ideally — but the cupboards yield only a rolling pin and a meat knife. I plumb for the latter and open the side door. Suddenly Helen is there, holding my arm, tears wobbling in her eyes.

'Why don't we phone Kyle?' she says. 'Or I can look for the tour operator . . . '

'And what are they going to do? It's two in the morning . . . '

'I know, but . . . I shouldn't . . . I shouldn't have woken you . . . '

I peck her on the forehead. 'Stay here. I won't be long.'

I step outside and wait until I hear the click of the door locking behind me. The dark is impenetrable, the only light coming from the moon and the stars. The garden is swallowed by night. No Coke-thieving monkeys to be seen.

I hear a noise to my right. Quick, stealthy strides headed towards the road. I move towards the sound, squinting. I can't see anything. The footsteps stop, and I hold my breath.

But then, movement on the hill that leads up to the road where our rental car is parked. It's difficult to see, but I can just make out someone or something moving briskly up the bank.

'Hey!' I shout, and the figure moves quickly. My heart is racing. I hold the knife in front of me and go after him.

4

Helen

30th August 2017

I'm wool-headed this morning after last night's escapades. Not nearly as sexy as it sounds. I woke up to use the loo around two in the morning and heard noises outside. I went to check and saw a man moving around in the garden. At least, I think I did. I was so sure last night and now I'm not. I feel so guilty. I woke Michael and he went after him. He was gone for over an hour. The longest hour of my life. When I saw him coming in through the door I almost collapsed with relief. He was sweaty and out of breath, but not injured.

'Did you find him?' I said, my voice trembling. I found myself looking him over for signs of blood.

He set the torch back in the block on the kitchen bench. 'No. It was too dark.'

'Didn't you take a knife? Where is it?'

He sank into a chair by the table and wiped his face. 'Dropped it.'

I waited for something more — where he'd been, details of a confrontation with an intruder, a fight. A narrative of any sort to put all the questions whirring through my head to bed. Michael wouldn't make eye contact.

'But . . . you were gone for *ages*. I was out of my mind . . . I was absolutely beside myself, Michael. Did you catch up with him?'

He rubbed his eyes, stifled a yawn. 'I followed him into the trees and then I turned back. I got a bit lost, though. Luckily I saw the lights from the bay through the trees and followed them home.'

I gasped. 'You were in the rainforest?'

He was tired, keen to shrug off the memory of it. 'It was pitch black. Couldn't see a thing. One minute I was on the road and the next I was surrounded by trees and frigging monkeys.'

I studied his face. He looked amused by the memory of being surrounded by monkeys, not bothered at all by the fact that he went racing out after a suspected intruder.

'I'm so sorry,' I said, deciding that I had somehow got it all wrong. I'd let my paranoia get to me. 'But . . . you really didn't see who it was?'

He gulped back a glass of water. 'That's what I said.'

'But who could it have been?' I said. 'Why would someone have been outside?'

'Are you sure it *was* someone?' Michael said, and I did a double take.

'You saw him, Michael. You went after him . . . '

'I was half asleep. I spent an hour walking in circles in the bloody jungle.'

And there it was again, the edge of guilt against my skin. I looked down, ashamed. 'Sorry. I think we were both possibly being paranoid.'

41

'Both of us?' he sniped back.

I fell silent. I had been absolutely sure that I had seen a dark figure, a man moving through the garden and up the bank, but just then doubt slipped in, like a lie sliding inside a truth.

'Let's just go to bed,' he said, rubbing his face. 'We've got a long drive back to the airport tomorrow.'

No one is happy when we shut the door on the beach hut for the last time. Reuben has his headphones on but is clicking his fingers and stamping his feet in the way he does when he's particularly stressed. Saskia is long-faced and holds Jack-Jack extra tight.

'Maybe we can come back next year,' Michael says cheerily, though I catch his eye and give a small shake of my head as if to say, *let's not make promises we can't keep*. I have no idea how we've afforded *this* trip, never mind how we could possibly afford round two in a year's time. We're still paying off Reuben's iPad, for crying out loud.

We spend the first hour of the drive to the airport in a gloomy silence. In reflection of our mood it starts to rain, and before long it's coming down in great sweeping chains. The air feels cooler, which is no bad thing. Grey cloud spreads out across the sky. It's been blue skies and belting heat for six weeks straight. Saskia decides she needs to wee every four minutes, so we pull over for the dozenth time and let her go at the side of the road.

'I'll drive for a bit,' I tell Michael as he heads back to the driver's side. 'You have a nap.' I'm not completely comfortable driving on the wrong side of the road but I feel guilty at the dark circles under his eyes.

The kids settle down in the backseat, Saskia holding Jack-Jack tightly and looking mournfully out the window, Reuben plugged into his iPad. Michael folds his arms and leans his head against the window. I find a British radio channel and turn the volume just enough to hear. *Enjoy the lack of traffic*, I tell myself, forcing optimism. *It'll be bumper-to-bumper when you get back home.*

About an hour into the journey a white van appears as we approach a bend, moving at high speed along the road towards us. Instinctively I press the brake as I reach the curve of the road. The van draws closer. It appears to be speeding up. Odd, I think. And dangerous. Why speed up on a bend, especially when the road is wet?

At the very last moment, the van veers sharply into our lane, two tyres lifting off the tarmac as it swerves and plunges straight into us.

There is no time to react.

An explosion of metal slamming into metal, the sound of tyres screeching like a wounded animal, the air slashed by screams. An airbag explodes in my face and the car careens wildly, glass shards whipping through the air.

5

Michael

14th June 1995

The minute I finish my exams I get the cheapest flight I can out of Heathrow. Luke and Theo are already gone — their parents got them first class tickets. I buy the most sophisticated climbing equipment I can squeeze into my tatty rucksack: shorts, T-shirt, hiking pants, sleeping bag and dry bag, tent and stakes, crampons, stove, towel, light, cutlery, thermometer, thermos, Swiss Army knife, rain gear, balaclava, goggles, sandals, granola bars, noodle packets, Chapstick, head-lamp, first aid kit, ice axe, carabiners, prusiks, harnesses, rope, flask, and my lucky bear claw.

I expected Chamonix to be a campsite. Instead the bus pulls up to a charming Alpine village with hotels, B&Bs, shops, restaurants with verandas and parasols, right in the crease of a mountain range. It's pretty mind-blowing here, like being on another planet. All around me are unimaginably tall, jagged peaks, like the spine of a massive dinosaur. I stand in the middle of the street looking up at them, awe-struck. They're so tall I suddenly feel scared. Ben Nevis didn't look this big. *That's because it isn't, you moron,* I tell myself. Mont Blanc is fifteen frickin' thousand feet tall. It takes me a moment to spot her, and then there she is: the almost-perfect triangle at the very top of the massif.

I dump my bags at the youth hostel and set about scavenging for grub.

I head into the pub and lo, Luke and Theo are standing right in front of me with a couple of beers. I can tell who's who by the choice of outfit. Luke's dressed like the eighties vomited all over him. Neon pink leggings, white leg-warmers, a Bon Jovi T-shirt and blue goggles over a black bandana. I wouldn't be surprised if he's wearing a leopard-print thong. Theo's dressed like he's recruiting for the SAS: khaki everything, even the boots. A girl is with them. She must be Luke's girlfriend, Helen.

When Theo catches sight of me he leaves the table and walks quickly towards me, wrapping an arm around my shoulders and effectively spinning me the whole way around.

'Hey,' he says, nudging us to a table on the other side of the pub.

'Theo, can you get off me,' I say, breaking free. I glance over at Luke who is deliberately avoiding eye contact. 'What's all this about?'

He sighs, puts his hands on his hips. 'Look, I know you had a problem with Luke's girlfriend coming on this trip. I just want you to . . . stay calm, you know?'

'I am calm. I'm as calm as a cucumber patch.'

He tilts his chin. 'You being sarcastic?'

He hates it when I rip the piss out of him. 'What are you, his bodyguard?'

45

I catch Luke glancing over to check out my reaction. Theo takes out a pack of cigarettes.

'Smoke?'

I shake my head.

'Go on, have one.'

I relent with a sigh. He lights it for me, sits down and invites me to join him. I won't, so he stands.

I met Luke and Theo two years ago, when we starting a degree in Medieval Literature at Oxford University. They're twins, both six foot two, blonde rugby-playing public schoolboys who scored straight As in their exams. Both on a full-ride scholarship. Not that they need it; their folks made a fortune in the tech boom in France. They're identical twins but you can tell them apart. Theo wears glasses, has recently grown a Musketeer moustache, and his personal style is somewhere between misunderstood genius and Kurt Cobain, but even if you closed your eyes you'd pick them out by their voices. They've lived all over the world but spent most of their lives at boarding school in Cambridge, though Luke's accent is still more Oz than Brit with the occasional French twist. Theo's is perfected Norf Landan.

It's their personalities that *really* set them apart. Luke's an arrogant git but can be good fun when the mood takes him. Theo's Luke's shadow, a classic introvert. He prefers to sit in a corner with a beer and a book but he goes to the pub with us out of duty to Luke. He can be weird. He sees a psychiatrist every week. Luke says Theo's Theo-ness is down to their time at

46

boarding school in Melbourne. A soft-natured three-year-old crying for his mum makes easy prey for bullies and cruel teachers and I reckon he's never shaken that complex.

And now it seems we're bringing one of Luke's groupies along. This *Helen*. It was only meant to be the three of us. I've never even met her. She lives in London and Luke only sees her at weekends. I've nothing against girlfriends, or girls for that matter. I'm sure girls can climb just as well as blokes. But she's never climbed before, and I know exactly what's happened: she's one of these possessive types that can't let Luke out of her sight. He tends to date girls who're messed up and needy, the ones who only came to Oxford because their folks pressurised them, wanting to make good on years of private school fees, but who are starting to go slightly crazy from the pressure. His last girlfriend got him into cocaine. I'm no angel but I draw the line at the hard stuff. That, and I don't have any money.

Anyway, the point is that this trip is no stroll in the park. It takes training, strength, stamina and experience — with a good dollop of common sense — to climb Mont Blanc, and if I'm honest even I feel a wee bit intimidated. People have died doing this climb. I've spent the last three months training to make sure I'm up to it. What if she has an accident, or freaks out? What if she decides halfway up that she wants to go home? It'll wreck the trip. A once-in-a-lifetime trip that's costing an absolute fortune. Luke and Theo's folks are loaded, so they don't care how much it costs. But for some of us this means

47

living on beans and toast for the next six months.

I thought Luke was kidding when he first mentioned about a girl tagging along. When it seemed he was actually serious, I tried to get him to see sense. Gently, then with more muscle. Meaning that I plied him with vodka.

'This new girlfriend,' I said, once he'd knocked back the fifth glass. 'The one who's apparently coming with us to the Alps. Won't she feel a little like a third wheel?'

'Fourth wheel,' Theo corrected.

'Don't get what you mean,' Luke said, lighting a cigar and swearing when the match burnt his fingers.

'Not exactly a girl's thing, is it? A twelve-day *peregrination* up a mountain.'

Luke sniffed at this. Peregrination was his word. He's such a snob when it comes to language. Why say 'trek' when you can say 'peregrination'?

Luke took a drag on the cigar and blew a thick O of smoke in my direction. 'Helen's up for it,' he said. 'She's into that kind of thing.'

'There aren't any showers in the Alps. Twelve days without washing, mate. Girls can be a bit funny about that kind of thing. You sure she's up for that?'

Luke leaned into me until his nose almost touched mine.

'Michael, my love, she'll be fine with that.'

'Can she actually climb?' I said.

A grim look. 'Can you?'

'This isn't a walk in the park, Luke. It's the highest mountain in Europe.'

48

'It's the highest mountain in Europe,' he parroted in a high-pitched voice. 'She's fitter than you are, mate. She's a ballet dancer. Fit as butcher's dogs, those girls.'

'I'm sure Helen'll *love* being compared to a dog,' Theo said.

'Dancing's hardly climbing, Luke.'

'What I mean is, she's athletic . . . '

'I'm not risking my neck with an amateur.'

He frowned. 'So you're saying you won't go if she does?'

I took a long drink of my beer, enjoying watching him sweat, his eyes turning nervously to Theo. The thing is, we work very well together as a trio, particularly as Luke finds his twin boring and strange. He spends most of his time trying to palm Theo off on to someone else, occasionally paying other guys to take Theo out for a beer, but Theo prefers to be in Luke's shadow. And I've a knack for getting on both Theo's and Luke's level, so I've assumed the role of go-between, a stepping stone for their disparate personalities. I'm able to bring out the best in Theo, thus making his constant presence ('like a frickin' tumour,' Luke likes to say) bearable and occasionally pleasant.

'Come on, Mikey,' Luke said, backpedalling. 'This is our epic adventure. It won't be the same if you don't come.'

I shrugged, gave him a look of sorry-but-that's-how-it-is.

He leaned back in his chair, glanced at Theo. 'We could ask Oliver if he'll take Michael's place.'

Theo nodded.

'Oliver?' I said. 'Who's Oliver?'

'He's in Theo's Old Norse class. Said he'd like to come. He could take your place, Mike. You could maybe even sell your plane ticket to him . . . '

'What?' I said panicking. 'No! I mean . . . '

Luke grinned. He knew he had me. He knew better than I did how much I wanted this climb.

'We'd prefer *you* to go instead of Oliver, mate,' Luke said, wrapping an arm around my neck and putting his cigar to my lips. 'But if you're a widdle bit afwaid of a girl . . . '

I shoved him off. 'Alright,' I said. 'I'll go. But on one condition. We stick to the walking trails. No climbing. No abseiling.'

'Piss off,' Luke said. 'You're suggesting we don't actually climb the mountain? What would be the point in going?'

★ ★ ★

Luke raises his head as I make my way towards the table. He gives me a big cheesy grin and actually stands up to give me a big 'come here, you' bear hug which we both know is an attempt to butter me up. I was sure she wouldn't come. Luke is all-or-nothing, always acting on impulse, so it was likely that his spur-of-the-moment decision to bring her along would be dropped as fast as it was raised.

'This is Helen,' Luke says. I grin at the girl beside him, who blushes and says *hello*. She's tall, about five foot nine, blonde hair worn in a

50

plait, skinny but not anorexic. A bit shy, and preppier than I expected, with a slender face and high cheekbones, a look of a librarian about her. 'I'm Michael,' I say, offering a hand as she seems the sort of girl who does handshakes. A surprisingly firm grip. 'Nice to meet you,' she says, and I try to force out the same response but can't. She's pretty, though, in a way I didn't expect. She seems . . . normal.

'Nice to meet you, too.'

The words stick in my throat. After all, I finished with Nina a month ago on the basis that I'd be heading off to the Alps for a fortnight and wanted to be free to do as I pleased. Nina *might* have mentioned that she wanted to see other people the night before but that isn't the point. I made sacrifices, dammit.

'I hope you don't mind me gate-crashing your trip,' Helen says, sliding her eyes to Luke who shakes his head as if to say, *of course not*. Git.

'Yeah, not at all,' I say, lying through my teeth. 'The more the merrier, right?'

Later, we head outside for a practice climb up one of the crags ten minutes from the village. It's the size of a skyscraper but still looks puny compared to the mountains. Seems we're not alone in this idea, either — about a dozen other climbers are scaling the crag with us. An older couple from New York City, a bunch of tie-dyed, weed-smoking hippies from Portugal, and some plaid-wearing members of a Welsh photography club.

Helen looks visibly nervous about climbing this size of peak and I have to bite my tongue to

51

stop myself from calling it out to Luke. *If she can't manage this, how's she going to manage Mont Blanc?* He spots it though, and subtly suggests we take the walking trail that winds around the side of the crag, avoiding the rocks. Theo finds a ledge about six hundred feet above the valley and we all take a breather, sitting on the big slab with our legs dangling. Luke produces a box of cigars from a pocket in his trousers and passes them round.

'Mate,' I say, my mood rising considerably. 'You're the best.'

'There's more,' he says, unzipping another pocket.

'What you got in there?' Helen says, wiping her face. 'A parachute so we can all just float back down instead of climbing?'

'Even better, my love, even better,' Luke says, pulling out a flask. 'I've got . . . whisky.'

Helen doesn't look thrilled but Theo and I are all over it, and in a handful of minutes Luke's tapping the bottom for the last dregs. I lie back, my legs dangling over the edge, nothing but air between me and death six hundred feet below. The moon is a Cheshire cat's smile in an inky, cloudless sky.

'There she is,' Luke says, leaning towards Helen and pointing at the whitest peak. 'Mont Blanc. The imaginatively-monikered 'white mountain'. Highest mountain in the world.'

'Western Europe,' Theo corrects.

'Highest mountain *in Western Europe*,' Luke says sourly.

We sit for a moment in the still warm air,

looking over the silhouetted peaks towering above us and the lights of Chamonix below, the hostels and alpine huts glimmering and small as a gingerbread village. To the right I can make out movement, or what looks like a stream of ants hustling along a narrow trail. I take out my binoculars and there they are: hordes of climbers already setting off on the trail.

'Feels like we're going on a pilgrimage,' I observe, stupidly.

'You bring your rosary with you, then?' Theo says.

I pass the binoculars to Luke and he glowers at the people heading off. 'This isn't a pilgrimage, it's a traffic jam.' He looks over the lights in Chamonix and I read his mind: we didn't think there would be so many hostels. 'Thought we'd be doing this alone,' he says. 'Just the four of us.'

'Like the four horsemen of the apocalypse?' Theo says.

'You're so competitive,' Helen tells Luke, rubbing his arm.

'You say that like it's a bad thing,' Luke says, kissing her hand.

'It's not like there's someone at the top handing out awards for whoever arrives first,' Helen laughs.

Theo shrugs. 'You never know.'

'The summit is its own reward,' Luke says.

'So you won't be bothered if I get there first?' Helen says, and I see Luke's face fall.

'Not at all.' He breaks into a beaming grin, then slaps me and Theo on our backs before tilting his head to the sky.

'I love you guys,' he says, then adding: 'and girl.'

'Luke, babe, don't take this the wrong way,' Theo says. 'But . . . I'm not snogging you. Don't care what you give me. I draw a line at tongues. Pecking is fine, but snogging — no. I'm your brother and it's wrong.'

Helen laughs out loud while Luke and I lie on our backs sending loops of smoke drifting into the night air. I don't say it, and this is a rare feeling for me, but right now there is simply nowhere else I'd rather be.

6

Helen

30th August 2017

'Mum!'

Reuben is running down the hospital corridor towards me, his arms spread wide. He presses his face to my chest and I give a loud cry of relief. There's a nasty bruise above his right eyebrow, some cuts and dried blood on his forehead, his T-shirt smeared in blood, but otherwise he seems fine. I start to sob — relief or fear, I can't tell — and he starts to cry, too.

'Can we go home now, Mum?' he says, trying to climb on to my knee. 'I want to go home, OK? Let's go home.'

'OK,' I whisper weakly, wiping tears off my face. 'We can go home. I promise.'

I tell him as gently as I can not to sit on my lap and hold his hand tightly. The nurse says something that I make out as an urge to keep going, so I tell Reuben to stand and we're off again, the nurse pushing my wheelchair briskly along the corridor as Reuben staggers alongside me with both hands holding one of mine.

When we turn into a side room I see a figure lying on the bed. Strips of white tape run across his nose, chin, forehead and cheeks, holding a series of tubes and valves leading from his mouth to a monitor by his side.

Slowly I'm skewered by the realisation that this bloodied, unconscious figure is Michael. It's a realisation that seems to stop time. Trembling, I move closer. A bloodied ear, a small patch of his beard, two blood-encrusted nostrils and a pattern of dried blood on his shin.

'Why's Dad not waking up?' Reuben says behind me. 'Wake him up, Mum! Wake him!' His cries wrench at my heart. I try to console him but I grow more and more upset by his distress.

A doctor comes into the room and introduces himself as Dr Atilio. 'This is your husband?' he asks me.

I'm gasping for air and my heart is racing. I'm in the grip of a major panic attack.

'He was awake when the soldiers brought you here,' I hear the doctor say, though he sounds distant, far away, as though I'm underwater. 'He is falling in and out of consciousness.'

It's only when I see Reuben from the corner of my eye and remember that he's in the room that I somehow find the strength to stop and hold myself together. I hear myself tell Reuben it's alright, everything is OK, but nothing could be further from the truth. I'm chanting the words over and over to help regulate my heart rate. The nurse moves me close enough to take Michael's hand. It is limp and covered in dried blood.

I can't believe this is happening. I can barely breathe. My thoughts whirr and strain to find answers, solutions. I remember with a hard punch to my chest the sight of Saskia on the ground in front of the car.

'Where is my daughter?' I shout frantically. 'Her name . . . Her name is Saskia. Saskia Pengilly. She's seven years old, she . . . she has blonde hair, she was wearing a stripy T-shirt . . . '

'We will take you to her,' the doctor says, and they wheel me abruptly out of Michael's room towards another ward further along the hallway.

The sight of Saskia on the bed is like a fist slammed into my face. She's hooked up to machines, there are blood stains on her pink cotton dress, her small, limp hands are bruised and painfully gashed. It is unbearable.

I start to shake, a strangled scream escaping from my open mouth. Even when Reuben starts slapping his head I can't stop. A nurse appears at my side, pulls the waistband of my shorts down below my hip and sticks a needle in my backside.

Blackness.

* * *

'The lady, she come here for see you.'

A nurse is leaning over me and adjusting a tube in my arm. The room is swaying. Another woman comes into focus. Slim, young. Bobbed black hair, red lipstick. Wide smile. A suit.

'I'm Vanessa Shoman,' she says, stretching out a hand. 'I'm from the British High Commission. The doctor told me that your family had a car accident.'

The knowledge of why I'm here hits me like a wrecking ball. An invisible force sweeping me off my feet and landing me somewhere else in time, outside my own body. Horrifying fragments of the crash flash painfully across my eyes. I wrap my arms around my legs and howl in the space between my knees. I remember crawling on all fours to reach Saskia. She was lying on the ground, about ten feet ahead of the mangled hire car. I remember it was raining and there was glass everywhere. Saskia wouldn't move. I was screaming for her to wake up.

'My daughter,' I tell Vanessa through gulping sobs. 'She's seriously injured. I . . . I don't know if she's going to survive.'

I can hardly bring myself to say the words aloud. I can't stop crying. Reuben is sitting back in his chair, knees to his chest. He looks stricken at the state of me but I'm too helpless to comfort him.

Vanessa rubs my back sympathetically and explains her role as an officer of the High Commission is to help people like me. She assures me she will contact my family and help us get home, but none of it brings any comfort. She tells me we are in a hospital just outside of San Alvaro, one of Belize's poorest towns. She says the hospitals in this region are understaffed, underfunded, but that a neurosurgeon is coming from Belize City today or tomorrow for Michael and Saskia.

My memories are an explosion of particles that I have to knit together, atom by atom. I remember coming to in the modernist sculpture that used to be the car. I remember Michael slumped like a beanbag in the seat beside me, his right shoulder twisted at an unnatural angle. I was certain he was dead.

What happened after that? How did we get to the hospital?

Vanessa tells me an army truck full of soldiers came across us after the crash. The soldiers dragged Michael and Reuben out of the car, dumped us in their truck and brought us all to the hospital.

'You were lucky,' she says. 'It's a very remote part of Belize. No towns or villages for many miles. You could have been there a long time before someone found you. Maybe even days.'

She tells me that the soldiers managed to salvage some luggage from our rental car. The bag containing our passports and money is in Michael's room, but we had other suitcases containing clothes, toys, souvenirs, our mobile phones. Irrelevant, of course, but Vanessa mentions that we were also lucky that the army managed to save them.

'Save them?' I say weakly. 'From what?'

'From the police. They steal all the time. How many bags had you in total?'

'I think we had four,' I say.

She writes this down. 'How much money did you have in cash?'

'I don't know.'

'Any gadgets? Laptops, smartphones?'

I bite my lip. 'I'm not sure.'

'Credit cards?'

'I think . . . maybe AMEX and Mastercard.'

Why does this matter? I don't care about money. I care about my family.

'We will check that these are still there. If not, we'll attempt to cancel the cards for you. But the other bags I don't think we will ever see again.'

Vanessa folds away her notebook, her information retracted. She pulls another packet of tissues from her bag and passes them to me.

'You poor thing,' she says, watching me dissolve into gulping sobs. 'But it's good you're awake. The police will want to get a statement from you as soon as possible.'

★ ★ ★

Reuben is huddled on the bed next to me. The lights go out, plunging the hospital into darkness. Somehow the darkness makes the sense of loneliness and disorientation ten times worse. I feel trapped in a nightmare. My heart starts to race again. I press my fists against my eyes and weep from my core. It feels like I've been torn apart.

I wish Michael was here to tell me that everything is OK. I wish someone could promise me that Saskia is going to make it through. I can't believe this has happened. I hate myself for being less injured than she is. I would give anything, absolutely anything, to trade places with her.

Earlier I caught my reflection in a broken mirror in the bathroom and had to look twice to check it was me. The left side of my face is yellow and puffed up so badly that my left eye is a mere slit in my face. My hair is pinked with blood and under the dressing on the side of my head is a painful gash. I think my collarbone and wrist are broken. My right ankle might be broken too. I can barely put any pressure on my feet and every movement feels like I've torn dozens of muscles.

But I'm alive. We all are. I have to cling to that. It could so, so easily have been otherwise.

Vanessa said that the army brought us here. As I sit up in the darkness I remember a pair of heavy black shoes next to my face as I came to by the car. My image was blurry but I definitely saw them. A ripped denim hem, like jeans. A crunch of glass underfoot.

Michael was unconscious. He was wearing flipflops, not boots. The soldiers would have been wearing fatigues, not jeans. I think the van driver came to inspect the damage to our vehicle after the crash. He was unharmed enough to walk. I'd identify his shoes if I saw them again. Black lace-ups, a scuff on the right toe.

But he didn't call the police. Vanessa said the army came across us by chance. The driver had left the scene of the crash long before then. I try to imagine him looking over our mangled car, our bodies covered in glass and blood. How could he have looked at Saskia on the ground like that and just raced off without calling anyone? How heartless would you have to be to leave her like that?

I know I saw someone outside the beach hut the other night. Michael questioned me and yes, it was dark but I *know* I did. He was wearing a white T-shirt and jeans. Dark hair. Short — about five foot eight — with black fuzzy hair. Dark-skinned, stocky. I didn't see his face.

And the telescope at the other hut that was pointed at ours. It freaked me out. I only stopped to catch my breath on the pier. Curiosity got the better of me so I went for a look around. I knew no one was staying there. But when I glanced inside the window I saw one of the bedrooms with clothes on the floor, the sheets kicked back off the bed as though someone had been sleeping there.

'I need a story,' Reuben says. 'Tell me a story.'

'I don't have any books, love,' I say weakly. 'I don't think the hospital has any either.'

'Tell me a story, Mum. I want a story. Tell me a story.'

I make him turn away from me so he won't see the tears running down my face. Then, in low whispers, I tell him the story of *Angelina Ballerina*. It's the only story I can recall because Saskia makes me read it to her all the time.

When he falls asleep I try to will myself to stand. My legs feel like jelly and I want to throw up from the pain but finally I'm able to pull myself upright. I need to go and check on Saskia. I want to make sure she's OK. I'm stricken by the thought that, if someone *has* struck our car deliberately, they won't stop there.

I try and will my body to do what I so desperately need it to do, but it won't. I used to be able to push through all kinds of muscle damage and foot injuries, but now I have no strength left and feel dangerously woozy. I sink back down beside Reuben and fall into darkness.

I dream of Saskia coming into our bed for a cuddle.

Morning, Mummy. Can I snuggle with you?

In the dream she curls up next to me and watches Netflix on an iPad while I read. Michael appears in the doorway with a tray laden with cereal bowls, toast, coffee, and a babyccino for Saskia. We stay there until it's time to take Reuben swimming and Saskia to ballet. The warmth of the blankets, her feet against my calves, her forehead against my lips, butter-soft, and her little fingers laced between mine, both of us wearing sky-blue nail polish flecked with glitter.

Mummy, please stay a little longer. I love our mornings.

7

Michael

31st August 2017

I can hear someone screaming. No, not screaming. A mechanical whine, a machine somewhere
that whirs.

I open my eyes and immediately bright light
squared off by a window blinds me. My eyes
adjust and I see I'm in a room with a small
rectangular window to my right. Plaster is
peeling off the wall beneath the windowsill. I can
hear shouting down the hall. All a bit Mad Max
in here. A white sheet is drawn across my legs.
My T-shirt and jeans are covered in dirt and
blood stains. There's dried blood all over my
arms. I feel like someone's beaten me with a
metal bar.

My mind flicks through reasons that I might
be in hospital like a slot machine spinning its
three wheels printed with cherries and bells.
Three sevens line up, and I remember.

The crash.

It comes to me in vivid, broken flashes. The
sound of the car whipping round. I was sure I'd
died. I was sure we'd all died. Did we hit a tree?
I remember the car coming to rest virtually

upside down. Helen was shaking like she was having a fit, her teeth chattering. I told her it was OK, that everything was OK. Her breathing slowed. After a few moments I managed to make out something she said.

He just came out of nowhere.

A tear slid down her cheek.

Who? I said. *Who came out of nowhere?*

The van. He just slammed into us.

I told her I loved her.

I love you too. I'm so scared, Michael.

I thought those were the last words I'd ever hear.

I think back to last night, when I chased after the guy who'd been trespassing outside our beach hut. I didn't want to make much of it to Helen but when I got to the top of the bank I saw someone running towards a white van that was parked about a hundred yards away from the hut. I shouted, 'hey!', and this guy turns and looks at me, holding his hands at either side of his shoulders as if to say 'what?'

I stopped dead in my tracks and gave a gasp. He looked exactly like Luke. Same sandy-blonde hair, same build, same face. I felt all the blood drain from my face.

'Luke?' I called out. 'What are you doing here? Luke?'

He took a few steps towards the van, then jumped in and took off, the tyres kicking up white stones. I was so stunned at the sight of him that I didn't react, at first. Then I started to run after him, thinking that if I could get the registration plate I could report him. He sped off down the path and took a right. There was no way I was going to catch up with him so I cut through the trees. Daft, on hindsight, but I was in a daze. Luke is dead. It could have been Theo. But why here? And why now?

I'm lucky to have made it out. The rainforest is fifty miles thick. One wrong turn and I'd have been in deep kimchi.

The bleep of the heart monitor tugs me back into the present.

I sit up and try to speak but my mouth feels full of cotton wool. I think back to the fire at the bookshop. The bookshop wasn't just my pride and joy. It was an offering, an act of supplication to Luke. And they burned it down.

We're not safe here. They won't stop until we're all dead.

8

Helen

31st August 2017

I'm woken by a man and woman removing my drip. Both are in plain clothes, the man dressed so casually that I jump when I see him standing so close. Jeans and a colourful Hawaiian shirt with a rosary around his neck. He speaks to me in Kriol.

'I'm sorry, I don't understand,' I tell him. He starts to gesture with his hand but I don't understand it. After a few minutes of confusion the nurse says 'X-ray' and I realise they want to take me for one.

'Yes. Yes, X-ray,' I say, nodding. They bring in a wheelchair, tell me to take off my clothes to be gowned. I'm so hot and filmed in blood and dirt that I virtually have to peel them off, which takes a while. Every movement makes me yelp in pain. When Reuben starts to follow after the wheelchair they shake their head and I try to explain that he has to come with me, but they won't hear of it. I look around desperately for Vanessa.

'My son . . . my son's autistic,' I say, stumbling over my words. 'He *has* to come with me because

I'm afraid someone will hurt him. Please . . . '
The nurse rubs my arm and tries to tell me it's
OK, he is safe here in a hospital, and then they
ignore me completely and wheel me down the
corridor while Reuben stands in the ward,
dumbfounded.

I'm crying and shaking all over when they
wheel me into the X-ray room, weakened by fear
and shock. The radiographer — a woman about
my age, slim, concerned — speaks good English
and asks me what's wrong.

'We were in a car accident,' I say, and I'm
trembling so badly I can hardly get the words
out. 'I'm afraid someone is going to come into
the hospital and hurt us.'

She bends down in front of me and listens.

'Who do you think will hurt you?'

'A man,' I say, gulping back air as though I'm
drowning. 'He was wearing black boots. He
crashed into us on purpose . . . he's going to
come here, I know it!'

She takes my hand and I manage to take a
breath. 'Is there security at the hospital?'

She frowns. 'Not really. But the police should
help. If you had a car accident they will want to
find who did this.'

This is comforting enough to help me stop
shaking. 'The police,' I say. 'The woman from
the British High Commission said they would
want a statement but they've not come to see me
yet.'

She smiles reassuringly.

'They will be here very soon. It is not a big
police force so they may be busy. But they will

help. If someone is trying to hurt you, the police will protect you.'

I lie on a cold metal table as she pulls the machine over my collarbone, then my legs and arms.

In my mind's eye I see myself standing in our ground floor flat in Sheffield. Reuben is in his high-chair in the room behind me shouting and throwing beans across the room. The postman pushes a pile of letters through the letter box and Reuben screams at the sound.

Most of the letters are bills, but there's a padded envelope sent on by our landlady, Lleucu, from our loft flat in Cardiff. Amongst the letters is a cream-coloured bonded envelope with 'Haden, Morris & Laurence' emblazoned in navy lettering across the back. It looks important, so I open it first.

K. Haden
Haden, Morris & Laurence Law Practice
4 Martin Place
London, EN9 1AS
25th June 2004

Michael King
101 Oxford Lane
Cardiff
CF10 1FY

Sir,
We request your correspondence in receipt of this letter to the address above.
Our clients desire a meeting with you

regarding the death of Luke Aucoin.

The time to meet about this tragedy is long overdue.

Please do not delay in writing to us at the above address to arrange a meeting.

Sincerely,
K. Haden

The letter drifts from my hand to the ground. Reuben continues to shout in the background. I feel like someone's run through me with a sword. Slowly I sink to the ground and pick the letter up again. Five words scream off the page.

The death of Luke Aucoin.

Those words chill me to the bone, turn my guts to mush. At one point I believed Luke was the love of my life. And yet I caused his death.

I turn and look at Reuben. My first thought is: they'll take him from me. I will lose him if I face this.

So, I hid the letter. And I persuaded Michael that it was time to move again.

I thought it would all go away.

The voices in my head remind me that there have been dozens of occasions in the past where something has gone wrong and I've connected it to these letters. When we lived in Belfast our cat Phoebe died. The vet said it was poison. I worked myself into a complete state, certain it was deliberate, payback for Luke, until a neighbour approached us and apologetically explained that he'd left out rat poison in the back garden and had spotted Phoebe near the tray on the day that she died. And the miscarriage I had a few years before Saskia came along . . . for about year afterwards I was trapped in the silent torture of being convinced that Luke's family had done it. I even had the scenario in my head. We were living in London at the time and I took the tube to and from work every day. I was seventeen weeks' pregnant. The first cramps started about ten minutes after I got off the tube. It would be easy to inject me with something that would start early labour. A light prick that I'd probably never notice.

It's difficult to explain paranoia. Saying something like that aloud — though I never did, not to anyone — makes it sound ridiculous. But the suspicion was like a monolith in my head, impossible to budge. We buried our little girl in the hospital graveyard, named her Hester. And when the voices of suspicion finally died down, a new one set in: Hester's loss was karma for Luke.

Other mishaps were similarly difficult to assign to chance: a slashed car tyre, the night I was followed home in Kent, a few weeks of silent phone calls at three in the morning, two bouts of severe food poisoning. On hindsight it's unlikely any of these were related to what happened to Luke, but at the time I was sure they were, and I carried that knowledge like a knife lodged in my chest. I could tell no one, not even Michael. My hair would fall out in handfuls and the smallest thing felt physically impossible. Cooking a meal, meeting up with friends . . . I felt incapacitated, barely able to look after myself, never mind my children. Life stalled and sputtered, but somehow hobbled on.

There is a point when fear is no longer a protective instinct, and it becomes sabotage.

No, I tell myself resolutely through tears. *The crash has nothing to do with that. It has nothing to do with what happened to Luke.*

I'm trying hard to convince myself, to drown out the other voices. But they're too loud for me to silence. They shout in my head like a Greek chorus.

But what if it is? You're alone in the hospital, completely vulnerable. If they want to come and finish you off they only have to walk through the doors.

⋆ ⋆ ⋆

When I return to the ward — with the news that my wrist is broken — I breathe a sigh of relief that Reuben is there, hugging a flat rectangular object with a blue rubber casing to his chest. His iPad. The glass is cracked in one corner but otherwise it seems OK. I ask him if he's OK, and he nods, but then tells me that a man came up to him and asked him where I was.

'Who was it?' I say. 'Was he a doctor? A nurse?'

He shrugs and moves his eyes around the room. He seems agitated, but of course he has every reason to be and I can't read him.

'Did the man say why he wanted me?'

'My headphones are gone,' he says.

'How did you get the iPad?'

'A nurse,' he says, but doesn't explain further.

I nod and study his face for clues. This is probably as much information as I'm going to get from him about the man who came. I look around the ward — it's unusually quiet, all the visitors gone and the patients asleep. Just the sound of the traffic outside and the ceiling fan.

'Let's go check on Saskia,' I say, and he wheels me quickly down the hall to her room. When I see her there in the bed it's a bizarre mixture of relief and renewed grief that hits me hard.

I take her little hand in mine, staggered by the confirmation by each of my senses that this is happening. Crescent moons of blood and dirt under her nails. Her closed eyes and the frightening chasm between each bleep of her pulse.

★　★　★

Night falls and every time I hear footsteps coming up the hallway I seize up with blunt, raw fear. The ward I'm in is right at the far end of the wing and there is no exit without going up the hallway, so if anyone came to get Reuben and me, we have nowhere to run. The hospital is like something straight out of a zombie movie — there is one bathroom that I've spotted and it was crawling with insects, no loo paper, and brown water pouring from the taps. No catering, very little drinking water. Both Reuben and I are weak from hunger. I've asked to be moved but the nurses either don't understand me or feign ignorance. Vanessa hasn't appeared and I'm worried that she won't return. She said a neurosurgeon was coming to see Saskia — why isn't he here?

There is no phone I can use and I don't have my mobile. Worst of all, they won't let me sleep in Saskia's room. Reuben and I take up too much space and the nurses need to be able to access her — it took half an hour of interpretive gestures for me to work out that this was the reason — but it's utter rubbish, because we only get seen once a day. I'm trying to be brave for Reuben's sake. He keeps saying, 'What's wrong, Mum? What's wrong?' and I have to tell him I'm fine, that everything is fine.

But it's a lie.

9

Michael

31st August 2017

My head hurts like a meteor has landed on it. Someone's knocking against the windowpane, a *thunk thunk* that seems to fall into rhythm with the banging in my head. I get up to see who's knocking and find it's an insect of some sort, the size of a small bird, trying to get outside. With a gasp of pain I yank the tube out of my arm and struggle forward to let the bugger out. He has a stinger about three inches long but he's more scared of me than I am of him.

I sit on the side of the bed and discover I'm wearing a snot-green hospital gown, tied at the waist and neck like a weird apron. Nothing underneath. Who undressed me? I'm in what seems to be a hospital, albeit a pretty nasty one. It looks like a building site. Smells like one, too. My back aches like I've fallen off a mountain. I'm covered in cuts and bruises. My first thought is that I'm here because of the fire, and my mind spins back to being trapped inside the shop, black smoke swirling. The sensation of my lungs being crushed.

And then the sight of Luke at the beach hut.

His hands out at either side in a half-shrug, as if to say, *what did you expect?* With a shiver I wonder if I saw a ghost. A more rational explanation is that I was half-asleep, or that the trespasser bore an uncanny resemblance to Luke. But it could have been Theo.

There's a black rucksack on the floor next to the bed. I pull it towards me and begin hunting through it. Not much in here. Someone's already been through it. Of course they have. I know I put Helen's passport in here, the kids'. All three are gone.

I remember putting my passport in the secret pocket at the back. It's still there, along with my wallet, a notepad, pen, and my mobile phone. The battery's dead. Damn it.

My checked shirt is rolled up in there, too. I pull off my bloodied T-shirt and use it to wipe my armpits and neck, throw on the clean checked shirt. I see my shoes on the floor by the door.

I see a nurse walking down the corridor and my impulse is to call out to her, tell her to contact our next of kin and tell them what's happened. But neither Helen nor I have parents, or any close relatives.

I sit back against the cold bars of the bed, weighed down by the knowledge that we have no one to call for help.

This is my family. I have to do it. There is no one else.

10

Helen

1st September 2017

I fight sleep for as long as I can, listening out for sounds of movement in the hallway. I have the distinct feeling of being watched. Not just a feeling — a gut-wrenching certainty. All the hairs on my body stand on end despite the crushing heat, my senses on high alert and my heart fluttering in my chest. I'm in excruciating pain and physically helpless against whoever is in the shadows, watching us. None of the nurses on the ward tonight understand me and no one helps. We are completely alone.

The white van coming towards us is a vivid, garish splinter in my mind, and my foot jerks, puppet-like, at an imaginary brake pedal every time I think of it. Over and over, this circular reaction, my body reacting to a memory that's stuck in the pipework of my mind.

When my body finally caves in to exhaustion I dive deep into dreams and surface again with a gasp into that same terrible realisation of where I am, and why.

I dream of the fire at the bookstore, black clouds of smoke billowing out of the windows of the shop, ferociously hot. Michael and I at the end of the street helplessly watching on as fire fighters roll out long hoses and blast the flames with jets of water. In the dream, though, it is the beach hut that's ablaze, not the shop. A figure running away from the scene, up the bank into darkness. I try to get Michael's attention.

Look! Do you think he was the one who caused the fire?

Michael's comment floats to the surface of my dreams.

Kids didn't start the fire, Helen.

There is a tone in his voice that I can't work out. When I wake, it continues to echo in my ears, making the slow transition from dream to memory.

★　★　★

A little after eight in the morning I hear voices down the hall: an ambulance is here to take Saskia to the hospital in Belize City. To my relief, they say that both Reuben and I can go, though for one terrifying moment I feel I'm abandoning Michael. He would want me to go.

But right as the nurses are helping me into the ambulance, Vanessa pulls up alongside us in her car. 'The police have requested that you go to the station right now to make a statement about the collision,' she says emphatically.

I tell her that Saskia is going for surgery right at this moment but she holds up her hands.

'It's not my call,' she says. 'The police have the last say. And they require you to go to them right away.'

78

It's a heart-breaking decision to have to make, but Vanessa insists I have no choice. She says I have a legal obligation to give information on the crash and that it has to happen right away.

'I'm very sorry,' she says. 'But this is out of my hands.'

I watch on, tears rolling down my face, as the ambulance pulls away with my daughter inside. It feels like someone is pulling off one of my limbs and dragging it down the street, out of sight. My instincts divide me, one shouting that at least Saskia will be safe in Belize City and the other shouting, *Are you nuts? You've just let them take her away! You have no idea that they're even real doctors!*

At least the police will protect us. I'll tell them about the trespasser, about the van driver who got out after the crash and looked over us without helping.

And perhaps they'll assign Saskia a police escort to ensure she's safe.

The police station is about half a mile outside the town of San Alvaro, which appears to be no more than a row of wooden shacks selling fruit, vegetables, and handmade rugs and clothing at the side of a dirt road. Children running naked in the streets. Stray dogs everywhere, their ribs protruding like comb teeth through patchy fur.

Inside the station, we are summoned to a small room at the end of the corridor. Vanessa pushes me in the wheelchair and a couple of police officers stop chatting at the front desk when they see us. Vanessa addresses them cheerfully in Kriol, but they don't respond, their eyes fixed on me and Reuben, who is clicking his fingers and being extremely brave in this hostile and foreign place.

'So, tell me what happened,' Superintendent Caliz says once Vanessa, Reuben and I are sitting down by his desk in the small room. His eyes are hidden behind darkened lenses, the corners of his mouth turned down in a deep frown. A pot belly stretching out his beige uniform, badges on the breast pocket. Photographs behind his desk show him being decorated for service in the police over many decades. He flicks his eyes across Reuben who has his attention fully on the row of glass bottles by the window, filtering sunlight across the floor in a kaleidoscope of colours.

I notice that Superintendent Caliz has no pen in hand to transcribe the interview, no tape recorder. I glance at Vanessa and tell him everything that I can recall: the trip to Mexico, our fortnight at the beach hut, the trespasser running up the bank. Then, my heart in my mouth, I tell him about the crash, recounting it with tears streaming down my face. I have to tell him this so he understands why the van driver standing at the scene of the crash, watching us, was so cruel. Recounting this feels like I'm right back on the ground again beside Saskia, praying for our lives.

'I feel afraid,' I say, trying to be as clear as possible in my use of language so he doesn't miss a thing. 'I feel worried that this man is going to come back and hurt us again.'

Superintendent Caliz purses his lips, nods.

'You were all wearing seatbelts?' he says.

'Yes,' I say, confused.

'Why your little girl go out the window?' He makes a motion with his hand. It takes a second for me to realise he's demonstrating Saskia being catapulted out of the windscreen of the car.

'We *were* wearing seatbelts,' I say, but my mind turns to the last time we pulled over to let Saskia go to the loo. Did I clip her seatbelt in? She was capable of doing it herself and I usually left her to it, but the rental car was old, a 1999 hatchback with tight, irritating seatbelts that she complained about. Guilt rivets me as I think that I didn't check it. If I had, she might not be in a coma.

'You were driving, yes?' he says.

I nod. 'Yes.'

'Why your husband not drive?'

'The other vehicle drove straight into us,' I say in a brittle voice. 'It wouldn't have mattered who was driving. He swerved into our lane, right at the last minute . . . '

He leans forward across the desk, his hands clasped, and gives me a murky look. 'You buy drugs here in Belize?'

'*Drugs?*'

Superintendent Caliz addresses Vanessa in Kriol. She falters, confused.

'We were told that someone has been arrested,' Vanessa interrupts, addressing him. I can't believe what I'm hearing. I had thought the police of all people would want to help, that the Superintendent would see the situation for what it is and offer to protect us. Michael lies

81

unconscious in the hospital. Saskia is seventy miles away, in a hospital surrounded by strangers. Reuben and I are completely alone.

'What's he saying?' I ask, and she hesitates before answering me.

'They've arrested the driver of the van that crashed into your car,' she says slowly.

I take a deep breath. 'Good.'

But she shakes her head, as though I've misunderstood. 'He is saying the crash was deliberate. The driver says he was *paid* to do this.'

A noise escapes my mouth. Every suspicion I've had has been correct, all my instincts ringing true. Someone *was* watching us. Someone wants us dead.

'So, you're completely sure,' Vanessa asks me again. 'No drugs purchased in Mexico. No reason for anyone to try and harm your family.'

'This has *nothing* to do with drugs!' I shout, the strength of my anger surprising everyone in the room, including me. 'I told you! Someone was watching us at the beach hut and the next day a man crashed into our car. You say you've arrested him. Who paid him to crash into our car?'

Superintendent Caliz leans back in his chair, laces his fingers together and barks something in Kriol.

Vanessa processes whatever information he has shared before tilting her head to mine, her brow folded in confusion.

'What is your husband's name?' she asks.

'Michael,' I say, confused. 'Why?'

'Michael Pengilly?'

82

'Yes, Michael. Why? What has that got to do with the man who crashed into us?'

My voice rises again in desperation. She repeats this to Superintendent Caliz, then listens intently as he replies in Kriol. The air is suddenly loud with suspicion and menace. I had expected to feel safe here but instead I feel in even more danger than I did at the hospital.

Vanessa fixes me with a dark stare. She chooses her words carefully. 'The van driver claims your husband paid him to crash into your car to kill you all and make it look like an accident.'

Her words are like a black hole, sucking me into it cell by cell, until all that's left of me is a scream.

11

Michael

1st September 2017

It's a shock to the system to be in a car again, right after the crash. I break into a cold sweat as we move through the streets, pushing through crowds of people — donkeys, too, and I swear some guy had an orangutan back there — and then a flood of cars that veer all over the place. The driver tells me there are no road lanes in this town. Looks like there are barely any roads either, at least not of the tarmac variety, despite the fact that there appears to be a car-to-human ratio of eleven-to-one. Dust rises from the tyres, making it impossible to see or breathe. Like driving through a sandstorm. The driver smokes weed, has some funky music playing loudly. He tries to strike up a conversation, asks if I'm a medical student at the hospital. I say yes and try to conceal the lie in my voice.

There's a white phone charger trailing into the back seat over a couple of Coke cans. It's a match for my phone. I say, 'Can I use this?'

'Yes, of course,' he says. I plug in my phone and within minutes the screen flashes white. I scroll through my photographs, past videos taken by Reuben. I click on one of them and find it's of the bookstore, pre-fire. The sight of it pierces me. His face appears large on the screen as he props the phone against the leg of a table, plucks a book off the shelf and then sits on the floor, cross-legged, filming himself reading. A pair of legs appears next to him after a few minutes. I watch as he glances up at whoever's standing there, then goes back to reading. It must be a customer. She's carrying a Sainsbury's shopping bag. She steps over him, like he's part of the furniture, then turns to him and snaps, 'Why are you just sitting there in the middle of the floor? Can't you see people are trying to get past?'

Reuben lifts his head and stares at her blankly before returning to his book.

'So rude,' the woman says off-screen, and instantly I feel an old urge to shout, *He's not rude, he's autistic!* Helen and I once said we ought to have that emblazoned on T-shirts and wear them whenever we went out as a family. One day Saskia came home from school and said her teacher had said she was very artistic. Saskia was quick to correct the teacher. 'I told her that doesn't mean I'm rude and ignorant, Mummy. Artistic people are just as polite as neuro-typical people. Isn't that right?'

We had a laugh at that one.

I scroll through his other videos, one of him playing Minecraft, another of him drawing. I know Reuben is an amazing boy. Despite society's obsession with status, personas, the endless barrage of visual culture, we still place a ludicrous amount of trust in what we see. On the outside my boy isn't normal, and that's still a problem. Helen and I vowed a long time ago that we would fight for our children to feel at home in this dying, messed-up world, to find their place in it. We would protect them.

And that's precisely what I intend to do now.

I scroll through my gallery to find the photographs I took of the letters. Helen doesn't know I opened them, but she knows we were receiving them. Why hide them from me? Every year, a new letter. And always on the date of Luke's death to make a point. As if I could ever forget.

I took photographs of the letters in case she got rid of them. And I needed time to think about what the letters said, about why she didn't tell me about them. There are many secrets in our marriage, but they pale in comparison to squirrelling away letters that contain so much threat. Helen's forever accusing me of avoiding confrontation, and yet she was the one keeping these from me. Why? What has she got to hide?

I start to panic when I can't find the images. There are photos of Reuben wearing a snorkel mask for the first time, giving a big thumbs up. Pictures of Saskia pirouetting in her *Trolls* swimsuit, her face all lit up when she spotted the dolphins. I try to flick past them as fast as I can but something in my chest gives and I have to look away so as not to start sobbing.

Finally, I pull up an image of one of the letters and zoom in on the cream page.

Sir,
We write again on behalf of our clients

regarding the death of Luke Aucoin.

Our records show that you signed for our previous letter. We request that you contact us immediately to avoid further consequences.

Sincerely,
K. Haden

A wave of anger rolls over me as I read the words 'further consequences'.

'Where to, man?' the taxi driver asks.

'The airport,' I tell him. 'Make it quick.'

12

Michael

16th June 1995

It's decided: we'll spend the next three nights in Chamonix learning stuff like what to do in an avalanche ('Duck?' Theo offers), crevasse rescue ('It's called chucking a rope down there, mate,' Luke says), and belay techniques, or in other words, we'll be drinking our body weights in vodka and singing German folk songs, with some token ice pick swinging in between.

This morning we're joining a crowd of fifteen other climbers led by a mountain guide named Sebastian who is taking us up the Aiguilles Rouges for some mixed climbing techniques. This part of the Alps reminds me of Ben Nevis in Scotland, or the Lake District — a palette of earthy brown and velvety green, with gentle rises and pockets of snow in the nooks of distant peaks. Mountains stretch as far as the eye can see, no sign of human life anywhere. Just our little group swallowed up in the mountains.

It's a warm sunny day without much of a breeze, but Sebastian has us all geared up as if we're approaching the summit — helmets, crampons, ice picks, the lot. Still, I get to watch the sun rise over the mountains, a rich, yolky light breaking over the crystalline towers, bright rays the length of motorways pouring across the valley. It's pretty awesome. Enough to make me feel more at ease around Helen.

'Where did you meet Luke and Theo?' she asks me amiably, once we've settled into our stride. 'I mean, I know you all go to Oxford but did you know each other before?'

'Nah. We're all on the University rowing team,' I tell her. 'Ugly here got us all into climbing. Didn't you, Luke? We did Ben Nevis last year.'

He grins. 'Dragged you and Theo kicking and screaming up Ben Nevis, more like.'

'We're doing Kilimanjaro next. Then Everest,' I tell her, and she looks impressed.

'Wow, Everest,' she says, glancing at Luke, who clearly hasn't mentioned any of this to her. 'I don't think I'll be going on *that* trip!'

Oh, are you sure? I want to say in a voice dripping with sarcasm. *What a pity.*

'Come on, you lot!' a voice shouts. The guide, Sebastian. He's made the group stop on a massive rock ledge overlooking a sapphire lake. We take off our helmets and rucksacks and start to set up the stove, but Sebastian shouts at us again.

'This is not the lunch stop,' he says. 'First, we learn how not to die. Second, we eat. OK?'

Sounds fair.

Helen stands close to the front of the group, watching Sebastian as he demonstrates how to make a top managed belay site.

'If you need to lower into a gorge, you need to

set up an anchor,' he says, looping a figure eight of rope around a tree by the edge. 'You clove hitch yourself into the shelf which enables protection at the edge. My belay device clips into the masterpoint. I need two lockers on the masterpoint — use a small carabiner for this to redirect the brake strand, OK?' He holds up a carabiner and links it to the shelf. I take a peek over the edge. Quite a distance to the bottom.

'Now, for a demonstration. Who will be my volunteer?'

A nervous laugh ripples among the crowd.

'You,' Sebastian says, gesturing for me to step forward.

'What, me?' I say, glancing around.

'We're going to cover what happens in the event of an *arête* shearing your rope, OK?'

Luke laughs and shoves me forward. One of the more outspoken blokes in the crowd — the South African fella with purple dreads — raises a hand. 'An *arête*? What is this?'

'An *arête* is a knife-edged ridge,' Seb says. 'If your rope is rubbing back and forth on this, what do you think will happen?'

'It'll break,' everyone murmurs.

He holds up a worn piece of rope and demonstrates. 'Snap!' He turns to me and gestures at me to lower down off the side of the cliff. I'm not feeling overly confident about this right now. Still, I hook myself to the rope and try not to look too terrified as I lower down, eyeing the rope fearfully as it tightens around the tree. He lowers me down about twenty feet — which feels like a hundred feet — when suddenly I feel the rope go slack. My feet slip against the smooth rock and I scramble wildly to find something to hold on to. There's a chink in the rock face and I dig my fingers into it, my heart thumping like there's a box of frogs in my chest.

A few moments later, Sebastian shouts at me to climb back up. The rope tightens and I scramble back up there like Spiderman.

Everyone applauds and I try not to faint.

'So, you see,' Sebastian informs the group. 'It's important you know how to make a secure anchor when descending, but even *more* important is making sure your rope doesn't run over any sharp edges. If you find yourself in a no-fall zone, the number one rule is . . . ?'

'Don't fall!' everyone shouts.

★   ★   ★

Back in Chamonix, Luke announces at the bar that he's paid for us all to sleep in one of the dorms — we'd been camping outside but he says it's a better idea to stay indoors. 'Call it insurance,' he says. 'We don't want *somebody* forgetting to stub out their cigarette because they're too drunk to think straight. We might all end up without any gear.' We both turn to Theo, who says, 'What?'

'Don't play innocent,' Luke says, shuffling a deck of cards. 'You know you almost set the house on fire last weekend. Every time you get drunk you get your cigarette on the edge of the sofa or on the frigging mattress.'

'Don't remember,' Theo says with a shrug.

'Don't remember?' Luke laughs. 'The corner of the sofa was on fire, mate. It was starting to climb up your trouser leg. I grabbed a glass of water that turned out to be vodka, almost chucked it over you. You can imagine how that would have gone.'

'You going to deal or what?' Theo says, a fag bobbing between his lips, nodding at the pack of cards in Luke's hands. He begins to deal.

'What are we playing?' I ask.

'What are we drinking?'

'Gin.'

'Gin rummy, then.'

'Why not poker?' Theo asks.

'Fine, poker.'

'Where's Helen?' I say. 'Isn't she joining us?'

Luke deals. 'She's reading. Doesn't want to impose.'

The gin has warmed me up, broken down my hostilities. 'Mate, I don't mind if she wants to come.'

Luke gives me a dark stare. 'I don't know what drug you're taking but it's making lies fall out of your mouth.'

'I'm serious. Where is she? Invite her down here.'

Luke shakes his head. 'She won't come. She's got an early start with one of the trainers on the slopes.'

'She's training?' Theo says.

'Yeah. She doesn't want to rely on me when we're doing the tough parts. She's independent, mate.'

I sit with that for a moment. A sense of guilt

92

has crept in, my words about her being a leech and a millstone starting to nip at my conscience. I figured that she was Luke's trophy girlfriend, but with every hour that I spend in her company I find all my assumptions being scratched away. She seems hard-working, independent, and pleasant to be around. Even better is that so far Luke has been on top form, joking around and insisting on paying for everything. I'm putting it all down to Helen being here.

I stare at my cards. Not a great hand. My high card's the queen of hearts.

'You seem really into this chick,' I tell Luke, only realising once I've said it how childish it sounds.

'Thanks, mate. She's my girlfriend so it's probably a good thing that I'm into her. If you know what I mean.'

'How long you been . . . you know . . . ?'

'Seven months.'

'A long time to keep her away from your best mate,' I say. I think about mildly accusing him of either lying or being possessive but think better about it.

He shrugs. 'She lives in London. And when she's in Oxford we don't exactly want any extra company, if you know what I mean.'

Theo and I share a look. 'So, we probably shouldn't bring up any of the one-night stands you've had in that time?' Theo adds.

'Not unless you want me to mention the essay I helped you write for Comparative Literature last term. The Dean might not like that so much.'

I play my queen of hearts. Luke sets down a queen of spades and an ace.

He wins.

The next day the three of us are badly hungover. Luke and Theo say they'll give the training a miss, but I spot Helen, all geared up in a fluorescent pink shell suit heading off to the practice slopes with the rest of the climbers.

'Hey! Helen! Good morning!' I say, waving like an idiot.

She turns to the sound of her name. Sees me, waves. 'Hi, Michael. Have a good night?'

I nod and slap my forehead. 'Paying for it now, though.'

Another smile.

I am restless all day. Even when I join another climbing group with some French dudes who are eager to practise rope skills I feel distracted, my thoughts spiralling off in all directions.

13

Helen

1st September 2017

I'm at the British High Commission, sitting in a leather chair opposite Vanessa's desk. I'm too numb for tears. I'm paralysed with fear and blind confusion at what has just happened. The walls seem to move in and out, exhaling. I don't trust anyone.

I watch Vanessa on the phone to her superiors asking for advice. At least, that's what she tells me she's doing but for all I know she's part of this. For all I know she's involved in the crash.

I want to go back to the hospital and find Michael and tell him what's happened. I need to leave, call someone, beg for help. Inside I'm floundering like someone tossed into the middle of the ocean without so much as a life jacket. When Vanessa looks up I ask if I can use one of the other phones to call my friend, Camilla, back in England, but she simply nods and holds up a finger, distracted by the person she's speaking to. My breath comes in short, quick bursts. I move in and out of my body, into the past and the future.

The shrill sound of Vanessa's mobile knocks

me back into the room. She sets the handset of the landline down and answers, then hands her phone to me quickly. It is Alfredo, the neurosurgeon, and suddenly I'm plunged seventy miles north, in the hospital with Saskia.

'We have done extensive scanning of Saskia's brain,' he says. 'We can see a number of contusions on the frontal lobe and signs of a diffuse axonal. What I cannot see just now is whether there is any bleeding or swelling in the brain.'

'Will she be OK?' I ask tearfully.

He gives a sigh, and my heart plummets. 'There's a possibility that the pressure will increase and slow blood flow to the brain. If this happens, something called cerebral hypoxia and ischaemia can occur. It means that the brain can begin to protrude through the skull, which we certainly do not want.'

I feel turned inside out by this news. My mind races with questions. *Will she survive this? Will she walk again? Speak again? What are the long-term effects?*

'What can you do to help her?' I say weakly.

Another grave sigh. 'She will need an operation to insert an ICP bolt to monitor pressure in the brain cavity.'

There's a long silence, and I realise he is asking for my permission to perform this operation. To put a bolt in my daughter's head.

'Yes,' I hear myself say, though instantly I feel terrified, flooded with doubt. Is this the right thing? Did I just agree? Can I trust him?

He tells me that the next twenty-four hours are absolutely critical for her survival.

'Yes, please do whatever it takes,' I tell him, apologising as I break into sobs. I tell him I will do anything, absolutely anything for her. I will sell my body, rob a bank, plunder a city. I will give her my organs. I will give her my life.

'You must leave this to me,' he says, and I realise with terrifying helplessness that Saskia's fate — her survival — is entirely out of my hands.

★　★　★

'Can you take me to Michael, please?' I ask Vanessa as she wheels me through the hospital doors. I'm so weakened with worry about Saskia that I feel sick, and although I am desperate to see Michael I have no idea how to tell him about the van driver's accusation. How will he take it? How will he cope with news of Saskia *and* this accusation?

As we turn towards the corridor linking to his room I hear a man's voice bark, 'Helen? Helen Pengilly?'

The man is white, broad-shouldered and sandy-haired, the sleeves of a white linen shirt rolled up to his elbows, his hands in fists by his sides. He seems restless, as though he's searching for someone.

It is Theo.

I give a sharp, high-pitched scream.

'What's wrong?' Vanessa shouts. I turn all the way around in the wheelchair and pull on her clothes, yelling at her to get me out of here.

'Oh my *Lord*, Helen!'

A woman's voice. My vision blurred with tears, I make out another blurry figure racing up the corridor towards me. A slim woman, early thirties, short red hair, a black cotton dress and yellow sandals. Her face is wet and streaked black with running mascara. My heart pounds in my throat as Theo walks briskly towards me, but with each step he reveals himself as someone else entirely. It's not Theo after all. For a moment everything turns black and I'm gasping for breath.

Moments later my younger sister, Jeannie, is on her knees in front of me, her arms reaching around and pulling me into a painful embrace. I can smell her, feel her lips on my cheeks.

'I can't believe it,' she says, fumbling to take my hand in hers. 'I just can't believe what's happened, Helen, I can't! It's so awful!'

She reaches up and pushes a strand of hair out of my eyes, then cups my face. I burst into tears and she pulls me into another embrace.

When she pulls back she seems to be looking at the man behind her with a frightened expression.

'This is my boyfriend, Shane,' she says quickly. 'Shane, my sister Helen.'

'How do you do?'

I flinch as he looks at me, half-expecting him to turn into Theo again. My heart is still doing somersaults in my chest in case I'm mistaken. But he remains Shane — handsome, mid-forties, surprisingly anodyne, at least compared to Jeannie's usual class of boyfriend — and offers a hand, as though we're meeting in a café or bistro instead of a ramshackle hospital halfway around the world. He shakes Vanessa's hand and pulls a banknote out of his pocket, handing it to her, before stepping in to take over the job of pushing my wheelchair.

'Vanessa's from the British High Commission,' I say.

'Oh, apologies,' he says as she looks down with confusion at the twenty-pound note in her hand. 'Shane Goodwin, how do you do? You guys do a terrific job.'

I stare at Jeannie, engulfed with relief at the sight of a familiar face, by the fact that I'm no longer alone. It doesn't matter how awkward it is, how fractured my relationship with Jeannie is — she has come all this way to be with me, and for a fleeting moment I feel like I've been rescued. The threat of someone walking through the hospital doors lessens as Shane chats amiably to Reuben, asking after the game he's playing on his iPad. Shane begins to push the wheelchair towards the ward while Jeannie makes a huge fuss over me.

'This hospital is *horrific*,' she says loudly. A nurse passing by gives Jeannie a sour look. 'Honestly, of all the places to have a car accident, Helen! It's like a building site. Where's Saskia, by the way? And Michael? Are they in a different ward?'

'Saskia's been transferred to another hospital in Belize City . . . ' I explain, but Jeannie doesn't hear. She frowns as she looks over the ward, commenting on the lack of chairs for visitors and the appalling smell.

' . . . we've just got off a twenty-two-hour flight,' she says bitterly. 'Business class, but still. And the drive here . . . Oh! I won't bore you with the details but it was horrendous . . . '

From the corner of my eye I can see Reuben growing anxious. He's like a sponge, absorbing my mood. Shane keeps trying to talk to him — in a way that tells me he has no idea about Reuben's condition — and he's inching closer to me and stamping his feet.

'Do you need the bathroom?' Shane asks him. He turns to Vanessa. 'Do you know if there's a bathroom anywhere for this chap?'

Reuben starts to shake his head. He doesn't stop. I intervene, taking his hand, pulling him on to my knee and whispering into his ear.

'It's alright, Reuben,' I tell him, 'you're safe,' but he bangs his hands hard against his ears and makes a brrr sound with his lips, like the noise of a toy car. I can already tell he's heading for a full-scale meltdown and I'm in no position to stop him. The people on the ward are staring, Jeannie is informing Shane and anyone in a five-mile-radius that *Reuben is autistic, bless him*. My heart is pounding at the thought of what is happening to Saskia as we speak. I'm struggling to breathe and Reuben is now bouncing on my lap, so hard that I give a loud yelp of pain. Shane steps forward to intervene but Reuben shouts, 'Get off! Don't touch me!' and Shane leaps back like he's burnt his hands.

I tell Reuben to take off his socks and lie down on the floor, resting his feet on my lap. Shane and Jeannie look appalled. My arms feel like lead, but quickly I run my hands up and down his shins, then the soles of his feet.

'It calms him,' I explain weakly, and they nod but Jeannie looks as though she might throw up.

Once Reuben has been calmed and we've waved goodbye to Vanessa, I settle back into my bed on the ward and Jeannie cordons off the space with a curtain. She and Shane make seats out of plastic containers and sit by the bed, and I wait until Reuben is sufficiently distracted by a game on his iPad before telling them in frantic whispers what happened. The figure I saw at the beach hut. The van I saw swerving into our lane. The gut-wrenching moment of impact, unimaginably fast and horrific, that moment where I thought we wouldn't make it, that this was it — the end. And as I describe it I recall more details, each one like a lash across bare skin, breaking me down into juddering tears. I remember screaming for help. I remember climbing out of the car and surveying the scene, taking in the sight of the crumpled car and the small figure of Saskia's body on the ground with such horror that I blacked out. The boots by my face.

Retelling this changes the air, making it fizz. Jeannie and Shane look horrified. She takes my hand and asks about Saskia, why she isn't here. I tell her about Belize City, that Saskia's in surgery as we speak. I tell them about the interview at the police station. How I had expected to feel safer once I'd relayed my fears to the police, but instead I felt much, much worse, as though they viewed me with suspicion.

'What fears?' Jeannie asks, and I have to close my eyes and steady myself before I say it.

'That someone's trying to kill us,' I say through deep, juddering breaths, and instantly I can see the look of disbelief on both their faces. 'The police arrested the van driver and he's told them that Michael paid him to crash into our car.'

'Say that again?' Jeannie says, her eyes widening, and once I've repeated it she sits back in her chair and shares a horrified look with Shane. 'Well, of *course* the other driver's going to say anything to get off the hook. I'll bet you anything he was drink-driving and now he's trying to get out of serving jail time. Can't say I blame him. I mean, if the hospitals are this bad you can imagine what the prisons are like.'

'Surely they don't believe a word the other driver says?' Shane offers, a little more gently. I tell him I don't know. I don't know anything any more.

'Does Michael know?' Jeannie asks. 'Have you told him?'

I shake my head. 'He was still unconscious when I left.'

I ask them to help me into the wheelchair so I can finally head to see Michael. My thoughts pendulum between breaking this hideous news to him and his fate, which seems to rest now on the word of a stranger. What will happen to Michael if the police decide to investigate? Will they arrest him? Will they arrest me? What will happen to Reuben and Saskia?

The thought of the police barging in to rip

Reuben from my arms makes my blood run ice-cold and my whole body tremble uncontrollably.

Shane offers to sit with Reuben while Jeannie pushes me in the wheelchair to check on Michael. The corridor is dark, a puddle forming in the middle from a drip in the ceiling and a single strip light that flutters, on the verge of giving up. Jeannie's chatter behind me is soothing in its buoyancy, the confident tone of her voice.

'We need to arrange a way home,' Jeannie is saying in a crisp voice. I notice her accent has changed again — it tends to change to match her environment — to a solid RP accent, just like Shane's. Last I heard she was working in London as a Programme Director for the National Opera. 'I've already spoken to the airline and re-arranged your flights. Shane was already in Mexico when I got the call. He said he'd fly down and meet me here. Do you think you'll be well enough to travel tomorrow?'

'*Tomorrow?*'

'Oh, ignore me. I forgot that Saskia's in a different hospital. That reminds me: I hadn't told you about Shane, had I? It must have been weird for you to see him earlier. He's my new boyfriend. Met him at a thing in Mayfair. He's handsome, isn't he? And guess what?'

'What?'

'I've got him into leech therapy. We're going on a GOOP retreat in January. A week in Bali with shamans, yogis and leeches. *Bliss.*'

My younger sister and I haven't always seen eye to eye, mostly on account of how different we are. She's demanding, opportunistic, and doesn't listen very well, unless you're sharing wild gossip, in which case she's all ears: a difficult person to warm to. Intuition whispers that she's not here for me at all but for the drama. Jeannie adores drama.

We'd not seen each for six years when the fire at the bookshop happened, and within twenty-four hours she was on my doorstep, eying up the destruction to our livelihood, and the niece and nephew that didn't recognise her, with unveiled glee. She stayed for two weeks, which was long enough for Michael to tell me to cut ties with her.

I wonder what he'll say when he sees her here. Maybe he'll be grateful. We need as many people fighting our corner as we can get right now.

'We must have the wrong room,' Jeannie says when we turn into Michael's side room.

I glance at the metal cupboard in the corner with the dent in the door, the flaking blue paint on the wall beside it making a butterfly pattern in the plaster. 'No, it's definitely this room. I remember it.'

The bed is empty, the covers flung back. Jeannie flicks on the light.

'Well, where is he, then?'

The ventilator, monitor and drip-stand are here, tubes hanging redundantly by their sides. I glance at the chair beside the bed where I spotted Michael's clothes and backpack. They aren't there.

'They must have moved him,' I say, and swiftly Jeannie walks out of the room and further into the ward to find someone to ask.

'We're looking for Mr Pengilly,' she tells a nurse, pointing at Michael's room. 'My brother-in-law. He was just in that room.'

The nurse walks a little way ahead of us and turns into the room. She lifts the clipboard at the bottom of the bed, scans the notes. 'Michael Pengilly,' she reads slowly, then looks again at the bed as if he might materialise.

'Excuse me, please,' she says after a few moments, then heads back down the corridor to find a doctor. We tell him the same thing, and again we go back to Michael's room, only to confirm the same: we had arrived to find the bed empty. Michael was last seen by a nurse at three o'clock. He'd been sleeping but otherwise stable. By all accounts, he should still be in the room. The catheter and IV have been removed but nobody had signed off their removal.

I spot some bloodied dressings underneath the bed, and Jeannie picks them up and thrusts them at a nurse who stands in the doorway, her mouth open.

Just then, a doctor appears by the nurse's side.

'We have been conducting an extensive search for Michael Pengilly,' he says, out of breath.

'And?' Jeannie says, throwing her arms up.

'We have searched the whole hospital, checked all the wards. Nobody has seen him. I'm afraid he has gone.'

14

Reuben

1st September 2017

I like hugs, like Olaf in *Frozen*, except I'm not a snowman and I'm much taller than he is. I also like pizza, animation, and hiding. I don't like tight shoes, umbrellas, people who stare, and hand dryers, because they go off whenever you get too close and it's like being shouted at only worse.

I also like the colour blue and robins, though they aren't blue but I saw this YouTube video once of a robin that waited by the same path for this man who walked his dog every day because he always brought food for the robin. Also 'robin' is one syllable away from being my name. I like whales now, too, blue whales in particular though they are the loudest animals on earth. Also, their tongues weigh as much as an elephant, though that wouldn't really bother me if I saw one.

I tell all this to the nurse and she has a look on her face that I can't read, sort of angry and sort of shocked. It's the same look that Mum sometimes has when she walks in and finds that I've used too much blue bath paint and then she'll chillax and say, 'You look like a Smurf, Reuben.'

I begin to ask the nurse if she thinks I look like a Smurf when Shane talks over me in a big voice. He tells the nurse that we're waiting on Helen, who is my mum, while she visits Saskia, who is my sister. Saskia hurt her head and is in a coma, which means she sleeps for days and nobody knows when she might wake up.

The nurse says something I don't understand. Everyone here speaks either Spanish or Kriol, which is a type of English but is the same thing as adding tomato sauce and onions and mince to spaghetti. The spaghetti is no longer just spaghetti but Spaghetti Bolognese.

I don't know where Dad is and him not being here makes everything louder.

The nurse is waving her hands now. She tries to take my iPad off me. Shane stops her and speaks to the nurse and me very fast.

'Reuben,' he says. 'I don't think you're allowed to film in here, son.'

'I'm not your son,' I say. On my screen the nurse's face grows whiskers and bunny ears. I tried to tell her I liked watching everything on my screen — and actually I was recording — because it made me feel better, and filters can make things that are scary less scary, even funny, but she was still angry and shocked and Shane took the iPad off me.

She said we could wait in a side room instead of the corridor and Shane said yes, though when we go into the room I want to leave again because there is a woman and a baby in there who is crying really loudly and it makes my ears hurt.

Shane tells me to stop smacking the back of

my head with my hand. I try to but it's really hard. My hand wants to do it even though I want it to stop.

'Will you do the feet thing?' I ask Shane.

He frowns at me. 'What's the feet thing?'

So I pull off my flipflops and lie back in the chair opposite and put my feet on his chest. His eyes are wide and he looks over my feet at me.

'Reuben, do you mind telling me what on earth you're doing?'

'You have to kiss my feet,' I say, wriggling my toes.

'Beg pardon?'

'And stroke my shins.'

Shane says a swear then and I think he's going to not stroke my shins and I think I might explode. But suddenly he touches my feet and I feel calm because my feet like being stroked. He's not doing it like Mum does and he won't kiss them but he rubs the soles of my feet with his thumbs in big circles which is nice actually and even the baby has stopped shrieking.

When I open my eyes the woman and the baby are looking at me with my feet in Shane's face and they're laughing. Shane turns bright red and jumps up out of his seat.

'Come on, Reuben,' he says. 'Let's go grab some air.'

We go out of the room and outside the hospital and get into the car where my new headphones are. He turns on the engine and the air con blasts out.

'Better?' he says, and I nod. I put on my headphones even though the car isn't too loud, but I hate being inside the car because I keep thinking that someone is going to crash into us again.

Shane is Aunt Jeannie's friend. He has cardboard-coloured hair with bits of grey in it and crinkly eyes and a nose like a paper aeroplane. He does not like hugs or the heat.

I tap the 'voice memos' app on my iPad and check it for the tracks I'd recorded of Dad. I want to hear his voice again but they aren't there.

'What's the matter?' Shane says. 'What's with all the finger clicking?'

'There is no Wi-Fi,' I say, and he takes out his mobile phone and lets me log on to his personal hotspot. As I log into my iCloud I get three hundred and forty notifications on all my new apps.

One of them is from iPix Pro, which is an animation app that lets you make drawings or even animations and then share them with your friends. I'm not allowed Snapchat or Facebook or any social media but I'm allowed iPix because you can create an avatar and a fake name and it's mostly about drawing. Some people have a million friends on there. I have six. Josh, Lily, Jagger, Lucas, Rach, and Malfoy. I open the chat box and there are some messages from Josh and Lily asking what I'm doing. I say 'Hi, not much' to both of them and they don't say anything so I open the one from Malfoy.

```
Malfoy:  Hi Reuben. Are you OK?
Roo:     Hey Malfoy. Yes am OK. Are
         u OK
Roo:     r u ther?
```

The cursor blinks for fifty-five seconds. He doesn't answer. I go to close the app and start drawing again but suddenly it says 'typing', and just over three seconds later a message appears.

```
Malfoy:  Yes I'm here. Are you alright?
         Where are you?
Roo:     Yes am OK. my little sis
         is not OK
Malfoy:  Is she still asleep?
Roo:     yes but for a long time
Malfoy:  ☹ Did the doctors say she'll
         wake up soon?
Roo:     idk
Malfoy:  How is ur mum?
Roo:     she cries a lot ☹ ☹
Roo:     Have you finished ur anima-
         tion of the pirate ship
         battle?
Malfoy:  Almost.
Roo:     Can I see?
Malfoy:  You bet. But can you do me
         a favour?
Roo:     k
Malfoy:  can you record your mum
         for me?
Roo:     Y?
Malfoy:  I want to see what your
         family is up 2 . . .
Roo:     thats a wierd request . . .
Roo:     u want me to interview my
         mum????
Malfoy:  no. don't let her know ur
         recording. Better if it's
```

```
          fly-on-the-wall stuff.
Malfoy:   Hey, I learned how to use
          Trapdoor Particular. If you
          record some stuff for me I'll
          show you. Would be perfect
          for your Mayan village . . .
```

The cursor blinks for twelve seconds.

```
Roo:      OK. I'll record some stuff
          + send it to you tonight.
Malfoy:   Thanks. Gotta go.
```

I sit for a few moments trying to work out why Malfoy wants me to record stuff. We've never met, not in real life, though he likes me and not very many people like me. He knows all kind of animation stuff. He showed me how to make palm trees move in the wind to make the village look like a real village.

I go to the camera app but then remember the nurse being weird with me. Mum says people don't like being filmed. I don't mind it. But I can record sound with the voice memos app and nobody ever notices.

I bring up the app. As Mum and Jeannie get in the car I say, 'Hi Mum,' and she says 'Hi.'

On my screen the 'record' light is flashing.

15

Helen

1st September 2017

Michael is missing. Actually vanished, missing, nowhere to be found. Nobody knows anything. I feel like I've slipped into a nightmare. My lungs feel crushed to the size of peanuts, my throat burns with fear, and I'm exhausted from pleading with every hospital worker we can find to tell us where Michael is. They look at me as if I've gone mad.

My first thought was that the police had already arrested him, that they'd turned up unannounced and hauled him off to the police station, but a phone call to Vanessa confirmed that this isn't the case. I told her that perhaps the van driver turned up to the hospital. Again, this isn't likely, given that the man is still in custody. Though maybe he didn't act alone. Maybe someone else is working with him.

When I start wheeling myself down the corridors in tears, screaming Michael's name, a doctor persuades Jeannie to take me to a side room.

'You *have* to calm down,' she says wearily. 'They're going to kick us out.'

'*Calm down?* How can I? He's been taken.'

'Taken? What do you mean, 'taken'?'

I can't stop shaking, adrenalin surging through my veins. 'I *know* he has. We're being watched, Jeannie.'

'Watched by *who?*' she says, clearly not believing a word I say, and I realise she's in danger, too.

I fall silent and concentrate on forcing my body to breathe. Blackness flutters at the edges of my vision, luring me to fall into it, but I have to stay awake. For Reuben's sake, for Saskia's. And for Michael. Jeannie knows nothing about Luke's death and I can never, ever tell her. She hasn't spent the last twenty-two years dragging the guilt of her dead lover behind her like a ball and chain. She hasn't had to grow eyes in the back of her head, or develop echolocation to detect the sound of another letter being penned, calling her a murderer. How could she possibly understand a word I'm saying?

Eight hours have passed since we discovered Michael was gone. I'm stinking with sweat and dried blood, overwhelmed by terror. Dawn begins to creep through the windows in a rich orange glow, the loud whirr of insects lessens. It's morning. I have not slept all night. The surgeon calls to say that Saskia is out of surgery, that it was a success. The news brings staggering relief, but it's short-lived. I want to go to her immediately but then Dr Atilio arrives, together with the hospital's Chief Physician, Dr Gupta, to help with the search for Michael. Flanked by nurses, Dr Gupta is a tall, rakish woman in her late sixties with full red lips and an air of authority.

'I can confirm Michael Pengilly is not in this hospital,' she says. 'We must now turn this matter over to the police.'

If it is possible to feel more terrified than when discovering your husband has vanished into thin air after a serious car accident, then this is it. I beg her not to call the police and start to tell her about Superintendent Caliz, how he didn't listen to a word I said about the fact that I saw the van driver at the scene of the crash, how he did absolutely *nothing* to help any of us. That someone is watching us. Of course, she looks at me with a mixture of pity and wariness, and I see myself through her eyes: I'm a ranting foreigner who sounds entirely like she's been doing drugs.

So somehow I find the strength to push all the emotions that want to thrash and flail in outrage and fear down, down into a corner of my heart, and I force myself to comply, go along with procedure.

Dr Gupta tells us that the hospital administrative manager, Zelma, has checked the hospital's CCTV cameras and spotted something that she wants to share with us. 'And the police,' she tells us. 'They have said they wish to see this also.'

Jeannie and I are taken to Zelma's office in the east wing of the hospital, a small room with a desk cluttered with framed pictures of smiling children and an old dusty computer.

'I asked all the staff and the patients where your husband go,' Zelma explains in a thick accent. 'Many of them didn't see anything. But there was one man, a janitor. He saw a white man walking on the road near the hospital.'

'What road?' Dr Gupta interrupts, and Jeannie writes it down. Orchid Street.

'Did the janitor give a description of the man he saw?'

'Yes. He say this man have dark hair and on him navy T-shirt with denim shorts and flipflops. Like Michael Pengilly have.'

'A few white men of that description are in this area,' she says. 'We have a training college here in the hospital. Cheaper here than in the US so a lot of American medical students.'

'Did the janitor say how the white man appeared?' Dr Gupta asks Zelma. 'It is not likely that Mr Pengilly was recovered enough to leave by himself. Did the man appear to be alone?'

Zelma looks perplexed. 'I'll ask the janitor again.'

A knock at the door. Dr Gupta steps across me to open it to two police officers and a man in plain clothes who doesn't introduce himself. My blood runs cold. It's Superintendent Caliz. I keep my eyes on the ground as he takes a chair behind me.

A minute later Vanessa comes into view, all beaming smiles in a navy skirt suit. I notice that she freezes as soon as she claps eyes on Superintendent Caliz.

'Hello everyone,' she says, quickly gathering her composure. She leans over and whispers in my ear. 'I have something for you.' Reaching into her briefcase she pulls out a slightly scruffy white teddy with a satin collar stained with blood, as though he's been garrotted. Saskia's Jack-Jack. There is something new on his collar, too, a little love heart tag that Saskia must have put on him recently. I draw a sharp breath and clutch Jack-Jack to me, breathing in the faint scent of Saskia that still clings to his fur. I'm trying so hard not to break down in front of everyone but I feel frantic.

'One of the soldiers brought him to me earlier,' she says. 'One of Saskia's toys, yes? I thought you might like to take it to her.'

An officious-looking man with a silver quiff and a sharp black suit follows behind her. Vanessa introduces him as Jim Kierznowski, the British High Commissioner. I watch as he shakes hands firmly with the police officers before turning to me and slapping a large square palm painfully on my shoulder.

'I'm deeply sorry to hear about what's happened,' he says. 'I know Vanessa is working very hard to ensure that you and your family can get home as swiftly as possible.'

I nod and thank him but inside I'm screaming. How can I even think about going back to England? Saskia is seventy miles away and Michael is missing. Every second that he's gone makes me think I'll never see either of them again, and it is terrifying.

'Shall we watch the footage you captured, Zelma?' Dr Gupta says, and Zelma manoeuvres the old PC monitor at the edge of a desk so that it faces us all. She brings up a new browser and points at some green digits at the side of the frame.

'This footage is from two days ago,' Zelma says, clicking play. Immediately I can see that the camera is angled downward at a fire exit.

'This is at an exit at the side of the hospital,' she says quietly.

'Which side?' Jim asks.

'The east side. About one hundred yards along the corridor here.'

We wait for the footage to reveal this. Finally, a figure comes into view. We all lean forward. A tall, dark-haired man with a backpack slung over his left shoulder walks slowly towards the door. He pauses at the exit, then pushes the bar at the fire door, opening the door outwards. A brief glance to his right shows that he is wearing sunglasses, his hair comes to his jaw, and he continues out of the door with a noticeable limp.

'Do you recognise this man?' Zelma asks me.

I squint at the screen. 'The angle makes it difficult to tell,' I say, and I feel Superintendent Caliz's eyes on me.

'Perhaps we might zoom in on the image?' Vanessa says mildly.

The footage begins again, zoomed and pixellated, and when the figure appears again his head almost fills the screen. The man is the same height and muscular build as Michael, dark hair, a hint of beard. At the moment that the man turns his face to the right, Zelma pauses the frame.

'Do you think that's your husband?' Vanessa says.

I recognise the shape of the backpack with the plastic handle on the top.

117

It's Michael.

Zelma unpauses the footage, and I watch, floating out of my body, as the footage shows Michael walking through the fire exit door. Another figure appears closely behind him. Another man, stocky build, protruding belly. Black, bald-headed and dressed in a short-sleeved shirt and jeans. From the angle of the camera, it almost looks as though the man behind is pushing Michael forward.

'Who is that?' I say quickly. This man has my full attention. I'm back in my skin, filmed in ice, my senses razor sharp. 'Who *is* he?' I say again.

Dr Gupta and Dr Atilio share a glance. 'We can find out.' Zelma rewinds the footage and we watch again, studying the movements. Every gesture, every frame is weighted with significance, because there is simply no way Michael should be in any of them.

'It does look like he's with Michael,' Jeannie observes, leaning forward and screwing up her face at the footage. 'Kind of forcing him out the doors.'

'So you think this man *is* your husband?' Dr Gupta asks.

'Yes,' I say, too distracted by the man standing behind Michael to think about my answer. Behind me, Superintendent Caliz clears his throat.

'Michael Pengilly was on medication, yes?' Jim asks Dr Atilio, who nods.

'Patient-controlled analgesia, which meant he pressed a button when he was in need of pain relief. We also gave him a mild blood thinner to prevent clotting.'

'This could potentially have affected his

mental capacities?' Jim asks.

Dr Atilio looks doubtful. 'I don't think so. We monitored him closely to ensure the dosage was correct.'

'If he was being monitored closely, as you say,' Jeannie interrupts, her a voice a little too loud, 'how exactly was he able to walk out of the hospital?'

'Or be forced to walk out of the hospital,' I say, though there's a voice of doubt in my mind about the way Michael is leaving that door. He doesn't look behind. He just leaves. A chill runs up my spine.

'What's clear is that this family has faced an extreme misfortune,' Jim announces in a way that seems to wrap up the session. 'A little girl's life hangs in the balance, another child and the mother are injured, and now the father is missing. We must all work very hard to ensure he returns safely.'

As Superintendent Caliz gets to his feet I'm sure he has a smirk on his face.

16

Helen

1st September 2017

Shane arrives back at the hospital with Reuben shortly after the police leave. I am haunted by what happened earlier when we watched the footage.

Why did I tell them that it was Michael? Why did I say that? If I'd said nothing, they might have believed me when I said we were in danger. That Michael's disappearance was proof of it. But I've confirmed that it was him, and the footage can be taken in such a way that he left voluntarily. Now the police have evidence, but not the sort I hoped. They have evidence that the accusation against Michael might be true. Because why else would he leave, if not to avoid being charged?

What have I done?

Reuben races into the ward shouting 'Mum!' and throws his arms around me. I see that his hair has been washed and he is wearing a new T-shirt and shorts, both blue, albeit with a misspelled Adidas logo, and a pair of new headphones hooked around his neck, also blue. I risk a glance at Shane — I'm unnerved by how much he reminds me of Theo — and he leans forward to give Jeannie a kiss. He looks exhausted.

'I must have driven around the hospital eighty times,' he says, rubbing his face. 'Kept driving on the wrong side of the road. Got lost trying to explore a wider perimeter. Drove out into the middle of nowhere.'

'So, no sign of him?' Jeannie frowns, and Shane shakes his head.

'Asked a few people too and they said they'd not seen anything.'

'I made a Mayan village on iPix,' Reuben says, showing me something on his iPad. 'Malfoy helped me. He showed me how to download Optifine.'

'Malfoy?' I say. 'Who's that?'

'He's one of my iPix buddies,' he says, and proceeds to tell me about the 3D Mayan village he'd designed, with jaguars and lizards and a king with a feathered crown. 'Can I go see Dad, Mum? Shane bought me new headphones. I want Dad to try them because he always tries them before we buy them to make sure they aren't too loud and aren't too quiet.'

I draw breath sharply and try hard to force a smile on my face. 'Dad's asleep at the moment, darling. We'll show him later, OK?'

His face sours and he murmurs a word of protest. Shane steps in. 'Reuben's also done some exemplary drawings on his device. Has he shown you?'

'Not yet,' I say, but Reuben shifts to hop from foot to foot and clicks his fingers: a stinker of a

121

meltdown isn't far off. He can tell we aren't telling him the whole truth.

'Can I see Dad when we come back from seeing Saskia?' Reuben asks, and I falter.

'You know, I found this amazing pizza place on TripAdvisor,' Shane tells me enthusiastically for Reuben's benefit. 'It's actually in Belize City. How about we go there after seeing Saskia? And then we can see your dad in the morning. Does that sound like a good idea to you, Reuben?'

Reuben nods reluctantly.

Afterwards, I replay the CCTV footage over and over again in my head. Maybe it wasn't Michael. I watched that footage after enduring one of the most horrific nights of my life. I have slept only a handful of hours in over two days, I have a head injury, and my daughter has just undergone brain surgery. I am not, you might say, in the best of minds right now, so it's likely that when I watched that footage, everything in me *wanted* it to be Michael. If it was him, it means he hasn't been flung into a prison cell by the police, or hauled off by one of the van driver's accomplices. I crave answers. I am desperate for Michael to be alright. So, it's possible that the footage showed someone else entirely and I was just willing it be him.

And yet, there's a part of me that says it *was* Michael in the footage. But the chances of anyone being able to physically walk out of the hospital right after a major car accident are slim to none. And even if he somehow was physically able, what reason would he have to leave? Neither of us have ever been to San Alvaro before. It's a completely foreign place. Michael would have no idea where to go. And he wouldn't just waltz out without saying something, even if only for a brief time. He would have come to see me first if there was a reason he had to leave.

It just doesn't make any sense. None of it.

The exit they say he left by is on the other side of the hospital, close to his room. There is an exit right by my ward marked with a bright 'fire escape' sign. If Michael came to find me and then decided to leave, he would have no reason to go all the way back to the east side of the hospital.

Why would he go?

17

Helen

17th June 1995

Waking up beside Luke is the most incredible feeling. We're on a single bed in a dorm filled with four other sleeping bodies, though there's a curtain to give us a little privacy. He lies beside me on his back, his head turned slightly away, gently snoring. I've never seen a more beautiful man. His bone structure is like one of those figures carved on ancient Greek temples. His hair is like spun gold and his skin is that shade of Bondi tan that's bone deep. His hands look like they could hold the earth, and when they're on my body I feel like a rare and precious stone filled with light and water and earth.

People are amazed when I tell them I'm dating someone who has an identical twin. They imagine that Luke and Theo are dressed the same, that their hair is the same, as though they're five years old. Luke showed me some of their old school pics and I was mesmerised — they really do look like clones, two adorable little boys with white-blond hair in sailor outfits, exact copies of each other. He and Theo are so different now. Theo's much skinnier, about an inch shorter, and his hair is long and greasy. He looks like he plays the bass in a grunge rock band. Luke, on the other hand, looks like he's been carved by Michelangelo, with floppy gold hair, sea-green eyes and a rippling six pack from all that rowing. The real difference, however, is on the inside. Luke isn't just gorgeous because of his physical attributes. I'm not in love with him for his body, perfect as it is. It's his personality. He's like fire. You just can't help but want to be around him. Though sometimes I'll admit I get a little burnt by getting too close.

I need to pee so I try to squeeze my way out of the slim space between Luke and the wall of the dorm, but he rolls over, a heavy, muscular arm slung over my waist, trapping me. I laugh lightly, pinned to the bed. I expect him to open an eye and prove he's awake, but he snores on, his lips puckered. I ignore the pinch of my bladder and lie there with my eyes closed.

I have always, always wanted to be loved as deeply as this. I used to see other people in relationships, their arms around each other and their smiling faces turned to each other, and my heart would drop. I never thought it would happen to me. But it has, and I won't let go of it.

My bladder won't hold off any longer. I manage at last to wiggle out of the bed and run on my tiptoes down the hall to the bathroom. I wash my hands. Someone's left a small tube of toothpaste with foreign writing on it — Russian, I think — so I squeeze out a pea-sized amount and rub it over my teeth and tongue. I don't want to have bad breath. Then I turn to the foggy mirror and try to tame my hair into sexy-bedhead instead of wild-witch-plucked-from-a-hedge.

I lick my fingertips and smooth my eyebrows, then pinch my eyelashes to give some definition to my eyes. I have such pale colouring that going without make-up is nerve-wracking. I worried that Luke might find me less attractive out here, bare-faced and frizzy-haired. But he always says I'm beautiful, I'm gorgeous, and sexy. That I have the most amazing body he's ever seen. Every other guy I've dated has been such a boy in comparison; clumsy and inattentive.

I broke up with Ian last year when I found out he was addicted to porn and generally made me feel like a piece of meat. Just . . . gross. I could almost laugh when I think back to how much courage it took me to break up with him. I didn't even find Ian attractive and he was boring. All he wanted to do was play his Nintendo and watch porn. But we had been going out for almost a year and deep down I worried that I wouldn't find anyone else. I'm nearly twenty, after all. It was almost easier to convince myself that Ian was better than he was just to avoid being on my own. But I found the courage and dumped him, and a month later I met Luke. Within two weeks he told me he was in love with me, and within three weeks I found myself daydreaming about being Helen Aucoin.

When I head back to the dorm everyone's awake and getting their bags together. The sun is rising, a long orange tail of light laid across the room. I walk over to Luke and peck him on the lips. He gives a stretch and says, 'Morning, gorgeous.' I feel a swell of pure joy inside.

We gear up and head out into the day, bright blue skies overhead and the mountains all around us like sleeping dragons. I'm feeling more confident about the climb today, though I know that the real challenges still lie ahead.

When Luke first asked me to come along I said no. I'm fit, yes, but climbing the Alps? I didn't feel at all capable. 'You'll be fine,' he said, moving his hands over my hips and kissing my neck. 'You're unstoppable. You'll tackle those mountains like they're escalators.'

I laughed and pulled away. 'It's a boy's walk,' I said. 'You and your mates. It'll be weird if I come.' He pulled a sulky face and I leaned over to kiss him. 'Seriously, Luke. What if I get mountain sickness? Or whatever it's called. You'll hate me and I wouldn't like that very much.'

'I'll never hate you,' he said wistfully, snapping the waistband of my leggings with a hooked finger. 'I'll just miss you, is all.'

I told him I had to get ready for dance rehearsals. He looked up from my bed and gave me a frown as I rifled through the pile of laundry on the floor for a clean towel.

'What about that Ian?' he said. 'He still in touch with you?'

I turned and tried to read his face. 'Ian? Funny you should mention him. He sent me a card last week. *Such* a moron.'

'I thought you broke up with him last year,' he said in a tight voice. 'How come he's still contacting you? Are you still sleeping with him?'

I stopped what I was doing, aghast. 'Are you serious? No!'

But he wouldn't make eye contact. His face darkened. He muttered something about Ian trying to worm his way back into my life and maybe I preferred him. I knelt in front of him and tried to get him to look at me.

'Luke, I will *never* get back with Ian, alright? It's just . . . I'm sorry, I shouldn't have said anything.'

He looked sheepish, finally raising his eyes to mine. He brushed my hair off my shoulder and gave me that look, the one no one else has *ever* given me, the one that seems to drink me in like something divine. I could drown in that look.

'I don't want to lose you, that's all,' he said. 'What if you decide I'm not worth your time when I'm away?'

'You know that won't happen . . . '

He dropped his head into his hands. I could see I was tormenting him. And what was so wrong with me going? I knew his brother Theo. I got on with him and I sensed that Theo liked me.

'Maybe I *could* come,' I started to say, and he looked up quickly, a big grin on his face. 'But only if you promise to be nice . . . '

'Yes! Yes! Yes!' he was shouting, climbing on to my bed and bouncing up and down on the mattress with his arms in the air.

'Keep it down, you two!' my flatmate shouted grumpily from the other room, thumping the wall. 'Not when I'm at home, remember? Jeez!'

'*And* I'll need climbing gear,' I said to Luke,

suddenly wary. 'I don't even think I'll be able to get any this late in the day.'

He pulled me in for a kiss. 'Don't worry about that. I'll buy it for you. I'll buy *everything*.'

I laughed and pulled away, glancing at the clock. 'We can sort that out later. Now, I really do have to go,' I said, finding a damp towel slung over the back of my chair. 'I'll see you later, OK?'

He gave me a come hither look. 'Where do you think you're going?'

'Rehearsals, sorry.'

He snatched the bag from my hand, tossed it into a corner. Pulled me in for a long, knee-jellifying kiss. 'You're not going anywhere,' he said.

18

Michael

2nd September 2017

The plane descends over the city, the Thames' grey ribbon and the Lego model streets and bridges shift gradually to human scale. I can make out tufts of black smoke rising from a large building on the outskirts of the city. Ever since the fire at the bookshop I'm hyper alert to fire hazards. Before, I never really paid much attention. When I went camping in my teens I always found it hard to get a good fire going, had to slip a few fire lighters beneath the logs on the sly. And even then, it would go out in the slightest gust of wind. But now, I look at a match and want to throw up. I see people lighting candles on their mantelpieces, people smoking, and I have to close my eyes.

When Mr Dickinson rang and said there was a fire at the shop I imagined a bunch of teenagers smoking out the back had triggered an alarm. Maybe one of them had set fire to the wheelie bin. Worst case scenario, I'd left a heater on and it had started a small but containable fire that we'd put out with a fire extinguisher before it did any significant damage.

Of course, that's not what happened. Helen and I drove down to find what seemed like an inferno, the windows all aglow with flames and thick black smoke rolling out from under the door like a carpet. All I could think about was saving the books. I even did a quick mental calculation of my most precious stock: first editions of Oscar Wilde and *Black Beauty* with a wooden frontispiece, some nineteenth-century folios with gold endpapers, a box of Victorian letters gifted by a local man in his will. I ran up the stairs to the small room at the back where I stored all the collectibles and antiquarian stock but the smoke was like a wall, or an actual living entity that plunged its fist inside my chest and pulled out my lungs. I can still feel that pain, months later. Like drowning or having a heart attack. I was blinded, stumbling down the stairs in a blind frenzy and dropping all the books I'd grabbed. So stupid. I could have died.

Helen pulled me out and we lay on the pavement outside, gasping for breath as flames chewed up everything we'd worked for. I'll never forget that sight. Only once before have I felt so completely helpless. That was a long time ago. It felt like Luke's death all over again. As though I'd never be free.

The plane bumps on to the runway. My family's faces flash across my mind. Helen. Saskia. Reuben. I came to in the army truck after the crash and looked over them all. I was lying flat on my back. Helen's head was on my chest and Saskia was laid out beside me, along my arm. Reuben was huddled in a corner, crying. I cupped Helen's face and she woke up. I told her everything was going to be OK. I told her I'd protect her and the kids.

But the distance from them now almost crushes me. I wish I could be with them so badly it almost turns me inside out.

In the terminal building I duck into a toilet to splash water on my face. I passed out on the plane and when I woke I felt like I'd been drugged — my vision was blurred and I was literally seeing stars, a bright crescent of them framing everything I looked at.

The mirror throws back a version of myself with a black eye, cuts on my forehand and blood encrusted around my nostrils. No wonder people on the plane kept asking if I was alright.

I pump soap from the dispenser and lather it across my face and under my armpits with warm water. My beard's too long, it makes me look aggressive. I need to shave it off. Suddenly I feel a shooting pain in my left side, just under my ribcage. It's like being burned, as though someone's driving a hot poker right through me.

The passport queue is about a mile long. Everyone looks miserable. I watch the officers at the desks as they check the passports, all of them stern-faced. This was a bad idea. They're going to take one look at my passport and haul me off to a cell. The family in front of me have a toddler, a little boy about eighteen-months-old with a Gruffalo backpack who is screaming his head off. His dad bends to pick him off the ground but he kicks him square in the face. When he recovers, the dad yanks the boy up into his arms and signals to an officer who has been strolling up and down the queue with his hands behind his back.

'Isn't there a line for families with young children?' the man asks. The toddler starts to shout again and the mum steps in, wrapping the boy's legs around her waist and pressing his face into her neck. He subdues.

The officer shakes his head. He mutters something about flight delays and six planes landing at once. When he walks on I feel his eyes on my face, taking in the state of me. I can't let the fact that my legs might buckle at any moment give me away. I need to come up with a story about why I look like I've been beaten to a pulp.

Finally it's my turn. I slide my passport to the officer and try not to let the stars in my vision distract me too much.

He's about thirty, stares at me, visibly trying to work out why the hell I look like I've been the victim of an elephant stampede. I point to my face and grin.

'Came off my bike,' I say. 'Don't know who came off worse, me or the pavement.'

A flicker of a smile. Hands me back the passport.

'Have a great day.'

Relief floods me. A second later I want to throw up all over the counter.

Luckily, though, I don't, and I make it all the way out into the terminal. A scree of familiar signs greets me: Boots, Dune, Costa, WH Smith. Out here, in the bustle of last-minute toothpaste and paperback holiday read buying, no one looks at me. But high above the heads of all the travellers are scores of CCTV cameras, and *they're* watching everything. At every exit there are at least three security guards, and walking towards me are two uniformed police officers. One of them frowns as he makes eye contact. I try not to look but his stare brings me out in a cold sweat and I have to sit down on the bench nearby. I pull out my phone, pretend to be checking emails. I wonder if I'm about to be arrested. But he keeps on walking.

With trembling hands I flick through to the image of the letter again. The address is there when I zoom in:

Haden, Morris & Laurence Law Practice
4 Martin Place
London
EN9 1AS

Google maps says the route involves two tube changes, a bus, and a bit of a walk. It's been a long time since I've been to London and everything looks different. As I head towards the train platform a memory of Helen rises up in my mind. We first met around that trip to Mont Blanc in our early twenties and after that I had never expected to see her again. But then, at a train station, I had seen a girl on the platform opposite, reading. Blonde hair in a side ponytail, a yellow scarf, navy mini skirt showing off those amazing legs. The familiar stance — her right leg placed slightly in front of her and bent with the foot tucked in at an angle. I remember my insides turned to jelly. I couldn't tear my eyes away from her. It was like being split right down the middle. Half of me wanted to yell out, call her name, the other wanted to run in the other direction. Instead I froze. Right as she looked up and saw me her train came screaming into the station and she was gone.

From the moment we had left Mont Blanc she had haunted my thoughts every single day. I had tried so hard to find her. This was long before social media so finding someone was virtually impossible back then. I had had a few relationships but they all petered out because I was so disinterested. I kept trying to find someone like her and failing miserably. So one day I had an idea to call every dance school in the country. She'd said she was a ballerina, quite a decent one at that, so surely someone must know where she lived?

It took thirteen phone calls. Finally I got through to a receptionist at the dance school in Leeds who'd heard of Helen Warren. 'I only work two days a week,' she said. 'The other girl who's usually here, Tessa, she knows Helen. She might have a forwarding address. She'll be in tomorrow.'

I got on the first train to Leeds. The next morning I turned up at the dance school with the biggest bouquet of flowers and a box of chocolates. I told Tessa I needed to give them to Helen Warren in person, and acted disappointed when she said Helen was no longer coming to the dance school. She was hesitant but didn't want Helen to miss out on the gift, so she quickly wrote down the last address she had for her. I thanked her profusely and headed back to the train station. I changed at Birmingham New Street. My train from there was delayed, so I bought a book and waited on the platform. Then something made me look up.

A girl was standing on the platform opposite. Helen. It couldn't be a coincidence. I ran to her and wrapped my arms around her. She was so taken aback that she jerked away until she saw my face. Then she stared at me for the longest time, before breaking down into tears and pulling me into a tight embrace.

★ ★ ★

The train for King's Cross pulls up. I have 6 per cent battery left and it takes all my strength not to call Helen, not to tell her where I am and what I'm doing. But they've probably bugged our phones. And I know exactly what she'll say. She'll tell me not to. It's why we haven't spoken about it all these years, isn't it? It's why she hid the letters. We risked losing the kids. If anyone found out what happened on Mont Blanc it would tear our family apart.

But that has already happened. There's no going back now.

Martin Place is a row of old six-storey Victorian buildings carved up into offices. The pain in my side is flaring again and my head is flooded with blinding, crushing pain. A couple of brass plaques on a doorway list the tenants.

Accountants, a literary agency, a number of legal firms. None of them called Haden, Morris and Lawrence. I spot the name 'Morris' in one of the other firms — Morris and McColl — and press the buzzer. A receptionist answers. I explain that I need to speak to Mr Morris.

'Who?' she says.

'Mr Morris. I'm guessing he's the partner of the firm?'

'That would be Judy Morris,' the receptionist says. 'Who shall I say is calling?'

'My name's . . . David,' I say. 'David Ashworth. I need to locate the new address for the Haden, Morris and Lawrence law firm. It's urgent.'

'I'll check if she's free.'

Ten minutes later I'm in a swanky office being offered a cup of tea by a secretary. I gladly take it. The office is old money — a solid mahogany desk with captain's swivel chair, towering bookcases in the alcoves and a marble fireplace. The woman who walks in and introduces herself as Judy is older than I expected. Late sixties. Short black hair, penetrating blue eyes. A black cowl-neck jumper and black trousers.

'You're looking for Haden, Morris and Lawrence, I believe,' she says, taking the seat behind her desk.

I nod. 'Yes. They made contact quite some time ago and . . . I thought maybe you might know where they've relocated.'

'I see. Well, I'm afraid I wasn't employed by that legal firm, despite my surname.'

'Oh.'

'I can tell you they didn't relocate, however.'

I perk up. 'They're still here?'

She shakes her head. 'They dissolved. About five years ago, after two of the partners passed away.'

My heart sinks.

She cocks her head. 'Is there something I can help with?'

I glance up at the portrait of Winston Churchill behind her. He's sitting on a chair, both hands on the armrests and his jaw tilted slightly upward, as though he's about to get up. It's a restless picture, the portrait of someone who wasn't keen on sitting down and staying still.

'Someone tried to burn down my shop,' I say. 'I think they're trying to harm my family.'

She gives me another quick scan, checking out my face. 'I see. Is there a particular reason why someone would want to harm your family?'

Now I hesitate. Am I ready to say it aloud?

'A friend of mine died some time ago.'

She waits. 'And I'm assuming you had something to do with it?'

I hesitate. 'Do you know of someone called Luke Aucoin?' I say. She clasps her hands, eyes her telephone. 'Is he alive?' I ask.

'I don't believe I know of anyone by that name.'

I have no idea whether she's telling the truth. 'I believe that someone related to Luke has been searching for me ever since the . . . incident. They sent threats via the Haden, Morris and Lawrence law firm. There was a signature at the bottom. K. Haden. I was hoping I could get in touch with the client, but if the law firm has dissolved . . . '

She holds up a hand. 'Keith was a colleague at another firm,' she says. 'He's dead now, I'm afraid. But I can try and contact his wife. Perhaps if you leave it with me I can send her a message?'

I nod. A flick of a smile.

'It won't be until tomorrow, I'm afraid, as I'll have to search for her number. Perhaps if you come back around noon?'

I rise from my seat and stretch out my hand to thank her. She hesitates before taking it.

'What did you say your name was?' she says, narrowing her eyes. 'David, was it?'

'Yes. David. David Ashworth.'

She smiles but I can tell she doesn't believe me.

★　★　★

I buy razors, scissors, a new outfit, food, and dressings for the cuts on my arms and face, then check into what appears to be the last hotel room in London, which is basically a cupboard at the top of a sliver of a Victorian terrace in Covent Garden. There I shave my beard, trim my hair, then fall into the deepest sleep imaginable.

I don't dream, but my mind circuits all night. I think of the Churchill portrait I saw in Judy's office, and from there I spiral into deeper trenches of memory. I recall something about Churchill's wife. She owned an estate that Luke's parents bought. I remember Luke saying it, that Churchill used to sleep in his bedroom. He joked about his ghost stomping up the stairs and that's why he never went home. It was an excuse he peddled to his mum, too, when really we both knew it was because he didn't like his stepdad.

I wake with a start.

I have to find that house.

19

Helen

2nd September 2017

Jeannie and I are in Dr Gupta's office Skyping a special branch of the CID at Northumbria Police, talking to Detective Sergeant Jahan, a young, sharp-eyed man with slick black hair, and Detective Chief Inspector Lavery, a Geordie woman in her late fifties with cropped grey hair and severe red glasses.

'The van driver has made a serious accusation against Michael,' Jeannie says, once I've filled them in on everything else. 'They said he paid for the other guy to crash into their car. It's ridiculous, not to mention bloody frightening. I know it sounds a bit out there but it really feels like the police here are trying to blame my sister and brother-in-law for the crash.'

'They emailed us scanned transcripts of the interviews they had with you and the driver of the van,' DS Jahan says. 'We had to twist their arm a bit but we've got them now.'

'What about the other driver?' Jeannie says. 'Have they charged him?'

'I'm afraid they've already let him go,' DS Jahan says, and I give a loud gasp.

'You're not serious,' Jeannie says. 'They *let him go?*'

I think back to the CCTV footage, and the man behind Michael who I suspected was forcing him out of the hospital. 'When did they let him go?' I ask.

'In the last hour,' DCI Lavery says. 'The law in Belize only allows them to hold detainees for a certain length of time. They either have to charge them within twenty-four hours or release them.'

So it's unlikely that the man in the footage was the van driver.

'But . . . why would they release someone who admitted to taking money to deliberately smash into another vehicle?' I say. 'How can they *not* charge him?'

'We have our concerns about this for a number of reasons, one of which is of course that Michael went missing right after the accusation was made against him,' DS Lavery says. 'We've got some notes here from chatting with Jeannie that you saw a man prowling around your rental accommodation a day or so prior to the accident. Is that right, Helen?'

'Yes,' I say. 'The night before we left, in fact.' Then, 'Maybe if I saw a photograph of the van driver I could decide whether he was the man I saw.'

'Leave that with me,' DS Jahan says, and I feel momentarily heartened that I'm contributing to a resolution, that I can put an end to even a fraction of the chaos that I've been plunged into.

'Just to clarify,' DCI Lavery asks. 'The man you saw in the CCTV footage from the hospital

— do you think it was the same man you spotted outside your beach hut?'

I falter. 'I don't think so.'

My head feels close to bursting. Saskia flashes across my mind. Her sweet face bouncing up to mine with excitement at the park close to our house. Her lips pursed as she blows a dandelion clock. Her eyes rolled back in her head as she lies on the tarmac surrounded by blood and glass.

'When was the last time you spoke to Michael?' DC Lavery asks.

'I can't remember,' I say, pressing my hands to my forehead. 'Right before the crash, I think. We were talking, and . . . '

Suddenly I hear the van smashing into us, a sickening crunch that seems to repeat over and over again on a loop. My own screams for help. Then something I hadn't remembered before; another sound unfurls in my mind, fresh and bright, as though it has edges. Michael. He spoke to me.

'I remember Michael saying something,' I say weakly. 'He said something right after the crash. Before I crawled out of the car. I must have blacked out straight after.'

'What did he say?' DS Jahan says, pen poised.

I strain to listen to the memory in my head. It feels like trying to hook on to a cool wind, or something scrambling to get away . . . But then, I seize it and the scrambled sounds come together. It wasn't just a moan of pain. Michael spoke. He said something.

I have to protect you.

Words uttered from far away, as though at the

143

bottom of a tunnel.

'This may well require a trip over to Belize,' DC Lavery says. 'Sounds like Michael Pengilly had some serious injuries, so it's important we get a search going out there,' she continues. 'We'll review the possibility of travelling over there in a week or so, if he hasn't made contact.'

Right then I'm lost in a memory from years ago, in our first home in Edinburgh. We were only just married, barely a few months. I had had a nightmare about Luke's death. I woke up screaming and the next morning he asked me why. I was broken, swollen eyed and snivelling over my coffee.

'I loved Luke,' I said. 'I think maybe we owe it to him to tell the truth. About what happened.'

'The truth?' he said in a hard tone. 'We both know the truth, Helen. We both know who was to blame.'

His face softened and he sat down beside me, took my hand, but I pulled it away.

'What do you mean by that?' I snapped. He looked away, not wanting to answer. I got up and stormed out, slamming the door behind me. I was disgusted with him, and deeply hurt. Was he suggesting I was entirely at fault, that he and Theo played no part? Perhaps he was right. Perhaps it was all my fault. This thought settled into me like rain seeping into the earth, transforming it into mud.

I wanted to leave. I wanted to run away to the ends of the earth with this new knowledge. I packed a bag, made it as far as the front door. But I couldn't leave. Perhaps I'd misinterpreted what he'd meant. I decided not to act rashly but to discuss it with him when we'd both calmed down. Neither of us had fully recovered from what happened on Mont Blanc, I knew that.

That night I woke up in the wee hours to the sound of banging. The space in the bed beside me was empty, the covers pulled back. I went out into the landing, saw the loft ladder was down. I looked up and could see a light was on up there, a rush of wind from the gap between the eaves that we'd never got around to fixing.

I climbed up the ladder and saw Michael sitting on a chair in the middle of the room, the single naked lightbulb casting an orange glow over his body. He was completely naked. The sight of him sitting there like that was so bizarre I let out a nervous laugh.

'Michael?' I said. 'What's going on?'

His face was contorted into an expression I'd never seen before. I saw he was holding something.

'What's that?'

He lifted it slowly. It was an old rope, looped at one end.

'A noose,' he said.

Why he should be sitting there holding something so peculiar was beyond me. I thought he'd found it up there and was waiting to show me.

As I climbed up to the final rung he shouted for me to stop. It was then that I felt my skin crawl.

'Michael, you're scaring me. What's going on?'

His face was shining with tears and sweat, his

hair ruffled, and there was something else in the air, wide in the room. Another presence.

'When you started talking about what happened to Luke,' he said, his voice breaking. 'I just . . . I can't take it.'

I thought back to what I'd said. I felt appalled at myself for bringing it up so casually. I hadn't meant to upset him.

'Michael, I'm sorry. I'm really sorry . . . '

'I'm not a killer!' he yelled. It was a plea to be let loose from something, as though he was trapped in a cage and was begging for the key to be let out.

He was sobbing and shaking, his head in his hands and his shoulders jerking up and down.

'Please, Michael,' I begged. 'Please . . . I never meant to make you feel like that.'

'It wasn't my fault,' he said, lifting the noose. 'It wasn't my fault, Helen.'

My own screams echoed in my ears. 'I know it wasn't, Michael. It was my fault. Please just come down from here. Please.'

Eventually he did. I never brought up Mont Blanc again. I didn't leave him, either. I adored him, and somehow I understood that his insinuation that I was to blame was motivated by pain, a wound that was so deep it lay beneath reason, instinct — even love.

And when the letters came, I made sure to hide them from him before persuading him we needed to move again.

Google Earth pops up on the screen, showing the area around the hospital here in San Alvaro. I recognise it as the pot-holed road that runs outside, surrounded by trees and empty buildings.

'We're using satellite technology to locate Michael's last whereabouts,' DCI Lavery says. 'We can see from this map that the exit he took out of the hospital leads directly to this road here, so we'll focus on trying to get the police to speak to people who were around the area at the time he left. We'll also try and get information about the owners of the cars parked at the time of Michael's disappearance. We're also working with the hospital chief to get all the data from the hospital's security systems to see who was inside the hospital that day.'

I take a breath and nod, reassured by the confident tone of her voice. She strikes me as someone who works quickly and efficiently, which is exactly what we need.

'The one thing that's a bit of a concern is this,' she says, dragging the arrow to the side of the room. A pixelated image of a shelter comes into view.

'What is it?' I ask.

'It's a bus stop. We've checked it out and it's a pretty major route, going all the way to Belize City and even the airport. Is there a chance that Michael had his passport with him?'

I swallow hard. 'I . . . I don't know.'

'What about cash? Or credit cards?'

The police probably stole them, I think, but say nothing. I began to type all the sort codes and account numbers for the business account and our personal accounts. Luckily I knew them off by heart.

Great, DCI Lavery types back in the chat box. *We will keep a close eye on this. We are gathering resources here and hope to launch a thorough inquiry with the Belizean police tomorrow afternoon.*

20

Helen

3rd September 2017

'Hello, Helen. How are you this morning?'

A woman is standing above me. I have no idea what day it is. Slowly the woman becomes familiar — she's the lady from the High Commission, Vanessa? — and the knowledge of why I'm in hospital arrives like a juggernaut, carrying me outside my body and landing me with a crack of bones back into the white noise fever dream that is my current reality.

Vanessa looks different today. No suit. A white strappy dress, white Converse, her black hair pulled into a ponytail. She holds up a cotton bag with some food supplies sticking out — bottled water, bread rolls, apples. I look around quickly, hating myself for falling asleep. When I can't spot Reuben I start to scramble painfully out of bed until I remember that Jeannie and Shane took him back to their hotel last night.

'I wanted to check you were alright,' Vanessa explains as I crawl back on to the bed. 'I live only two miles away so I thought I would come by.'

She opens a bottle of water for me, which I drink in one go. It's scorching hot in here, like being slowly baked alive. It was forty degrees when we were at the beach hut but the sea breeze made the temperature bearable. Here, in the city, it's as though the heat is melting everything. Even the insects look like they're wilting.

I can't imagine Vanessa living somewhere as impoverished as San Alvaro. She always looks so smart, with her sparkling earrings, pristine suit and glossy red nails. I can well imagine her going out with a group of friends to a nightclub after work, a Pilates class. Not walking along the dirt path lined with shacks and stray dogs that makes up the town of San Alvaro.

'My parents are both blind,' she says, opening a packet of biscuits. 'Trust me, I pleaded with them to move to the city so I could look after them. But they've lived in San Alvaro their whole lives and refuse to move. Here, would you like a Johnny cake? They're a Belizean specialty.'

I take one so as not to offend her and nibble at the corners. 'I'm sorry about your parents.'

'Oh, they're fine. I still have my own place in Belize City but when my mother lost her sight last year I moved home to make sure they were both looked after. My father only retired a few years before the river became polluted. Many people went blind in that year.'

'What river?' I say, and she tells me about a river that runs the whole way through the country that is used by big corporations as a dumping ground for toxic waste. They were well aware that many rural towns in Belize still use the river for washing, drinking, and cooking, as

150

they had done for generations, but it didn't stop them polluting it.

'Is that what why your mum went blind, too?'

She gives a sad smile. 'My father insists that she was just feeling left out so her eyes stopped working. But in truth, it's most likely that the river caused her blindness. My parents never got treated.'

I reel at this. 'Why not?'

'By the time I persuaded them to go to the hospital it was too late. Babies went blind, too. Many children left with . . . how do you say it . . . disabilities? Nobody has the money to prove that it was the pollution, or that the corporations did it.' She sighs and opens another bottle of water for me. 'Everywhere has its problems, I guess. Belize has incredible riches in terms of her ecosystems, her cayes, her barrier reef, her rainforests. And of course, archaeological treasures. But we have problems with pollution. And corruption.'

She glances to check that nobody can overhear us before pulling her chair closer to me. 'My father was a cop for thirty-five years. I spoke to him about the police here, about what they said to you.'

I sit up straighter. 'Go on.'

'My father says he is almost certain the police took a bribe. From the man who hit your vehicle.' She's barely whispering, and I have to stare at her full lips to make out what she is saying. 'It happens often. And you are not local, you understand. Nobody knows you. Nobody will challenge them if the blame is put on you.'

151

'They took a bribe,' I say, as if saying it out loud will make it easier to stomach.

She leans closer. 'My father said he remembered a case, eight or nine years ago, just before he retired. A British couple were murdered about ten miles from here. My father was a Detective Sergeant then. The cops had the murderer, they all knew they did, but he offered a bribe. It wasn't even a lot of money but they let him go.'

Her words colour my surroundings, painting vivid possibilities for the reason I am here, the reason we're in this nightmare. It's at once terrifying and absurd, but my body reacts to the possibility that the police are trying to set us up. Vanessa flicks her eyes at a nurse who had come in to check my charts. We both wait until the nurse's footsteps vanish down the corridor before Vanessa turns back to me.

'I will try to find out the van driver's name,' she says. 'But I can't promise anything.'

'What should I do?'

'The British police *may* be able to put pressure on our police,' she says. 'But I wouldn't count on it. Many of the police officers in San Alvaro are only interested in what's in it for *them*. If they don't have to do something, they won't.' A beat. 'Not all of them will be that way, though. My father was a good cop. He never took the bribes. He believes in karma. You know this word?'

I nod. 'Karma, yes.'

' 'What goes around, comes around.' That's why he isn't bothered about fighting the big corporations. This will come back to them. If you

152

continue to do good things for other people, sooner or later good will come to you.'

She opens a brown bag of sea grapes and lets me devour them. I don't know how long it's been since I ate properly. My clothes feel loose.

'Tell me about where you come from,' she says, smiling. 'I've never been to London. What is it like?'

I tell her that I used to live in London, but now live about three hundred miles north.

'There's a place in London I've always wanted to go to,' she says. 'And I hope you've been there at least so you can tell me what it's like and I live the dream through you.'

'Where's that?'

'Harrods,' she says, dreamily. 'It looks like heaven. I think if I ever go to London I'll need to take a trillion dollars with me just for shopping.'

I explain to her that there are lots of shopping malls all over England, many of them every bit as nice as Harrods, but she doesn't seem convinced. Finally, I say, 'If you can find my husband and get me out of here, I'll take you to Harrods. I promise.'

Her eyes light up. 'You would take me to Harrods?'

'I'll even pay your airfare.'

She laughs and claps her hands. 'Now I'm the one accepting a bribe,' she whispers, and a shiver runs up my spine.

'You live in San Alvaro,' I say. 'Do you think the locals might know the man who crashed into our car?'

'I will try and find out.' A pause. 'The thing

you have to remember though, is that *if* the police have taken a bribe, they will be extra vigilant about making sure blame is pointed at you. You're a tourist, you understand. They will try and say you were drunk, or driving dangerously.' Another pause, longer this time. 'This is why I'm concerned about the claim against your husband.'

'But it's a complete lie,' I say, and she nods.

'Yes, but it complicates things. It technically creates more work for the police.'

'What do you mean?'

'Usually they would just take a bribe and that would be that. By stating that the driver made this claim, they have an obligation to search for your husband to question him.'

Surely they have an obligation to search for him as a missing person, I think, and Vanessa clarifies her meaning. 'What I'm saying is, if *someone* paid a man to hit a vehicle for whatever reason, the police would have a possible manslaughter or murder case on their hands. As the named perpetrator, Michael is someone they have a responsibility to look for. They could have taken the bribe, not mentioned the accusation, and avoided having to do anything at all. Brush off the crash as an accident.'

I struggle to follow this. 'So . . . why you do think they haven't done that?'

She sighs. 'I'm very confused by it. I will speak to my father again. He will work it out.'

★ ★ ★

At the hospital in Belize City Vanessa wheels me to the ward and there is a child lying completely still and silent on a bed surrounded by foreign tubes and machinery. Saskia.

I move close and take her hand in mine, speaking to her softly, telling her I'm here. One of her fingers jerks, flooding me with hope that she's about to wake. But she doesn't, and for a long time I sit pleading for her to open her eyes.

Was it really only days ago that she was laughing and shrieking on the sand at the beach hut? I press her hand to my face and send silent prayers to the universe that she'll be OK. That somehow she'll recover from this. That somehow she'll still dance and laugh and play exactly as she used to. And then fear sets in that the future I want for her has been erased for ever and I feel like my heart might break.

Reuben produces a small Bluetooth speaker, sets it on the table next to her bed. 'I've made you a podcast, Saskia. Check it out.'

He presses a button on the MP3 player, and after a moment or two the sound of waves rolling across the beach arises from the speaker. Voices in the background. My own voice, calling *Kids! Come and get some food!*

'I thought she'd like to remember what a fun time we had,' he explains.

Another voice, female and high-pitched. 'Come and look at this!'

It's Saskia's voice. She is laughing, her voice dipping in and out of audibility as she runs across the sand.

'No, no, not like that,' she says, 'like this.' My

own voice is somewhere in the background, asking her questions. I remember she was showing me how to build her sand theatre. We were making a stage with columns, then seats and an orchestra pit, and she was directing me how she wanted them done. Always so precise, so particular. She has such a strong, wilful character and as I watch her on the bed, impossibly still, I will that dimension of her personality to help her through this.

Then Michael's voice. *Shall we go in now, kids?*

I hear him chatting to Reuben about whether or not there are great white sharks out there, what they would do if they spot one. *What if,* he asks him over and over. *What if you saw a fin? What if you couldn't get away?* It strikes me that since Reuben's diagnosis we've lived in the future, always wondering what lies ahead for our boy. When we learned Reuben had autism the consultant told us to prepare ourselves for what he *wouldn't* do. He wouldn't be able to live independently, wouldn't have a career, wouldn't get married, may never speak. Suddenly we were mourning a future that we'd imagined for our son. *There is no cure for autism,* they said, and the boy we'd held in our mind graduating, travelling, scaling his life's dreams, was swept away in an instant.

Eventually, of course, we came to terms with it, but that sense of always looking forward, always living in the future tense — it has never changed. Until now. Now the future looks very different indeed. Now I think that living in a constant state of 'what if?' was utterly pointless. In fact, it angers me that I have spent so long living like that.

Reuben presses pause on the iPad and looks at me with a confused expression, and I remember: he has no idea that Michael is missing.

'I'm fine,' I say, clearing my voice. 'It's just . . . Saskia's voice, that's all. It makes me very emotional.'

Reuben considers this, then skips to another file. This time it is his own voice laced with another man's voice as they chat about ancient ruins. It takes me a moment or two to place the voice. Shane. Reuben's asking him questions.

'Are you a policeman?' he asks.

Shane laughs. 'Why do you think that?'

'Your hair is silver and you have policeman boots.'

'Do I? Well no, I'm not a policeman, actually. I'm an academic.'

'An epidemic? Isn't that where you make loads of people sick?'

'Um . . . I lead research on political theory and work in middle management at a university.'

'What's political theory?'

'Um, well, it encompasses discourses on human rights, justice, government, ethics, what protection ought to be in place for minorities in majoritarian democracies . . . '

'What about the Mayan-Toltec civilisation? Do you research that?'

'Umm . . . '

' . . . the name 'toltec' actually means 'master builders'. That's because they built a lot of big

157

buildings. My dad took me to Chichén Itzá. It's an ancient Mayan site dating back over a thousand years. Have you been to Chichén Itzá?'

'I've never been to Mexico,' Shane says. 'Perhaps one day.'

I ask Reuben to replay the sound fragment and fall silent when he asks why. I listen again.

Never been to Mexico?

But Jeannie said he was just there on business. Why would he lie?

21

Michael

18th June 1995

It's 6 a.m. and freezing cold, which is a good thing for starting off so early. There is nothing like the ghostly presence of the mountains and that brisk alpine wind to get the blood flowing and the body forgetting its aches and pains. Luke and Theo are in shorts and T-shirts. I've opted for tracksuit bottoms with a thermal base layer and a fleece jacket. Helen has obviously taken the advice given by the other climbers seriously and is already geared up in climbing pants, thermal layers, and protective gloves. She flashes me a smile and I give one back.

'Alright, boys,' she says at the hut doorway. 'Let's be off.'

Theo is our designated map person, being the most nerdy and organised of the four of us, though there are plenty of signs posted to give us an idea of where we should be headed. The path is still gentle and surrounded by trees, though I can see clouds not too far above us, now. It's kind of surreal. Mont Blanc still seems staggeringly high, shrouded by wispy cloud, her pointy nose just touching the moon.

Our route takes us towards a hut a quarter of the way up the ascent where we'll rest for a day or two. For all our preparation, this part of the climb seems deceptively easy — the valley splays before us in shades of emerald green, the mountains verdant and veined with snow. Meadows of buttercups, bunnies and zig-zagging dragonflies scale down our 'expedition' to a stroll on a warm summer's day. Twenty minutes into the walk Luke and Theo get into an argument about something or other and I find myself walking alongside Helen. I try to keep a couple of steps ahead but she matches my pace, throws me a nervous smile. 'So how did you and Luke meet?' I ask to break the silence.

'We met at an Oasis concert at Earls Court,' she says. 'He tried to chat up my friend Anna but she wasn't having any of it.'

'I did not chat up Anna. She has this huge nose,' Luke shouts. I forgot he has the hearing of a bat. 'She looks like a bloke.'

'That explains it,' Theo says, glancing behind. He's fed up with arguing with Luke and walks alongside me.

'I was . . . manoeuvring,' Luke says when we catch up with him. 'The old charm-the-best-friend approach.'

'So, it was love at first sight, was it?' I say. I don't know why I say this. It just comes out.

Helen arches her head to grin brightly at Luke.

'I'm going to take that as a no,' I say.

'Love at first sight for her, maybe,' Luke says, taking her hand. 'Isn't that right, babe?'

'Oh, I don't think so,' she says, smiling. 'I don't believe in love at first sight. *Lust* at first sight, maybe.'

Neither of them look at me. Their eyes don't leave each other. It makes me uncomfortable. Luke's never been touchy-feely with girls but now he reaches out to her, wrapping his arm around her waist and kissing her on the cheek.

'Oh, the hubris of the madly loved. Hundred per cent agree with that one.'

Theo and I look at each other in shared irritation as Luke whispers something sexy in Helen's ear that makes her giggle.

'I take back what I said,' Luke says then. He raises his arms above his head and walks backwards. 'When I say it was love at first sight for her, what I mean was she quickly realised I was a tosser and changed her mind. For me, it was love at second sight, and third sight, and fourth sight, et cetera. The attempt so hard, the conquest so sharp, the fearful joy that ever slips away so quickly — by all this I mean love,' he says in chorus with Theo. It takes a moment to register that they're quoting Chaucer.

'It's from *The Parliament of Fowls*,' I murmur to Helen when she looks confused by Theo and Luke's chorus. 'It's a poem from the fourteenth century about love and Valentine's day and all that crap.'

'*Th'assay so sharp, so hard the conqueringe, the dredful joye alway that slitso yerne,*' Luke shouts, and she laughs.

'What the hell language is *that?*'

'It's old English,' Theo tells her. 'That's how

people spoke back in medieval times.'

'Seriously? Why?'

I go to explain, but Luke grabs her and lifts her up on to his shoulders. I look away, embarrassed.

'By all this I mean love!' he says, spinning her around as she shrieks. Then he sets her down and pulls her into a deep kiss. I'm just about to tell Luke to get a room when he raises his hands above his head in a victory salute and shouts, 'I love her! I love this woman!'

'Yeah, all right, mate,' Theo says.

'We get the point,' I add. 'Pack it in until we're back in England, alright?'

Luke reaches out to take Helen's hand but she grips on to the straps of her rucksack, her eyes darting at me. She's sensed the resentment radiating off me and Theo and wants to calm Luke down a bit.

Theo stops, consults the map.

'Thought you'd be happy for me,' Luke says to him. 'Finally finding someone I really like.'

'Finally?' Theo says, not looking up from the map. 'Well, I suppose you've already slept with the entire Oxford campus. You don't have to be a mathematician to work out that sooner or later you'd come across one that would put up with you for more than a week.'

Helen gives a nervous laugh. Luke glares at his brother, who is studying the map. I go to ask him if we're lost but think better of it.

'Isn't it lunchtime?' Helen says, keen to change the subject. 'I'm hungry . . . '

'You know we're moving in together?' Luke

says to Theo. 'So you'll have to find a new place when we get back.'

Theo looks up from his map, pushes his glasses up his nose and stares at Luke. 'Oh, I think you'll find Mum put the flat in my name. So you'll be the one moving out, Luke.'

Luke slaps the map out of his hands, sending it into the air like a wing. There's another fight brewing, this morning's bickering unresolved. They don't fight often but when they do, it's pretty nasty.

'Mates, let's just calm down for a second,' I say, slipping between Luke and Theo and grinning like an idiot.

Helen approaches Luke, tries to pull him away. His face is burning red, his fists clenched. 'When you insisted that I come along on this trip,' she says, 'I said I'd come on one condition: that you'd be nice.'

I turn to Helen. 'Sorry, what did you say?'

'Did you just say that Luke 'insisted' that you come along?' Theo adds, adding air-quotation marks.

Helen frowns in confusion. Her peace offering hasn't quite worked as planned.

'You insisted that she come along,' I repeat to Luke, and he won't meet my gaze. 'That's not the story we heard.'

'Well, no, I didn't want to come,' she says again, stuttering. 'At least, not at first. It's a major expedition, isn't it, so I . . . well, I wasn't sure I'd be up to it . . . '

She trails off, turning her eyes to Luke. 'I said I would, on the condition that I get some training first.' She looks around, gives a nervous laugh when she sees the grim expressions on our faces. 'What's wrong with everybody?'

'Oh, nothing,' Theo says. 'We were worried that you might not want to come, weren't we, Luke?'

I slap him lightly in the gut. He winces but doesn't retaliate. He knows he's been rumbled. *Liar*, I think.

★   ★   ★

After a few hours the deceptively gentle forest trail graduates to uneven scree. We find a clutch of dry rocks just off the path and choose it as a lunch stop. We shake off our backpacks and set up the stove. I make us cups of tea while Theo very helpfully makes himself a roll-up cigarette.

'Want one?' he asks no one in particular. Helen and I both shake our heads. I've decided to scale back on smoking for the duration of the climb. Luke accepts, though.

It's windy, so Luke and Theo step to the side of a larger rock where the wind is re-directed. I can hear them murmuring from over here, moaning about the crowds of people we can see joining the trail in the distance.

I boil up some noodles, hand Helen a mug-full with a spork, then make my own. An awkward silence. She keeps hanging around, as if she expects me to make conversation. I pretend to take an interest in the stirring of noodles to avoid eye contact.

'What do you study, then?' she asks, repeating

it when I pretend I don't hear.

'Lit,' I say briskly. 'Same as those two.'

'Medieval literature or some other kind?'

I can't help myself. 'There is no other kind.'

Her face breaks into a grin. 'Ah, I see.'

'See what?'

'Why Luke is so fond of you. He's a med lit geek, as I'm sure you'll know.'

'Yes. We've been friends for a while now.'

'I'm sorry to have intruded,' she says after a moment's pause. Then, biting something back, 'It's so beautiful out here. I mean, look at it.'

She turns to look down at the valley from whence we came. The clouds separate just long enough for a shaft of brilliant blue sky to reveal itself and filter panes of sunlight all the way to the valley floor.

'They say Sibelius heard his Fifth Symphony when he looked on a mountain range like this one. It's no wonder.'

'Who's Sibelius?' I say, immediately regretting it.

'He's a composer. I like classical music.'

'You want to be a composer, then?'

She laughs and sits down on the rock next to me. I've no idea what I've said that's so damn funny.

'I'm a dancer, actually.'

Do I look like I care?

'Luke wants to open a bookshop when he graduates. I suppose there's little else you can do with a degree in literature.'

'Oh, I don't know,' I say, bristling. 'I suppose those of us who are stupid enough to study

165

something as useless as literature might make a life for ourselves. Maybe as bin collectors or toilet scrubbers, seeing as literature degrees are so useless.'

She falls silent, stung, then stands up sharply and moves away. Suddenly I feel moved to apologise. I watch as she makes her way towards the grassy verge on the other side of the path for a clearer view of the valley and, I know, to put some distance between us. She has only just crossed the path when suddenly a group of a dozen or so young guys from Russia come marching up the path like a frickin' platoon, their heavy boots shaking the ground. I hear a scream and look over to see her being knocked sideways by one of the Russians. There's a scrambling sound as she topples down the snout of the hillside.

It's a sheer drop from there to the valley.

'Luke!' I shout, racing towards her, glancing down from the edge of the path. I can see her lying on her side on a rock jutting out, but she's on a bank of moss, visibly struggling to hold on, and beneath her the drop isn't nearly so gentle. Luke rushes over and looks down.

'What the hell happened?'

'I . . .'

'Luke!' Helen shouts.

He tries to climb down but catches his boot on a crag and isn't fast enough to loosen it. Quickly I lower myself down after her, grasping on to the reeds and crags for leverage. She crawls towards me, reaching with all her might until I'm able to grab her hand and pull her towards me. Luke and Theo lie flat on their bellies, pulling us both back on to the path.

When she scrambles up the bank Luke wraps his arms around her, kisses her forehead, and immediately makes it all seem like a big joke.

'Babe,' he says, ruffling her hair like she's four years old. 'What did you leap off the mountain for?'

Helen visibly clings to the levity, scaling down from out-of-her-mind terror breath by breath.

'You know, if you want to dump me you can just say,' Luke continues loudly, giving us all a big performance. 'You don't have to go jumping off the edge of a cliff.'

She laughs, and Luke announces he's brought Cuban cigars and this seems the perfect time to light up.

'Good job you were there, mate,' he tells me later, handing me a bottle of scotch. 'I want you to point out which of those Russian guys knocked her over, alright? She won't tell me.'

I stop, search his face. 'Why?'

Stupid question. His face darkens and he looks away. 'You know why.'

'Luke, we're not here to start a fight, alright? I'm sure it was an accident.'

'Just point them out, alright?'

I nod. 'Alright.'

22

Helen

3rd September 2017

We are pulling into the hospital car park at San Alvaro when Jeannie's phone rings. She answers it, then mouths 'Vanessa' at me. I watch as she listens, her face tightening into a scowl. When she hangs up she tells Shane to keep driving.

'Keep driving?' he says, perplexed. 'But we're here. Have I come to the wrong hospital?'

'No, just . . . go!' Jeannie shouts, and he starts up the engine and pulls off, flustered.

'Where am I going?' he says, pulling on to the wrong side of the road. A car sounds its horn and he swings back into the right lane, waving an apology to the other drivers who flash their lights and yell abuse out the window. I'm curled up in the seat, my hands pressed against my eyes. Any minute I'm expecting a white van to appear in the windscreen, the same explosion of glass and metal as before.

'That was Vanessa from the High Commission,' I hear Jeannie say. 'She said the police are on their way to the hospital.' A pause. 'They want to arrest you, Helen.'

I open my eyes. 'They want to arrest *me?*'

Jeannie's eyes are wide, her voice shrill with horror. 'She mentioned drugs. They think Michael has done a runner and they seem to think that arresting you will bring him back.'

'Google it,' Shane says loudly, his eyes flashing up in the rear-view mirror at Jeannie. 'Google the Foreign and Commonwealth guidance for tourists in Belize. Google drug penalties in Belize.'

'A bit late for that, don't you think?' Jeannie says, but she searches on her phone and says, 'Uh oh.'

'What?' I shout.

She reads her findings aloud. ''Penalties for possessing, using, or trafficking drugs in Belize, even unknowingly, are tremendously severe. A life sentence is not uncommon.''

'What's a life sentence, Mum?' Reuben asks. 'Is it the one that begins with a verb?'

Right then, a police car with flashing lights sweeps by. I turn and watch it pull into the hospital.

'What do we do?' Shane says. He's gone a bit pale around the eyes.

'Take a left here,' Jeannie says, and despite the traffic light changing red Shane veers left and accelerates hard, all of us thrown back into our seats.

'Where are we going?' Shane says when he hits a motorway. His knuckles are white as he holds the steering wheel as though it might fall off the dashboard. As we reach ninety miles per hour I close my eyes and try not think about the fact that we're in a car. A glance at Reuben shows

169

that he's loving the rocking of the car from side to side and is filming it all on his iPad. My heart is hammering so fast in my chest that I think I might pass out.

'We need to go back to the hospital at Belize City,' Jeannie says, and for once I'm glad she thrives on extremes, for whereas my thoughts are fireworks of handcuffs and hard labour she remains razor-focused on a strategy. 'We need to get Saskia,' she says firmly. 'And then we need to fly home.'

Home? I can't just abandon Michael. I try to tell Jeannie this but she cuts me off.

'Helen, I need to ask you something,' she says, exasperated.

'What?'

She leans close in case Reuben catches the conversation. 'This accusation against Michael.'

'What about it?'

'Do you think . . . I mean, is there even the slightest possibility that Michael might have actually done this?'

I feel like I've been slapped. 'Of *course* I don't think that! How could you even ask such a thing?'

'Well, this whole situation is just bizarre,' she hisses, flustered. 'Michael has vanished into thin air. We saw on the CCTV that he literally just got up and left you all in the hospital without even checking to see if you were alive. And now the police are out to throw you in some manky jail cell for the rest of your life. And frankly you're acting very weird. I have to look out for you if you won't look after yourself . . . '

I check that Reuben is immersed again in his tablet before answering in a suppressed scream. 'Jeannie, I'm *acting weird* because my little girl has just had major brain surgery to save her life. I'm acting weird because I'm in a foreign country in a cockroach-infested hospital, with no clean water or washing facilities, because someone tried to kill us. I'm acting weird because my husband has disappeared and the police are trying to arrest me for drug trafficking.'

I'm surprised by how loud and angry my tone is, and Jeannie seems equally taken aback by how her meek and placating sister has actually put her in her place. She nods quickly, chastened, and I'm reminded of how immature she is. Jeannie's all bark, no bite, all persona and social airs and shockingly little substance. Our relationship has always been complex. We're half-sisters, technically, the only physical signature of our genetic match in the form of our slightly pointy chins.

I ask Jeannie if I can borrow her phone and call Vanessa. She confirms it: the police contacted her at the British High Commission and asked if I was there. She acted casually, explained I was still being treated in hospital. The officer blurted out that I was to be arrested. He mentioned 'suspected drugs'.

And now I'm a fugitive.

★ ★ ★

At the hospital in Belize City a nurse pages Alfredo and explains that we wish to take Saskia back to the UK for treatment. He agrees readily

171

that she would be better cared for in the UK, and before I know what's happening Jeannie is arranging a medevac air ambulance, and a team of consultants are drafting a systemic procedure for Saskia's transportation and care while in the air. I'm so caught up in the frenetic pace of things, one eye on the hospital entrance for any sign of the police and another on Saskia, that before I know it Jeannie's telling me that the air ambulance will arrive in the hospital parking lot at dawn and that Shane has found us a hotel close by for the night.

I look at her, wondering if I've heard her right. 'But what about Michael?'

Jeannie tries to talk me down, telling me I have to think about what's right for Saskia, and at this I explode.

'How can you *possibly* know what's right for my children?' I roar. We're in the corridor. Nurses turn and stare but I don't care. 'You have no right to try and force me to abandon my husband in a foreign country!'

Her cheeks burn and she looks around, feeling the eyes of the nurses and doctors watching us.

'I want to Skype the police back home,' I say, composing myself. 'I want to tell them what's going on and get their advice.'

She nods, silently pulls out her phone, and hits a button. A few moments later we're in a side room speaking to the detectives online. They tell me that they've found the man we'd seen in the CCTV footage at the hospital, the man who had walked behind Michael and who I'd suspected was pushing him out the door. His name is

Apolonio Martinez and he was visiting his wife in the hospital. His alibis all ring true: his wife was being treated for kidney failure and he came to the hospital every day. They confirm what Jeannie says: that Michael appears to have left the hospital voluntarily without checking to see if me or our children were even alive. They say he's back in England. That he flew to Heathrow without us.

Impossible.

'Michael's passport was scanned at Heathrow airport yesterday afternoon,' DS Jahan says. 'Unfortunately there was a technical fault, which meant that they didn't detain him there and then. We're reviewing CCTV footage to work out where he might have gone. But he's definitely in the UK.'

I stare at the screen, wondering if I've heard them correctly. I can't fathom it. Why would he have flown from Belize to Heathrow? Why wouldn't he have come to find me?

'He did have a head injury,' DCI Lavery adds. 'People often do strange things after accidents like this.'

I nod, mutter a reply, but my brain is doing cartwheels, filtering and piecing together every fragment of information that the police provide in the hope of working out how anything makes sense.

★　★　★

Saskia is last to be manoeuvred on to the plane, assisted by Alfredo, a team of nurses and the paramedics. So far, the ICP monitor in her head is signalling that she is in a stable condition. Alfredo tells me he will have a meeting online with the neurosurgical team back in the UK to update them on her procedure and subsequent care.

I keep watching out for Superintendent Caliz but, mercifully, he doesn't appear.

The medevac team insist on giving me a sedative for the journey to help me sleep, and finally I relent, laid out beside Saskia, holding her hand. Reuben clasps her other hand. I can hear him making noises, a series of repetitive drills with his tongue matched by stamps of his foot. He's trying to keep his anxiety in check. I lift my head to offer him as much of a reassuring smile as I can manage and he smiles back.

The plane takes off with a roar.

23

Reuben

4th September 2017

Planes are noisy but not as noisy as a blue whale. A jet engine is 140 decibels at take-off. A blue whale calling underwater is 230 decibels. I think that, if I ever swim with a blue whale, I'm going to need to design noise-cancelling headphones that can be used underwater.

I feel sick when we lift into the sky, and when the internet signal drops out my belly starts to bubble up again. I want to be on the plane home but I don't want to be. My dad is not here. He should be here. Mum says he's coming home soon but I don't think he is because Shane drove us around San Alvaro forty-six times looking for Dad and we wouldn't be doing that if Dad was coming home. I filmed a hundred and twelve minutes of people shouting at us in their cars, plus fifty-four seconds of when someone's monkey got loose in traffic and almost got squashed by a van full of melons.

I log in to iPix Chat to read my messages but the 4G on my iPad dropped out right as I was typing a message to Malfoy to tell him I'd recorded more stuff for him. He said he'd give me rendering software for my animations if I did, so I sent it as soon as I could. I recorded me and Shane searching for Dad and then some old footage of me and Saskia making a Mayan sandcastle.

No messages. Major suckage. Wait — there's one message. And it's from Malfoy! He's sent a link to a download with a password and I'm able to download Trapdoor Particular for free. *And* he's sent a link to a YouTube tutorial. Awesome!

Mum is asleep on a stretcher next to Saskia. Her hand is holding Saskia's hand, but all of a sudden, her hand goes limp and falls down in the gap between the beds, knocking Jack-Jack to the floor.

The floor is dusty. Jack-Jack will get dirty. So I get up and stagger a bit as the plane is still moving upwards slightly, but I manage to get Jack-Jack and dust him down.

He's still got the love heart on his collar. Some girls at school passed Love Heart sweets around on Valentine's Day and I got a yellow one that said 'True Lips' and a white one that said 'Be Mine'. I didn't know what that meant but Lucy thought it was funny.

When I look closer I see Jack-Jack's love heart isn't a Love Heart. It tastes and feels like plastic, for a start, and the name on it is 'TRKLite'. I don't know what that means. Is it a word?

I go online to Google it and then remember the 4G isn't working. There's another signal though from the plane so I click it and in four seconds I'm online. I type 'Trklite' into Google and four thousand two hundred results come up.

There's a website, www.trklite.com, so I click it and it tells me that for just forty pounds I too can own a TRKLite in a range of colours, including baby pink, like the one Jack-Jack wore around his collar. The website says, *An easy and versatile way to track keys, luggage, phone, and valuables via Bluetooth! Just download our free app and never lose your keys again!*

I download the app to see how it works. It's genius. A red circle appears on a map, locating the love heart. I watch the screen for four minutes. The red circle blinks on the digital map on my screen as we fly over a place called Calakmul. The love heart is a tracking device. I've seen those online. They're really cool. You can attach them to something and then find them with Google maps anywhere in the world. So that's what this is.

But that doesn't make any sense. Why would someone put a tracking device on a teddy?

PART TWO

24

Helen

5th September 2017

Grey streets. Car horns. Crowds.

Helen, love. We're just going to give you a sedative, alright my lovely? Sharp scratch. That's it.

Blackness.

I am trapped in my body, locked inside a glass cage, unable to speak or move.

White coat, face full of pity.

Photographs of smiling children on her desk.

You experienced a delayed reaction of shock, Helen. It's common for people who experience trauma overseas to cope whilst away only to have a breakdown when they come home. Sometimes the familiar makes what happened abruptly real. We'll assign you a trauma counsellor. Liz will visit with you every day, OK?

I shake my head. I don't need a trauma counsellor, I need Reuben to have his father back, and his sister. I need my husband to come home. I need my daughter to live.

I lie flat on my back as they slide me into the white hoop of the CT scanner. I want to enter another time zone, reinsert myself into the past.

The cut in my head is healing and I have a mild concussion. Whiplash, a fractured wrist and torn ligaments in my foot. My head wound is healing nicely. My bladder is fine. Bruised, the doctor says, like most of my body, but whole. Unlike my heart. I imagine my heart under a CT scan. A hundred broken fragments, each bearing my daughter and husband's names.

I am discharged with a prescription for heavy duty painkillers, and a bandaged foot, a wrist brace, crutches, and a sheet of daily neck exercises for my whiplash. I hate myself for surviving when Saskia is at death's door. It's wrong. I would do anything, anything to trade places with her.

★   ★   ★

I'm sitting in a wheelchair in scrubs at the foot of Saskia's bed, watching the rehabilitative and respiratory nurses and Saskia's neurologist, Dr Hamedi, busy about the machines around her, attempting to break her out of the coma.

'Ready?' I hear a voice say, and on an exhale I tell myself, *ready.*

Under the honeycomb lights she looks lunar white, angelic, as if she already belongs more in heaven than she does on earth.

They stop the sedation. The hum of the machines stalls, and my heart lurches. They fold over her, calling her name.

Saskia, are you alright? We're just waking you up now. Mummy's here, sweetheart. Would you like to see her?

I rush out of the wheelchair and stagger towards her, my own voice echoing off the tiled floor, shrill and half-crazed with desperation.

'Saskia, love, I'm here. Mummy's here, darling. Mummy's here.'

Her eyes flip open, milk-pale, as though she's been ripped from a nightmare.

'Can you hear me, darling?'

But I can tell she doesn't see me, doesn't see anything but the dreamscape she inhabits. Suddenly her legs and arms begin to flail and crash against the bars of the gurney.

'Saskia!'

I reach frantically to calm her, seizing her hand, and as she locks her wide grey eyes on me for one heart-splitting moment I say, 'Please! Please stay, darling!'

But she continues to convulse. I have to move back, back, to allow the nurses space. I watch in horror as they reinstate the tubes, switch the machines on, begin to re-sedate her.

She slides back under, adrift in the darkness and watchful stars.

★　★　★

Dr Hamedi brings a cup of water into the room, sets it on the table in front of me.

'Sometimes the patient simply isn't ready to wake up,' she says gently. 'The brain needs a little more time to rest and heal.'

I'm curled around the hole in my chest where my heart used to be. Tears drip slowly down my face.

I cannot think about what I will do if Saskia dies. I cannot accept a world without her in it.

⋆ ⋆ ⋆

Our street.

Detached stone houses surrounded by gardens.

A marble sky of mourning.

A large crowd of familiar faces armed with balloons and banners are waiting outside our house: my friends Camilla and Rosie, Lucy and Matilda, the two students we'd employed to cover weekends at the bookshop, a large group of Saskia's friends from school and ballet, two dozen parents and children from St Mary's Primary School. Andrew Cheek, Michael's accountant and business mentor, is there, and I notice Jim and Simon, a couple of the school dads that Michael had a beer with a few times. I'm at once moved by the show of compassion and terrified to face everyone in case I collapse into tears.

'Who are all those people, Mum?' Reuben says, peering out the window.

'I think they've come to see us,' I tell him, bracing myself.

'Why?'

Nope. I'm not strong enough. I turn to Jeannie. 'I don't think I can face them.'

'It's my fault,' she says quickly. 'I got a phone call from the school and I told them we were leaving the hospital . . . '

'No, no, it's fine,' I say, taking deep breaths. But I crumble. It's all so strange. The sight of familiar faces confirms that what happened in Belize was real. That I'm returning home without half my family.

'Leave it to me,' Jeannie says firmly. 'I'll tell them you need some space . . . '

I see the kids' banners, the effort they've put in to make a huge poster with 'WE MISSED YOU' and 'GET WELL SOON' spelled out in bright colours. Everyone looks so keen to see us.

'I'll be OK.'

'Why are those people in our garden?' Reuben asks.

As soon as I step on to the kerb I burst into tears. The children surround me in the front garden and bombard me with hugs, kisses, and concern.

'Mrs Pengilly, why is your face like that?'

'What happened to your arm? Are you better yet?'

'When are you coming back? Will you be at school on Monday?'

'Did you get my picture? I painted butterflies on it and a rainbow.'

Jeannie steps forward, holds up her hands like she's talking down a terrorist. 'Now, kids, I know I told you I will *personally* see to it that every single painting, canvas and sand picture is displayed in Mrs Pengilly's house, but right now I think she needs to have some rest, OK?'

The kids look disappointed but the parents take their cue to usher them all back into their cars. I feel terrible but relieved. A handful of people have showed up to see Reuben. Several teachers from his school, Mr Aboulela and Mrs

Abbott, and the Head Teacher, Dr Angier. Lily, a girl from his year who acted motherly and protectively towards him, and Jagger. But no sign of Josh. They surround him and say hello, but he takes out his iPad and films them as they attempt to ask him how he is. I don't intervene.

Saskia's friends, Amber, Holly and Bonnie, are there with their mothers. The Formidable Foursome, we called them, bursting with opinions and exuberant forthrightness, a mutual love of ballet and small animals. I often turned my mind to Saskia's group of friends when I felt despondent about the future — *these girls*, I thought. *They'll put the world to rights.* They would hold play dates with their pets and despite the logistical hassle I indulged it because it was simply adorable.

'Where's Saskia?' Bonnie asks, her little face full of confusion, and when I glance at her mother it dawns on me: nobody knows just how ill she is.

'But why is she in the hospital?' Amber cries in a shrill voice when she overhears me mumble a tear-stricken explanation. 'Has she got tonsillitis? I had tonsillitis, didn't I, Mummy?'

The mothers don't know what to say, and when Holly asks me with tears in her eyes if she will ever see Saskia again I can't speak. It is excoriating, unbearably sad. Amber's mother apologises and tries to drag her away, but she grows frantic.

'Saskia!' she screams at the gate. 'Where's Saskia?'

★　★　★

Jeannie opens the front door and I ask her whether or not it was locked beforehand. She can't remember.

'What's wrong?' she says, following my gaze across the living room and kitchen.

'I think someone's been here,' I say quietly, looking over the chair that's lying on its side by the dining table. Has Michael been here? Or someone else? There's an unwelcoming presence, the trace of something sinister.

It looks as though someone came in through the back door and knocked the chair over. I spot mud on the floor, too, and there's a pile of papers on the kitchen table from a drawer, which has been left ajar. The bills drawer, where we keep all our receipts and household paperwork, including birth certificates, Reuben's SEN stuff. I rummage through it, my stomach flipping and my heart racing.

'To be fair,' Jeannie says, glancing around. 'Your house always looks like it's been burgled.'

I look over Saskia's toys in a corner, her toy pram filled with teddies. Michael's boxes of books from the shop. His coats in the hallway. Her pink wellies at the back door, her ballet bag hanging on the back of a chair. Photographs of us on the walls, strategically positioned, I remember, to cover Reuben's drawings on the paintwork.

A line has been scored in the universe, cleaving my life into Before and After.

I curl up into a ball in the middle of the living room and cry.

Jeannie and Reuben are talking in the kitchen. She finds a frozen pizza in the freezer and puts it in the oven for him. After a while she kneels beside me and rubs my back.

'Can I make you some tea?'

I wish I could take Saskia's place.

'Alright. Then why don't you go to bed? A good night's sleep always makes me feel better. Come on. I'll help you upstairs.'

'I can't go to bed,' I tell Jeannie.

'Why not?'

'Reuben doesn't go to bed until nine. He'll not break his routine. I have to stay up with him.'

She gives a chuckle. 'That's what *I'm* here for. I've arranged time off work and rented an Airbnb around the corner, so I'm all yours, OK? If Reuben needs a little longer to settle I'll wait for him. We can go pick up the pets from your friend's house. And I'll tidy downstairs while I'm at it. Come on, let me help you.'

She helps me shuffle along to the bathroom where I brush my teeth at the sink. Michael's razor is in the cupboard, tiny bristles caught between the blades. His shampoo and deodorant in the basket. His smell clinging to a towel.

'Do you want me to wash your hair?' Jeannie offers. I can't remember when I last washed it and I certainly can't manage it now. I lower myself painfully to the floor, tipping my head backwards over the side of the bathtub while she lifts the shower head and scrubs my scalp. I don't think Jeannie has ever done this for me. It's a small act but it lifts me considerably.

I move at a snail's pace along the hallway upstairs, past more framed photographs of happy times on the walls towards Saskia's bedroom. In the doorway I stand and look over the pretty ballet-themed haven that she spent hours in, transforming her four-poster bed into a theatre where her dolls performed *Swan Lake*. Jeannie makes me sit down, then takes Saskia's hairbrush from the dresser and offers to blow dry and plait my hair. My hair is much too thick and long to be worn loose, and I don't feel like me unless it's braided.

'Did you know I never once told Saskia that I danced?' I say weakly. I'm not sure who exactly I'm speaking to, but Jeannie answers.

'You can still tell her,' she says, tugging at a tat in my hair.

'When she said she wanted to take ballet lessons I didn't think much of it. Her friends all did ballet. She liked dressing up. But she's so good at it. A born dancer. I started to think that maybe one day she'd go to dance school. And I'd tell her that I used to do that. I used to picture her expression when she saw the posters of me dancing in London, Prague . . . She'd probably not even believe me. But I thought maybe she would be proud.'

'She *will* be, Helen.'

She helps me take off my clothes and pull my nightie over my head. I get a clear view of my body in the mirrored wardrobe door. I've lost weight and am floral with bruises. The trace of the seatbelt runs diagonally across my chest and belly in a turmeric stripe. The contours of my face are reconfigured in shades of plum and merlot. Every movement is astonishingly painful.

I pull back the bedclothes and automatically

189

lie on my side of the bed, as though Michael might appear and climb in beside me. A peck on the forehead. *Goodnight, love.* The impossibility of his absence, his strange and sinister departure not just from the hospital but from the country in which, for all he knows, me and the kids were stranded, maybe even incarcerated, has me in a near-constant state of bewilderment. Like being on a merry-go-round someone has set to spin much too fast, and on which I have to stay while attempting to cope with everything else. Saskia's failed resuscitation. Reuben's anxieties about his father's whereabouts. The unshakeable certainty that even here, in my own home, I am being watched by someone who wants to kill me.

Jeannie is telling me how she'll take Reuben to school and collect him at the end of each day, how she'll drive up and down to the hospital to see Saskia. I look her over, and gratitude blooms in me like a peony in a field of thistles and briars. When did she become this person, a helpful, selfless adult?

When my mother brought Jeannie home from the hospital I was over-awed with protectiveness and maternal love. I even named her after a woman who worked at my school and who was always very kind. Mum was an alcoholic, and true to my expectations she quickly went back to her old ways, leaving Jeannie and me alone for days at a time. I was only ten years old but became very adept at looking after her. It was the school holidays so nobody noticed, but when I had to go back to school in September I was terrified at what might happen to the baby. A teacher challenged me about my absences. Two weeks later, Jeannie and I were in foster care. I insisted that we wouldn't be separated. I remember the foster family complained that I was 'interfering' because of how I fought to care for Jeannie.

I guess I've always mothered her, and in ways that made her increasingly entitled and manipulative. Michael found out I was still sending her money every month and hit the roof. I knew it wasn't normal to still pay your little sister's rent when she was in her mid-twenties and working full time, but I felt guilty. And even when I finally recognised that she was using me, I didn't think there was anything I could do about it.

Perhaps she's using you now, a voice whispers in my head, but I push it away.

No, I won't sabotage this. People can change.

Michael's books are on his side table. A spiral notebook sits on the top of the pile with a pen lodged in the metal spiral binding. I ask Jeannie to pass the notebook and flip through it, just in case there is something there. To-do lists for the bookshop, a few quotes from the books he was reading. Some notes about his dreams, which I didn't realise he kept track of. Dreams about Saskia running away, Reuben getting lost. Again and again, a dream about a door of flame with paradise on the other side. He's underlined a comment.

This time I asked Helen if she'd open it with me. Woke up before she answered.

'What's that?' Jeannie asks.

'He wrote down his dreams. I never knew he did that. Eighteen years together and I'm still finding stuff out about him.' *Except why he left.*

She looks over the notes, squints. 'A door of flame? What's that about?'

'I don't know.'

On one page I find sums that have no clear context but which I guess are to do with bills. But on the next page, the numbers resemble dates, with phrases written next to them in Michael's barely-legible scrawl:

> *5/4/17 — same guy as yesterday outside   shop just hanging around*
> *7/4/17, 3.15pm — same guy, black car, black coat, around corner from shop. Pakistani? Think taking pics!!!*
> *8/4/17, 8.05am and 6pm — man in black car again outside Post Office*
> *13/4/17, 11.17am — outside Reuben's school*
> *14/4/17, 6.30pm followed me home*

'Are those dreams, too?' Jeannie says, craning her head to look. 'Followed me home?'

I frown at the notes, trying to make sense of the dates. April. 'I don't know.'

A noise downstairs. The front door. It opens and closes. Quickly I get out of bed and look out the window at the street outside. A black car is parked haphazardly on the pavement. My guts churn, bile rising to my mouth. A man's voice calls up the stairs.

'Don't panic,' Jeannie says when she sees me looking alarmed. 'It's just Shane.'

'Hello?' Shane calls upstairs.

'Hi, darling,' Jeannie calls back. 'Just upstairs.

192

I'll be with you in a few moments.'

'Shane?'

I stare at her, speared with sudden anger that she's invited him into my home without asking first. Who *is* he? When did things turn so serious between them? My mind turns to the recording of his voice on Reuben's iPad.

Never been to Mexico.

25

Reuben

5th September 2017

Roo: Malfoy u there??
Malfoy: Yes. Are you OK?
Roo: Yeah back home now
Malfoy: In England?
Roo: Yeah In my bedroom Dad's not here tho
Malfoy: Do you know where he is?
Roo: no. Some policemen came today to talk to mum it made my tummy funny ☹
Malfoy: What did they say? Do they have any leads?
Roo: Leads?? Why would they have leads???
Malfoy: I mean information on your dad's current location.
Roo: I thot you meant computer leads! No they don't. Nobody nose anythin
Malfoy: That's a shame.
Roo: Thanx for sending me trap-door partcualr btw. Its amazing!

Malfoy: You're welcome. Thanks for the recording of your mum and all the people outside your house.

Roo: They all came 2 welcome us home

Malfoy: Where's your mum now?

Roo: I'm gunna do an animation of a blue whale instead of a Mayan village

Malfoy: Oh? How come?

Roo: idk. I liked doing the scale model of the Maya temple but Saskia liked the whales we saw and I thot it wud be nice 4 her to see an animation of them when she wakes up

Malfoy: I bet she'd love that.

Roo: U think so?

Malfoy: Definitely. And blue whales are v interesting creatures.

Roo: Am learning lots about them! They're enormous! And endangered and nobody nose much about them and theres hardly any YouTube footage of them b/c their hard to find and so big that you cant get to close in case u get hurt

Malfoy: I can help with your animation if you like? Are you planning on showing the whale breach?

Roo: I think so. Can blue whales breech? There like 100 ft long!!!!!

Malfoy: do some research. It would be amazing to have an animation of it breaching but you want it to be realistic, too. If it *does* breach, I think you'll need Cinema 4D. It's a software for more complex movements. I can give you that.

Roo: YES! ☺ ☺ ☺ ☺ ☺ ☺

Malfoy: Where is your mum right now?

Roo: She's downstairs y??

Malfoy: Is she alone?

Roo: No aunt jeanie's here.

Malfoy: I'd like more footage of her. Can you send me more clips?

Roo: k. What of?

Malfoy: Your mum and aunt.

Roo: k

Malfoy: Reuben, I feel I should tell you something but it's potentially very dangerous. Do you think you can keep a secret?

Roo: Yes

Roo: What is it?

Roo: You can tell me

Malfoy: Never mind.

Roo: Malfoy, are you still there?

Roo: Malfoy?

26

Michael

5th September 2017

The train lights flicker in a garish Morse code as we enter the tunnel, all the colours muted by the absence of daylight. The lights go out completely, the minty glow of the EXIT sign transforming the carriage into something out of a David Lynch movie.

I think about the dream of the door of flame, how the door is always both a relief and a terror because it is a light amidst the darkness of the world I'm trying to leave behind. That's always the pull — to move past pain and terror with my family to a better life. Maybe this journey is what the dream was always about. Luke's family have been hunting me for years, and now they know where we live. The door of flame is that pain barrier of confronting them. Of facing the past.

There's a woman a couple of seats in front of me, heavily pregnant. She looks uncomfortable and keeps trying to shift position to accommodate her massive belly. I think back to when Helen was pregnant with Saskia, the bigger her belly got the more stressed out Reuben became. He didn't understand what was happening to her body. It was heart-wrenching and cute at the same time. He was six, still in nappies, spoke no more than a handful of words. *Mummy. Daddy. OK. Love you.* Our beautiful boy, with flopping brown hair, a sweet, freckled face, and large chocolate-brown eyes that would soften the heart of a monster.

Helen and I didn't need language to communicate with our son because we knew him through and through, and because those beautiful eyes of his told a thousand stories. But it was as though there was an imperceptible membrane between him and the rest of the world, and for the most part he was happy there. Until he saw Helen's belly turning slowly into a mountain and he freaked out.

When Saskia was born I was worried that Reuben might harm her by accident. I knew he wouldn't intend to do it, but he was still prone to epic tantrums and occasional violence. At twenty inches long and a mere six pounds four ounces she reminded me of a little bird, starkly tiny and fragile in contrast to her tall, heavy-handed seven-year-old brother. I had to watch him like a hawk and be on guard at all times.

But he was incredibly tender with her. He kissed her and fretted when she seemed unsettled. When she screamed the house down he covered his ears with his palms but didn't scream and rock as he often did with other noises. He'd go into the other room and wait until it was silent again, and then he'd return and watch her with an awe-struck expression.

We're coming out of the tunnel, now, a

198

needle-head of light ahead dilating. The pregnant lady takes a sigh, rubs her belly and winces as an elbow or foot momentarily makes a shape in her black T-shirt, kicking her from the inside out. She's got both legs straightened, laid on the seats in front. With a smile I think of the last few weeks of pregnancy, how Helen struggled with it. Couldn't sleep, couldn't eat for fear of acid reflux, couldn't tolerate the slightest amount of incompetence.

Some of our friends broke up shortly after having a child. I don't blame them. Having a kid changes the quality of your relationship completely. It's like walking on a tightrope and then suddenly having to carry a python or a seal while still navigating that thin, wobbling path to the other side. But in our case, the kids brought us closer together. Maybe, deep down, Helen and I are equally determined to make sure that our children don't experience the same childhoods as we had.

When I was younger my goal was to be a footballer. I was crap at it. I always got good marks in English Literature, though, and I had this teacher who I secretly pretended was my real dad. Mr Biscup. He was so passionate about Chaucer that it rubbed off on to me. He encouraged me to apply for university, so I did, and somehow I got a place at Oxford. I thought someone was having a laugh. But I loved it, every second of it. My goal was to do a Master's degree then a PhD, and one day end up as a Professor of Medieval Literature.

One decision derailed that dream for ever.

After Mont Blanc I dropped out and spent years pinballing from one dead-end job to another: cleaning fish guts in a factory, scrubbing toilets, then a fairly long stint in crisis clean-up, which involved cleaning the gore left behind after murders, suicides, biohazard accidents and unattended deaths. Surprisingly well paid. It exposed me to a world very much like the one Chaucer inhabited during the Black Plague. Better than reading about it at a distance — an Oxbridge distance, at that. People starving to death because their benefits hadn't been paid and decomposing on a sofa. Or a life blasted all over a room, the narrative of that life and its trajectory turned to detritus. We were the first ones there, straight after the police or forensic guys. I can't explain why it felt good to clean up something as gruesome as those scenes, restore order, but it did.

The tunnel ends; a patchwork quilt of green fields fans out beyond the window. In the glass of the window I see a man sitting a few rows in front on the opposite aisle wearing a black baseball cap, 'NYC' in white letters. He's looking directly at me, his face twisted in a scowl, and when I turn to stare back he lowers his head. A fierce twitch runs all the way across me. I only caught a glimpse of him but he looked familiar. I slide my eyes back to the glass without turning my head and sure enough he's lifted his head and is looking straight at me again. I don't move a muscle but inside I'm screaming. I know his face. I'd know it anywhere, I'd know it. His face, his voice, his mannerisms — Luke is branded on my memory for ever.

I'm just about to get up and change cabins to see if he follows when he gets up, picks up a black backpack and sidesteps into the seat directly behind me. I'm sweating like a tap. I hear a zip being pulled across the backpack and I wait for it, resigned to the inevitable.

Be quick about it, Luke.

A female voice on the tannoy announces loudly that we're arriving into Gare du Nord. In my head I count quickly to three and jump to my feet, striding towards the doors of the carriage. All my senses are on hyper-alert, and although it only takes a few seconds for me to reach the doors and stride through to the next carriage I know he hasn't followed. He's zipped up the bag again, returning whatever he removed, whatever he intended to use. The train slows and I slam the button to open the doors. The platform is full, everyone squashed together like sardines. They don't move so I push through, stepping on a guy's toes and almost knocking over some old dear.

'Sorry!' I shout behind me, and I race on without looking back.

I see a sign for the toilets and I head there on autopilot. For years our bathroom has been my sanctuary, the only space in our house where I could escape, lock the door, regroup. I do that now, only the gap beneath the cubicle yawns wide. It's cowardly to hide in here.

I open the door, scan the sinks. No one around. I hold my wrists under the cold tap to cool down. Footsteps squeak across the tiles. An

NYC baseball cap. My stomach clenches. He steps into a cubicle, thinks better of it, tries the one next door. I turn around to get a better glance. My certainty that it's Luke begins to wane. When he catches my eye I realise with jolting relief that it's not him at all. Same jawline, same hair, if he somehow maintained the same hairstyle from over twenty years ago and avoided grey hairs. *Of course it wasn't Luke, you moron.* I give another sideways look just to be sure. He looks again, his brow furrowed as if to say, *what you staring at?*

I press my palms on the edge of the sink and take a deep breath. *Get a grip, coward,* I tell my reflection. *Luke is dead, mate. Luke is dead.*

I head to an internet café and do some searches. I Google 'Luke Aucoin' and 'Theo Aucoin' and a promising number of results flick up. I spend a good half hour trawling through them all. Half are to do with fashion, the other to do with a chef called Maurice Aucoin who turns out to be no relation at all.

I try 'Churchill house Paris France'. 475,000 results. With a sigh I start scrolling. Lots of hits about the war, about Churchill's stint as a cavalry officer, about places he stayed. Roquebrune-Cap-Martin appears a few times. I click on a link. A house owned by Coco Chanel. Luke never mentioned anything about that, and it's in the south of France. Did Luke say his folks were from the south? Where did I get Paris from?

'*Tu es fini,*' a voice says. I look up. A man is standing beside me. Greasy hair, heavy glasses. He points at the clock. 'Your time is up. We have other customers waiting.'

I scrape back the chair and stand up, digging in my pockets for more money. It's all in sterling. I'll have to go withdraw some euros from the bank.

★ ★ ★

When I'm starting to feel woozy in a café on Rue La Fayette I recall Luke telling me about the time he ran away from home. He was nine or ten, bored to tears of his parents and Theo, so got up from the dinner table one evening, packed his bag and left the house. He managed to get all the way to Paris before a train inspector stopped him at the gate and alerted his parents. It took him two hours on the train, he said. Two hours.

Quickly I jump up and head back to Gard du Nord, looking over the departure board. It means nothing to me, so I move to a map mounted on the wall. Normandy. Two and a half hours away. I go to the ticket desk and buy a ticket for the next train. It's not until tomorrow morning, but I buy it anyway and head back through the darkening streets, intent on finding a room for the evening.

It's raining, and everywhere is full. I don't know enough French to ask if anyone can point me in the direction of a hotel with rooms, and my legs are aching. I need to lie down. I take the metro to the final stop, Place d'Italie, and head past a row of shops that are shutting up for the night towards a sign for a hotel. *Hôtel du*

Paradis. Sounds exactly what I'm looking for.

As I cut down a wet, narrow alley I hear the sound of footsteps behind me, then a voice. As soon as I turn a fist plunges into the side of my head, knocking me clean off my feet. One second I'm upright, the next I'm face down in a puddle. I see three of them reflected in the dark water. A foot moves back, goes to kick me in the ribs. I manage to block it and tip the guy over but his friends don't like that so much. There are four of them gathered around me now like a pack of wolves. They all start booting me then, and I curl up into as tight a ball as I can. Someone stomps on my head and with an explosion of pain behind my eyeballs I fall silent.

All the lights go out.

27

Helen

6th September 2017

I wake with a start. A slash of light through the curtains falls on a blister pack of pills on the bedside table. Sleeping tablets. When did I buy those? I'm fairly sure I didn't. I don't remember taking them last night either. The digital clock on Michael's bedside table reads 13.24. I don't know what day it is.

I pull myself to the edge of the bed. All my muscles feel pulverised. I cling on to the walls and make my way slowly to the top of the stairs.

'Reuben?'

No answer.

My heart is racing. I take the stairs in a bum-shuffle, the way Saskia did when she was learning to walk. At the bottom of the stairs I can see the front door is open. With a shudder of fear I creep towards it, wondering if someone is already in the house. I step outside, look up and down the street. No one is around. The sky is grey, the first nip of autumn in the air. Reluctantly I head back inside. The house no longer feels welcoming and homely. My mind spins to all its hiding places. To the cellar we never use. The attic.

I inch across the creaking floorboards of the hall to the kitchen and find the largest knife I can in a drawer, bracing myself to hold it in front of me as I check every room in the house before recognising that even if I find someone here my soupy muscles and bruised bones wouldn't stand me in much stead against an intruder. So I take to the downstairs bathroom and lock the door before lowering myself to the ground, shaking and weeping.

After a half hour or so I open the door half an inch and listen for any sound. Nothing. I can see the landline handset on the kitchen worktop. Quickly I reach for it and call Jeannie. She answers on the third ring.

'Hello, darling. Are you alright?'

'Reuben's not here,' I whisper. 'Have you seen him?'

'Yes, this morning,' she says. 'I took him to school. I think he was glad to go actually. I'll be back in an hour. I'm just picking up some more groceries for you. Stay in bed, OK? Enjoy the peace and quiet.'

A knock at the front door interrupts our conversation. I ask Jeannie to stay on the line and hold the handset in one hand, the knife in the other, as I inch into the hallway. Three figures behind glass. Slowly I open the door a half-inch and peek through. A short woman with purple glasses and close-cropped silver hair and two men. All in suits.

'Helen?'

'Yes.'

'I'm Detective Constable Fields,' one of the men says in an earthy Yorkshire accent, his eyes flicking down to the knife in my hand. 'Have we come at a bad time?'

I open the door fully and let them in, quickly setting the knife on the console table with a faltering excuse about chopping apples.

DC Fields tells me he's been appointed as my FLO — our family liaison officer. He insists that I stay on the sofa with a mohair blanket around my knees while he makes me a cup of tea, though I'm still mentally peeling myself off the ceiling. I feel adrift without something to do, so I end up making the tea and enlisting DC Fields' help when I can't lift the kettle. DS Jahan and DCI Lavery sit in the living room and offer small talk about the weather, about how long we'd lived in Northumberland, about the bookshop.

'I can't face the bookshop just yet,' I tell DC Fields, and he throws me a sympathetic smile. 'I know it's five minutes from here but . . . ' I tail off, the thought of having to confront that black, destroyed space that was our beautiful book haven flooding me with fresh dread.

I take a Citalopram and two Ibuprofen when no one is looking to stave off the brain zaps I've been having as a result of antidepressant withdrawals and the ache of torn muscles down my back, shoulders, and wrist. I hadn't experienced pain from the whiplash until now, but the doctor said that shock was a powerful blocker of pain.

Once I've settled into an armchair and everyone has exhausted their pleasantries,

Detective Sergeant Jahan flips open a notebook. He is younger than I'd noticed on Skype, smartly dressed in a grey suit, pristine white shirt and navy tie. He has these dark eyes that seem to see all the way to the other side of the Universe. Detective Chief Inspector Lavery is short and lithe, with silver hair cropped neatly to her scalp. She's wearing navy slacks with a white shortsleeved shirt, runner's veins roping all the way around her arms and neck. I know they're here to help, but I feel a lurch in my stomach at their presence. I've never dealt with the police before, and certainly not plain-clothed detectives. After Luke's death I've always broken out into a sweat anytime I spotted the neon stripes of a police car.

'We wanted to talk to you about the next steps,' DCI Lavery tells me. 'A key aspect of the search for your husband will be to speak to witnesses in San Alvaro, and we'd like to do some searches of the house.'

I blink. 'Search the house? You mean, *this* house?'

'To search for any correspondence Michael might have had,' DS Jahan says. 'Letters, emails, text messages . . . '

' . . . most importantly, his devices,' DCI Lavery says.

'His mobile phone and laptop were destroyed in the crash,' I say.

'What about desktop computers or tablets?' DS Jahan says. 'Does he have a home office?'

'His office was in the shop. But it's been destroyed in the fire.'

Blank stares. 'Well, there may be hard copies of correspondence that will help.'

I'm still lost. 'But . . . correspondence with *who?*' DS Jahan frowns. I know how uptight I sound. 'Sorry,' I say. 'I'm just trying to work out what this search is for.'

'We know he took a flight out of Belize and landed in Heathrow,' DCI Lavery says. 'We're still trawling through data from Heathrow to find out where he might have gone but that's going to take a while. In the meantime, we'd like to form a picture of Michael's life leading up to the crash.'

'We spoke with your sister Jeannie earlier this morning,' DS Jahan says. 'She said you seemed quite paranoid before you went on holiday. She said she was worried about you before you left.'

'Worried?' I say. 'Well, I suppose she was worried about the fire . . . I hardly saw my sister before so I'm . . . I'm not quite sure why she would have said that I was acting paranoid.'

'You mentioned that you felt watched before,' DCI Lavery says. 'When you were on holiday.'

I nod. 'Yes, and clearly that *wasn't* paranoia, it was fact . . . '

'What about before the holiday? Did you feel watched then?'

Of course I did. The letters came every year.

'No. I was perfectly fine before we went on holiday.'

'I suppose the fire would have added to Michael's stress levels,' DS Jahan says.

'Well, yes. The fire added to *all* our stress levels,' I say. 'We still don't know if the insurance company is going to pay out. We have a huge mortgage on the shop and if they don't pay . . . ' Already my heartbeat is quickening and I can feel my colour rising.

'Can you tell us what happened?' DCI Lavery asks. 'With regards to the fire?'

I close my eyes and clasp my hands tightly. It's no easy thing to talk about. 'We got a call in the middle of the night. We raced down there but the fire was bigger than either of us anticipated. We'd thought we should bring a couple of fire extinguishers that we keep at home in case of an emergency . . . ' The memory of the thick black smoke curling underneath the shutters comes back in a horrible rush. My chest tightens, my blood runs cold. 'Michael went inside, tried to tackle it,' I say, my voice growing hoarse. 'There was nothing we could do. He loved that shop. It was his baby.'

'And you don't think anyone started it maliciously,' DCI Lavery asks.

I shake my head. 'The investigation is still in progress. One of the firefighters said it was probably just one of those things. A bookshop unfortunately contains a lot of inflammable material.'

'Do you think Michael could have had anything to do with it?' DC Jahan says bluntly. It takes me a moment to understand what he's asking.

'You mean, could Michael have started the fire?' I say, incredulous. 'No! Absolutely not.'

'We checked the village CCTV cameras,' DCI Lavery says. 'Michael's car is a green Vauxhall

Zafira, correct? Registration NP03 TRF?'

I nod. She flips through her notes. 'The fire started around midnight. A green Zafira appears on the CCTV at thirteen minutes past midnight heading down Fraser Street, which is the route between your house and the shop.'

'There must fifty green Zafiras in the village,' I say quickly.

'Five,' DS Jahan says. 'Two were out of town, one was in the garage. That leaves just yours and one other on the road. Your sister said that Michael often worked late. Was he working late that night?'

My thoughts are churning, my heart thudding. 'I don't know. He could have been. I really don't think . . . '

'We have a note also that Michael had been involved in a fight with another parent shortly after the fire,' DCI Lavery adds coolly. 'Benjamin Trevitt, father of Joshua Trevitt. Reuben's friend, I believe. Mr Trevitt filed a complaint of assault.'

I look over their faces, my throat tight. 'I didn't know Ben had filed a complaint.'

'Tell us about Michael,' DCI Lavery says, leaning forward, clearly wanting to avoid upsetting me too much. I won't be much use if I fall apart. She glances around the room, taking in the pictures on the walls of our family in happy times, the mess of Saskia's toys in the corner. I start to tell them about the bookshop, about how dedicated Michael is. How he's set up weekly reading groups for new mums and pensioners, writing competitions, school visits — more a social enterprise than a mere shop. She smiles.

211

'Aside from his job, though. What's he like as a husband, a father? Behind closed doors?'

I'm a bit confused by the question — or the reason she's asking it — but I go along, slightly wary. 'Michael's a good husband. A great father. He was the one who suggested we go to Mexico. For Reuben, you know?'

'Expensive trip,' DS Jahan says. 'Was it something you'd been planning for a while?'

I shake my head. 'No, it was kind of last minute . . . '

He looks down at his notebook. 'Michael booked the trip after the fire, isn't that right?'

I nod, and he holds my gaze.

'I don't know about you, but if I'd just lost my livelihood in a fire I wouldn't be booking a two-month family holiday in the Caribbean.'

His stare pins me to the seat. I feel my breaths quicken, my skin turns to ice. I start to answer but he cuts me off.

'What about before the fire?' DCI Lavery asks. 'Were either of you stressed about finances?'

I don't like what she's implying. 'No more than anyone else,' I say. 'We have mortgages on the house and the shop but no credit card debt or anything like that.'

It seems to be the right answer, because they share a look and move on, asking for more details about the beach hut, about the butler and the touring company we booked with in Mexico.

Then: 'We do have an update about the driver of the other vehicle,' DCI Lavery says. 'Vanessa Shoman — the lady at the British Embassy? She was able to pass on a name and after some

212

probing, the police in Belize confirmed that this was the man they'd interviewed. We asked another police force in the area to run some checks on the van, so we're eighty per cent certain this is the individual we're after.'

I look from DCI Lavery to DS Jahan, wondering why they didn't mention this before now.

'Well, who is he?'

'His name's Jonas Matus,' DS Jahan says, flipping open his tablet. 'Does that name mean anything to you?'

My hands are shaking and I can barely breathe. It feels as though a monster is being given a human shape. I feel nauseous. 'I've never heard that name before,' I say weakly.

DCI Lavery consults her notes. 'He's local to San Alvaro. Has some previous convictions. Theft, fraud, assault.'

'I remember his shoes,' I say in a tight voice. *His boots. Right there by my face. A scuff on one toe.*

'His boots?' DC Fields says, and I explain.

'We don't have a full body photograph, I'm afraid,' DS Jahan says, tapping on the screen of his tablet. 'The police sent us this mugshot.'

He passes me the tablet. On the screen, a man with dark, blank eyes, overlapping teeth, a distinct underbite. A wave of revulsion rolls over me. I stand up and begin to pace slowly across the room. DCI Lavery asks if we should stop, take a breather. I go out to the porch and stand in the cool breeze urging myself not to faint.

A hand on my shoulder. 'Are you OK?'

DC Fields. 'I know it's really, really difficult to

face this,' he says gently. 'But the sooner we get a clear idea of what went on in the time leading up to the crash, the better. Do you think this is the trespasser you saw at the beach hut?'

He is holding the tablet with the mugshot of Jonas Matus staring back at me with a gaze that might burn my eyes out. I take deep breaths, force myself to stay focused. Is he the man I saw running away from the beach hut? 'I didn't see his face,' I explain.

He swipes to another image of Matus' white van, obviously taken before the crash. I have to turn away and cover my mouth, because immediately a memory of the van lunging into my lane flashes across my mind, sharp as a razor. I feel it slamming into me, the spin of the car. I see it in a haze at the far end of a mosaic of shattered glass, on the other side of the road, upright, the bumper crumpled and the windscreen shattered, steam rising from the bonnet. It's the same van.

'We spoke to the people who were staying at the beach resort at the same time as you,' DS Jahan says. 'One guy said he spotted a white van in the area just before you left. It seems there aren't a lot of vehicles out that way which is why he noticed it.'

'If Matus *was* watching you, though,' DCI Lavery says thoughtfully, folding her arms, 'how did he know where you were staying? If hardly anyone knew you were in Belize, much less your actual address, and if you say Matus had no connection to you . . . how would he know where you were?'

'Maybe he didn't,' I hear myself say. 'Maybe the crash was an accident and he's making up this claim to avoid blame.'

They consider this, but even I don't believe my words. The instinct I had in the beach hut of being watched is back. I feel like something is just within my blind spot, and if I look close enough at my memories I'll see it, bright as the noon day sun.

'Are you alright?' DCI Lavery asks, seeing my face blanch. I feel faint but I tell him I can manage. I need this to be over.

'So . . . just thinking about the fight with Mr Trevitt,' DCI Lavery says, sweeping her eyes across our family photographs on the walls. 'You have a lovely home and a lovely family. Would you say that Michael wasn't normally a violent guy?'

We're back to this again. Why can't they see that Michael has nothing to do with Jonas Matus?

'Michael said he was trying to protect Reuben,' I say slowly. 'I'm not exactly sure what the threat was but . . . we have to be careful with Reuben in certain social situations. I suppose it's been a long time since he was invited to a birthday party. In fact, I think this was his first invitation in fourteen years. Michael was probably being over-protective and . . . '

'Has Michael been violent before?' DCI Lavery asks. Then, more gently, 'To you, maybe?'

I shake my head. 'Absolutely not.'

'Not even in an argument? After a few drinks?'

'*Every* couple argues, especially when you've

215

been together for as long as we have . . . '

'What were your arguments about?'

I shrug. 'Same as everybody else's. House-work. Money.'

'You were happy, then?' DC Fields surmises.

I stare at my hands. At my wedding band. 'We had our ups and downs.'

'How bad were the downs?'

'Michael didn't like to talk about things. He could be . . . distant.'

'What about the painting?' DCI Lavery says slowly. 'Your sister mentioned that Michael destroyed an expensive painting he'd bought you. Can you tell us about that?'

My mouth falls open. Jeannie actually brought that up? She mentioned the painting?

I look around each of them and I know my cheeks are burning, a red glow all the way from my cleavage to the tips of my ears, the mark of stress. I want to dodge the question, come up with an excuse. But they're all looking, and I don't want them to suspect me of lying. Why has Jeannie told them about this? I had forgotten that I'd confided in her.

'It was a long time ago, before we had Reuben,' I say in a shaky voice. 'We went to an antiques market in Venice and came across this painting that I fell in love with. It was of a ballet class, a row of dancers at the barre. The man said it was a lost Degas. It was five hundred euros, and neither of us were sure that it was actually a Degas. Even so, Michael insisted on buying it for me.'

It was a beautiful Autumn day, and we went to

Murano, the beautiful island in Venice with rainbow-coloured streets and the bones of a slain dragon in the floor of a church. Michael and I were deeply in love, locked in a mutual gratitude at having found each other, at finding peace after so much anguish. I remember that holiday marked a change in how we dealt with the past, with the guilt of Luke's death. The painting captured for me not just the beautiful image of dancers, reminding me of my ballet days, but of the promise of a future where we could be happy together.

'Michael destroyed the painting, is that right?' DCI Lavery prompts. I nod, on the verge of tears. The memory of it almost turns me inside out.

'Can you tell us why?'

It burns in me, the fact that I told Jeannie what happened. I might have known she would tell someone, use it against me right when it would hurt most.

'We got a new head teacher at the school where I worked,' I say, clasping my hands rightly. 'Scott Renzi. Michael started coming out with strange comments about the way Scott looked at me, where I'd been if I got home five minutes late. I didn't really think anything of it. Michael isn't the jealous type. I knew he wasn't sleeping at the time.'

'Sleeping?'

I nod. 'He has bouts of insomnia, usually when he's stressed. It can be very severe unless he gets medication for it, and even then . . . Anyway, I made a comment one evening

217

about something Scott said. He'd praised me for something I did at work. I can't even remember what it was, now. Michael didn't say anything at the time.' I'm stammering, my words blending one with another. Nobody speaks. 'The next day, I got home from work and saw that . . . he'd destroyed the painting.' I draw a breath and wring my hands, pained by the memory. 'I knew that Michael felt betrayed. That in his head I was cheating on him with Scott, that I was going to leave him . . . ' I start to explain about Michael's mother leaving when he was little, how I knew this was something he'd never really dealt with, but it all comes out jumbled. 'Anyway, I knew this was his reaction in the heat of the moment. He'd put the painting in our fire bin and . . . incinerated it. But when I tried to talk to him about it, he was so wounded and apologetic that I ended up just letting it go. I mean, it was only a painting.'

My voice has tapered to a whisper. I don't want to talk about this any more. Michael isn't here to defend himself. It feels terribly unfair, and an agonising reminder of that out-of-body moment when I realised what he'd done.

'How did you feel about that?' DCI Lavery asks.

'I was . . . bewildered,' I say, tears beginning to prick my eyes. *But the thing is, I know how paranoia feels. I know it can drive you to think something is real when it isn't. And he was sorry, so very sorry.*

I press my hands against my face and start to cry. DC Fields moves to the space on the sofa next to me and places a hand on my back.

'Forgive me for saying so,' he says. 'But that doesn't sound at all like something a 'good husband' would do. It sounds like the work of someone very cruel and manipulative.'

'He was sorry,' I tell him, wiping my face. 'It was a spur-of-the-moment thing. Not like Michael at all.'

I can't tell him anything about what happened on Mont Blanc. Michael is not a bad person. He was insecure, and out of his mind without sleep. I knew he was sorry for what he did.

'Everyone has dark colours in their character,' I say. 'Michael would never lift a hand to me, never hurt me.'

'And yet, he attacked Benjamin Trevitt,' DCI Lavery says.

I can see now why they asked about the painting. To portray Michael as violent. It's not true.

'The fight with Ben Trevitt wasn't long after the fire so I know Michael was under a lot of stress,' I say. 'I did try and speak with Ben but he didn't want to know. He just blanked me. What does *that* say about him?'

My last remark is a little bitter, I'll admit, but it's true. I called the Trevitts after the fight but they wouldn't answer. I saw Ben Trevitt at the school gates — I remember wincing at the bruise on his face, a horrible black eye — and waved at him but he stalked off angrily. What else could I have done?

But a question has rolled into the room, the missing piece of the puzzle wedging itself

219

amongst the others to form a picture. What if Ben Trevitt had something to do with the crash? Reuben Skyped Josh from the beach hut, I remember that. It was likely that Josh knew exactly where we were staying. He could have told his parents. And when Michael punched Ben Trevitt it was in front of his own son, in front of all the other parents, and I knew from our brief exchanges at the school gates that he had an ego, very Alpha Male . . .

Was he so humiliated about it that he was driven to take revenge?

28

Michael

20th June 1995

We spend the afternoon at the Mer de Glace, a glacier almost five miles long. I say aloud that it looks like a trail of white feathers winding through black crowns. Luke gives me a slow clap for my poetry while Helen comments on how my description fits the scene exactly. We take a cable car above the glacier to reach an ice grotto, the work of a lapidary. A long, polar-blue tunnel carved into coruscating ice. It is like stepping inside a gigantic blue agate, the walls inside made of quartz instead of ice. And the deeper we get, the architecture shifts to something almost human, almost umbilical, like we are re-entering the womb.

I think better of saying this out loud, given the company I keep.

'Father Christmas is at the other end, isn't he?' Luke jokes as we walk through the tunnel.

'Do we get to meet Rudolph?' Theo asks anyone who'll listen.

We head back to the trail after lunch and spot loads of weird horned creatures eating on a grass ridge.

'What *are* they?' Helen asks aloud, stopping to look at them.

'It's like a badger mated with an antelope,' Luke observes.

'Chamois,' Theo says, lighting a roll-up. 'A species of goat-antelope native to the Alps.'

'Huh.' Luke arches an eyebrow at his brother. 'They dangerous?'

Theo shrugs. 'I wouldn't try to cuddle up to one at night.'

Helen coos to the small one that gingerly pads over the rock towards her. Reaching towards a tuft of grass she rips it out and holds it towards the animal. It approaches with its face down and Helen laughs as it takes some of the grass from her hand. Just then, a bigger one — the parent — comes clopping over the stones and we all notice the size of its horns.

'It's like the Billy Goats Gruff,' Theo says.

'Just watch out for the troll,' Luke adds. Then seeing Helen inch closer to the bigger animal, 'What the hell are you doing?'

She motions to it with another fistful of grass. The smaller one gets closer and I see the bigger animal stamp its feet.

Luke grabs Helen's arm in a firm grip and pulls her out of the way. I see her wince, as though in pain, though she lets him pull her away from the animal. She shrinks at the look of anger on Luke's face.

'You want to get yourself killed?' Luke shouts.

'Chill out, babe,' Theo tells him. 'You want a smoke?'

Luke stomps off ahead. I notice that Helen is

shaken, rubbing her arm.

'You OK?' I ask. She flicks the corners of her mouth up but I can tell she's shaken.

Later, when we stop for a snack, Helen pulls her hair out of its tight bun and tugs her sweater over her head. I notice the spot on her arm where Luke had gripped.

Four long yellow bruises there, spaced close together.

That was why she winced: he gripped a sore spot on her arm.

'What happened?' I say lightly.

She pulls her arm to her chest, covers up the bruises. 'I . . . I fell.'

'Fell?' I say, pulling off my boots to get a stone out. 'Looks like finger marks.'

Her eyes lift to Luke, who is having a smoke with Theo about ten feet away. His mood is shifting, I can read it. It's like the anger boils up in him and then has to find a way out. Sometimes it's by starting a fight, occasionally by getting so drunk he passes out in a doorway, and usually by smoking something that smells too sweet to be wholesome.

'It's nothing,' she says, but as she lifts her sweater to put it back on I notice another bruise on her right shoulder, a black crescent-shaped mark. She traces the direction of my stare, throws her sweater on. Luke stomps over, full of the joys.

'Hey, sweet cheeks,' he says to Helen, and she looks up. Her eyes contradict her smile.

'Hey. Feeling better?'

He gives a deep inhale, pounds his chest with

223

his fists. 'Yup. Shall we get going?'

'Helen hasn't eaten,' I say. 'I was just boiling the kettle . . . '

He glances at his watch. 'We've got to get going if we're to make it to the refuge for supper.'

'I'm not hungry,' Helen says quickly, getting to her feet. I go to protest more but she throws me a look that makes me shut up fast. I swallow back the remainder of my own noodles, put my gear on. Theo and Luke are already ahead, Helen trailing behind.

I never thought I'd say this, but I'm starting to feel sorry for her. Why did Luke force her to come along? One minute he's all over her and the next he treats her like he doesn't want her here.

We reach the refuge eight hours later. It's built on a large outcrop with a glass wall overlooking the massif, affording breath-taking views. Hard to believe we're still on planet earth. More like Mount Olympus up here. The sun is beginning to sink into foamy cloud, glossing the ridges and crests of the Alps in a beatific gold. We had planned to stay in one of the dorms inside the hut but, this being summer, the place is heaving. The camping area behind the hut is filling up fast so we take our spaces and set up our tents. I don't mind camping — much cheaper than sleeping in the refuge, though I don't admit this to Theo or Luke. They could probably afford to buy the place outright.

We encounter some of the people we met at the previous hut: the group of Italians who caught Luke's attention by speaking loudly about drugs, and the old French guys who told us about the campsite in the first place. One of them looks around a hundred years old, Santa Claus beard, craggy face and teeth that would look good on a donkey. He invites the four of us to join him and his pals for a beer around the campfire later on. Tiresias, he says his name is, which isn't lost on Theo, Luke and me.

Helen is sharing a tent with Luke and I'm sharing with Theo. We originally agreed to share my spanking new three-man tent purchased specifically for the occasion, and as I help Theo erect the one he'd brought for us — a tiny, inadequate offering that I suspect won't withstand the harsher winds close to the summit — I feel a flush of anger.

And as I watch Helen climb into the tent, followed by Luke who throws us both a victory salute — he always does this when closing in on a skirt — another emotion catches me by surprise. Jealousy. I am jealous of him.

Get a grip, mate, I tell myself. *This time last week you hated her guts. Now you've got feelings for her?*

I try to tell myself that I'm missing Nina but I know it isn't that. It isn't Nina, and it isn't the mountain air.

It's Helen.

29

Michael

6th September 2017

I come to. It's stopped raining but I'm lying on my side in a large puddle in a back alley. Someone's chucking black bin bags into the dumpster beside me. He stands in front of me, looks down. A big guy in whites. Shouts something that sounds a lot like he thinks I'm drunk and wants me to get out of here.

I roll on to my hands and knees. Blood drips down from my ear into the water beneath me. I lean against the wall, make my way to a standing position. The man is still shouting and gesturing at me to get lost. I see two of him. '*Barre-toi!*' he shouts, waving a fat hand. '*Dégage!*'

'I got mugged,' I mumble, but he picks up a broom and starts jabbing the end of it in my ribs. I double over in agony as he jabs the spot where they kicked me. It feels like I've a couple of ribs broken, at least. He pulls out a mobile phone and punches a number into it.

'*Gendarme?*'

That, I understand. I look around for my bag but I know it's gone. He's phoning the police. I tell him I'm sorry and stagger off.

It's daytime. I have no idea what time. It looks like people are heading to work. Lots of cars and scooters on the road, lots of people on the pavement. I look down and see the Seine running alongside me. Notre Dame in the distance. The Eiffel Tower. I wish Helen was here. I wish I could tell her. I dig my hands in my pockets, shot through with a need to call her.

But there's a moment of blind panic. Everything was in my backpack. My passport. All my credit cards, the money I drew out.

My train ticket.

Gone.

I check my pockets again, just in case. Way down in my front pocket I find my phone. There's a small slip of paper, too, a few coins, about four Euros. With a sigh of relief I see it's the ticket I bought for Normandy.

The ticket reads 08.46. Have I missed the train? I start heading back to Gare du Nord, scanning the buildings for a clock. Finally I stop a few people and try to recall my French GCSE.

'*Escusez-moi . . . Um . . . quelle heure est-il?*'

No one will give me the time of day, quite literally. Eventually I spot the screen of a woman's mobile phone. 08.43 appears in white digits.

'Thanks,' I tell her, and hasten my pace to the station.

The train is waiting on platform 4. I have seconds to spare. '*Pièce d'identité,*' a guard barks.

Another commuter pulls out a driving licence, someone else produces a passport. I hold out my hands.

'*Non . . . non passport.*'

'*Pièce d'identité*,' he repeats, and I'm sweating now, but despite my pleas he stands firm.

The train pulls out of the station without me on it.

30

Helen

6th September 2017

I close the front door behind the detectives, numb with shock. They took the desktop computer from upstairs and my Kindle. I told them I only use it for reading but they took it anyway. DC Fields promised me I could call him anytime if I wanted to chat about anything. All I can think of is that they've got the wrong end of the stick. Michael has done nothing wrong. He's missing, and seriously injured. He is potentially in a lot of danger. But somehow the emphasis seems to have shifted from finding him to pinning blame on him.

My sister's comment about the painting has fuelled it.

I drag myself back upstairs and crawl into Saskia's bedroom. I curl up on her pink rug and scream into the fur of one of her unicorn teddies. My grief has converted to white-hot rage. What the hell is Jeannie playing at? I confided in her. When Michael destroyed the painting, I was absolutely distraught. I remember pulling the charred bits of painting out of the fire bin in utter horror. Even then, I believed that he was playing a horrible trick, that he'd burned a different painting and was going to pull out the one he'd bought in Venice. That he'd tell me he was joking. But he wasn't.

Just then, I hear a noise in the hallway.

'Helen? Where are you?'

Jeannie. I hear the sound of the front door locking behind her. Then another voice.

'Hi, Mum!' Reuben shouts. The buoyancy of his voice is jolting. 'Is Dad back?'

The question hits me flat in the chest. 'No,' I say, and I stumble over an excuse about why he's not here, but he has seen. His eyes search my face, see that I've been crying.

'When is Dad back?' he says, looking past me and up the stairs. 'Where is he, Mum?'

'I . . .'

He holds up his iPad. 'Malfoy's finished his pirate ship. I want to show Dad.'

'Who's Malfoy?' Jeannie asks Reuben, taking his coat off his shoulders. 'Isn't that someone from Harry Potter?'

'He's my friend on iPix,' Reuben says, showing me a drawing on the screen. 'He's helping me with my blue whale animation. Is Dad upstairs?'

How badly I want to say yes. I say nothing, and he heads up there, taking the stairs two at a time, calling, 'Dad! Dad?'

Jeannie and Shane are speaking in low voices, full of affection. I'm still unsettled about their relationship. He's an academic, or so he says. He wraps an arm around her waist, whispers something in her ear that makes her giggle. He's light years from the type of guy she has tended to date — fiery, gorgeous, self-centred, abusive men, usually actors or dancers. Jeannie seems different, too, though I have no doubt it's just a role she's playing right now. Gone are the crop tops, pink hair, and slashed jeans. Today she's wearing a forest-green Hobbs dress and black brogues. Her short red hair is styled and parted to one side, and she's wearing full make-up: thick mascara, autumnal eyeshadow, glossy red lips. She's had a manicure, too. How can she think about getting a *manicure* when my world is falling apart? I struggle to picture the scenario. Popping in a salon to get her nails done while Saskia lies in a coma in the hospital. Chatting to the beautician about the turn in the weather. It's absurd.

I notice Shane's boots. Black boots, just like the ones I saw when I came to on the road after the crash. I give a loud gasp.

Jeannie turns to me, sees me standing with a look of horror on my face.

'Helen,' she says, walking towards me. 'Come here. I have something for you.'

She takes me by the hand to the dining room where a display of flowers sits on the table. It's not a bouquet of roses or lilies, but bruise-coloured thistles, garish strelitzias, bloody-hued poppies, and purple foxgloves that look like open mouths, round with shock. Behind the bouquet I notice the edge of a gold frame. When I see what it holds I gape in abject horror. It's a framed print of the painting that Michael destroyed and which the police have just questioned me about. The timing is staggering.

I draw a hand to my mouth. Jeannie folds her arms and gives me a sympathetic smile.

'I had to drive to Newcastle this morning to get it,' she says, beaming. 'When I found it online I rang the shop first thing to check they definitely had it. I couldn't help myself. I should say, it's not a Degas like you thought. Edouard Sylvester, one of Degas' pupils. Still gorgeous, though.' She turns to Shane, glowing with pride. 'See? I *knew* she'd love it.'

She clasps her hands together and beams at her handiwork. When I don't stop crying she puts a hand on my shoulder.

'What's wrong? Has something happened? Helen?'

With a terrific burst of energy I reach for the print, lift it above my head and bringing it crashing to the floor. The glass sprays outward, skittering under the table and on top of my feet. Jeannie gives a loud noise of horror, a choking sound. I bend down and pick up the frame, shaking the remaining pieces of glass loose. Then I tear out the print and scrunch it up into a tight ball.

'You think I don't know what you're trying to do?' I say, throwing the scrunched-up print in her face.

'What are you talking about?' she cries.

I look at Shane, at his boots. Both of them knew our location. They knew exactly where we were staying in Belize. He said he was never in Mexico, but he was. He was there all the time, watching us. Making sure the job was done. And now they're here, in my home.

'I'm going to call the police,' I say in a low voice, heading towards the handset on the console table. 'Perhaps you'd like to tell them what you were doing at the scene of the crash, Shane.'

He looks up sharply. 'What?'

'You *watched* us,' I tell him, my vision blurred by tears of anger. I smash my fist down on the table. 'How *could* you?'

'What?'

'You lied to Reuben! You said you'd never been to Mexico and yet Jeannie said you were there right when the crash happened!'

He trips over his words. 'I . . . I haven't been to Mexico . . . '

'Just stop it!' I shout. 'I know it was you! You had those boots on . . . I woke up and saw you there. And you did nothing!'

'New Mexico,' Shane says after a moment. 'I was at a conference in Albuquerque giving a plenary on totalitarian enmity. I've never been to Mexico. You can check my passport, if you like.'

He pulls out his phone and starts showing me photographs he took out there. There's one of him with a group of men standing outside a sign that reads 'The Fifteenth Association of Political Thought Conference 27-31st Aug, Albuquerque, NM'.

'My paper was on the thirtieth,' he says, scrolling through more photographs. 'That was the day of the crash, I think. You can ask the other two hundred and fifty delegates whether I was there or not.' He gives a short smile, infuriatingly polite. 'I don't hold the accusation against you. I lost my father in a car accident when I was ten. I'm well acquainted with the impulse to assign blame.'

I'm halfway between wanting to punch his smug, plenary-on-totalitarian-enmity face and collapsing to my knees and begging for forgiveness. I opt for a seat by the dining table to gather my senses. Jeannie follows suit, pulling out the chair opposite, and Shane copies her.

'Helen, I need to be really honest with you,' Jeannie says, laying her hands flat on the table. She turns to Shane. 'And I'm glad you're here, because if we're going to move in together and make a deeper commitment then I think you need to understand a few things about me.'

She takes a breath, the famous Jeannie-dramatic-pause. I bite back a noise of irritation.

'OK, I have a little speech prepared,' she says, taking a yogic breath, hands sweeping air into her nostrils. 'I know that I have been a petulant, selfish, and ungrateful *diva*,' she says. 'I knew how to guilt you into giving me things and I did it over and over. I thought I was being clever, that you owed me, somehow. In the back of my mind I thought I was getting compensation for not having a proper Mum.' Her voice is slower, her Northern accent more pronounced. Tears roll down her face but she doesn't make a show of dabbing at them. She seems . . . genuine.

'When I told the police about the painting, I wasn't doing it to spite you,' she says. 'I was wracking my brains, trying to think of anything I could that would help you. They asked so many questions. I remembered what you'd told me

234

about Michael destroying the painting he bought you. It really shocked me because he seems like such a good person.'

'Alright, Jeanne,' I say, leaning back in my chair. 'I know you always hated Michael. You don't have to over-egg the cake . . . '

Her eyes widen in feigned innocence. 'No! I don't hate Michael . . . Alright, so I was jealous of him. Happy? He came along and took you away from me.' She folds her arms, bites her lip, her mask slipping at last. 'I was only thirteen, remember?'

I hesitate. I was twenty-three when Michael and I got together so yes, Jeannie was only thirteen. Can that be right? She seemed so much older . . . In any case, it wasn't like I kicked her out. She was living with a foster family. I fought to act as her legal guardian once I reached eighteen but the courts rejected it. The family we were with then — John and Amanda Carney — were decent people, an older working class couple from Grimsby with a smallholding: Shetland ponies, rescue hens, an irritable ram called Rodger, infinite vegetable patches. Jeannie loved the animals, loved the vast outdoor space. I thought it was in Jeannie's interests to stay there until she turned eighteen.

'I thought you were happy at the Carneys,' I say, faltering.

She lowers her head. 'I missed you. I mean, it was a long time ago but . . . Anyway, it's all in the past.'

As I watch her eyes moisten I'm suddenly sifted by remorse. When she moved out, I paid her rent for almost a decade. She rang me up, told me she wanted to go to drama school but couldn't afford the fees. I told her I'd pay. I'm still paying off those damn fees. Guilt money. Deep down I knew she was miserable when I left the Carneys' home, but I'd been accepted at dance academy and nothing was going to stop me.

'And you're completely right,' she says, wiping her nose on her sleeve, as though she's nine years old again. 'In hindsight it was a poor choice on my part to tell the police about the painting. It was ages ago. Yes, fine, we all know I have a tendency to exaggerate and dramatise a bit. It's been something I've been trying to work on for a while. I think I worry that people won't find me worth being around if I'm not extra-special or exciting . . .'

Shane says nothing but takes her hand, watching her with interest.

'Are you telling me the truth?' I ask her.

She nods, then lifts her eyes to mine. 'I swear on Mum's life.'

I double-take. It's a phrase we used as children whilst in foster care. Our mother was a mythic being, at once a construct that we created of a loving maternal figure who wanted nothing more than to rescue us from a steady stream of uninterested foster families, and a fragile, disintegrating woman who we never knew, snatched up by the claws of addiction. Jeannie might say many things, but swearing on our mother's life is not something she did lightly.

'If you're not convinced by that,' Shane says. 'I

can tell you that Jean paid for the Medevac trip back to the UK.'

'Shane . . . ' Jeannie says, disappointed.

I straighten. 'You said the Medevac was crowdfunded.'

He shakes his head. 'Fifty grand. She knew it would be unlikely that we'd raise the money in time and she needed to get you home.'

'You really paid for us to get home?' I say, astonished.

She gives a small nod and bites her lip. 'You put me through RADA. It meant everything to me, absolutely everything. I always promised myself that I'd pay you back.'

I am so moved by this that I don't know what to say. I'm suddenly flooded with remorse for ripping up the print and for everything I've just accused them of.

'Jeannie, I'm sorry,' I say. 'I'm already plundering through my coping overdraft and . . . ' She reaches across the table and takes my hand, giving it a squeeze.

'Please don't say sorry, Helen. I think the time to stop apologising for yourself is long overdue.'

31

Reuben

6th September 2017

```
Roo:     Malfoy are you there?
Malfoy:  Yes. Are you OK?
Roo:     Yeah I'm here but I'm wor-
         ryed bout wot u said
Malfoy:  What are you worried about?
Roo:     U said u wantd 2 tell me
         somethin that woz danger-
         ous??
Malfoy:  Did I?
Roo:     YES
Malfoy:  I think it was a code I
         had for unlocking a Minecraft
         secret
Roo:     I don't believe u
Malfoy:  ur right, it was something
         else. But it is a dangerous
         secret and I'm not sure I
         can trust you with it
Roo:     You can trust me
Roo:     Malfoy?
Malfoy:  Tell me what's going on in
         your life. How are you feel-
         ing?
```

Roo: Mum is 🙁 a lot. Sask still in coma. Idk if she will ever wake up again. Miss my dad.

Malfoy: You miss your dad? Does anyone know where he is yet?

Roo: No but I think he left because of me.

Malfoy: That's not true.

Roo: How do you know?

Malfoy: Trust me, I know things. The footage you sent of your mum and aunt shows a happy family.

Roo: Maybe on the surface.

Malfoy: ?

Roo: My dad worked all the time even tho he didn't need to.

Malfoy: Did that make u sad?

Roo: 🙁

Roo: Did you know that ketchup used to be used as a medicine?

Malfoy: You'll see ur dad again.

Roo: U don't know that! U shouldn't say things like that if u don't know

Malfoy: I DO know

Roo: u no where my dad is?

Malfoy: Yes.

Roo: No way

Malfoy: Yes way.

Roo: You have to tell me where he is!

Roo: And yo have to tell me how

239

u know wher he is !!!!

Malfoy: I will, I promise. But first you have to do something for me, ok?

Roo: yes

Malfoy: I want you to record more footage of your family.

Roo: y?

Malfoy: It makes me happy. Try not to make anyone aware that you're recording because it'll only make them upset.

Roo: -.-

Malfoy: What is that?

Roo: Morse code for the letter 'k' which also means 'OK'.

Malfoy: -.-

Roo: ☺

32

Michael

21st June 1995

A large campfire blazes about thirty feet away and the other walkers soon leave their tents to gather round. Darkness shrouds the Alps, the sky is alive with galaxies and shooting stars, and a strange pink glow zigzags and kinks like an eel in dark water, just above the horizon.

I watch as Helen sits on a rock near the fire. Luke takes the spot next to her, wrapping his arm across her shoulders. I look down, freshly stung as he whispers something into her ear that makes her giggle.

Music starts up — yes, someone has actually brought a frigging ukulele up the frigging Alps — and some people begin to clap, but shortly after the music falls silent and a commotion rises up. A German-speaking group have arrived at the camp with one of their members on a makeshift stretcher.

'What is it?' Helen asks, getting to her feet. It was difficult to see but someone was shouting for a medic.

'Looks like a girl,' Luke says. 'You got a flashlight, Theo?'

Theo hands him one and he turns it on. About twenty feet ahead I make out a girl, about our age, with a badly damaged leg, her shoes and the stretcher soaked in blood. Another flashlight reveals a piece of bone sticking out of her ankle.

The guy next to me throws up.

'Nice,' Luke says. Then, glancing around: 'Isn't anyone going to call the rescue guys?'

When no one moves he stubs out his tab angrily and races inside the refuge to use the emergency telephone. The girl moans and cries on the stretcher. Helen approaches her, takes her hand. Theo debates with someone whether to give her some weed to help her deal with the pain. In the end, he decides not to risk getting into trouble. The French police can be funny about drug-taking in the Alps, apparently.

Twenty minutes later a helicopter arrives, the wind whipped up by the blades blowing dust all over the campfire. The fire goes out. A scramble to get the girl onboard. I notice that she's no longer crying but motionless, her eyes closed.

'Do you think she's dead?' Helen asks with a gasp.

'Nah,' I say, coolly. 'She'll be worn out from the pain. She'll be fine.'

But secretly, I wonder if she is dead. My stomach flips.

The helicopter drifts into the night. The music is gone, the mood subdued. I notice Luke doesn't light up again. The girl's group look tearful. Even Luke seems moved by the girl's plight. One of the guys mentions an avalanche.

'An avalanche?' Helen says, throwing a scared

look at Theo. 'I thought that was only when there was heavy snow.'

Tiresias gives a laugh. 'It snows pretty much all year round at the top of the mountains, so avalanche is a constant threat. As long as you have awareness of the signs, you should be OK. But even then, people get caught out.' He nods at the remaining members of the German team who'd had to deliver one of their climbers to the helicopter.

'That girl was lucky. They'd taken the Cosmique route, which is a little more dangerous this time of year. Definitely not for amateurs. We've had heavy rains over the last week, some big winds. My advice to anyone attempting the summit is to wait out the rains. Hang back 'til they've passed. Don't try and climb when bad weather hits.'

'I think we're taking the Cosmique route,' I say, glancing at Luke. 'Aren't we?'

'Which is the safest route?' Helen asks Tiresias.

He scratches his beard. 'I would have thought you'd already have your route planned by this stage.'

'We're taking the Gouter route,' Theo says.

'And where are you acclimatising? The Gouter hut?'

Theo slides his eyes to Luke. We'd never discussed acclimatising, but now that he said it, it made sense. The old guy gave a laugh and shook his head in disapproval.

'You will get altitude sickness,' he declares. 'If you don't give your body a chance to adjust to the lack of oxygen in the air you'll get so ill up there that you'll fall into a state of delirium and lead the rest into peril. A climber who is not acclimatised is a liability.'

'That's just an old wives' tale,' Luke says, and Tiresias turns to him archly, his eyebrows raised.

'An old wives' tale?' he says. '*Mon Dieu*. Do not underestimate the ability of the mountain to kick your ass. She will throw rocks as big as houses at you, pour snowfields down on you, and if she really doesn't like you she'll have your babymaker drop off from frostbite.'

Luke gives a big belly laugh with his arms folded as if the whole thing is a big joke, but the man is deeply serious.

'Any fool who doesn't give her the respect of waiting a few days before attempting the summit is almost certain to get the sickness.' He glances at Helen. 'He is your boyfriend, miss?'

She nods. 'He is.'

'He is foolish, this one,' he says. He sweeps his eyes across the crowd. 'I think you should forget this foolish boy. I think you should try someone else. Maybe this one.' He fixes his eyes on me. I give a nervous chuckle when I see Luke's expression darken. He rises to his feet, and for one awful moment I think Luke is going to attack the old man, but he stalks off. Helen gets up and goes after him.

'I only speak the truth,' Tiresias mutters, lighting a tab. Someone passes me a bottle of beer and I move closer to the fire, which has grown strong and beautifully warm again. A few moments later she returns and sits next to me.

'Luke's just getting a drink,' she says, though when I glance over at the refuge I spy him chatting to the group of hippies we met the other day. It doesn't take an Oxford education to work out that he is blagging weed. As we watch, he hands something to one of the guys and a few moments later is lighting up, sending that familiar sickly-sweet cloud of smoke in our direction.

'Funny looking drink,' I say. 'Do you smoke?'

She shakes her head. 'No. I don't usually drink, either. I dance with a ballet company and we have a fairly brutal rehearsal schedule.'

'Luke did tell me you're a ballerina'

'I prefer 'dancer'.'

'You any good?'

She shrugs. 'I was the lead in *La Sylphide* last year at the London Coliseum.'

I'm genuinely impressed. 'Wow. How did you ever end up with someone like Luke?'

'You mean other than his magnetic personality and stunning good looks?'

I take a swig of my beer, then offer her some. She refuses. 'You know what I mean,' I said. 'You seem so . . . levelheaded. And clearly talented. Luke's a bit of an eejit.'

She laughs uneasily. 'Not exactly. He's an Oxford student.'

'OK. He's an academically brilliant, emotionally thick-headed numbskull.'

'I thought you were friends,' she says, smiling.

'We are,' I say. 'But you're not his usual sort. Let's just say that.'

She looks away, turning her face to the fire. 'I

245

know Luke is fickle. And he likes attention. Particularly from other girls.'

'Mmmm,' I say, half-tempted to correct 'thick-headed' with 'obnoxious, egotistical asshole' and to point out that he'd been with dozens of girls while she was away dancing for the good people of London.

She draws her knees up to her chest. 'He makes you feel like the sun is shining on you.' She rubs the spot on her forearm that I remember is bruised. 'But then sometimes it's like a switch flips in his head and he . . . ' She doesn't finish the sentence.

'Luke's my best mate,' I say. 'Love the guy. But if I had a little sister, I'd probably not want her anywhere near him.' Then, in case I'd gone too far: 'But I mean, he must really like you if he insisted that you come along on this trip.'

'I think it was more that he wanted to keep an eye on me,' she says carefully. 'He's very possessive. I was flattered by it. It's nice to be wanted.' She bites her lip. 'Well, I don't have anyone else.'

'What do you mean?'

She shrugs. 'I mean, I have friends, but I don't have any family. My little sister lives in Grimsby. She's only nine. I've no idea who my father was. Our mum was always a bit . . . '

'Useless?'

'Alcoholic. She died a few years ago. Emotionally she abandoned us a long time before she died. My sister and I grew up in foster care.' She shifts in her seat, as though her own words surprise her. 'Sorry,' she says, covering her

246

mouth. 'Luke's always saying I say the wrong thing and he's right. Why don't we talk about the weather or something?'

'You're not saying the wrong thing,' I say quickly. 'My mum left me a long time ago, too.'

She searches my face, the flames of the campfire glinting in her eyes. 'She did?'

'Yeah. I didn't know why for a long time. It was Dad's fault. He was always controlling her, punishing her in stupid ways. Like he'd lock her in their bedroom all day and she couldn't get out until he came home from work.'

Her eyes widen. 'That's awful.'

'Yeah.'

Now it's my turn to be surprised. Why am I saying all of this? I haven't told anyone this stuff, ever. Saying it aloud makes my whole body tremble and my teeth chatter. A strange reaction. Luckily, Helen doesn't seem to notice, though she looks concerned.

'Did he . . . you know . . . beat her?'

I shake my head. 'I don't think so. He always made a point of saying he never laid a finger on her, like this made him a hero or something. All I knew was that one morning I got up and got dressed, and she wasn't there.'

She reaches out and puts a hand on my shoulder. 'How old were you?'

I swallow hard. 'Nine. It took a day or so to realise that she'd left. About a month before I considered that maybe she wasn't coming back. And she never did.'

'What did your dad say?'

'He didn't even acknowledge it.' A swirl of

anger boils up in my stomach. I try not to let it show. 'I kept asking where Mum was and he kept changing the subject. It messed with my head. After a while I actually wondered if she'd ever existed. He threw out every photograph, every piece of clothing that she left, even her shampoo.'

'That's terrible,' Helen said.

Her pity is like a knife twisting in my gut.

'That's . . . that *would* mess with your head,' she says. 'You were just a little boy . . . it was so manipulative of him.'

I nod vigorously. She's just put into words the base note of my entire adolescence. It feels like a cool rain washing on my bare skin to be heard, to be finally understood. To say that I had a mother.

'Did you ever find her?' Helen says, and I take a deep breath. I'm trembling all over like I'm terrified and I don't want her to think I'm going to burst out crying or anything.

'Four years ago,' I say slowly, 'I found a stack of letters under his bed. All from her. All to me. They said that she'd tried to see me, tried to take me away from him. Dad told her to stay well clear, made threats, said she was a terrible mother for abandoning me. He'd never told me any of this. He hid her letters.'

Helen shuffles closer and puts her arm all the way across my shoulders, her other hand clasping mine. To my horror I realise that snot and tears are streaming down my face.

'She'd written that she thought Dad was right,' I say, unable to stop spewing this verbal diarrhoea. 'She said she was a terrible mum.

She'd left because he made her feel trapped and that he might kill her one day. She said he'd held a pillow over her face the night before she left and she was convinced that her life was in danger. So she'd left but tried to get access to me. Dad had told her I didn't want to go.' I break down then. It feels embarrassing and good at the same time.

'And what happened?' Helen asks. 'When you found the letters did you go looking for her?'

I give a rueful laugh. 'She had died shortly before I found the letters, hadn't she? She'd found a place in Liverpool, got a job as a secretary. Went to night school. Became a personal assistant. Met a guy. Then got cancer.'

I swipe tears from my face. 'I remember her. She was such a nice person. Nervy, anxious, but now I know why. It was Dad's fault. She was a wonderful mum. I was going to confront my dad about it, actually thought about beating the crap out of him for what he'd done to her. And for the lies he told me.'

'Lies?'

'About Mum. But other things, too. He made out that he was a good man, cared about his family. He said, a strong man protects his family. That was his reason for keeping her away. He was protecting me. It was all lies. I promised myself that I never wanted to be like that. I would be a good man, and I would protect my family. But not like that.'

She rests her head on my shoulder. 'I'm so sorry you didn't get to see your mum before she died, Michael. She would have been so proud to see how you turned out.'

I turn to her then, pricked by her words. The nine-year-old in me is suddenly there, and he's on his knees, pleading for her to be right. Pleading for Mum to be proud of me. I couldn't bring her back but I hoped that, wherever she was, she was glad I was doing something with my life. It was why I'd gone to Oxford — my mum had always wished she'd been able to go to university, to the *best* university. She talked about people who went to Oxford like they were royalty.

The gold glow of the fire passes over Helen's face, and as she lifts her head our faces are so close that I can feel the warmth of her breath on my cheeks, and I have the strongest desire to kiss her. The urge is so strong. Her hand finds its way into mine. I feel something pass unsaid between us, a decision that's made by the language of our bodies.

'Hope I'm not interrupting you,' a voice says behind us, and Helen gasps and pulls her hand from mine. Theo steps forward, a look of anger on his face. He looks at me.

'Comfy, Michael?'

'Theo . . . ' I can't think fast enough. I need to come up with something, give him an explanation, but the gears of my brain are rusty.

'We were . . . we were just chatting, Theo,' Helen interjects in a tight voice.

His expression darkens. 'Yeah. Looked like it and all.'

He turns on his heel, heading back to the hut where Luke is. I laugh it off but Helen looks shaken. She won't meet my eye. I rise quickly to my feet and race after Theo. He keeps walking, and I jog in front of him.

'Theo, wait,' I say. 'No need to cause a fuss, mate. I wasn't doing anything.'

'What or *who* you do is your business, Mike,' Theo says. 'Move.'

'Mate, don't go telling Luke what you saw,' I say, standing in front of him. 'Yeah? It really was nothing. We were just talking, that's all. Nothing more.'

He lifts his pale eyes to mine. A muscle in his jaw twitches. 'I can't have you stealing my brother's girlfriend.'

'That's *not* what I was doing . . . '

'It's what it looked like.'

'I promise, Theo. Please. The last thing we need on this trip is a bust-up between mates. Alright?'

He gives me a final grim look before stomping off. I know he's seen sense but I feel uneasy for Helen's sake. I think quickly about the bruises I saw on her arm and shoulder. I'm fairly sure Luke's been hurting her, and instantly my panic turns to fury. If I find out he has there will be no stopping me.

My father was right, in some ways. A good man does protect his loved ones.

He was never speaking about himself.

★ ★ ★

Later, when I open my sleeping bag, the smell of chamois dung hits me like an open sewage pipe.

It's so powerful I can taste it. Theo has stuffed my bag full of it, and even when I shake out the contents and climb inside the stench is strong enough to make me hack and gag all night.

It's punishment for talking to Helen, for stepping on his brother's territory.

Luke comments on the smell the next day, clearly unawares.

'Michael, mate. You feeling alright?'

I narrow my eyes at Theo, who is whistling a merry tune, well chuffed with himself.

'Had a bit of tummy trouble,' I mutter to Luke. 'That's all.'

'Gee whizz, mate,' Luke says, beating the air with his hand. 'You want to see a doctor tout suite. You smell *terrible*.'

33

Helen

6th September 2017

I go upstairs to check on Reuben. He's sitting at his desk drawing what looks a blue whale on his iPad.

'Your face looks puffy,' he tells me, glancing up. 'Like a mattress.'

'Are you hungry?' I say.

He shakes his head. 'Where's Dad?'

I catch my breath, choose my words carefully. 'I spoke to the police this morning. They are working out the very best way to find Dad and bring him home. OK?'

He shuts off his iPad and stares at me. His eyes are dark and sunken and his bottom lip trembles. 'I heard the doctors say that Dad walked out of the hospital. Was it because of me?'

'Of *course* it wasn't.'

He nods as if he wants to believe me, then starts to wail and hit his head with his fist. I have to do the feet thing. It's the only way to get him to be calm. I get him to lie back on his bed and sit opposite him, cross-legged, with his feet on my lap. I pull off his socks and stroke his feet.

Within a few seconds he's breathing normally.

'Reuben, sweetheart. Dad didn't leave because of you. I promise you that.'

'Then why did he leave?' he sniffs, staring up at the ceiling.

'I don't know. But we're going to figure it out, really soon . . .'

'Is it because of what happened with Josh's dad? Because I would have said sorry. I didn't mean to say horrible things to him. It was just . . . ' His face crumples again.

'Helen?' Jeannie calls up from downstairs. 'Helen, love, are you up there? Dinner's ready.'

'I'll be down in a sec,' I call back, gently pulling Reuben's socks back over his feet. I move to sit on the side of the bed beside him, holding his hand.

'I know it's really difficult,' I say gently, and very, very slowly, 'but . . . do you think you can tell me what happened . . . at Josh's party?'

'Joshie's party was stupid,' he snaps tearfully, and I consider telling him alright, we don't have to talk about it. But I press on, because I have to know. I wasn't there, and I never got the full story from Michael. We have to talk about this.

'Please, Reuben,' I say, my voice on the edge of a whisper. 'Can you tell Mummy what happened? You're safe here. It won't ever happen again, I promise.'

He keeps his eyes on the ceiling and remains silent for a few minutes as I stroke his shins and feet.

'Dad took me to Josh's birthday party,' he says on an exhale. 'I gave him the postcode on the birthday invitation. Dad was . . . confused when we got there. He . . . he kept asking where the party was.'

'It was at the Simonside Hills, wasn't it?' I say.

He nods. 'Josh said we had to meet in the car park. His dad had all the gear. Everyone was there. Jagger, Dylan, Lucas. Most of the class and their parents were already there.'

He starts to stutter and grow upset at the memory of it.

'It was a hike, wasn't it?'

'Yes but no. Josh said it was a hike but he was being funny. The pick-up time was seven o'clock that evening. Dad's face was all worried when he saw Josh's gear. He said, 'You're just walking, yeah?', and I said yeah. But then Josh's dad came over and told Dad that he had helmets and harnesses for everyone. He said we'd only be doing a small abseil today, nothing major.'

'You were abseiling?' I say, and he nods. The order of events starts to lace together in my mind.

'Dad held up his hands and his voice got really shouty. He started going on about how it was dangerous and if he'd known that he would have turned around and taken me home. All the other kids and their parents were staring. I said, 'Dad, settle down, I'll be fine,' but he started trying to pull me away.'

'And what happened with Josh's dad? Did he say something to Dad?'

Reuben grows upset, his face crumpling. He covers his eyes with one hand, the other clicking, faster and faster, like a racing heartbeat.

'It's OK, Reuben,' I say, reminding myself how delicate he is, how gentle I need to be. 'It's OK. You don't have to tell me.'

He slips out of my grasp, his dark hair damp with sweat. Picking up his Minecraft models from the shelf he sits down on the ground, placing the models around him in a tight circle. I wait patiently until he has them ordered the way he wants. I can see the stillness this brings to him, having his precious items near to him and in order.

'I don't know,' he says, calmer now. 'Dad scared me. I was trying on helmets to get the right size and then I turned around and saw Dad punch Josh's dad in the face and Josh's dad fell to the ground. I've never seen Dad act that way.'

No wonder Reuben reacted so badly. A flash of that afternoon comes to me in a rush. I was surprised to see the car pull up in the driveway. They weren't due back for hours so I thought Reuben must have left something at home. Reuben raced in ahead of Michael, went to his room, slamming the door behind him. In an instant I heard the sound of yelling and crashing from behind his door. I approached Michael. *What happened? Why's he so upset?*

'He was yelling and shouting at Josh's dad,' Reuben continues.

I can see it's beginning to upset him, recalling it. He lifts his Minecraft models and shifts them about, creating a tighter circle.

'Did you hear what he shouted?'

He shakes his head.

'Josh said it was going to be fun,' he says, his

voice breaking. 'We were going to climb up to the top of the cliff and he'd use his drone to capture us as we abseiled down. He said it'd be like nothing we'd ever done before but it would be safe because his dad was a climber and knew all about it.'

His voice peters out with confusion and pain at the memory of it and he curls up into a ball on the ground. I lie down next to him and his breaths lengthen and slow.

'Reuben, I promise that Dad didn't leave the hospital because of anything you've done. This has nothing to do with the fight at Josh's birthday.'

'But I didn't speak to Dad for a long time. I hated him. I told him that I hated him. What if he left the hospital because he thought I didn't love him?'

'I promise you, Reuben,' I say gently. 'Dad knows you love him. And he loves you.'

A flash of anger. He looks up, his eyes full of pain. 'Then why isn't he here?'

I have no way to answer him.

When I get up to leave his room a thought comes to me. I turn and say, 'Reuben, when Dad and I decided to leave Cancún to stay at the beach hut, did you mention it to anyone? Like Josh, perhaps?'

He looks up, an expression of fear on his face.

'It's OK,' I say quickly. 'I promise you're not in *any* trouble.'

He lowers his eyes. 'I guess I told Malfoy.'

'Malfoy?'

'My iPix buddy. And Josh.'
'You told Josh?'
He nods. 'Yes. I told Josh.'

34

Helen

22nd June 1995

I stand by the window and drink in the view. Towering peaks right there in front of me, so tall that they throw perspective into disarray — it's only when I see that the small white thread in the distance is actually a gushing waterfall that I really grasp just how big they are. I can tell which of the mountains is Mont Blanc, or the White Beast, as Theo calls it. I have to admit, I'm quite daunted by the fact that I'm going to climb to the top. It looks incredibly high — literally as though you could reach up and touch the sky from the tip of it.

I make coffee on the stove and one of the other climbers, a German guy, offers me some sort of German muffin. It looks like it's made of sawdust. I smile and quickly say *'nein, danke'* — I picked this phrase up last night — in case Luke comes along and sees. He might think I'm flirting. The German guy cracks a joke and I laugh but he could be saying I have a huge backside for all I know. This is the problem when you try and communicate with people who speak a different language — you always have to find a way to backpedal from complex conversation.

Last night in the tent wasn't too bad. Luke and I kept our gear on for warmth and held each other like an old couple. It was blissful. But I kept thinking about Michael. I thought he was such a grandad when I met him, so stiff and uptight. He barely looked in my direction. Luke said Michael was really excited for me to come along on their expedition and couldn't wait to meet me, so I was shocked by how cold he was towards me. I'd had the impression that Michael was a great guy. He's Luke's best friend, too, so I was eager to meet him and make a good impression. I can't describe how disappointed I felt when he snubbed me.

At least, at first. And then last night he opened up to me.

Turns out that he *is* a lovely guy, just like Luke said. We had a heart-to-heart that made me feel like we covered a lot of ground and grew closer. I felt a bit weird, to be honest, when Theo saw us. I hadn't meant anything by it at all, but the dynamic of the group is all out of kilter up here and I can't seem to find my boundaries. We're certainly not the only ones climbing Mont Blanc but even so, it feels very much like the four of us against the world, against the elements. Mother Nature is more mercurial and ruthless than I'd ever imagined until I came on this journey. Luke, Theo, Michael and I are dependent on each other. Every day is harder than the one before. Time seems to be contracted up here, too. It's strange to think that just a handful of days ago I met Michael for the first time. The four of us having a drink in Chamonix, as though we were about to have a walk along the beach and not up the hard spine of a mountain, passing into another realm.

Theo comes into the kitchen as I'm rinsing out my cup. I smile and say, 'Morning,' but he stiffens.

'Morning,' he mumbles under his breath. I watch, a little dumbstruck, as he pours water into the kettle and keeps his back to me. Why is he acting so strange, as if I've done something wrong?

He whistles to himself — an attempt to avoid conversation — and I set down my glass and walk outside. Luke's folding up the tent and chatting with Michael, who looks like he's dry retching. I approach them both, a little guarded. Luke sees me but carries on chatting with Michael. My heart sinks. Sometimes I feel like I'm a puppet and Luke's the one pulling my strings. When he tells me he loves me I could melt in his arms. This love is so passionate that I'm bruised from it. Before we left for Chamonix, he held me so tightly that he left hickies on my arms and shoulders. He likes to leave them all over me like signatures. 'Don't you mean like a dog, leaving its mark?' I laughed, and he pinned me down and sucked the skin on my hipbone until a black moon appeared. 'There,' he said. 'It's skin writing for 'Luke was here'.'

But he leaves deeper, unseen bruises when he ignores me, or withdraws his affection. Those bruises are on my heart. It's unsettling, how much I crave him. But something tells me that this isn't how love should be. Not this pendulum between extremities. But then, I wouldn't know. No one has ever loved me before. Not my mother. Certainly not my dad, whoever he was. None of the foster carers. Just Luke.

I approach him and give him a tight smile. He tilts his chin, acknowledging me like someone he vaguely knows, and I feel a shadow pass across my heart. Michael is rolling up his sleeping bag and there's a foul smell in the air. He turns and grins at me and his smile is just enough to lift the shadow and make me feel like I'm whole again.

35

Helen

6th September 2017

Downstairs, Jeannie is bent over at the dining table sweeping up pieces of glass. I still feel a mild sting of guilt for destroying the print she bought me. She sees me, straightens.

'Do you want some food?' she asks.

I tell her perhaps later, and pull out a seat at the table. She tips the broken glass into the bin and joins me.

'Is Reuben OK?' she asks.

'He said he's been chatting with someone called Malfoy. He's mentioned him before. He said he told Malfoy that we were in Belize.'

She studies my face. 'Malfoy? Is this an actual person or a bot?'

'He said it's a friend on iPix. Have you heard of iPix?'

She thinks, shakes her head. 'What is it? One of these new musical.ly things that all the kids are into now?'

'Musical.ly? I don't think so. We don't let him have social media. I thought iPix was a drawing website but it seems to allow him to connect with other people. Can you look it up, see who he's been talking to?'

She pulls out her phone, Googles it. The site is mostly videos of drawings and photographs. She types 'Malfoy' into the search bar but nothing comes up.

'I think we'd need Reuben's log-ins. A fourteen-year-old's hardly going to be your first port of call for the car accident, though.'

'Someone knew we were there, Jeannie. I know you think I'm paranoid but the simple fact is that the only way anyone knew where we were is because someone told them.' I see the apps on her phone for Facebook and Twitter. 'Did *you* tell anyone we were in Belize?'

She looks up. 'Well, Shane, obviously. No one else.'

'What about social media? Did you mention anything there?'

She brings up her Facebook page, bearing a profile picture taken by a professional photographer and headed by her Deed Poll name: Jean Kensington-Smith. One of many attempts to erase her humble origins as Jeannie Warren. The page shows a few cute photographs of her and Shane, some 'sign this campaign' messages and rants about the obscene amount of traffic wardens in Northumberland. Nothing about Belize.

'You can see here that there is *nothing* about you and your family being on holiday,' she says. 'I know you *hate* Facebook so I never put anything about you or the kids on here.'

I tell her what the police had shared about the van driver, that his name was Jonas Matus. She stares at me for a long moment before typing his name into the search bar with her thumb.

'What are you doing?' I say.

'Searching for him.'

'You can do that?'

She raises her eyebrows in a look of amused pity. I'd never have thought of searching social media accounts. Michael and I silently agreed we wouldn't broadcast our identities online, and we had Lucy do all the online stuff for the bookshop so I'm completely out of touch with how these things work. I watch, a little mystified, as Jeannie brings up a list of people called 'Jonas Matus' on Facebook, then Twitter and Instagram. There are some Jonas Matuses in Australia, several in the UK, another in Israel.

'He's probably deleted his account,' she says, frowning. 'But you never know.'

I squint hard at the pictures, trying to match them to the mugshot DS Jahan showed me. I watch as she clicks on each profile and sends a 'friend' request.

'What are you doing?' I say.

She shrugs. 'Can't hurt, can it? Not illegal to friend people.'

With disappointment I notice that none of the people on the list are based in Belize. 'Reuben told me what happened between Michael and Josh's dad,' I say, thinking back to what the detectives said about Ben Trevitt.

She holds my gaze, reads my mind. 'Do you think he might be involved somehow?'

'Is he on Facebook?'

She types 'Benjamin Trevitt' into the space bar

and instantly his face pops up alongside Josh, an arm around his shoulders, Northumbrian landscape in the background, both grinning. Jeannie scrolls down his page. He isn't an avid poster, but one status in particular grabs my attention. 'CROSS ME AND GET WHAT'S COMING' in bold white lettering against a black background. Jeannie scrolls down the comments beneath.

```
Sam N Sue Muir: ☹
Lewis Ure: Have it!
Philippa Crewe: Did someone
  cross you, m8?
Shayee Peeke: I heard bout this.
  Joshie's birthday party!!
  Awful . . .
Lewis Ure: What happened?
Ben Trevitt: I'll DM you.
```

'When did he post that?' I ask.

'July twenty-fourth,' Jeannie says.

'That was just after the fight. We were in Mexico by then.'

'Look,' Jeannie says. She's clicked on Ben's friends list. There's someone called 'John Matos' named there. I feel my heart pound in my ears.

'Reuben said he told Josh that he was in Belize, too.'

'That's quite the coincidence,' Jeannie says. 'I can't see where this John Matos guy is based, though. No picture, either. He must have his security settings set really high.'

I get up then, too anxious to sit still.

'Where are you going?' she says.

I step out of my slippers and into a pair of boots. 'I'm going over to speak to the Trevitts,' I say.

She watches me rummage for my car keys. 'You're not allowed to drive, Helen.'

'Watch me.'

She sighs. '*I'll* drive you.'

She calls Shane and asks him to come back and stay with Reuben while she drives me over to the Trevitts on Larkspur Lane. I've taken Reuben over there a few times before so I know where they live. A pretty stone cottage close to the school, surrounded by gardens, a large fir tree outside that they string with lights every Christmas. The perfect family home.

Jeannie parks a little way up the street and we make our way to the front door.

'I don't have a good feeling about this, Helen,' she says, looking around. 'Why exactly are we here again?'

My confidence is waning but I don't want to admit this to Jeannie. 'If Ben Trevitt has something to do with the crash, then I need to know. This accusation against Michael is gaining traction and I have to slow it down.'

'Mmm. So you want to go knocking on the door of someone who potentially tried to kill your whole family. Call me crazy but maybe just calling the police and telling them about it is the best way forward . . . '

'I'm not going in there all guns blazing,' I say firmly. 'I'll play it cool. The police said the Trevitts pressed charges against Michael. I should have confronted them as soon as the fight happened. Nipped it in the bud.'

'That's what this is, is it? Nipping it in the bud?'

I get out of the car before I lose my nerve. A silver Porsche Cayenne is parked in the driveway, but there are no lights on in the front room. Jeannie texts Shane, mumbling her message aloud.

'If you don't hear from me I've been murdered at 13 Larkspur Lane . . . '

We ring the doorbell and wait for a few minutes. No answer.

'Try the side entrance,' Jeannie says.

We make our way to the right side of the house where, sure enough, there's a smaller exterior door that seems well used, a kitchen visible through the window. I knock on the door — there's no doorbell — and the door pushes back into the kitchen. I glance at Jeannie before pushing the door open further and calling, 'Hello?'

No answer. I take another step inside, then another.

'What are you doing?' Jeannie hisses like I've lost my mind. 'We can't just go inside someone's house.'

'I'm just having a look . . . '

She gives me a wide-eyed look of warning, and I know I'm acting dramatically out of character. I would *never* normally be so bold as this, would never dream of doing anything illegal or offensive. It's like I'm two people, one half watching on in curious bewilderment while the other is spurred on by a searing heat in my bones, an itch to find something that locates Michael. To prove he had nothing to do with the crash.

I move through the kitchen quickly, ignoring Jeannie's loud, alarmed whispers, demanding that I stop.

The living room is dark and has a level of tidiness that makes me feel like a slob. A grand fireplace with an open fire, an ornate gold mirror and ornaments of hearts and stars. A quick glance tells me there's nothing here of any relevance to what I'm searching for. I step into the next room where a glass dining table sits surrounded by metallic chairs. A large maple sideboard at the far side of the room. I open one of the drawers and find a silver laptop. I flip it open and it boots up. Jeannie takes a step closer to me, waves of fear radiating off her.

'Helen, we've got to leave *right now*,' she says, breathless. 'Do you realise how much trouble you could get us into?'

But the temptation is too strong. I'm already clicking on the email icon, scouring through them as I had done Michael's. I type the name 'Jonas Matus' into the space bar. Nothing comes up. I try Michael's name, then 'Belize' and 'John Matos.'

Nothing. Maybe I'm doing it wrong.

'OK, you've checked, now let's go,' Jeannie says, fidgeting with nerves, but as I close up the laptop there's a loud noise from the side door.

' . . . I'm just grabbing my purse, give me one second,' a woman's voice shouts. Kate Trevitt. Inside. The. House.

Jeannie and I stare at each other for one

terrifying, wild-eyed moment, before ducking down and crawling quickly under the dining table. Jeannie gets stuck as she tries to squeeze through the legs of a chair. I shove the chair to help her through but immediately a loud whine of metal against metal rings out across the room. The footsteps in the kitchen stop.

Jeannie signals at me not to move, and we both hold our breath — me under the table, Jeannie behind it, completely visible to anyone who might come into the room — as Kate's heels click-click on the kitchen tiles towards us. I don't dare breathe or move a muscle.

Through the legs of the table and chairs I see Kate's leopard-print pumps as she walks quickly through the house, still speaking to someone behind her.

'Hannah's at Ava's house, I told you,' she says loudly in irritated tones, and I allow myself to exhale. She hasn't seen us. The creak of a cupboard door in the hallway sounds. She begins to rifle through coats hung there. 'I've got a meeting later,' a man's voice booms from the kitchen. I freeze. Ben Trevitt. They're both here.

My heart beats in my mouth. We left the side door ajar, I'm sure of it. Did I leave the sideboard drawer open? I try to twist around from my position on all fours but I can't see. If they find us here they'll call the police, no question. Or something much, much worse. If Ben is guilty of arranging the crash, he won't just phone the police. He'll take revenge into his own hands.

'We won't take long,' Kate shouts back,

grabbing a large white handbag and glancing inside. 'Where *the hell* did I put it?'

She comes into the room. I squeeze my eyes tightly shut, waiting for the scream as she spies Jeannie behind the table. Her feet shuffle towards the table and there's a jangling sound directly above my head. She's reaching into the glass bowl in the centre of the dining table and plucks something out.

'Check that she's in before we head over there,' Ben shouts from the kitchen. 'You should have arranged it first.'

I force myself to open my eyes and watch her walk slowly back into the hallway, distracted by something. I don't dare breathe.

From the hall I hear a bleeping sound — numbers being punched into Kate's phone. A thought crosses my mind that it has all been a bluff, that she *has* spotted us and is calling the police. My stomach leaps. But a second later, my phone buzzes in my pocket. I almost jump out of my skin. With a trembling hand I reach to turn it off, and as I pull it out and find the 'silent' button I see 'Josh's mum' in tall white letters on the phone's screen.

I turn to Jeannie and we share a look of sharp despair. The kitchen door clicks shut and, without really knowing what I'm doing, I hit 'answer'.

'What are you doing?' Jeannie mouths at me as I press the phone to my ear and mumble 'Hello?'

'Hi, is that Helen?' Kate says, and in the background I hear the car door slam. The sound of tyres across the driveway. 'It's Kate Trevitt here. Look, we wanted to stop by for a chat, if you feel up to that. We were thinking of coming by in the next ten minutes?'

'Sure,' I say, covering my mouth with my hand. Then: 'I'm just out at the moment but I'll be home soon. Reuben's in.'

'Oh *good*. We have Josh with us so I'm sure those two will want to spend some time together. See you shortly.'

I hang up and take a hard gulp of air. Jeannie and I crawl out from under the table and make our way quickly towards the door. For one terrible moment I think it is locked, that we are trapped inside. I give a hard pull, then another, and with a swell of relief we are outside.

Inside Jeannie's car we both look at each other and burst out laughing.

Then, falling serious: 'You've got to promise me you will *never* do that again,' Jeannie says, her voice trembling. '*Never*. You have officially just shortened my life by five years.'

We drive slowly through the streets to my house, where a Porsche Cayenne — silver — is parked outside. Ben and Kate are already here.

36

Helen

6th September 2017

We find them in the living room with Shane. Reuben sits at the kitchen table with Josh, both hunched over their iPads. Jeannie and Shane leave quietly while I busy myself with making a pot of tea. It's an attempt to buy time in order to calm myself. Maybe they saw us in the house after all. Or perhaps they'll spot Jeannie and me breaking in on a security camera. My hands shake as I stir the tea. *What on earth was I thinking?*

I take the rattling tray with cups, spoons and the teapot into the living room and set it on the coffee table. I can feel Ben's eyes on me as I pour two cups of tea with shaking hands. He's a reserved guy with ginger hair and glasses. Works in civil engineering. Kate's a slim, black-haired nutritionist. We've previously had conversations about our boys, about paediatricians and St Mary's, the school Josh and Reuben both attend.

There's a moment's awkwardness as we sit in a triangle, the silence swollen with subtext. Kate and Ben share a long, uncomfortable look, as though neither knows how to begin. My stomach

273

clenches with fear. I still don't really know why they're here. It's about the fight, of course.

'Are you here to tell me that you've pressed charges against Michael?' I say in a small voice.

They share another look. 'We had to press charges,' Ben says, 'but that's not why we came.'

'We heard about what happened in Belize,' Kate says gently. 'Not long after what happened at the shop, too. You've had such an awful time. We wanted to come by and see how you're doing.'

I'm taken aback by this. As I stumble over my response I notice two scratches on Ben's right cheekbone, just beneath the frame of his glasses. A remnant from where Michael punched him. His own eyes are drawn to the black brace on my wrist and the bruises on my face.

'I was very sorry to hear about Saskia,' Kate says. 'How are you and Michael coping?'

'Michael is missing,' I blurt out. 'I expect that's who you came to see. He's not here.'

'*Missing?*' She sounds genuinely puzzled, though I thought our situation was common knowledge in the village by now. 'What do you mean, missing?'

I swallow hard, trying to read the tone of her voice. She sounds genuine, but I daren't trust her.

'It's a long story,' I say, wringing my hands and keeping my eyes on the coffee table. 'But the police are still looking for him.'

They both look confused. 'When did he go missing? We just heard there was some horrific crash overseas.'

I tell her about the hospital, about Sas, about the claim made against Michael by the van driver. I watch both of them carefully for their reaction, for any sign that they might not be telling the truth, but they seem genuinely shocked.

'So . . . Michael's still in Belize?'

I can feel myself starting to grow upset. 'He could be. Everything's up in the air at the moment. The police are investigating . . . '

'Is there anything we can do to help?' Ben says. 'I know Mike was mates with a few of the other school dads. They went on that pub crawl not so long ago. Maybe we could ask around, see if he said anything that . . . '

'That what?' Kate asks, and he shrugs.

'Well, I don't know. It just seems out of the ordinary. Mind you, the smack he gave me at Joshie's birthday party was out of the ordinary, too.'

I think back to what Reuben told me about the fight. 'Michael said he was protecting Reuben when he hit you. Is that true?'

Ben widens his eyes. 'Protecting Reuben? I don't know what he thought he was protecting him from but blimey, it was me that needed protecting.'

I swallow hard. 'Tell me what happened.'

He shares a look with Kate. 'Well, it was like I literally didn't know what had hit me. One minute we were chatting and then pow! He's whacked me square on the jaw, a nasty uppercut.' He demonstrates by raising his own fist to his jaw. 'That wasn't the punch that did the damage,' he said. 'I staggered backwards with the first one but then he hit me again. I think I blacked out for a moment or two with that one because the next thing I knew I was on the ground with lots of people standing over me. Josh was crying, begging me to wake up.' He shakes his head. 'It was madness.'

I try to envisage Michael doing these things. Attacking someone. Punching someone to the ground. He's such a sensitive guy. A memory rises up of him punching Luke.

But that was different.

'What happened when you got to your feet?' I say.

'Well, that's the thing,' he says. 'Mike just legged it. No apology, no explanation.' He glances at Kate again, and I see her face is flushed. She's upset at the memory of it. 'My glasses were broken. Party was cancelled, obviously. I took Josh home, tried to shake it off. The next morning, though, I could barely move my neck. Real bad shooting pains right into my shoulders. My jaw was swollen, too. I went to the doctor and ended up having to go to hospital for a CT scan for possible brain trauma.'

I am horrified. I manage to ask if he *had* brain trauma.

'Luckily, no. Whiplash injuries, yes. All about the way he hit me, you see. I'd to take three weeks off work, had acupuncture, physio. Got new specs. All that doesn't come cheap. So yeah, I spoke to a solicitor and filed charges.'

He's growing upset the more he speaks, his voice getting louder, his eyes moving across the room as though he expected Michael to leap out again and attack him.

I say, 'I need to understand what might have caused Michael to walk out of the hospital. I tried to talk to him about what provoked him at Josh's birthday party that day but he wouldn't open up. I guess I thought you must have said something to make him lash out like that.'

Ben reaches up to touch his jaw again.

'I've gone over it in my head a thousand times,' he says. 'Your husband strikes me as an alright kind of bloke. Packs a mean punch, though. True what they say, isn't it — it's the quiet ones you've got to watch.' He folds his arms. 'An apology wouldn't have hurt, though. I kept expecting a knock on the door, a phone call . . . '

'I tried to speak to you,' I blurt out. 'I sent flowers . . . '

'Yeah, but that kind of thing needed to come from him, didn't it?' Kate says. 'But then we heard you'd all gone to Belize. And I thought, well, that's nice. Here's my husband having to sleep bolt upright and being jabbed by an acupuncturist while the man who decked him is off having the holiday of a lifetime.'

I draw a sharp breath. I should have tried harder to make Michael talk about it, to confront the Trevitts. Letting things linger is never a sensible resolution.

I turn to Ben. 'So, what happened immediately *before* he hit you? Why did he react like that?'

'Like I said, I don't know . . . ' He pauses. 'He seriously didn't want me taking Reuben up

277

there, that's for sure. I tried to tell him it was perfectly fine. I knew what I was doing. I wouldn't be taking my own son up there if I didn't.'

I nod. 'And what did Michael say to that?'

Ben scratches his head. 'He said no, Reuben's not climbing, we're going home, see ya later. Alright, so maybe I told him not to mollycoddle Reuben, to let him man up and join in with his friends. A poor choice of words, on hindsight. But it was Joshie's birthday party, for heaven's sake. Mike just flipped.'

His words confirm everything I already suspected, but hearing it aloud feels like a kick to the chest. Michael didn't expect the birthday party to be a climbing trip, it was as simple as that. Ben is a nice guy but he pushed the issue, tried to force Michael's arm. But there was simply no way he would have let Reuben go climbing.

Not after what happened on Mont Blanc.

'Excuse me,' I say, and I run as fast I can to the kitchen sink, making it just in time before I throw up.

37

Michael

24th June 1995

I keep a careful distance from Helen to prove to Theo that I'm not attempting to steal his brother's girlfriend, though to be fair, Luke is way more interested in cosying up to the Italians who evidently have more marijuana in their backpacks than climbing gear to notice.

My sleeping bag holds on to the smell of chamois dung for dear life. I have no spare, so I've no choice but to climb in night after night and attempt to distract myself from the awful stench, though generally I dry-retch myself to sleep. Theo has paid for a room inside the refuge, the git. At nights, when the campfire is in full blaze, I notice people will sit down next to me, then get up quickly and move away. I don't blame them.

Luke pisses himself laughing when Theo tells him why I smell so bad, though he keeps quiet about *why* he stuffed my sleeping bag with dung.

'That's amazing,' Luke says, crying with laughter and high-fiving his brother. 'Chamois dung. Genius, mate.'

Theo beams with pride at Luke's approval.

But there is something different in the air when we leave the camp site, a shift in the dynamic of our group. I put it down to the heart-to-heart I had with Helen, but there's something else. A shadow has crept between Luke and me, and between me and Theo. It's as though they can read my feelings for Helen, despite how hard I've tried to stamp them down.

I think I'm falling in love with her.

The sun is just beginning to rise, a belt of liquid gold across the horizon. We walk in silence. After an hour the trail fades to crumbling scree, the level path modulating to a pitched slope that makes my calf muscles and knee joints scream. We swap our walking boots for crampons, our T-shirts for thermals and duvet jackets, strap on our helmets and harnesses. The terrain is lunar, hostile, a platform of cotton clouds exactly level with our altitude. We can almost reach out and step on to it.

We find a fixed line and grasp on to it like the last survivors of a sinking ship as we make our way along the mountain's shoulder to the next refuge hut.

I think about my conversation with Helen. I opened up to her in a way that I've never opened up to anyone before. I feel a connection, a pull towards her unlike anything else. I've never been in love but it feels like I'm definitely at the foothills. And yet it's pointless. She's with Luke. When I look up to see him holding her hand, I feel the sting of jealousy.

Pull yourself together, mate.

The climb gets harder and harder, the air

thinning so drastically I have to gulp down each breath to stop from feeling woozy. Doing this for hours makes you believe you are literally drowning, and the panic instinct it releases in the body is an exhausting battle in itself. My lungs feel like they are being slowly but surely crushed. We are no longer walking so much as scrambling along a sideways slope, gradually drowning hundreds of metres above sea level.

And then, within a handful of minutes, the bright sunlight thins and the blue skies close up, shielded by black cloud. Suddenly there is a tremendous roar.

'Rock fall!' Theo shouts from ahead. 'Take cover!'

We all scramble under an overhang as the ground trembles and the sound of thunder grows louder. In an instant the ground all around is pelted with boulders.

The noise is deafening, and it's so foggy that we can barely see one another. It starts to rain, too, and within seconds rivulets of water accompany the falling stones, veining the slopes. What was it Sebastian said to do in the case of rock fall? I know he covered it but I can't remember. I start to slide and scramble at loose rock. *This is it*, I think, seeing nothing but my own feet scooting down the mountain. *I'm actually going to die here.*

Luke hurls two pick-axes deep into the ground. He hesitates as I slide past him, then holds out a hand to me and I cling on.

I look up. 'Thanks, babe.'

He grins. 'You're welcome.'

Even so, I'm not sure how long I can hold on.

One false move and I'm gone, sleighing down the rock face to certain death.

But as quickly as it arrived, the thundercloud passes, the fog creeps back, the blue skies re-appear, and the rocks stop barrelling down.

By the time we gather ourselves back on track the distinctive whomp-whomp of a helicopter sounds overhead. We watch as it circles an area about three hundred feet above before coming to land, whipping up pillars of dust.

'Someone must be hurt,' Helen pants, wiping mud off her face and tilting her head up to see. We can just about make out some people by the helicopter and a stretcher carrying someone inside.

'Looks like it,' Theo says.

The helicopter lifts off again. No one says a word as it drifts back to the valley.

It's dusk when we arrive at the hut, all of us exhausted and out of puff. The hut isn't as busy as the previous refuge, though just as big, with a spacious kitchen and dining area, ten dorms, a large communal area filled with flags and notes from previous guests, a gear room and even a small library. The sight of other people just sitting around, breathing, not drowning or dying, is strangely reassuring.

I force myself not to watch as Helen and Luke go off to find their room. *Don't think of her, mate. This isn't love, it's mountain fever.*

I occupy myself by finding a good book — a rare edition of *The Iliad* — and a coffee and curl up next to the log fire, intent on leaving Helen and Luke well alone and enjoying every square inch of the hut's luxuriantly flat ground.

A while later, once I've eaten and napped in a chair by the kitchen table, I get up to dig out my sleeping bag from my rucksack in the gear room. I head down the corridor looking for Theo. A couple of groups are visible in the dining area, but the communal area seems empty.

I duck my head around the door and think I spot Theo by the fire. But then I spot Helen, and I realise it's Luke.

He and Helen are both on their feet, facing each other. Helen has her arms folded across her body protectively and her head bowed. He is pointing at her, his arm at a forty-five-degree angle. Accusing, and full of menace.

I hear her say, *Stop it, Luke.* And then he lifts his hand and she turns her head, and from where I'm standing it looks like he's smacked her across the face.

Before I know what I'm doing I'm on the floor on top of him, my hands grabbing fistfuls of his T-shirt. 'Don't you *ever* hit her!' I yell. 'Don't you dare!'

It doesn't take long for him to shove me off.

'Have you lost your bloody mind?' Luke pants when we're both on our feet. He dabs his nose with his hand, finding blood, then gives me a flat look that says, *You've crossed a line, mate.* But I don't flinch. He's the stronger of the two of us and we both know he could win a fight. The fire blazes nearby. For a moment I think he might reach out and grab a log, stab it in my face.

'You don't hit her,' I say again, pointing at Helen.

'*Hit* her?' Luke says. We both turn to Helen. She looks from me to Luke, gives a small shake of her head. 'I never hit her, you idiot. We were arguing about you, as it happens. About how cosy you two got the other night.'

He sees my face fall. 'Theo told me all about it,' he says.

'She's got bruises on her arm, Luke. I saw! And I saw you hit her.'

Helen shakes her head and goes to speak, but Luke gives me a hard shove with both hands, knocking me backwards. Somehow I don't fall over.

'What's going on between you two?' Luke says, glancing at Helen. There's a sob in his voice, and when he turns back to me he no longer looks angry. Just wounded. And I feel terrible.

'*Nothing* is going on,' Helen says wearily.

'Nothing's going on between us,' I repeat like a robot. 'I thought . . . it looked like you hit her. It's one thing for you to cheat on her but hitting, I won't tolerate.'

'Cheating?' Helen says, tearing her eyes from me to Luke. 'Cheating on who?'

I turn my eyes to Luke but say nothing. I've made a right mess of things now. Too late to backpedal.

'What does he mean, 'cheating'?' Helen pleads with him. He can't deny it. He bunches his fist, looks like he wants to knock me out. I almost want him to. In this moment I've chosen Helen over him. A girl I'll never see again over my best friend.

I hear a noise to my left and turn to see Theo

standing there, summoned like Luke's frigging genie. I have no fear of Theo doing anything and I suspect he's a little caught off guard by the fracas to do much.

An explosion goes off in my head from where Luke slams his fist into my skull.

In an instant I'm on the ground, his hands around my neck. I hear Helen shout at him to stop. Luke's on top of me now, his hands squeezing so hard that the room starts to fade. The fire is close, burning hot. I can hear Theo murmuring, 'Luke, take it easy, mate! He can't breathe!'

'I'm no fool,' Luke says in a strange voice.

'Luke, stop it!' Helen yells.

He loosens his grip just enough for me to push him off and roll over, gasping for breath on all fours. I can see stars. My neck feels broken. With a last disgusted look at me he stomps out of the room. Theo follows shortly after, his side already chosen.

38

Helen

6th September 2017

I rinse my mouth with a glass of water and return to the living room.

'Sorry about that,' I say. Kate and Ben both look horrified.

'Is everything alright?' Kate asks.

'Something you said made me realise why Michael might have reacted the way he did at Josh's birthday party,' I say slowly.

I sit down again, my movements unsteady. Kate watches me carefully.

'What was it?' she says. 'Drugs?'

'I really don't think the attack was an act of malice,' I say unevenly, my mind racing as I speak. 'The fire at the bookshop . . . it really broke us, you know? Michael wasn't himself. And when he was much younger he was into climbing. He did Ben Nevis, the Alps . . . ' I find I'm shaking as I say it aloud. 'He lost a friend to climbing. It was terrible. *That* was why I threw up.'

Kate seems moved by this, and as I hear my own words echoing in my head it occurs to me with a shiver that it's true: the fire at the book-shop, then Ben getting over enthusiastic about taking our son on a climb. It was just the right combination to make Michael take drastic measures.

'Do you think that's why he's gone missing?' Kate says. 'Was it something to do with this friend he lost when they went climbing?'

I go to say no, but then I hesitate.

In a flash I'm back in our flat in Cardiff opening that first letter. Every year on the twenty-fifth of June, the same letter. The anniversary of Luke's death.

'I don't know anymore,' I tell Kate, my voice breaking. 'I believed that he'd have contacted me by now, at least to check we're all OK and let me know he's alive. But he hasn't.'

'Let us know if there's anything we can do, OK?' Kate says. '*Anything*, OK?'

I try not to think what might happen if she discovers that just hours before I'd been in her house, trawling through her cupboards for anything that might implicate her husband in the car crash.

Ben calls Josh downstairs and a moment later he comes, smiling and bright-eyed, telling us excitedly about Reuben's animation of a breaching humpback whale.

'We can have Reuben stay at ours some time, if you like?' Kate says, and I glance at Reuben who brightens. Reuben has never been to another child's house, has never had a birthday invitation or a playdate. For many years I've told myself that, even if he got an invite, it would be awkward. What if he had a toilet accident, or a meltdown?

Kate puts a hand on my arm when she sees

me falter. 'And don't be worried about anything he does or says. We know all about it, don't we, Ben?'

As they say all of this Josh is by Kate's side, asking on repeat for the car key. She ignores him until she's finished her sentence, then faces him and says, 'can you count to thirty, love? I'll give it to you once you reach thirty.'

Josh nods, begins to count. 'One, two, three . . . '

'I think Reuben would love that,' I tell them.

When they leave, Jeannie creeps downstairs and looks me over.

'Well?' she hisses. 'Are they axe murderers or not?'

'Not,' I say, wearily. 'Look, I need to ask a favour.'

'Anything.'

'Yes. I . . . Can Reuben and I come and stay with you? Is there a spare bed at the place you're renting? It's just weird, being here . . . '

'Of *course*. Man, how thoughtless of me. I'm getting Shane to turn around right now.'

I manage to persuade Reuben to pack a small overnight bag, though he insists on bringing a large suitcase with all his Minecraft models and books and every piece of blue clothing he possesses. I don't mind. I pack the most comfortable clothes I can find and lock the door behind me.

I can't tell Jeannie, but as we drive away from our house I shudder with relief.

★　★　★

The morning is bright, a sloe-blue sky with rich sunlight that falls on the cathedral spires, coming to rest in the valleys and fields that are beginning to burn golden. Autumn is my favourite time of year in Northumberland. Michael's too, not least because the bookshop sales spiked. Author events and book groups are always well attended, too, and we installed a wood burning stove in the café with two sofas beside it for customers to sit down with a hot drink and a new book.

I ask Jeannie to take me to the bookstore on the way to visit Saskia. Outside, I make her turn off the engine so that I can get out and look at the exterior of the shop. It is heart-breaking to see it so damaged. Sunlight makes the destruction all the more painful, a syrupy light swirling across yellowing leaves on the cobbles in acute contrast to our pitifully incinerated bookstore. Weeks after the blaze, a throat-clutching stench of black smoke still on the back of the wind. Our cosy book-filled haven morphed to a blackened wreck. Everything Michael worked for gone overnight.

Jeannie gets out of the car and reluctantly stands beside me, looking the place over. She wraps her arm around me.

'I'm so sorry, love,' she says. 'Maybe we can get it fixed up again soon.'

I take a step towards the door, pulling back the police tape and trying the handle. It's unlocked. I push it back.

'What are you doing?' she says. 'Helen . . . '

'I want to go inside.'

'Helen, you *can't* go in there!' she says loudly,

but I have to. I have to see if they're still there.

The shop is unrecognisable. The floorspace is littered with charred books, toppled bookcases and debris from the floor upstairs, which had partially collapsed on the far side. The books that remained on the shelves are all but turned to charcoal, the till table stacked high with burnt papers and ash. It hurts less than I'd anticipated, to see it like this. Saskia's life hangs in the balance; the shop can be replaced. And I didn't come here to work out what could be salvaged. I came here to find something I hid a long time ago.

'Helen . . . ' Jeannie says, placing a hand on my arm, but I want to see it. I want to take it in, absorb the mess. Remember it. I want to see if any trace of the fire's origin had been left.

'You've got to be careful,' Jeannie calls after me as I shuffle through the papers and book spines scattered on the floor. 'You don't know what structural damage has been done.'

I take the stairs slowly, clutching the thick wooden banister. The banister and stairs are remarkably intact, and although the stair runner has been obliterated by a heavy layer of soot, it looks as though the fire ventured close enough to lick the first step before turning away. The staircase was what made Michael fall in love with the shop — it was the original mahogany staircase, dating back to the 1830s and sweeping up to the next floor in a dramatic twist. The newel post at the bottom of the stairs is about twenty inches in diameter, a proud, hand-carved signature of the shop's former purposes. The inscription of a cross to mark its years as a hospital, a quill to signify its time as a school. Michael will be glad that the stairs had survived.

'Where are you going?' Jeannie calls after me as I continue upstairs. 'Helen, half the floor is gone up there! You need to come down *right now!*'

'I'll only be a minute,' I tell her, and I move faster in case she thinks to come up after me.

Upstairs is even worse than the ground floor. The beautiful leather sofa and chairs I bought at the beginning of the year are destroyed, the springs sitting up out of the bowels of black chairs. The air is thick with soot and already I can feel it on the roof of my mouth. Scattered amongst the ash and dust are odd things that have somehow survived — a single plastic polyester lily, still white, lying amongst a pile of ash. Coffee mugs, a copy of Mary Oliver's *Selected Poems* almost pristine, a browned edge the only sign that it was here during the fire.

I cover my hand with my mouth and move to the next staircase, a narrow spiral that leads to Michael's office. I'm taking a risk going up there, I know it, but I have to look.

The attic is like a coal mine, the chipboard wallpaper that we were unable to remove now the texture of charcoal, though a celestial-bright ray of sunlight fingers through the shattered Velux window, providing a source of breathable air. Michael's desk is badly burned, the computer and paperwork turned to ash. The filing cabinet is warped, too, locking it tight.

I move towards the narrow end of the room and reach up into one of the exposed rafter beams. I have to see if it is still there. The box that I placed there, hidden.

My fingers strike tin.

It is still there.

'Helen, what are you *doing?*' Jeannie shouts. 'I'm getting filthy down here! Can we go now, please?'

I don't answer her but lift the box down and blow ash off the lid. Although the beam it sits upon is badly burned, the box has remarkably escaped damage. I pull the lid off, hold my breath. Blood thuds in my ears. Downstairs, I can hear Jeannie still urging me to come down. She's on the first floor. I can't tear my eyes away from what's inside the box. I had placed all the letters we'd received over the years there, always addressed to 'Michael King' instead of Michael Pengilly.

I only opened one letter. The rest I stored intact.

But all the letters have been opened, their envelopes torn and placed back inside the box.

With shaking hands, I unfold the letter at the top of the pile.

K. Haden
Haden, Morris & Laurence Law Practice
4 Martin Place
London, EN9 1AS
25th June 2012

Michael King
101 Oxford Lane
Cardiff
CF10 1FY

Sir,
I await your response to our previous
letter.
We are growing impatient.
We are prepared to do whatever it takes
to bring you to justice.
Please respond within forty-eight hours
of receiving this letter to avoid conse-
quences.

Sincerely,
K. Haden

Most of the letters were redirected from our
Cardiff address. When we moved from Wales to
Sheffield — then Belfast, London, Kent, and
finally here in Northumberland — I had our post
from Cardiff re-directed to a PO Box. And every
June, when the letters came bearing the same
postmark, the same addressee — Michael King
— I hid them away. Someday, I thought. Someday, when life slowed down enough for Michael
and me to be able to face up to things, we'd read
them together. We'd put it right.

But 'someday' never came. The years spun
away from us like a ball of wool flung into the
distance. And I never once suspected that Michael
might find the box, that he might actually open
and read the letters.

But it seems he has.

I unfold another letter, the one sent in January. A letter comprised of a single word in black marker, the letters screaming off the page.

Murderer

My stomach churns, my veins run cold. I force myself to stay focused, to not let the panic overcome me. I remember opening the letter with confusion, wondering why or how they'd sent it here. I knew it was from Luke's family. No invitation to come forward, no polite hint of threat. Just this hideous accusation. They'd found us.

At the time I was so paralysed with fear that I didn't know what to do. Who could I tell about it? I couldn't go to the police. Reuben was going through a really rough patch at school and his behaviour had become more challenging. He lashed out at me one night and then wet himself in the supermarket the next. When we looked into the cause we discovered he was being bullied at school. I got caught up in that and managed to push the letter to the corner of my mind. I didn't dare look at it again. As long as I kept it hidden, out of sight, I could almost pretend I'd never come across it.

Shaking, I look over the envelope. It's badly crumpled but I can make out a French postmark. A row of stamps bearing the Eiffel Tower. And on the back is a water-damaged label with something scribbled for customs. A name. The writing is a scrawl, but I squint closely, turning to the light at the window to see it better. I can just make out a name:

Chris Holloway

'Helen? Where are you?'

Jeannie's voice sounds from the bottom of the spiral staircase, making me jump and knocking me out of my memories, back into the charred attic.

'Coming,' I call. 'Don't come up here, Jeannie. It's too dangerous!'

Quickly I lift the letters out of the box and stuff them inside my coat. I haven't told Jeannie about them. How could I? How could I even begin to explain what they relate to?

'What the *hell* do you think you were doing?' Jeannie says once we've hurried out of the shop to her car. 'Honestly, Helen, do you really think my heart is up to something happening to you, too? What could *possibly* be so important that you had to go all the way into the attic?'

Discovering who paid Jonas Matus to crash our car.

Chris Holloway.

That's who I have to find.

39

Michael

25th June 1995

We get up at 2 a.m. and start walking an hour later, once we've re-fuelled and geared up. Theo tries to kill the palpable awkwardness by being extra talkative about the route and attempting some jokes. *What do you call a pile of kittens? A meowntain. What's the difference between a guitar and a fish? You can't tuna fish. What do you call a fake noodle? An impasta.*

Finally, he shuts up and talks about the summit. It's a big day, one we've planned for almost a year.

'How'd you sleep?' I ask Helen.

A tentative smile. 'Fast.'

Luke's stare is beginning to burn a hole in my back, so I leave it at that.

We have only a thousand metres of elevation to clear before reaching the summit, but the air is so thin and the snow so dense that every step feels like a mile. Even so, once the darkness lifts, we have to stop and look out in silence at what stretches out in front of us.

The blanket of clouds that has been adjacent for so long is now far below, the sunrise a bright red sliver across the horizon, the moon a white dot in the blue. The peaks snake out of the cloud like the spine of an ancient monster, like fossilised waves.

We reach the summit at nine. It is an incredible moment, a feeling of relief and disbelief. Looking down on the world so far below is dizzying and exhilarating. Even the clouds are hundreds of feet beneath us, a thick white carpet. Mists rise and fall from the peaks as though the mountains are breathing. I've already decided they are living entities instead of rock and stone. As for the four us, we no longer look human but like aliens, our faces obscured by sunglasses, face scarves, and helmet straps. The whole thing feels surreal. And yet we've done it. We are *here*.

'Woo!' Theo shouts, both arms high above his head. 'We made it! We actually made it!'

Luke takes a French flag from his backpack and plunges it into the snow, crossing himself once before high-fiving Theo.

I find a space far enough away from everyone so I can do my summit thing in peace. As has been my plan for ten whole months, I recite the poem that Percy Bysshe Shelley wrote when he visited Mont Blanc in 1860.

The everlasting universe of things
Flows through the mind, and rolls its rapid
  waves,
Now dark — now glittering — now reflect-
  ing gloom —

I stop when I see Helen about thirty yards away. She's built a small pillar of snow, and quietly takes something out of her pocket, sets it on top. A piece of sea glass. I can't take my eyes off her. I want to know so much about her, to ask question after question. I want to tell her everything.

I see Luke approach her, his arms out wide. My gut flips. He leans in for a kiss but she pulls away sharply. Theo turns his head to me, watching on. I turn away. In that small series of gestures I read the signs: our relationships are over. I never want to see Luke or Theo again, and I'm sure the feeling is mutual.

But, there's a minor problem: we still have to get back down. It will take two days, maybe three. We all have to put our differences aside and work together if we want to reach Chamonix in safety.

Fortunately, the thin air and physical exertion has knocked the fight out of us, Luke included. When the adrenalin hit of reaching the summit begins to subside we approach the edge of the route that will take us across the shoulder of the mountain and back to Chamonix.

'Can't we just ski back down?' Luke says, looking over the snowfields below, the thick white carpet that sweeps before us for what seems like miles. I know how he feels: looking up at the mountain from the emerald, sun-swept valley of Chamonix, it hadn't seemed that far. Walking through snow — upwards or down — is the single most difficult thing I'd done in my life. These snowfields are like being on the moon, a completely different realm to the rest of the planet. I will never take walking unencumbered for granted again.

We have to keep moving, though the urge to sit down and sleep is constant. After an hour, we reach an outcrop which seems a good place to boil up some snow for our noodles and refuel, but by the time we finish eating a dense fog has closed in. There is no warning. No thundercloud, no rain. Just a creepy grey veil drawn across the sky, the valley, the black faces of the mountains studying their guests.

'I think we should wait it out,' Helen says, glancing around. 'It's too thick to see anything.'

'No,' Luke counters. 'We keep going.'

He turns and starts walking. He only takes five or six steps before the fog gobbles him up. We follow after. I turn on my headtorch to cut a path through the fog but it merely bounces back. We have to use our poles to tap a way forward.

Two hours of blind walking later, the fog lifts, like a chorus of silver curtains lifting in a vast theatre. Blue skies again, though heavy mists marble all around us, potent with threat.

'Dude, we got a problem,' Theo says quietly.

'What's that?' Luke says, wiping sweat off his face.

Theo has the map out. He looks at it with his nose scrunched, then looks up. Looks down again, turns, looks up.

'We are completely and utterly lost,' he says.

We all turn around in a circle on the spot, as though a sign will appear telling us the way to go.

'We seem to have reached the end of the path,' Helen says, and I can see that ahead of her is a

299

sharp drop of rock. A cliff, basically.

'Unless we develop the power of flight, we ain't going nowhere,' Theo surmises.

'You seriously don't know where we are?' Luke asks.

A cough. 'We're, uh, meant to be on a gradual decline. Not a rock face,' Theo says, squinting at the map.

Helen approaches, takes off her backpack and traces the map with her index finger. She turns and squints into the distance.

'Is *that* where we should be?'

She points at an angle of the mountain some distance away that winds down to another refuge hut. Theo's silence suggests she's right. We've taken the wrong path. But no time to start blaming anyone, though we all know who's at fault.

'We should head there,' I say, panting. 'This descent is too steep. And look.'

I point at black cloud behind us.

'Storm's coming,' Helen says. There is fear in her voice.

Luke kneels to inspect something at the edge of the cliff. 'This is a faster way down. Look. Anchor points right here.'

'Check the bolts,' Theo says. 'Are they spinning or secure?'

'They're secure,' Luke says, though I don't see him check the bolts. He takes some carabiners from his rucksack, then his rope.

'What are you doing?' I say.

'Avoiding the storm,' Luke says. 'You got a better option?'

I don't answer. Luke sets about making a quad

anchor with the carabiners and rope. I am not convinced. There are anchor points in the rock all right, but they looked old and rusty, and there is no fixed line.

'This isn't safe,' I say.

'It's completely safe,' Luke counters.

'What's going on?' Helen says, glancing from me to Luke.

'We are getting ourselves down the mountain,' Luke says cheerily. 'We're creating an anchored line that we'll harness ourselves to and gently lower down, using our crampons and axes as leverage. Okey dokey?'

'How far is the drop?' Theo says, hesitating.

'It'll be about a hundred feet, mate,' Luke says.

'You're guessing,' Helen says. 'Seb said not to guess anything but always to . . . '

'I don't think we have much alternative,' Luke says, and I take a walk up and down the path to find one, but can't.

'We'll have to rope together,' Theo says finally. I can tell that he's suddenly nervous, reluctant.

'Look, we aren't experienced in this,' I say. So far we've managed to avoid such steep descents. Something in my instinct says we are best heading back to the original route, but it is so, so far away, and every single step is exhausting.

'Michael, there is a storm,' Luke says testily, pointing at the wall of black cloud behind us, inching closer.

'Yes, but . . . ' The air has become so thin that it's difficult to speak. Every word requires more breath than my lungs can manage.

301

'Tell you what, Michael,' Luke says, panting. 'You go and take the path. We'll call it a race, eh? Off you go.'

I watch silently as Theo steps forward and harnesses himself, then lowers down over the edge of the cliff.

'I'll go next,' I say when Luke steps forward.

'Too scared to go off on your own?'

'No,' I say, lowering myself down.

Luke tries to help Helen harness to the rope but she does it herself. Silently, he follows.

I'm relieved to find it is OK, at first. The footholds are decent, with nice deep hollows to get a grip. As long as I don't look down I'm hunky dory.

Before long we are eyeballing the bank of cumulonimbus that looks like a fluffy white quilt from above.

'How far until the bottom?' Theo shouts.

'Too much fog,' Luke says. 'I'll try throwing something and we'll listen to the drop.'

He chucks a rock down. I don't hear it land.

'That's more than a hundred-foot drop,' Theo observes.

'It probably landed in a bush,' Luke says dismissively. He says something else, but we don't hear it, because right then rocks come chucking down, hundreds of them, as though the mountain is disintegrating. Helen screams, and we all grip on to the rockface as tight as we can, keeping our bodies flat to stone as the rocks plunge down around us like rain.

Suddenly the rope jerks wildly, and in an instant I see Luke peel away from the cliff and fall down, down. It happens so fast, my legs and arms smashing against the rock. Theo manages to loop his end of the rope around a tree that is jutting out of the rock, holding us all fast and saving our lives. But with a horrifying jolt, the rope lashes upwards, slamming us all against the jagged angles of the cliff again as the rocks continue to fall.

After a moment, the dust settles.

Everything is still. I open my eyes. Nothing I see makes sense.

'Luke?' Theo shouts. 'Luke!'

It takes me a moment to realise that I'm hanging upside down. My helmet is barely hanging on, the blood rushing to my head. I see cloud, then Helen, clinging to the rope for dear life, whimpering, and above her Theo, latched on to the escarpment, star-shaped.

I arc my head and glance down. Luke is there. Why is he *beneath* me? It doesn't make sense. Just a moment before he was at the *top* of the rope. Now he's upside down, like me, his neck arched and his arms flung backwards, like a puppet dangling from a string.

He isn't moving.

'Someone help!' Helen shouts. 'Help us!'

I try to gather my senses, but just then rocks start hurtling down again, infrequent but too close for comfort. I can see that Luke is still harnessed to the rope but the anchors have come away from the rock. They are visible at the end of the rope, caught against his harness. They've clearly detached from the rock and pulled Luke down the rockface.

The only thing keeping all four of us from plunging to our deaths is Theo, hanging on to the rope above.

'Theo!' I yell. 'Have you anchored us?'

'Just about,' he answers in a tight voice. 'I can only hold this for so long. Any ideas?'

Helen is shouting about her fingers. She's been hurt.

'Helen! Are you OK?' Theo shouts, and I arch my head back.

'My hand,' she gasps. 'I think my hand is broken!'

'Keep against the wall,' Theo shouts then. 'I can hear rumbling!'

The rope is swaying dangerously, the weight of Luke's body beneath us clearly too much.

'Luke!' I shout. 'Luke, are you with us?'

I need him to wake up and grip the rock. He gives a low moan. When he spins around again I see his helmet is missing. It must have been knocked off in the rock fall.

'Theo, we need to create another anchor,' I say. 'Can you do that from your end?'

'I'll try.'

'Helen, how are you doing?' I say, giving a thumbs up.

She nods, but is holding on grimly to her hand.

'Luke?' she shouts. 'Tell us you're alright!'

'Luke, are you OK?' Theo yells. Nothing.

'I think he's taken a hit to the head,' I say. 'I can't see his helm . . . '

I don't finish my sentence. The rope drops again, making us all scream. The tree that Theo looped the rope around is beginning to peel away from the rock.

'I can't hold it!' Theo shouts. I shout at Luke to wake up, but he doesn't stir. Theo is screaming about not being able to create an anchor in time, he is trying so hard but can't, the weight beneath him is too much. The rope drops again, and this time I know it is all over. I crane my neck to look up at Helen one last time. One last look before we all fall.

She locks eyes with me. 'Cut it!' she pleads in a tear-stricken voice. 'Cut the rope!'

I don't have time to think. I don't have time to do anything but act on instinct. Luke is badly injured, and I see a bright splash of blood on his forehead. He won't wake in time to find a grip in the rock. This is the only way we can survive, the one chance we have to make it.

I quickly filch the Stanley knife from the thigh pocket in my trousers. I pause as I press the blade against the rope.

'Luke, *please!* Wake up!'

Nothing.

I slice the knife against the fibres of the rope. In an instant it snaps, whipping upward as the weight beneath me slips into shadow.

There is no scream from Luke, only a rushing sound as he plunges downward. A series of sickening thuds as his body hits the side of the cliff on the way down.

'No!' Theo screams. 'No no no no no!'

For a long time, we hang there in the fist of horror, in harrowing stillness.

The storm passes.

The rain stops.

The sun comes out.

Somehow we manage to descend to an outcrop where Theo launches himself at me and punches me to the ground, almost knocking me off the edge. Helen screams at him to stop, but I don't want him to. I want him to push me off. I sent Luke to his death.

I killed him.

'Michael had no choice!' she tells Theo. 'We all would have died!'

Theo doesn't respond. He's hysterical. Tears roll down his face and his lips curl into an expression I've never witnessed before. He howls terrible anguished cries that bounce off the indifferent rockface, the quiet, watchful peaks. His cries penetrate me, entering my bloodstream, braiding my DNA.

Changing me for ever.

⋆   ⋆   ⋆

We follow a path.

We don't stop for food or water.

We don't speak.

Theo cries.

I am numb, completely in shock. Helen is sobbing.

When we finally convince her to take off her glove, it's clear that her right hand has been crushed by the rockfall, her fingers already blue and grossly swollen, the bones shattered.

We reach a refuge, raise the alarm about Luke.

A medic attends to Helen's hand, bandaging it

to the size of a boxing glove. A mountain rescue unit is sent by helicopter, and for a whole evening and night we live in a supernatural, fatigue-induced hope that maybe, just maybe, Luke will appear in the doorway of the hut. He will beat the living daylights out of me for cutting the rope, but that will be fine because he'll be alive, and we'll all have a beer and joke about it being the most epic climb ever.

The rescue team arrives back in the helicopter and the three of us bail out into the night in a shared vision of the helicopter door flinging open to reveal Luke with perhaps an arm in a sling and a cheers-for-dumping-me look.

But instead we watch in a gut-wrenching silence as the men in helmets and boiler suits pull a stretcher out, a body covered loosely by a weighted blanket.

Theo goes ballistic. He races at it, tears the blanket off. In the garish white light of the rescue hut's emergency light I see Luke's body. Not Luke at all. No sign whatsoever of the larger-than-life glow he emitted, but a mushed-up skull and face, his arms and legs stiff. Helen falls to her knees and cries without sound. Theo has to be pulled off him.

They hand us cups of watery tea, ask again what happened. 'For the *gendarme*,' they say, pens and paper in hand.

Helen manages to answer when Theo and I stay silent.

'Rocks came tumbling down. They hit my hand. We . . . we think they hit Luke's head.'

Theo breaks down again in horrible, anguished

sobs. He sounds pitiful, like a little boy.

They nod, say they have to phone Luke's parents.

Theo is the one who breaks the news to them.

I get on a plane without saying goodbye to Helen or Theo.

I land at Heathrow, then barricade myself in a shoddy motel for a week with enough vodka for the Red Army.

Somehow I survive.

But I don't sleep.

I find myself on a bridge looking down at a river a few weeks later and realise I have a choice. I can die, which would be a relief from the emotions that besiege me. Or I can do something worthwhile with the life that has somehow been given back to me. It could easily have been me at bottom of that rope.

A split-second decision has changed the entire course of my life, and ended Luke's.

40

Michael

6th September 2017

The hotel room is tiny, a segment of loft with a sloping roof and a small window overlooking rooftops and blue sea. Yellow wallpaper, an old-fashioned dressing table, half-shut blinds throwing a ribcage of light on the wooden floor. A leaflet on the table says 'Hôtel de Côte Fleurie.'

It takes a few moments for the images in my head to disperse, for Theo's yells to stop ringing in my years. I can hear him so clearly, the timbre of his voice, the pain in his yells. *No!*

After Luke's death I dropped out of Oxford. I changed my last name, not out of a conscious attempt to hide but because every cell in my body was changed by the fall. Michael King died on Mont Blanc.

I never contacted Theo again, or Luke's parents. Years later, I woke from a cold sweat and realised that the right thing would have been to contact them, to offer condolences and, more importantly, the full story.

Some years after that, I realised — much too late — that my silence suggested that I was guilty

309

of something much worse. Something intentional, deliberate.

That I had murdered him in cold blood.

And sometimes, in my nightmares, I wonder whether I had. Whether some vile part of my subconscious wanted Helen enough to cut the rope and clear the path to her. Whether I had simply obeyed what she shouted in the darkness.

I squeeze my eyes shut. As though at the far end of a corridor, I can see another image.

A dreamscape.

The door of flame.

Its heat travels the length of the corridor, warming my face. I'm terrified to go near it and yet I am pulled there.

⋆ ⋆ ⋆

I take a shower, standing for a long time under a hot jet of water against my forehead, blasting the fatigue that aches in my skull. Then I get changed, head downstairs for breakfast. The receptionist sees me, raises a hand.

'Sir?'

I approach the desk. 'Yes?'

She blushes. 'We had a problem with your credit card. It was declined. Can you try another?'

'Certainly.'

I pull the wallet out of my back pocket, find an American Express card. *Please God, let it work.*

She swipes it in the machine. Smiles. 'It worked.'

I try not to show my panic. The card isn't

mine. It's only a matter of time before the police trace that transaction. I'm not planning on staying here for long.

'Enjoy your breakfast,' she says.

'*Merci.*'

Yesterday morning I watched the train pull away from the station at Gare du Nord. I went to the ticket office to see if they'd change my ticket to a later train, but it turns out my understanding of French is even worse than my spoken French, and although I had my phone there was no battery left to try and use Google translate. I was, as they say, up the creek without a paddle.

I was starving, sore all over from the beating I took, and freezing cold. France is a hell of a lot colder than Belize so the clothes I'd changed into — a T-shirt and jeans with flipflops — weren't useful. I sat down on a bench in the station, wondered what to do. I wanted to go home. I thought of Helen and the kids. If my phone had been working I'd have rung her then. The urge to speak to her, to tell her I love her, burned in me.

I decided to go and hunt around the shops and stalls for a phone charger. I had four euros. Maybe I could get one for that, or haggle. I hobbled to a mall in the city, looked in all the shops. Phone chargers were around twenty euros. Right when I was actually considering stealing one — I've never stolen anything in my life, but desperate times — there was a big commotion at the entrance of the shop. Shouting, and a scuffle. I took a few steps up the aisle and saw a young girl with pink hair and a parka being searched by a security guard. The retail clerk seemed to be accusing her of stealing. The girl denied it loudly even as the security guard started digging stuff out of her pockets. Boxes of perfume, a couple of watches, a wallet.

All of a sudden the girl burst out of the shop, running like the clappers. Reaching out to the window display she pulled a mannequin down with a clatter behind her to stop the security guard and retail clerk from catching up. A few other shoppers stood and gawped, and just then I spotted something on the ground. A leather wallet. One of the girl's spoils. She must have dropped it during the chase.

Quickly I scooped it up, walked quickly out of the mall. I headed to a supermarket and plucked a phone charger off a rack. Some food, a coat. A clean pair of socks. At the checkout I dug one of the credit cards out of the wallet and gave a charming, an Oscar-winning performance of 'I can't remember my pin' by hand gestures. The sales clerk let me scribble a signature.

It felt strangely exhilarating.

And then I got a train to Normandy, found a hotel. Charged my phone. With huge trepidation I dialled Helen's number. It rang and rang, went to voicemail. I hung up and climbed into bed. Cried myself to sleep.

⋆ ⋆ ⋆

After breakfast I use the guest computer in the front lobby to look up the address for Luke's parents' place. Google reveals nothing. I spend an hour thinking up different search terms and each one yields no results. The receptionist sees me swearing at the computer, approaches me tentatively.

'Sir? Can I help?'

I rub my eyes. 'I'm looking for an address,' I tell her, but then I fall wary. I don't know who to trust. She's young. About twenty. Sweet-faced, a soft pink cardigan, earrings in the shape of cup-cakes. She puts me in mind of an older version of Saskia. My throat tightens.

'Which address?' she says. 'You're looking for a friend, maybe?'

'Yes. An old friend. His name was — is — Theo Aucoin. His parents owned a big house that once belonged to Winston Churchill. I know it was in this area.'

She thinks, then her face lights up. 'Ah.' She turns and heads back to the front desk, returns with a leaflet.

'This house?'

I look at the leaflet, spending a handful of seconds trying to find the house behind the castle before I work out that the castle *is* the damn house. Château du Seuil. An estate with forty acres, multiple outbuildings. A frigging lake.

'They do tours during the day,' she explains, showing me the price list.

'I don't think this is the place,' I protest, but she nods, adamant. 'Theo Aucoin? Your friend is called.'

'Yes?'

'The Aucoin family have owned that house a

long time. They still live there.'

'But, the tours . . . ' It looks like a National Trust property, not a family home.

'They live in the east wing,' she says, nodding, emphatic. 'Just a small section. The rest is public.'

41

Helen

6th September 2017

The letters sit inside my coat like beating hearts, alive and tormenting. Jeannie spies that I brought something down from the attic and I tell her it's just tax stuff and insurance certificates that I managed to salvage from the filing cabinet. One lie after another, threaded together like a pearl choker.

We head for the hospital. I'm aware that I've fallen silent but can't manage to find mental space to drum up some small chat. I was never any good at pretending. Jeannie fills the silence with small talk about how we could set up a pop-up bookshop in the meantime to keep the business going, that she could look into funding to pay temporary staff. Perhaps we can even re-employ Matilda and Lucy, who both worked so passionately at the shop and had been devastated by the fire. Then, mid-sentence:

'You don't think it was either of them that started the fire, do you?'

I stare at her. 'What, Lucy? Matilda? They're the loveliest girls you could meet. Why would they . . . ?'

She shakes her head, unable to finish her sentence, before signalling to turn on to the A1.

'Word about town is it was malicious,' she says. 'What do you make of that?'

I straighten. ''Word about town'?'

'When I was collecting your mail at the Post Office the teller mentioned Sam Jennings,' she says. 'Do you know him? The retired fireman who lives around the corner from the shop?'

The name is vaguely familiar.

'Apparently he reckons it was malicious,' she continues, clearly enjoying being the source of information. 'She said he'd been down to have a look around, found V-shaped patterns.'

'V-shaped patterns?' I say. 'What the hell does that mean? That a cult started the fire?'

Her voice falters. 'It's about the seat of the fire or something like that. He said if you find V-shaped patterns you've located the source, and usually in an accidental fire they're around an old heater or electrical socket or what have you. He said the patterns weren't anywhere near a source like that. In his experience, that meant that someone started it with firelighters or ignition fuel.'

'Well if *Sam Jennings* knows all this,' I say, 'what's taking the insurance company so long?'

'I had a look when we were inside,' she says, turning into a narrow back alley that joins two main streets. 'I didn't see anything V-shaped. To be fair, the teller said Sam's a sandwich short of a picnic so it could all be a pile of nonsense.'

I can feel my skin turning cold, anxiety beginning to claim me. 'The investigation has been going on for months. I'm starting to think it'll never end.'

She looks over at me, confused. 'Didn't you read the letters?'

For a moment I think she's referring to the letters held snug against my chest, infant-warm, and my heart drums in my ears.

'Never mind, that's what I'm here for,' she says proudly. 'The insurance company says they're waiting on a report from the arson investigator. They've got some results from the forensics team and are speaking to the police.'

I double-take. 'An arson investigator? So *they* believe it was malicious?'

She shrugs. 'They didn't say. If the Fire Service hasn't found the cause then maybe this is the next step?' She takes a deep breath. 'Hopefully they'll resolve it in the next couple of weeks. That would be something, wouldn't it? I seriously cannot believe one family can be hit with so much misfortune all at once.'

At the hospital, I take Saskia's hand and read one of her unicorn books aloud, talking to her as if I am reading her a bedtime story. It's useless — my voice is thin and high-pitched, wobbling on the brink of tears. Coming back to see her in the hospital is devastating. It steals away the hope I'm able to muster when I'm at home, surrounded by her toys and pictures. More machines than I could have imagined possible are keeping her alive, all with intricate names and functions that I've memorised: a transcranial doppler, cardiac parameters, a Brain Tissue Oxygen Monitoring System, the ICP and a

Saber cerebral blood flow sensor and jugular bulb oximetry. How anyone could survive such injuries is beyond me, let alone a little seven-year-old girl. And yet, she is still here, fighting on. I try to cling to that but I have voices in my head telling me I'm stupid for hanging on to hope, that I must prepare myself for a life without my daughter.

But I can't. I have no idea how to do such a thing.

The rehabilitation nurse, a young woman with expressive green eyes named Heather, tells me that reading to her like this and posing questions was a really effective way of activating the brain. Within a couple of days of Saskia being moved here we organised a rota, with many of my friends, Saskia's teachers and even her friends' parents all signing up to come and read to her for an hour or two per day. At night, the nurses set up an MP3 player plugged into donated speakers with the sound recordings that Reuben made for her so that she could hear familiar voices, including her own.

We have been told to talk to her, too, and ask questions as though she might respond. 'It can feel really strange,' Heather counsels. 'We know that the brain responds to these questions and begins to form patterns in areas that are damaged by trauma. Talking to her can also help her body fight infection. She may *seem* unresponsive, but what's happening inside her head is completely the opposite.'

I am telling Saskia about Chewy and Oreo when my mobile buzzes in my pocket. I recognise DS Jahan's voice immediately.

'There's been a development,' he says. 'A transaction made on one of the credit cards. Can we come and talk to you about it?'

The detectives are waiting outside my house when we arrive back from the hospital. Jeannie helps me out of the car and they follow after. They smile and ask after Reuben, but I can tell from the stiff smile on DS Jahan's face that the news isn't good.

'How's your little girl?' DCI Lavery asks, taking a seat in the living room. I catch my breath before answering.

'They're still monitoring her very closely,' I say, steeling myself so I don't cry. I'm tired of crying in front of strangers. 'She's starting to move her fingers and make noises, which is a positive sign.'

'Is that her teddy?' DCI Lavery asks, looking at Jack-Jack on my lap.

I dust him down. 'He's her favourite teddy. Unfortunately we've had to bring him home as they don't want anything synthetic lying around. There was a chance he might get binned by one of the cleaners.'

'You said there was a transaction?' Jeannie says, impatient.

DS Jahan nods. 'A withdrawal from a bank in Paris.'

'*Paris?*'

'Do you have any connections there?' DC Fields asks.

I shake my head. 'No, none.'

'No family or friends based out there?'

A shiver runs down my spine. Luke had family out there. Maybe they've taken Michael, forced him to leave.

Should I tell them my suspicions about who has taken him?

'What about friends or colleagues? Mistresses?'

'Of course not.'

They all wait in case I decided to change my mind.

'This isn't about either of us having an affair, I can assure you.'

Michael's never cheated. I've wondered a few times but my snooping yielded nothing. I've never been tempted to. Everything orbits around Saskia and Reuben. Our careers, home, day-to-day routine, even our marriage — it's all about them. And even if either of us had the inclination we certainly lacked the energy.

'OK,' DS Jahan says brusquely. I see him slide his eyes at his colleague at how I've suddenly shut down. 'I'll show you what we've got.'

He pulls out a tablet, clicks on a file. 'This was taken yesterday afternoon in a bank near Place de la Concorde.'

Immediately a video image appears of a queue of people lined up in front of three ATMs inside a bank. A man in a baseball cap is visible, his hands in his pockets. The camera is clearly mounted on a wall, pointing down. I hold my breath, waiting to see Michael. The queue shuffles forward and the man in the baseball cap approaches a bank clerk. I notice he has a limp.

'Is that Michael?' I say.

'That's certainly the man who made the withdrawal,' DS Jahan says.

He hits pause, then rewinds the footage to the beginning. I watch again with a sense of disappointment and frustration. I can't tell for certain if it's Michael. He's wearing black jeans and a white T-shirt with a logo across the chest. He looks too thin to be Michael. But then I catch a momentary turn of his head, an almost invisible movement, and I know it's him. It's Michael.

At the end of the queue there's another man, broader across the shoulders, also wearing a baseball cap. He's dressed like Michael, too. He keeps his head held down at the screen of his mobile phone. Michael approaches the ATM, punches a number into the keypad and receives a bundle of notes. Michael turns to walk away from the machine, and the other man nods at him.

'Who's that?' I say loudly. 'That man. Is he with Michael?'

DS Jahan rewinds the footage and zooms in. 'You recognise him?'

'No, but he signalled at Michael. Look.'

We all lean forward to study the screen.

DCI Lavery says, 'OK, he does seem to nod at Michael.'

'He could just be saying hello,' Jeannie offers. 'One stranger to another.'

'Or they could be together,' DS Jahan says. 'It's hard to tell. Either way, Michael withdrew five hundred euros.'

'He could have been forced to make that

withdrawal,' I say, because Michael has never been the sort to withdraw money from our account without asking me, and certainly not that amount. Five hundred euros? Are they sure? Isn't that more than the daily ATM amount? DS Jahan tells me that unlike British ATMs, many French ATMs don't have caps on withdrawals, but still, I'm having a hard time understanding why Michael would be withdrawing that amount of money of his own volition.

'Maybe this man was there to make sure he withdrew the cash,' I say, and my stomach flips.

'We'll look into the identity of the guy who gave Michael the nod, just in case,' DS Jahan says. 'We're in touch with the French police.'

The sight of Michael in the footage leaves me shaking from head to toe, my heart beating in my throat.

'Have you any idea where he's staying?' I ask in a shaky voice. 'Have you checked out the hotels?'

DS Jahan draws a sharp breath, and I can tell he's frustrated, that something isn't going the way he wanted. 'Ordinarily these kind of searches are straightforward. We can use ANPR or cell-site analysis to get an address fairly quickly. But in this case, Michael appears not to be using his mobile phone and he seems to be using public transport.'

If the man in the footage had kidnapped Michael, he wouldn't be staying at a hotel, or even a hostel. They'd keep him in a house somewhere, in a basement. Chris Holloway. He has Michael. He is forcing his hand, bleeding him dry. Chris knew about Mont Blanc. And he isn't going to stop until he gets revenge.

And yet I can't tell the police a word of this. They'll ask questions. Why would someone be seeking revenge? And everything would unravel, picking our world apart piece by piece. That's why Michael is in France, playing along, doing whatever Chris says. He's protecting our family.

'We're just beginning to see what resources the French police can pull together,' DS Jahan says, his voice clipped with frustration. 'It's a little more complicated when a charge hasn't been brought against someone, but that's in progress.'

'A charge?' Jeannie says, glancing from me to the detectives. I'm so lost in my thoughts that I don't figure out what she's asking. DCI Lavery laces her hands, takes a breath.

'We investigated the other bank accounts in yours and Michael's names,' she explains. 'And we also looked at the JustGiving account that was set up for the bookshop. We know that just over eleven thousand pounds was raised for the bookshop, so we wondered why that money never reached your business account.'

I look across their faces. 'What do you mean, never reached our business account?'

'The bank details appear to have been changed sometime in the last couple of months to redirect the money to another bank account based in the Caribbean,' DS Jahan adds. 'We're still looking into it but one of our team working on crimes committed via the dark web thinks it's a familiar transaction.'

I reel. '*The dark web?*'

I assume that the dark web is something to do with the internet. 'I don't do social media or anything like that,' I say quickly. 'I'm a bit of a Luddite so not up to speed with everything online.'

'It's basically an underground internet for criminals,' DCI Lavery explains. 'You've heard of eBay, I'm guessing?' I nod. 'Well, imagine an eBay for people who want to sell their services as an assassin, or a kidnapper. That's basically what one of our teams investigate online. We have a list of flagged names and offshore bank accounts where payments are often made before being bounced on to the bank accounts of the crims — like a Paypal for bad guys, if you will. The account that the bookshop money was transferred to was one of those flagged accounts.'

I try to process this. Jeannie reaches out and takes my hand. A moment or two when she meets my eye, a look of sadness and solidarity there.

'Can I ask a question, Helen?' DS Jahan asks. I notice DCI Lavery lowering her eyes.

'Of course.'

'Did you really not know that the money from the JustGiving fund hadn't reached your account?'

Silence falls like a guillotine. Both DCI Lavery and DC Fields have their eyes fixed on the carpet. Why is he asking this?

'No,' I say. 'No . . . '

'You had access to the business account, didn't you?' he presses. 'It's in both your names.'

I nod. Is he suggesting I had something to do

324

with the transfer? 'Yes, I . . . it's Michael's business . . . '

'But — a joint account. And the company has both of you listed as directors.'

'Yes. But I work as a primary school teacher. I don't have the time to do that *and* manage the business. The shop is — was — Michael's baby.'

DS Jahan begins to answer but DCI Lavery cuts him off.

'We spoke to Dr Fowad, your family GP at Lilyfield Medical Centre. It seems that you've had a prescription for antidepressants running back ten years. Do you mind if I ask why you were taking antidepressants?'

'I've had anxiety issues ever since Reuben was born,' I say. *And a long while before that.*

'And what about Michael?' DS Jahan says. 'We've another note saying he had sleep issues.'

'Sometimes, yes,' I say cautiously. 'But generally he was absolutely fine. Michael's a kind, sensitive man. He puts our family first in everything . . . ' I think back to the moment I reached into the fire bin in the back garden and saw the destroyed frame of my precious painting, a few fragments of canvas revealing the dancers' faces. He bought me that painting to bring me hope that, one day, I might return to dancing. I might accomplish the dream I had of opening my own dance studio. By destroying it he knew he was symbolically destroying my dream, and *that* was the real anguish, the real pain that entered my heart and never left.

'We have a confession from the van driver in Belize naming Michael as the instigator of the

325

crash,' DS Jahan says carefully. 'We've checked Matus' bank accounts. A recent transaction of what equates to eleven thousand pounds was made prior to the crash.'

'There is simply no way that has anything to do with us . . . ' I stammer, but DCI Lavery continues in a slow, firm voice, as though she's speaking to a child.

'Helen, our investigation has led us to believe that your husband arranged for someone to crash into your vehicle after a final, magical family holiday in an attempt to take his own life along with those of his children.' She pauses. 'And yours.'

I feel the room tilt, the air change. '*What?*'

'When that was unsuccessful, we believe that he slipped out of the hospital to avoid charge.'

I stand up, head towards the window. I need air. I need to get out of here.

DCI Lavery rises and stands close to me. I hold on to the window ledge to stop myself from collapsing. My knees are weak and it feels like my lungs are going to explode.

'Are you alright?' she asks, and I shake my head. She's shorter than me. The sunlight makes a halo of her silvery hair, picking out indigo shards in her eyes. Her tone is one of pity. 'Murder-suicide is a massive problem all over the world among white males in their thirties and forties,' she says, and I nod as if I might placate her by agreeing to this statement. 'Occasionally, parents of children with complex needs form a plan together. Did he discuss anything like this with you?'

With a sickening twist of my stomach I realise what she is saying. *Did Michael ask you to make a suicide pact?*

I blurt out a wild laugh. 'You're wrong . . . This isn't . . . '

'Sometimes, it's the people who are closest to you that will shock you the most,' DC Fields summarises from across the room.

I focus on the children playing on the street. Lucy and Daniel from number forty-two. Lucy and Saskia played together often, and I see Lucy glancing at the house every so often, as though searching for her face in the window.

'You're implying that Michael transferred the money from the JustGiving fund to the van driver,' I tell DCI Lavery. 'But . . . there would have to be an email from Michael to someone organising this, or a foreign number on his phone bill. I've checked his emails meticulously.'

'Emails are easy to delete,' she says with a sigh, and I begin to tell her that I had also read the bookshop emails, hundreds of them, line by line, both sent and received, in case I might find a clue, some hint of where he was, and why.

'He could have an email account that you don't know about,' DS Jahan says from the sofa. 'Communications on the dark net are done through a dedicated chat system. It would be highly unlikely that a dialogue of this nature is going to turn up in a Hotmail or Google account.'

Of this nature.

'We have a specialist team of forensic psychologists working alongside us,' DCI Lavery says, turning back to the sofa and slipping the tablet back into its case. She glances at me to follow, have a seat, and I comply. 'The data they're presenting on this type of crime is shocking. Usually heterosexual men with mortgages and families. Ordinary people facing exceptional circumstances. Losing their job, not being able to provide for their family — it can just make them snap and act completely out of character, but with extremely tragic consequences.'

I sit down, trying to ignore the listing room. 'Michael's livelihood has been destroyed but that doesn't mean he . . . '

'I think you need to consider the possibility that Michael started the fire at the bookstore, too,' she says. 'We're fairly confident that the green Zafira captured by the village CCTV on the night of the blaze was his car.'

I feel my throat and lungs constrict to nothingness, my heart stuttering at the suggestion that the fire has added to the suspicion around Michael, that they actually believe my husband is capable of such a hideous, unthinkable act as killing his own family.

Because Michael was completely right. The fire wasn't started by kids.

The fire was started by me.

PART THREE

42

Helen

12th December 1995

I pulled out of dance school yesterday. I haven't been in six months so I can't imagine they expected anything less. I didn't tell any of my classmates. I told Ronnie, Medbh and Judith that Luke died, that there was an accident. They showed me a newspaper article. There were five photographs of him and a headline:

Oxford Student Dies in Climbing Accident

I was hysterical. Seeing it confirmed in black and white was too real. It was like watching him fall all over again.

I don't know how I survived the first few days back from Chamonix. My memory of those days is virtually nonexistent. Ronnie brought me food, left it on my table. I moved out, taking only a small bag of belongings, slept on friends' floors. I'm skin and bone, a plastic bag caught on the wind. My hair has fallen out in handfuls. This grief is planetary. I don't feel like I'm alive. His absence is the only tangible, real thing. The knowledge that I will never hold him again, never touch him again, shatters me into a thousand pieces every single moment.

Madame Proulx came to see me this morning. When I peered through the crack in the living room curtains I was so shocked to see her there in her velvet turquoise cape and feathered hat that I let her in. I'm at Medbh's house, sleeping in the spare room. I knew Madame Proulx was here to urge me to continue dancing. I remember when I was about ten and going through that awkward phase, she said that a true dancer had to be like fire. Flames only exist because they dance, she said. When they stop dancing, they become ash. I had to imagine myself as fire, and every time my muscles burned and my feet bled I imagined them as part of the dancing flames and it helped me persist. Plus I have a lead role in *The Nutcracker* all through the Christmas period. We have twenty-nine shows lined up. Kate's a good understudy but Madame Proulx always preferred me. I knew she was really only here to talk me into going through with the show.

She had brought me a basket of bread and cheese and grapes. I looked like I'd gone ten rounds with Mike Tyson, my face swollen from crying, still in last week's clothes, tissues all over the place. She looked at me and the state of my room with unveiled pity. 'My dear,' she said. 'The loss of someone you loved is a wound you will carry for the rest of your life. But it *will* become bearable.'

I nodded and pretended I agreed but I knew she had no idea what this felt like. How could she? No one has ever loved another person the way I loved him. Crazy, obsessive love. I loved him more than I loved myself.

I told Madame Proulx I would come back to dance school and she was reassured enough to leave with a smile on her face. She said she would be back next week to check in on me and made me promise that I would eat and sleep. I have no intention of going back to dance school, nor do I intend to eat or sleep.

I put on my clothes, then write a note for Medbh that I'm not coming back and not to worry about me. I tell her she can have my red corduroy jacket for letting me stay and taking care of me. It always looked better on her anyway.

It's two in the morning, pitch black with snow on the ground. The ice pinches at my toes and cheeks as I walk down the street. It's a good feeling, a relief to be numbed, to have my thoughts pulled towards physical pain. I walk to the train station and walk towards the tracks. Then I lie down, pull out the Polaroid of me and Luke on our half-year anniversary, and wait.

The stars overhead gleam and twinkle. I remember singing 'Twinkle Twinkle Little Star' to Jeannie when she was a baby. She's ten, now. I haven't seen her since Easter. She's settled with the Carney family and they much preferred her over me. I was the stroppy teenager, Jeannie the cute eight-year-old who still enjoyed teddies and cuddles. I couldn't wait to leave that place.

I think of them telling Jeannie and me that our mother had died. I didn't blink. I might have said, 'Good,' though I didn't mean it. I wanted to be defiant, to show that Mum had no hold over me, not even in death. Jeannie burst into tears. She cried for days, kept asking where Mum had gone. She hadn't seen our mother for two years before that and even then Mum was distant and distracted. She only saw us for an hour a week, and with a social worker lurking in the background. Still, Jeannie was always so eager to see her, to please her.

I think I can hear a train coming. I squeeze my eyes shut and pray it'll be quick.

Jeannie was unsettled after Mum's death. She kept crying for me to come and pick her up but I couldn't bring her all the way to London. I'm a student. I couldn't possibly care for a child *and* go to dance school. And she'd been happy at the Carneys before.

I think of her hearing the news that her sister has died. I'm all she has, now. How will this affect her?

A horn sounds. I sit upright and see a white dot of light in the distance. I'm so cold I can hardly feel my arms and legs, but somehow I manage to shuffle to the side of the tracks right as a train thunders through the station, the suck of the wheels incredibly strong, almost pulling me under. The Polaroid of me and Luke is ripped from my hands and shredded by the force of the train. I curl into a tight ball and hold on to a piece of iron jutting up from the ground to stop myself from being dragged under.

When it passes, I know I can't do this. I can't do it to Jeannie.

So I go home, and when Ronnie questions me about the note I tell her I'm moving out. I'll get a job closer to Grimsby and visit Jeannie. I'll give Luke a second funeral in my heart.

Somehow I have to forget him in order to survive.

43

Reuben

6th September 2017

Malfoy: I think your whale looks amazing. The breach is super-realistic. Just need to work on the waves. Did you check out that free stock footage website?

Roo: ☺ ☺ ☺ I'm glad you like the whale! I was worried that you'd think it was rubbish. Your pirate ship was WICKED.

Malfoy: I *love* it. I can send you a YouTube link to some tutorials for shape tweening. Waves are hard to get right :/

Roo: Thanx

Malfoy: I need you to send me the footage I asked for in exchange for the YouTube link.

Roo: What footage?

Malfoy: Did u forget?

Roo: No. Maybe.

Malfoy: You didn't record the police

	interviewing your mother?
Roo:	Oh yeah I did ☺
Malfoy:	Phew.
Roo:	It's audio only tho is that a problem
Malfoy:	No. Send it now.
Roo:	Is this the dangerous thing u were going to tell me bout?
Malfoy:	What?
Roo:	The police interview. They asked about my dad a lot.
Malfoy:	That depends.
Roo:	On what?
Malfoy:	Well, I haven't listened to the interview yet so I don't know what they asked your mum.
Roo:	For me to send this u hav to tell me your real name.
Malfoy:	hahaha
Roo:	what's so funny?
Malfoy:	this is iPix, nobody uses real names. Only avatars.
Roo:	Yeah but this is different. I have to be able to trust u so tell me ur real name so I know u aren't a bad person
Malfoy:	I promise you I'm not a bad person.
Roo:	so tell me ur name then
Malfoy:	David.
Roo:	David who?
Malfoy:	David Reynolds.

```
Roo:      I don't beleive u
Malfoy:  That is my name.
Roo:      Y  do  u  keep  asking  me  to
          record my family??
Malfoy:  For your protection.
```

44

Helen

7th September 2017

I toss and turn all night, wracked with grief and guilt. I can hear Reuben grinding his teeth in the room next to mine. I go into his bedroom and slip his mouth guard between his teeth, ending the awful crunch of molar on molar. Then I go into Saskia's bedroom and lie down on her rug, breathing in the smell of her, dissolving quickly into tears.

The narrative that the police have constructed is that sometime during our family holiday, Michael contacted someone in Belize and said, *Here's eleven thousand pounds. Make it look like an accident.*

I tell myself that there is simply no way Michael is capable of such a thing.

A voice in my head whispers, *But what if he knew you burned down the bookshop?* I feel a deep terror creep upon me. What would he do if he found out? It was a thought that never crossed my mind at the time, but then I never expected the fire to grow so big. I feel stupid, utterly consumed with self-hatred. Michael built that shop from nothing and took immense pride in how successful it became. And when the public library closed down, our shop became even more vital and popular. Before, Michael had worked long hours to pay the bills. Now, he was working seventy or eighty hours a week to keep kids interested in books and to support local community groups.

And I destroyed it all.

What if that's what he discovered in the hospital? What if that's the reason he left? Michael's anger is the dangerous kind. Whereas mine is quick to show and just as fast to burn out, Michael's temper simmers for a long while, then erupts. A volcanic fury.

I can't sleep now, and it's not guilt that sends me down the stairs and peering out the windows, expecting to see a shadow outside.

It's fear.

I open the front door and step outside, looking over the street. No one is around. Smoke wafts gently from several chimneys in the distance, the smell of turf clinging to the cool, damp air. I'm barefoot, but I step out into the garden and walk out on to the street. I can feel it, now. The eyes that follow.

We both know kids didn't start that fire. He said that right before the accident, when we were lying in the hammock at the beach hut. I remember the bitter tone of his voice. I remember the way he looked at me when he staggered out of the blaze. He'd gone rushing in to try to put out the flames but quickly realised the blaze was already too big, bursting out of the windows and consuming the shop floor.

At the time I raced inside to help him. He had an armful of books that he was trying to salvage and was filmed in soot. My lungs screamed for air. When we reached the cool air outside we fell to the ground, gasping and choking. I rolled over and saw him on all fours, looking across at me.

That look. I tried to dismiss it at the time. It was a look that spoke volumes. *What have you done?*

There is nowhere I can go. Even here at Jeannie's AirBnB, he'll find me. With a deep, gut-churning shudder, I turn back inside, lock the door behind me, and climb into bed with the letters spread over the sheets. Michael read these. What must he have thought? How furious must he be with me?

For a long time I consider that showing these to the police is my only option. I can show them, tell them Michael is innocent. And yet they will only ask questions. Who was Luke Aucoin? Why did the writer call you a murderer?

I can never tell them the whole story. It was the reason we chose silence in the first place. To protect our family. We risk losing Reuben and Saskia.

'Helen?'

Jeannie appears in the doorway of the bedroom with a tray of coffee and buttered toast. I'm still surrounded by the letters, spread over the sheets. I make to tidy them away quickly but she sees.

'What are these?' she says, picking one up.

'They were sent to us over a number of years,' I say hesitantly. 'I got them from the bookshop

341

the other day. I think they have something to do with Michael's disappearance.'

She flicks through them, absorbing the content, her eyes widening when she sees the word 'murderer'.

'Who's Michael King?' she asks.

'Michael,' I say, my voice trembling. 'His name was once Michael King.'

'Michael *King*? When did he become Michael Pengilly, then?'

'About twenty-two years ago. He changed it to his mother's surname.'

'Why?'

I begin to cry. She takes my hand, looks over the letters a second time.

'Helen, what is going on? Why has someone sent you these?'

I tell her. In great blustering sobs I tell her about the trek twenty-two years ago. About Luke and Theo, meeting Michael for the first time. About the fall.

'Luke was unconscious,' I say, shivering with waves of shock as I recall it. 'He was hanging on the end of the rope. We were calling to him . . . the rope was about to break any second.'

We never talked about what had happened. We never wanted to face up to it.

And yet, it had lived with us every day of our lives. It was with us in the room when Reuben was born, a shadow that reminded me that all of this — my marriage, my newborn son, my life — could have, and perhaps *should* have, ended that day on the mountain. Every moment of happiness was a debt.

Jeannie sits down on the bed and says nothing while I tell her everything, confessing it. Again and again she refers to the letter, looking over the envelopes, absorbing the awful truths I'm divulging.

'You were only nine,' I say. 'Michael and I never told anyone a word of this. We were so young at the time.'

'Did you speak to the police?'

I shake my head, tears spilling down my cheeks. 'We never told anyone. It was so horrific . . . We both just disappeared.'

'But . . . how did you and Michael end up getting together?'

I tell her about bumping into each other on the train platform. How it was both awkward and like a homecoming, because we were the only two people on the planet who knew the dimensions of grief at Luke's death. Our knowledge of what the other was going through, of that terrible guilt, was a powerful intimacy. It was Michael who brought me peace, who taught me to love again.

'Michael and I, we never spoke about it,' I say. 'It wasn't murder. But we never spoke to Luke's parents and told them the truth so heaven knows what conclusions they drew from that . . . '

'You said Luke had a brother,' she says, shuffling through the letters. 'He was there, wasn't he? When the fall happened?'

I nod. 'He was destroyed by it.'

She nods, visibly struggling to keep apace. 'But . . . if Luke's brother was *there*, wouldn't he have told everyone that it was an accident?'

343

'I thought he would have,' I whisper. 'But time distorts everything, doesn't it? Maybe he started to think differently about it. Maybe he started to think that Michael and I planned it or something.'

My throat tightens painfully as though a fist is squeezing my windpipe. I've seen Theo many times over the years. On the tube, in the supermarket, on TV. At our wedding in Gretna Green — Michael in a charity-shop suit and me in a tulip-print dress off Tesco's sale rack — I broke into a cold sweat when I saw Theo brooding in the cloisters. I was so shaken that I stopped the ceremony halfway through and wandered off to have a look. Michael gave a nervous laugh, made a joke about me getting cold feet while the registrar cleared his throat. It wasn't Theo at all, of course — just a floral arrangement on a long black stand. And then at Reuben's baby group, one of the dads got a bit freaked out when I kept staring. He was Theo's double.

'Do you think he's the one sending threats?' Jeannie asks. 'This Theo.'

'I don't know. His name doesn't appear anywhere. I found this.' I show her the envelope signed 'Chris Holloway'.

'Does that name mean anything to you?'

I shake my head and draw my knees up to my chest. 'He's been sending letters every year to one of our old addresses. And then this year, he found us here.'

'The twenty-fifth of June . . . why does that ring a bell?' she says, looking over the postmarks.

'Was that when the fire happened?'

I nod. Her eyes widen.

'Then why didn't you show these to the police?' she says, exasperated. 'Helen, this is crazy. You have proof that someone was watching you, that someone was making serious threats. And that the date of the fire coincided with these. The police want to *charge* Michael with bloody murder-suicide! Why didn't you show them these?'

I can't answer her. She looks at me as if I am insane.

'What are you not telling me?' she says.

Right then a bleeping sound cuts through the room, the repetitive chime of a digital alarm or mobile phone. She looks around. 'Is that your phone ringing?'

I pat the pocket of my nightgown. My mobile phone is there, still as a stone.

The bleeping continues. We lift cushions and books to find the source, peer beneath the duvet and mattress. Just then, Reuben comes in. He's wearing his *Star Wars* pyjamas and holds his iPad in front of him.

'Are you OK, Roo?' Jeannie asks.

'Sssh!' He waves his hand at her. She jerks back in her seat, silenced. He keeps his gaze on the screen and shuffles towards the spot on the bed where Jeannie is sitting, then plunges his hand beneath her. Jeannie gets up with a shout. Reuben draws up the object making the sound: Saskia's teddy, Jack-Jack.

'Ha!' he says, tapping the screen of his iPad. Immediately the bleeping stops.

Jeannie and I look on in bewilderment as he makes to head back upstairs with the teddy clutched tight to his chest. He looks over at me sheepishly. 'I like to sleep with Jack-Jack,' he says. Then, so quiet I can barely hear: 'So I can be close to Saskia.'

I scramble out of bed and approach him, my eyes fixed on the screen of his iPad. 'What was that noise just before? Why was Jack-Jack bleeping like that?'

'Look,' he says, tapping the screen. 'It's cool. You can track him *anywhere*. If you lose him you can bring up a map and it tells you where he is. Well, not exactly. It didn't tell me he was down the side of the bed but that's why there's a noise on it, so you find his exact location.'

I turn to Jeannie. She bought Jack-Jack for Saskia, and I know it's upsetting for her to see it. She reaches out for the teddy and as Reuben passes him to her I notice something different about it.

A round baby-pink tag on his bloodstained collar, about the size of a ten-pence piece and twice as thick.

'It was a good idea to put that tag on him,' Reuben says then, glancing up at me. 'Pity he wasn't wearing that when we were in Cancún. We wouldn't have had to spend hours and hours looking for him.'

'This tag?' Jeannie says, finding it with finger and thumb. 'It's a name tag, isn't it? Funny name for a teddy, though. I thought she named him Jack-Jack?'

I step closer and finger the tag.

'I never put this on him,' I say. Jeannie raises it

up, and I see the lettering on the tag. TRKLite.

'How did you know it makes a sound?' I ask Reuben, and he tells me that the tag can track Jack-Jack anywhere in the world. He says he was able to bring up the digital map locating Jack-Jack as we left Belize and followed his journey all the way back to the UK on the Medevac plane. The more he explains the more bewildered I feel, and when he sees me growing upset he starts to click his fingers and stumble over his words. Jeannie intervenes, widening her smile and coaxing him to sit down on the bed.

'Reuben, darling,' she says impatiently. 'Explain it to us again? You can connect to the tag on Jack-Jack's collar with your iPad . . . '

He nods, then brings up the website for TRKLite and shows it to us.

'It's a crap website,' he says, disgusted. 'I could have done it *much* better.'

Flashing on the screen, an image of small round tags in various colours, and a banner that says, 'TRKLite! The new Bluetooth tracking device! Only £39.99!' A video featuring a smiley blonde woman explains it to us: you can attach it to keys or luggage and keep track of it anywhere in the world, just as Reuben said. All you have to do is download the app to a mobile device, *et voila*, a little red dot blinks on a digital map, locating your belongings.

When Reuben goes back to his room, Jeannie studies me with narrowed eyes. 'How did that tag end up on the teddy?' she says slowly.

The tag and collar lie on the bed in front of us like an explosive device.

45

Helen

7th September 2017

'How long has the tag been on the teddy?' Jeannie says.

It's like asking me how big the universe is. 'I have no idea.'

'Was it there when you were in Belize?'

'I can't remember.'

'What about when you were in Mexico? Could one of the people on the tour group have done it?'

I put my face in my hands, my mind racing. 'I don't know.'

She folds her arms, flustered. 'Maybe we should ask Reuben . . . '

'It'll be in the photographs,' I say. 'Michael took loads of photographs.'

'Wasn't his camera destroyed in the crash?'

I nod. 'But Reuben set up a thing called Dropbox so we could upload all our photographs. Michael uploaded all the photos to save storage on the camera.'

'Where is it?'

'It's online.'

She rolls her eyes. 'I *know* Dropbox is online. I

mean, where's your device? Have you got a tablet or were they all destroyed in the crash?

'We can use Reuben's iPad. I think I just have to sign in.'

We call Reuben back into the room and ask him very gently if we can borrow his iPad. He's reluctant to give it over but Jeannie offers to buy him a pair of top-of-the-range headphones, then promises to get his iPad's cracked screen fixed, and he agrees. Luckily he recalls the password, too, and within seconds I'm back on our holiday, confronted by over four hundred images of Before. Images of the humpback whales, of Michael and Saskia posing on the boat, their arms around each other and their faces lit up with smiles. Images from just three, four weeks ago, and yet a lifetime ago.

'It's OK, Helen,' Jeannie says, rubbing my back when I start to cry. 'Stay focused. Deep breaths. We're just looking for the tag, remember?'

There are hardly any images of Jack-Jack. There is one on the plane at Heathrow, a blurry picture of Saskia in a window seat with the teddy on her lap, giving Reuben a cheeky grin. I figure out how to zoom in — the tag is there, a small but definite round shape at his neck.

'Progress,' Jeannie says.

I find images from before the holiday, from months ago. Christmas photographs: Michael captured bleary-eyed and mid-yawn in our living room on Christmas morning as Saskia rips Santa-themed wrapping paper from her new toy pram, eyes wide as saucers. Jack-Jack is on the floor amongst the shredded paper, but no sign of a tag. Another image of Saskia at the dinner table pulling a face for the camera, her hands perched under her chin, her beautiful blonde hair in bunches.

On the table, just by her elbow, is the white shape of Jack-Jack. No sign of the tag. I zoom as much as I can to be sure, but it definitely isn't there. I note the date of the image file. July 14th. One day before Michael punched Ben Trevitt and eight days before we flew to Mexico.

I want to reach into the images and stop us from boarding the plane. I burn to scroll back, keep us frozen in time, re-spool the flames from the bookshop back into the head of the match in my hands. I ache to keep hitting the little image of a trashcan to delete everything bad that happened, right to the moment I met Michael.

If only the past was as easy to erase as photographs.

'So,' Jeannie says, re-ordering the images. 'This photograph is taken on April thirtieth, and the teddy has no tag. The next image we have of him is July twenty-third, on the plane to Mexico, and he has the tag on his collar. So sometime between May and July, while you're still at home, the tag appears on his collar.' She fixes her eyes on me. 'You know what that means, don't you?'

'Someone would have had to get close enough to Saskia to put that tag on him,' I say slowly, and every hair on my body stands on end. A skin is ripped from the world I knew, revealing another filled with eyes and malice.

Jeannie covers her mouth with her hand, turns her eyes to the screen. I know the thoughts that are spinning across her mind, because they're my thoughts, too. Why would someone go to that much trouble to keep tabs on our location? In a horrible rush, it comes to me: if someone wanted to take out our car, make it look like an accident, they might put a tag on an object that's going to be with us the whole time. And what better way to conceal it than a child's toy?

'Didn't Saskia say anything about the tag?' Jeannie says, scrolling frantically through the images. 'She's not the sort of kid who'd fail to notice something different about Jack-Jack.'

I swallow hard. A new angle presses into the air, one I can barely allow myself to think. Chris Holloway spoke to Saskia. He persuaded her — or forced her — to put the tag on Jack-Jack. *Oh, God.*

'What's this?' Jeannie says, bringing up a folder marked 'Josh's drone'.

I'm gulping back air at the thought of someone forcing Saskia to put the tag on the teddy. I try and imagine her reaction. She'd scream, run away. She would have told me, wouldn't she? Even if they threatened her.

'Helen, look,' Jeannie urges, tapping the screen with a fingernail.

There are thirty-eight video files between twenty seconds and twenty-six minutes long. I click on one and immediately find myself looking down on our village from about fifty feet in the air. The drone moves over the chapel, the fountain in the middle of the village, then drifts up the high street towards our shop.

As it circles back towards the town a black car is parked around the corner from the shop. I can just make out a man sitting in the passenger seat, a small thread of cigarette smoke curling up from the open window.

I have Jeannie click on more videos. Aerial footage of the countryside and the coast, the pretty seaside towns of Berwick-upon-tweed and Alnmouth captured during a golden sunrise. Several others of the village.

'The car is in this one, too,' I tell Jeannie. 'Look.'

It's a week after the previous video. This time the man is pacing the street, occasionally glancing up at the shop. He's got black hair and a long black coat, white trainers. Michael comes out of the shop, looks up and down. I'm almost certain he must catch a glimpse of the man, who jumps back around the corner and ducks into his car, slamming the door. As the drone turns back, Michael keeps his gaze in the man's direction before turning to look at the shop.

I note the date stamp. 7/4/17. Didn't Michael write that date in his notebook? Something about a man watching him?

'Do you recognise him?' Jeannie says when I press 'pause', freezing him at the moment that he goes to get into the car.

I shake my head. She reverses the footage and we watch again.

'He's certainly sneaking around, isn't he?' she says, zooming in. 'Look. He's taking pictures. See that, in his hand?'

She zooms in to 50x, and although the image is badly pixelated I see something small and black in his hand. I give a deep shudder. The last letter had been sent to the bookshop. No redirection label from our Cardiff address. They had found us.

'Maybe if we can find his registration number, we can look him up,' she says.

It takes a few attempts, but eventually we catch a frame where the registration plate at the rear of the car is just visible. WD61 OWE. A black Renault Megane.

'I had to do this in January,' Jeannie says, opening up a browser on the screen and tapping the registration details. 'Someone reversed into me on Parson's Street and drove off. My dash-cam caught the bugger's details, thank you very much. You go to the DVLA website, fill in a form, pay some money, and they can give you limited details. A name, sometimes an address, depending on what you say you need it for.'

She downloads a form headed 'Trying to establish the condition of a vehicle before purchase'.

'Says it can take up to four weeks for the information to come through. But at least we got this.' She fixes me with a hard stare. 'Promise me you'll take it to the police first, Helen. No more breaking and entering.'

'I promise.'

Just then, a chime sounds from Jeannie's phone. She looks up from her phone to me.

'Is it from the DVLA?'

She beams at me. 'Yup.'

'What does it say?'

She rubs a thumb up the screen, her face aglow with the light of the screen.

'His name is Kareem Ballinger,' she says, her

353

brown eyes glinting with excitement. 'Shall we Google him?'

To:
info@smartsurveillance.org.uk
From: h.pengilly@bookmine.co.uk
Subject: Michael Pengilly
Sent: 7th September 2017 22.31

Dear Kareem
I'm sorry this email comes out of the blue but I wish to ask you about my husband. It seems you own a Private Investigation firm and I have discovered that you were in our area recently.
Our family has experienced a terrible accident and are investigating the cause. If you feel able to, I'd like to find out more about what you were investigating in our village?

Kind regards
Helen Pengilly

To: h.pengilly@bookmine.co.uk
cc: info@smartsurveillance.org.uk
From: kareem@smartsurveillance.org.uk
Subject: Confidential
Sent: 7th September 2017 22.48

Dear Helen
This is interesting. I was indeed

investigating in your village.

Before I say more, can you tell me what 'terrible accident' you are referring to?

Best, K

To: kareem@smartsurveillance.org.uk
From: h.pengilly@bookmine.co.uk
Subject: Re: Confidential
Sent: 7th September 2017 22.51

Dear Kareem

My family was involved in a serious car accident in Belize that appears to be a deliberate attempt on our lives. My husband is now missing and we fear he may have been kidnapped.

Did you have anything to do with this? Do you know where he might be?

Helen

To: h.pengilly@bookmine.co.uk
cc: info@smartsurveillance.org.uk
From: kareem@smartsurveillance.org.uk
Subject: Confidential
Sent: 7th September 2017 22.55

Dear Helen

That is very alarming news.

I do have information that may

prove useful. I would prefer not to disclose this information via telephone or email but wish to meet you in person. Please can you meet with me at York Train Station as soon as possible? I can meet tomorrow morning.

Sincerely,
Kareem Ballinger
CEO Smart Surveillance

46

Helen

8th September 2017

We are on the 10.04 from Newcastle-upon-Tyne to York.

Jeannie takes the plastic lid off her coffee and pours in two sugar sachets. She's still wearing yesterday's make-up and looks tired. Neither of us has slept very much.

'We should have told the police,' she says, turning her eyes to the man at the table across from us who is typing furiously on his laptop. 'Or at least sought legal advice.'

'I don't have time,' I say flatly. 'I don't need anyone's approval to speak to someone who was clearly spying on us. He's a private investigator. Someone hired him.'

'Can I ask you a question?' Jeannie says in a low voice.

'No.'

Her face falls. 'Oh.'

'Of course you can ask me a question, Jeannie.'

'Oh, OK. Well, you know Michael's dream diary? And all that stuff about the door of flame?'

'Yes?'

'Did he dream that before or after the fire at the bookshop?'

I narrow my eyes at her. 'I've no idea. Why?'

She visibly bites something back. Replaces it with a more tactful observation. 'Well, it's a bit weird to be dreaming of a door of flame right before the bookstore mysteriously goes up in flames, don't you think?'

I know what she's implying. 'Michael is no arsonist, Jeannie. He didn't start that fire.'

She holds me in a deep look, arches a perfectly drawn eyebrow. 'You're sure of that?'

'I'm sure.'

She leans forward, lowers her voice. 'Would you have said the same thing about the painting? That Michael would never have destroyed it?'

I turn away. The memory pierces me.

'And by the way,' she continues, having heard my answer in the silence. 'Technically *that* was arson. So don't say Michael isn't an arsonist.'

I can't tell her about the fire. I can't tell her I did it. She'll never understand.

'You can tell me anything, you know,' she says, suddenly obsequious. 'I know you still see me as your irritating little sister making stage sets out of bean poles and shower curtains, demanding everyone watch me perform. But I'm thirty-one now. I'm actually able to keep secrets these days.'

For a moment, I consider. I say, 'I've told you my biggest secret.'

She leans back in her seat, sips her coffee thoughtfully. 'All this stuff on Mont Blanc happened so long ago. Why didn't you confront

358

it at the time? Or a few years afterwards, even?'

'I was deep in grief after Luke died,' I say quietly.

'You were in love with him,' she says. It's not a question. I sense that she's delighted to learn that Michael wasn't my first love.

'I was only nineteen,' I say. 'It was reckless, obsessive love. Not the sort Michael and I have.'

She considers that.

'I felt so guilty,' I say, wiping away a tear that comes out of nowhere. 'I didn't know how to handle it. Fight or flight.'

'But what about when you started getting the letters?' she says, lowering her voice. 'Why not just contact the people who sent them?'

Her wide grey eyes are fixed on me but I can't meet her gaze. *How can I explain?* I speak slowly, picking through my words as though they're covered in glass shard. 'We had Reuben by then. The letters were obviously sent because they thought we'd killed Luke, that his death wasn't an accident. Luke's family were filthy rich. They'd obviously hired some big legal firm to take us to court. Michael and I had no way of fighting those big lawyers. We thought . . . ' My throat tightens at the thought of it, of losing our children. 'It could still happen.'

'It's just . . . hear me out,' she says, when she can see that I'm overwhelmed. 'What if Michael hasn't been kidnapped at all?'

I shake my head, refusing to consider it. 'I don't think he would have left us in the hospital in Belize without saying something.'

'But . . . you said he saw the letters. Do you

think he's gone to see this man? This Chris Holloway?'

I fall silent. 'It's possible, yes. Michael would do anything to protect the kids.'

She raises her eyebrows. 'And you? Do you think he'd do anything to protect you?'

I don't answer. The truth is I don't know anymore.

★   ★   ★

'Kareem?'

'You must be Helen,' the man says, rising from his chair and extending a hand.

'This is my sister, Jeannie.'

He shakes her hand. 'I know.'

The footage from the drone was grainy, and yet I recognise him: the dark, greasy hair that turns out to be a comb-over, the slightly irregular posture, long, feminine fingers. It jolts me, meeting someone I caught in the act of watching our family. My first instinct is trepidation, wariness, until I see stains on the thighs of his trousers and feel reassured that he is, after all, just a human being. A Yorkshire accent inflected with Pakistani. Jowly, droopy eyed, a small shaving cut on his left jaw. A wedding band. We're in a small café just outside York station: very public and loud.

'Would you like anything to eat?' he asks politely. Jeannie and I shake our heads. Food is far from our minds.

He asks about the train journey, Jeannie remarks that she's not been to York before. A moment's faltering silence. Finally, I whisper,

'Thanks for emailing me back.'

He smiles, gives a small nod. 'Pleasure. You mentioned a serious car accident. What happened?'

It's difficult to slide this narrative into conversation with someone I don't know, and particularly someone whose relationship with my family appears to be voyeuristic and implicitly predatory. I offer the least emotional account of the last two weeks as I possibly can in order to avoid breaking down again.

'My husband and I took our children on holiday to Belize,' I say. 'We were involved in a serious car accident. Except, it was no accident. We were being watched. The person driving the other vehicle knew our precise location. Takes some skills to track someone down, especially when they're in a foreign country. Were you involved in this?'

For all my side-stepping and emotional retraction that hot lump of lava arrives back in my throat, right on cue. I don't take my eyes off him as he processes what I've said.

'I was approached in February by a client who wished to locate you and your husband, Michael,' he says.

I thought I was prepared for this and yet a shiver runs all the way up my spine, a full body shake. Jeannie glances at me and puts her hand on mine. She speaks for me.

'Did they say *why* they wanted you to locate them?'

'Not at first,' he says, frowning. 'They gave me an address in Cardiff, but it quickly became clear

361

that Michael King had not lived there for some time.'

Jeannie leans across the table. 'Who was the client?'

He gives a smile and leans back in his seat, avoiding Jeannie's gaze even though she's right in his face. 'My client informed me that they had made a number of attempts to find Mr King,' he says. 'They had spent a lot of money already. I found him, of course, in Northumberland, and I told the client.'

'Was your client called Chris Holloway?' Jeannie says. 'Or perhaps Theo Aucoin?'

Hearing Theo's name on Jeannie lips is a whole new level of weird. Kareem gives a mild flicker of his eyes. 'I operate a very strict ethical policy, and I must say upfront that I had nothing to do with the events that occurred in Belize,' he says, a little too formally, as though he suspects we're recording him. 'I discovered that you and your husband had planned a holiday in Mexico and informed the client. That was my remit. Nothing more. My business is information. It has never been about violence.' He holds up his hands, as though to prove he has no blood on them.

'On the contrary,' Jeannie says. 'This is entirely about violence.'

Kareem softens, lowers his eyes. 'Indeed. A young child has been seriously injured and I believe your husband is missing. I am very distressed to hear this outcome. I'll show you what I have.'

He reaches down into his briefcase, pulls out a laptop and slides it in front of me. A slideshow of images flashes up on the screen.

'You took these?' I ask. He nods.

There's an image of Michael at the door of the bookshop, turning his key in the lock and glancing straight at the camera with a frown. He's wearing his green parka and mustard-yellow beanie so it must have been taken around March, when the mornings still had a keen nip in the air. There's an image of me, Saskia and Reuben walking to school, Saskia's hair in bunches and her face angled up to mine. Jack-Jack in her arms. No sign of the tag on his collar.

The next image is a screenshot of an email sent to our bookstore account. An airline ticket to Mexico City with Michael's name in it.

'You hacked into our email account?' I say, incredulous.

'No.'

'Then how did you come across our plane tickets for Mexico?'

A small, curious smile, as if I'm very stupid. 'This kind of information comes cheap. Faster than hacking into your personal email account.' His voice is so calm and mild I can imagine a lucrative side-line in hypnosis, or curing people of insomnia by talking at them. 'Before the internet, being a private detective was pretty tough. But now you buy something online and someone somewhere has eight pages of information on you. Your credit history, your address, bank balance, what you eat, et cetera.' He glances at the screen. 'This cost me twenty pounds to pull off a data website.'

'Some ethical policy,' Jeannie says.

'Please. I was only doing my job.'

'Who was the client?' Jeannie says, banging the table lightly with her hand for emphasis. 'Tell us his *name*.' Kareem holds her in a long stare, until Jeannie gives a huge groan of disgust and plucks a thick white envelope from her handbag.

'Two thousand pounds, cash,' she says, ignoring my whispers of protest. 'Tell us who paid you to spy on my sister's family or we walk away.'

Kareem's eyes fall on the envelope. He reaches out for it but Jeannie doesn't let go.

'Chris Holloway. That was the client.'

My heart flips in my chest. 'How much did he pay you?'

'Six thousand pounds.'

'Six thousand pounds to kill our family?' I say, a sudden urge to cry sweeping across me.

He cocks his head, a look of disappointment. 'No, no, no. Of course not. Please. The request was to trace Michael King and find out the names and occupations of his network. Michael King wasn't to be found.' A pause. 'But Michael Pengilly was.'

'And Chris Holloway was satisfied with that?' Jeannie asks.

He takes a drink from his cup, dabs his mouth. 'I believed so. But I started getting emails about the image of the plane ticket I'd sent. One asking about surveillance in Mexico City.'

I feel my sphincter tighten, my hands forming fists. 'My daughter had a tag on her teddy. A tracking device. Was that you?'

He shrugs. 'I know nothing about a tracking device.'

'What about Jonas Matus?' Jeannie asks. 'You

know all about him, don't you?'

'Who?'

'Jonas Matus,' Jeannie repeats tersely. 'Oh, come on. He's the driver who crashed into their car.'

A blank stare. He shakes his head. 'I have never heard of this person.'

'What about Malfoy?' I say then, recalling the name Reuben mentioned. The friend he'd told about Belize. Kareem looks even more confused. He mumbles something about Harry Potter but it's clear he doesn't make a connection.

'So . . . Chris Holloway paid you to find out information on Michael,' I say. 'And that was it?'

Kareem nods.

'You're lying,' I say, he holds up his hands again and I can sense he's itching to take that envelope and walk.

'Look, my husband is gone,' I say, growing emotional. 'We think he's been kidnapped and I *know* your client had something to do with it. Who is Chris Holloway? Where is he? What has he done with Michael?'

'She, not he,' Kareem says. 'Chris Holloway is a woman.' He eyes the envelope. 'I might have her address . . . '

'The address or no money,' Jeannie cautions.

He holds out his hand and Jeannie places the envelope in his palm without letting go.

'She lives in France.'

'Write down the address,' Jeannie says.

Reluctantly he lets go of the envelope, pulls a pen from his shirt pocket and writes something on a napkin. Jeannie hands him the envelope and

365

he tucks it discreetly into an invisible pocket inside his jacket.

'We have to pass that information on to the police,' Jeannie says, reading the napkin.

She pulls out her mobile phone, but Kareem raises his eyes to me. 'I don't think Helen will like that. If you tell the police too much they'll start looking in places that you'd rather they didn't.'

Jeannie looks confused. 'What?'

He turns back to his laptop and taps on the pad, clicking through to the next image. 'Your call, whether or not you want to see,' he says, his face serious. 'But I should warn you that my client has this information.'

The screen shows our bookshop. Late evening. A woman coming out of the shop, wrapped up in a scarf and heavy coat, pulling the shutters down.

Kareem clicks through to the next image, and the next, showing the first signs of the fire, an orange glow appearing behind the shutters. I want him to stop. Smoke barrelling out of the door in heavy black spirals. Flames creeping through the windows upstairs.

'Your client set the bookshop on fire?' Jeannie hisses, fear streaked through her voice.

'I have withheld this information from the police,' Kareem tells me. 'But my client knows.'

'Your client knows what?' Jeannie says. 'Who started it?'

'I thought that this was the reason why they wanted me to watch your family,' he says, curiosity etched on his face. 'I assumed they must have known somehow what your plans were. That they wanted proof that you planned to burn it down.'

Jeannie stares at the screen. 'What is this? Why were you in the shop when the fire started, Helen?'

I can barely bring myself to look her in the eye. I can see her turn from me to Kareem, reading the shame all over my face and the satisfaction on Kareem's. In a handful of seconds her worst suspicions are ringing true.

'Did you . . . Helen, tell me you didn't have anything to do with the fire?'

I keep my head hung low, a hand pressed to my mouth.

'Helen. Tell me you had nothing to do with that fire.'

'I can't,' I whisper.

When I look up her mouth is open and her eyes are dark with horror. It's as though she's seeing me for the very first time.

'You can't be serious,' she whispers. 'You . . . you set fire to the shop? Like, on purpose?'

I nod and squeeze my eyes shut. I can't bear to see the way she's looking at me.

'Why?' She shouts it and looks at me as though I've gone mad. 'Why would you do that?'

'I was trying to talk to Michael about his insomnia,' I blurt out. 'I knew he hadn't been sleeping and suffering because of it . . . I wanted him to try a new medication. I started talking . . . and . . . he just clammed up. He walked out of the room. I was just . . . I couldn't take the silence anymore . . . '

Her forehead is bunched into lines of confusion. 'So you . . . went to the bookshop and burned it to the ground?'

I give a shrill laugh. It sounds so absurd. My laughter turns into a sob.

The eyes of the mountain were watching. I felt them in every corner of our lives, in every triumph, in every sadness. In every 'I love you' I heard myself shout 'Cut the rope!', and every time I uttered our children's names I heard Luke's name. These things might not have been. This love might not have happened. It could have been me hanging off the end of that rope, at the mercy of someone else's self-preservation.

'Michael didn't speak all night,' I tell Jeannie in hurried whispers, palms pressed across my eyes. 'He went to bed, I opened a bottle of wine. I went to the bookshop with the intent of pulling all the books off the shelves. He did this thing when . . . anytime we got into a serious conversation about something he'd lock himself in the bookshop and stock the shelves, make all the books the same height or some stupid thing like that. I had this idea of just trashing the place to make a point, of forcing him to see how angry I was. And then, once I was there, I saw a box of matches. I thought, I won't re-arrange the books, I'll burn them! That will really wind him up. Force him to *talk*. And then I left and it got out of control.'

I felt them watching, and I wanted them to see. I wanted them to accept it as supplication. We would lose everything. An offering. Retribution.

'But . . . what about the JustGiving fund? What about Michael? You said . . . the police said he went crazy *because* of the fire. And you started it?'

Jeannie rises to her feet, anger and bewilderment radiating from her in hot waves.

'I don't believe anything,' she says, lifting her bag to her hip. 'I don't believe a word you've said. Everything is *lies*.'

'Jeannie . . . '

But she turns on her heels and walks quickly across the station towards the stairs.

I turn to Kareem, apoplectic. 'What do they want? Why go to such lengths? My daughter's seriously ill. We could have died . . . Why are they doing this?'

'I was right in one respect,' he says thoughtfully. 'This is about retribution. Many of my clients seek this. It's why they pay me to investigate. They want justice for a wrong that's been done to them.'

'You call what happened to Saskia *justice*? She's an innocent child!'

He holds me in a strange look. 'In my line of work, context is everything. Perhaps if I jog your memory a little you'll change your perspective.'

'I don't care about context. You said I'm in danger. After everything we've been through, you're suggesting this client of yours wants to inflict more pain?'

'You do realise,' he says, leaning forward so that his voice is only audible to me, 'that my client believes *you* murdered their son?'

47

Reuben

8th September 2017

I'm standing at the front of the classroom by the whiteboard and every time I look up I think I'm going to puke. Miss McKinley is standing to my right with her arms folded and a big grin and I wonder if she's laughing at me, even though Miss McKinley is nice and says things like, *You did a super job, Reuben!* My legs are shaking and my teeth chatter as though I'm freezing.

'Today my presentation is called *Nomads in Deep Blue* and it's about a whale. A blue whale. Blue whales are the largest animals on earth . . . '

'A whale is a fish,' someone shouts out. Oliver Jamieson. I can see him rubbing his nose on the cuff of his sleeve. Miss McKinley says, 'Try not to shout out of turn, Oli. A whale is a marine mammal, and it technically is an animal.'

Oli scrunches his face up. 'What's the difference between an animal and a mammal, then?'

'Mammary glands,' Lily says, and everyone starts to laugh. Someone shouts 'whale-sized boobs' and I wonder if I should sit down now.

'Continue, please, Reuben,' Miss McKinley says.

I look down at my iPad. I hate speaking out loud like this. My voice always sounds different to the voice I think in.

'Blue whales can grow to a hundred feet long and weigh over two hundred tons. They are very solitary creatures but they do talk to each other with an A-call, which sounds like a rave drum beat . . . '

'Whale raves,' someone else sniggers. Miss McKinley urges me to keep going.

' . . . or a B-call, which sounds a bit like Chewbacca.'

'Excellent description,' Miss McKinley says, folding her arms.

'They have accents, too, depending on which ocean they live in. Some live in Southern California. They used to live in the Antarctic but in the 1920s people kept bombing them until they were almost extinct.'

People are talking. Sebastian Edu in my last school said I sounded like a vacuum cleaner. I stop talking and ask Miss McKinley to turn out the lights. She flips a switch and the classroom goes dark. I bring up my animation and then say, 'It's not quite finished yet.'

I press play.

The animation starts with a drone shot of an ocean. From above it looks like a blue carpet but then it moves down so you can see the waves and the whale from above. The camera moves to the side and runs along the length of the whale. I studied lots and lots of videos on YouTube to get this right and also pictures from National Geographic. Even though it's an animation I didn't want it to look like a silly cartoon — I wanted it to be as real as possible, as though it was real-life.

It was Malfoy's idea to have the whale breach, though it was my idea to show the breach in slow motion, with the whale breaking the water in a spiral, showing the three hundred baleen plates that stripe along its jaw, and the camera passing overhead like a drone to get a good shot of the blowhole. The blowhole of a blue whale looks like a giant human nose, it's weird. Last night I decided to have the whale shoot out a big jet of water as the drone passes overhead, with specks of water hitting the lens for super-realistic effect. I was so excited that I sent it to Malfoy and messaged him like forty times but he didn't answer.

After that the camera plunges underwater and runs the length of the whale to its tail. I added some dolphins to give a sense of scale. They jump in and out of the water and the camera moves all around the whale to show its body. At the end the whale flips its tail right close to the camera and splashes down, with the whole screen wobbling as though the whale has hit it.

And then the animation finishes. Miss McKinley turns the lights back on and claps loudly. There's a pause, and I feel a drop in my chest, as though I've failed.

'I've still to add some music,' I say quickly. 'And the movement of the waves needs a bit of polishing. I need to use an onion skin to check the arcs . . . '

'That was *wicked*,' Oliver Jamieson shouts out.

'I like what you did with the breach,' Savannah McArthur says. 'It was really cool.'

'Can we see it again?' Dashiell Marden says.

Miss McKinley says we can see it *one more time*, so I dim the lights again and we watch it and I chew my nails. Maybe it's not that bad. When the lights come up everyone is excited and talking about whales and someone says it's epic.

'See?' Josh whispers when I sit back down. 'Told you it was amazing.'

I go to say thank you but my throat is so tight with fear that I can't speak. I'm sweating so much that my palms leave a wet print on the table.

At lunchtime I log on to my iPix account to tell Malfoy how it went. He told me to tell him and he'll be excited when I say it was mega.

```
Roo:      Malfoy!!! R u ther???
```

I wait for six minutes and forty-seven seconds. There is no response. Lucy is online and says hi but I don't want to talk to her. All she talks about is musical.ly and how she thinks I should do a music video but I don't like music. At seven minutes and ten seconds the word 'typing' appears beside Malfoy's name and I tell Lucy I have to go.

```
Malfoy:  Hi Reuben. I'm here.
Roo:     Hey Malfoy . . . GUESS WOT?
Malfoy:  what?
Roo:     My presntatoin was EPIC ☺
         ☺ everyone loved it it and
```

```
             My teacher said she ws
             super proud of me
Malfoy:      That's great.
Roo:         I'm buzzin ☺ ☺ ☺ ☺
Malfoy:      What did your mum say?
Roo:         My mum's not here ☹
Malfoy:      Where is she? R u at home?
Roo:         Yeah I'm at home but my mum's
             in France! !
Malfoy:      France? Why?
Roo:         Dunno
Malfoy:      Whereabouts in France?
Roo:         I can find out
Roo:         heres a screengrab of the map
             — I put a tag on her bag so
             I could see when shes comin
             home
             [A FILE IS AVAILABLE TO VIEW]
Roo:         Malfoy?
```

48

Helen

8th September 2017

I can see Paris from my window seat, a sprawling grey web veined with rivers. The plane begins to descend into Charles de Gaulle.

I have all the instructions written down on a piece of paper, an old Nokia phone with a pay-as-you-go SIM card for emergencies. Jeannie pressed a Platinum Mastercard into my hand and told me to use it. My phone bleeps with a message from her.

```
Pin is 7612. Be safe. J x
```

I thought she was so disgusted with me that she wouldn't want to see me again. The old Jeannie would have flounced off, no contact for years, but when I boarded the train at York she was already on board and in the seat next to mine. Naturally, she was upset, her face marked with angry tears, but the cool air outside had helped her calm down. She wanted to hear me out.

I told her again about how the fire started. I told her about my frustrations with Michael building up until I wanted to scream from my toes.

'Kareem gave me this address just outside Paris,' I said, showing the piece of paper to her. 'Normandy, actually. It's close to where the CCTV footage showed Michael withdrawing money at the bank.'

'And?'

I took a deep breath. 'I'm going.'

She frowned. 'Where?'

'To France. Tonight.'

She looked to the ceiling in despair and gave a groan.

'You *cannot* go to France . . . '

'If the police find him first they'll charge him with murder-suicide . . . '

She nailed me to the seat with a fierce look. 'Helen, take a minute and listen to what you are saying. You've just been in a horrific car crash. You are in *no* fit state to run off to France and rescue anybody.'

I told her what Kareem had said before I left the café. 'He doesn't believe that Chris Holloway has kidnapped Michael.'

'And you believe that? A decade of threatening letters and you think they aren't behind this?'

'I don't know. I don't know, Jeannie. Maybe they are.' I took out the piece of paper with the address, spread it on the table. 'But how can I sit here and do nothing when I know where Michael is?'

Truth be told, I didn't want to go. I didn't want to leave Saskia and Reuben for a second. But greater than that was the urgency to fix all of this, to clear Michael's name. Jeannie looked online, found a flight leaving tonight. Only an hour and fifteen minutes from Newcastle-upon-Tyne to Paris, then a train from there to Normandy. Jeannie insisted on coming with me but I told her no, I needed her at home. There was no one else I would feel comfortable with looking after Reuben and holding Saskia's hand.

At home, Reuben saw me packing and asked nervously where I was going.

'I'm going to get Dad back,' I told him.

'Where is he?'

'He's in France, sweetheart. It's only an hour by plane. I promise I'll be no more than a day or two, OK?'

'A day?'

His eyes were wide and shining, and I had to swallow back a sob as I promised him it would go quickly, that we'd go swimming as soon as I got back.

'Can Dad come swimming too?'

I nodded, less certainly this time, and he saw. Brave boy. He visibly braced himself as I pulled the suitcase downstairs and waved goodbye from the window, still a little child at heart. I thought my heart would break as I pulled off down the street.

★   ★   ★

At Charles de Gaulle Airport I focus on the people around me, on the departure boards, a young boy flailing on the ground while his beleaguered mother begs him to calm down. I can well imagine how he feels. I feel overwhelmed, not sure where to go. At an information desk I ask how to get to the address Kareem gave me. The clerk explains it in English, then prints out a list of instructions: I'm to take a train to Gare du Nord, then a train to Caen and a taxi.

When I manage to hail a taxi outside the station at Caen I'm filled with relief. I pass the address to the driver and he gives me a thumbs up. Outside the sky is navy and portentous. The first specks of rain flick against the windscreen.

We drive out of a small town towards countryside, sprawling fields at either side of the car and narrowing roads with no traffic. The taxi pulls up outside a set of tall gates. I lean forward. The headlights bounce off the iron railings but beyond them I can see what looks like a sprawling estate. Château du Seuil.

'There's a noticeboard,' the taxi driver says, shining a torch on the pillar beside the gate. 'Opening hours are 9 a.m. until 5 p.m., week-days only.'

'Opening hours?'

'Oui. This is not a private address. It is a tourist destination.'

A tourist destination? My stomach twists and I feel a flash of panic. Jeannie was right. I had no reason to trust Kareem. The address was wrong. He has led me, quite literally, to the middle of nowhere. I feel sick.

'Can you take me back to the airport?'

'Airport?'

'Charles de Gaulle?'

The driver laughs. 'That is a long way for a taxi.'

'The train station, then. I'll take the next train to the airport.'

He reverses, begins to drive away. Through the trees I see lights on in one of the rooms of the castle.

'There are no more trains to Paris this evening,' the taxi driver says dismissively. 'Let me take you to a bed and breakfast, huh? Then in the morning you can go to Château du Seuil.'

★   ★   ★

With a heavy heart I walk up the steps to the guesthouse and pay for a room for one night. I can't shake the feeling that this has been a wasted journey. That I've come all this way for nothing.

I slip the key in the door and find a small, dark room with a single bed. The emptiness feels like a slap in the face.

Sinking down on the bed I close my eyes, fighting back tears. Somehow I'll have to come to terms with the fact that I'll never see Michael again. That perhaps I drove him away.

A few moments later, a knock at the door makes me jump upright, my heart hammering.

'Who is it?' I say. Someone tries the door handle, but it's locked. My throat tightens.

'Who is it?' I demand.

'It's me.'

I recognise the voice. In an instant I open the door and see a man standing in the dim corridor.

'Helen?'

49

Helen

8th September 2017

I take a step back and look him over as he stands in the doorway. It is Michael but not Michael, a facsimile in flesh-form. His hair is shorter — an uneven buzzcut, silver filings glistening amongst the dark — and the beard he grew out in Belize is gone, revealing the fine jaw I've not seen in a long time. I don't recognise the black coat he's wearing. But more than anything I don't recognise the look in his eyes.

He reaches out to me, presses his face into my shoulder and sobs. There is nothing more wonderful and terrible than this moment. We are together. He is alive. Our life has been ripped apart and I cannot imagine how it will ever be the same.

'Are you OK?' I whisper, wiping my face and leaning back to look him over, to confirm that he's really here, this is really happening.

I reach out and tentatively cup my hand against his cheek. He flinches and in a sliver of sunlight I see the cause: a dark bruise against his cheekbone, another on his hand. His nose looks broken, his lower lip is painfully split open. I don't remember his nose being broken in the hospital, nor his lips being so damaged. He looks dreadful.

'What happened?' I say when he takes a few uneven steps across the room and sinks down on to the bed. 'I saw the CCTV footage at the hospital in Belize. Did they blackmail you into leaving? Where did they take you?' I start to grow upset, questions spilling out of me. A need for answers burns me. 'Who *did* this, Michael?'

He looks stunned. I wonder if he's been drugged. There are fresh bruises on his face. Has he been tortured?

'Nobody blackmailed me,' he says simply.

I wait for something more. 'But you left the hospital . . . and the police showed me footage of you drawing money out of a bank in Paris . . . '

He looks away. 'I had to.'

I'm not sure I heard him right. 'You *had* to?'

'I read the letters,' he says simply, returning his eyes to mine. There's a light gone out of them and I try not to think about what that means.

'I'm sorry,' I say. 'I should have told you . . . '

'I know you were scared,' he says. 'They've been searching for us for years. Luke's family.'

'Because of what happened on Mont Blanc,' I say, and he nods.

In a terrible outpour I tell him everything that has happened: the police interviews in Belize, the terrible suspicion. Saskia's surgery, the Medevac. Returning home and feeling that I was going out of my mind.

He listens to all of this, keeps his gaze on the wall opposite. His eyes are haunted, his lips slightly open. It's the expression of a scream too harrowing to be uttered. I take his hand.

'Michael?'

His eyes shift slowly to mine, but I'm not sure he's seeing me.

'How did you know I was here?'

'Reuben,' he says, matter-of-fact.

'Reuben?'

'I've been communicating with him on iPix.'

'iPix?'

'As Malfoy. I set it up a while ago, remember? When he had no friends to play with on there and we wanted to encourage his drawings?'

In a moment it comes to me, and I remember it.

'He was able to show me a lot that was going on in Belize.' He raises a shaky hand to his face. 'I knew about Saskia. It almost tore me apart.'

His voice breaks and he starts to weep, his shoulders rising, huge, drawn-out sobs. I hold him tight, tell him that we have each other. We can be together. We are a family, always.

I tell him about Kareem. About the address I have for Chris Holloway.

'A private investigator?' he says, his voice rising, when I tell him how I knew to come to France. 'What information did he have on us?'

'They knew we were going to Belize.'

His face contorts. 'But . . . how would they know that? We only decided to go to Belize on the spur of the moment . . . '

I nod. 'Yes. But someone put a tracking device on Saskia's teddy.' I explain how Reuben had found the tag on the teddy's collar. His eyes widen in horror and he falls silent.

Why put the tracking device on Jack-Jack, and not inside my wallet, or Michael's keychain? Whoever had put that device on Jack-Jack to track our movements had to have known that Saskia wouldn't lose the teddy, that he was important to her, otherwise they risked losing our location.

I notice Michael is panting slightly, a hand lifting to his ribs.

'Lie down,' I say softly, but he shakes his head. 'We haven't got time. I know where they are.'

'Who?'

'Luke's family,' he says, swallowing hard in pain. 'I found the house.'

I frown. 'Château de Seuil. I went there.'

He looks up. 'You went there?'

'Yes. But it was a public property.'

'They still live in one of the buildings there,' he says, shifting his position until he finds a way to sit that eases the pain. He tilts his head back, eyes on the ceiling. 'I've already been. I spoke to a groundsman. He says they're expected back tomorrow.' He lowers his head, rests his eyes on me. 'There's another thing.'

'What?'

He hesitates. 'I found Theo.'

★ ★ ★

'It's here, thanks,' Michael tells the taxi driver. The estate looks different in daylight. The tall gates I saw last night are cast iron and marked with gold lettering: Château de Seuil. Beyond thcm I can see a sweeping landscape: a large lake surrounded by trees, gardens, and a towering castle at the end of a long driveway.

I follow Michael silently across a gravel path towards a wooden hut, where a girl stands, a roll of tickets in her hands and a vest emblazoned with the Château de Seuil logo. She thinks we're here to go on the tour.

Michael pulls out a wallet, buys two tickets. I don't ask him whose credit card he's using, though it's not his name along the strip.

We head towards the castle. I notice his limp is pronounced, his face pale and his breath laboured. He doesn't look well.

'Michael, I think you need to go to hospital,' I say, but he shakes his head.

'Nearly there.'

We reach a long garden fringed with bedded plants and small trees.

'Where's Theo?' I say, glancing around. Is he really here? Are we just going to walk up to him, shake hands? Talk about the weather? Perhaps my many sightings of him over the years weren't imagined after all. I'm sick at the thought of meeting him after all these years.

Michael staggers towards a clearing in the soil. I make out a stone angel, covered in moss. And a marble tombstone with clear gold script.

Luke Augustus Aucoin
22.8.1976 — 25.6.1995
and his brother, Theo Charles Aucoin
22.8.1976 — 25.6.1999
Fratres in aeternum numquam seorsum

I take a few steps forward and fall to my knees on the grass, weeping as I take it in. It's a grave. Theo died on the fourth anniversary of Luke's death. *Suicide*, I think, remembering how he had howled when the mountain rescue unit at Chamonix told us they'd recovered his body. *It must have been.* He was devoted to Luke. *This was all my fault. Both brothers, gone.*

I can hardly bear it.

★ ★ ★

At the bed and breakfast Michael removes his shirt, letting me trace the damage caused by an unnamed attacker across his ribcage and stomach. Beneath fresh bruises, older traces of the crash: the mark of the seatbelt, cuts across his forehead from shattered glass. A superimposition of trauma.

I kiss his scars, his broken lips, cradle his face in my hands as he weeps.

After, we lie together, our hands interlaced. Neither of us speak. He has not said whether or not he knows about the fire and I have not confessed it.

A long distance stretches between us, a deep fissure riven by silence and lies.

50

Reuben

8th September 2017

Josh is at my house and we're putting the finishing touches to our animations. The deadline for the competition is tonight so we're working really hard to get everything rendered and uploaded in time. We didn't even eat dinner, just came home from school with Aunt Jeannie and went upstairs to get our animations finished.

Josh's animation is of a fire-breathing dragon who transforms into a man and vice versa. He has called it *Return of the Phoenix* which I think is a wicked name. It shows this guy walking towards a cliff edge and then he jumps off and you think he's plunging to his death but instead he transforms into a dragon, and the camera zooms right into him as his arms grow red scales and turn into wings and you see his nose becoming a snout and his hands turning into claws. Right as he's about to hit the bottom of the cliff his wings span out and he soars upwards and then Josh shows the clouds and a sunset and the view of the valley. It is epic.

'Yours is good, too, though,' Josh says, but I know he's just being nice and that's OK because people sometimes don't say what they mean out of kindness.

It's seven o'clock and I'm famished. I go downstairs to toast a couple of the bagels Aunt Jeannie bought for me. I set my iPad on the coffee table. Aunt Jeannie is at the kitchen table with a large glass of red wine and her laptop open. She's wearing glasses which reflect the screen. I can even make out the Google logo.

'You searching for something?' I ask, and she looks up and smiles, though her eyes are sad.

'Always,' she says.

The bagels pop up. 'You want me to get those for you?' Aunt Jeannie says, but I say 'no thanks' and cover them in butter and then a big dollop of strawberry jam. Then I go into the living room. There are two iPads there, one on the coffee table and one on the sofa. Josh must have come downstairs.

'Josh?' I say, but there's no answer. He must have come down and then gone back upstairs. I put both iPads under my arm and carry them back to my bedroom, and as I'm walking up the stairs an idea hits my head like a stone. I tell this to Josh and he tilts his head to check if there's a lump where the stone hit me.

'I've just decided I'm going to be a marine biologist,' I tell him.

'You just decided that right now?'

I nod and give a big laugh, and there's a warm feeling in my arms and legs, a good feeling. Ideas start to pour into my brain as if someone's turned on taps.

'Blue whales are endangered, right?'

387

'Yes, they are,' he says.

'The reason they're so endangered is because ships crash into them all the time because they're so big. Well, if I become a marine biologist, I could use a tracking device like the one on Jack-Jack's collar and then give the app with the digital map to the people driving the ships so they can avoid crashing into them.'

Josh thinks about this. 'But . . . how would you get the tracking device on to the blue whales?'

I click my fingers and think. 'A drone,' I say. 'I'd use drone to zoom down and drop them on to the blue whale. I'd have to figure out how to get them to stick on.'

'I think it's a good idea,' Josh says, biting into his bagel.

There's a knock at the door. I hear it and I think Aunt Jeannie is going to get it but then someone knocks again so she must be busy. I go downstairs and look into the kitchen. She's got the oven fan on. I open the front door and there's a woman and a man standing there in suits.

'Hello,' I say.

'Hello,' says the lady. She's got short white hair and glasses. The man is much younger and very tall and makes me think of Snape. The lady says, 'I'm Detective Chief Inspector Lavery. I don't believe we've met. You're Reuben, aren't you?'

It always makes me feel funny when people say stuff like this because I don't know how they know me or why they do. I stare and she smiles.

'Is your mum in, Reuben?'

I shake my head. 'My mum's in France.'

The lady's eyebrows shoot up towards her white hair. 'France?'

'Yes.'

She looks behind me. 'I see. Are you on your own, Reuben?'

'My auntie's here. Do you want some tea and a Kit Kat?'

Mum always gives people tea and Kit Kats when they come to our house.

They say 'no, thank you' and I go to tell Aunt Jeannie that Detective Chief Inspector Lavery and her boyfriend are here, but then I remember something. I told the lady that Mum is in France but I haven't checked her location in over an hour so she could be somewhere else by now. I race upstairs and get my iPad and bring it back downstairs to show them.

'I put the TRKLite tag on Mum's bag,' I say, but they look puzzled. I bring up the location map with the red dot, showing exactly where Mum is. She's not even in Paris! She's in a place called Luc-sur-Mer. I can even see the street she's on. I show it to them.

'She's here,' I say. And I begin to tell them about the TRKLite and how cool it is but they're on their mobile phones, telling someone called Guv that my mum's in Luc-sur-Mer.

51

Michael

9th September 2017

I wake before sunrise. Helen's still asleep. I sit for a long time in the wicker chair by the window, watching her lying there so still. She's on her left side, one palm pressed into the mattress, quietly snoring. Her hair is slightly spread across her face, the duvet is wrapped around her waist. Her face is messed up from the crash but she's still beautiful to me. Every day for the last eighteen years, I have asked myself what I did to end up with this woman. I really don't deserve her.

My dad took me to see my grandfather a few times when I was about ten. I'd never met him before but he squatted down to eye level and pinched my cheek, called me 'a good lad'. He had a glint in his eye, a spring in his step. His house overlooked a wood and a river and we went out there and did a bit of fishing. The next time I saw him I was shocked. He was in a rocking chair by the fire, a blanket over his knees. He couldn't remember my name. I thought he was playing games. How could he not remember who I was? It had only been about eight or nine months since we went to see him. And then the next time I saw him he was in hospital, no more than a skeleton in a bed. I couldn't believe someone so thin and so sick could still be alive. They kept pumping him full of antibiotics. He was terminally ill, Dad said. I thought, *why are they keeping him alive?* Even as a boy I could see he was never going to recover, never going to have any kind of quality of life. Dad told me he would need care every second of every day. In hindsight, I can see I was angry at how people saw life and death. My grandfather had served honourably as a fighter pilot in the Second World War, won medals, buried friends, children, a wife. He came home and spent his life working on a farm. My grandma died giving birth, and my grandfather raised my dad and his brothers on his own while working from dawn until dusk. His life had been full and rich. He believed strongly that he'd see my grandma on the other side. Keeping him alive in that terrible, skeleton state was cruelty, not preservation.

It made me realise that life and death are a matter of perspective.

My life with Helen has been the most amazing eighteen years I could have imagined. Few people experience love like I have. I could have died on Mont Blanc, right after I met the love of my life. Fate made me find Helen a second time. So I don't consider the sacrifice of my life a death of any kind. How could I? Luke's parents want retribution, and they'll have it.

I remember the dream I had of the other side of the door of flame. I dreamt it right after the bookshop burned down and it brought me such comfort. A sweeping landscape of green fields and valleys bathed in gold light, a narrow road cutting through them. At the end of it was our house. Chewy was there, barking and furiously wagging his tail, telling us in doggy language to scoop him up and give him a cuddle. Saskia was in the back garden in her tutu, performing a little dance on the flagstones. Reuben was sitting under the apple tree with his iPad. When he saw me he lifted a hand and waved, *Hi, Dad*. Helen was kneeling by the edge of the garden, filling a trug with fresh strawberries. Everything was washed in an eternal light, an infinite summer.

I woke up from the dream in the middle of the night and saw Helen sleeping, just as I am now. I lifted a pillow, put it over her face. She moaned and turned away. I tried again. But I couldn't go through with it. What if she woke up in the middle and realised what I was doing? How would she feel about that? It would be the ultimate betrayal because she wouldn't understand. I was always bad at explaining things.

It had to be another way. After a holiday. After a celebration of our lives.

We had a book in the shop about accessing the dark web. I went online and found it quickly, found the right source. Made a connection, a payment.

He told me to buy a tracking device to make it seamless.

A few days later a package arrived at the shop. Saskia was helping me open the letters and she found a padded envelope amongst the pile.

'What's *this*, Daddy?' she asked, opening something that had a foreign postmark and a small round tag, baby pink. 'It's pretty,' she said, and I watched as she fastened it on to Jack-Jack's collar. Behind the fog that veiled my brain I recognised what the tag was. It would enable us to be located at the right moment, after our last big family holiday, and taken through the door of flame.

I knew everything would be better. No one would separate us. We would always be a family.

Except it didn't work out as planned.

When I woke up in the hospital I knew what I had to do. They had been watching all this time. I would find Luke's family and kill them. They were planning to hurt us. They wanted to take Saskia and Reuben away from us.

I lift the pillow and hold it out, lowering it to Helen's face. She moans, tries to push it away, and I press harder. I'll have to do this twice more for the door of flame to open and let us in.

But something stops me.

Not now, a voice says in my head. *Not like this. Not until it is done.*

⋆ ⋆ ⋆

The taxi pulls up at Château de Seuil. It's a beautiful day. Blue skies and lush countryside all around, a nip in the air drawing blood to our cheeks. Helen looks shaken as we step out of the taxi and face the entrance to the estate.

'I promise you,' I tell her, taking her hand. 'This will all be put right.'

'But what if they call the police,' she says, wiping tears off her face. 'What if they take Saskia and Reuben from us? Reuben would never cope in a foster home, Michael. He wouldn't cope . . .'

I pull her close to me, hold her tight. I know exactly how she feels.

'That won't happen. I swear on my life it won't happen.'

We follow the tour group towards the castle, then duck around the side to the house at the back. A few hens are pecking in the yard. I see the small white rectangle of a doorbell and press it.

For a long time, nobody answers. Helen visually contemplates walking away, eyeing up the road beyond, as though we could turn back and forget this ever happened. We know how that went.

But then the door opens and a woman's face appears there. She appears to be in her late sixties, maybe early seventies, stylish white hair to her jaw. A beige turtleneck, expensive slacks. Twinkling diamond earrings. Something about her eyes is familiar. She looks over Helen and me with curiosity.

'*Oui?*'

'We're looking for Chris Holloway,' I say. 'Can you help us?'

She looks taken aback. 'I'm Chris,' she says in perfect English. 'Can I help you?'

'I'm Michael Pengilly,' I say slowly, extending a hand. 'I was Michael King. I think you've been wanting to speak to me.'

The woman's mouth falls open. She ignores my hand and says something I don't hear, then shouts up the stairs. 'Paul?' Another shout, this time in French.

Helen flinches beside me and eyes up the road again but I hold her hand tightly. We have to face this. We have to follow through.

'Please,' Chris says, stepping back from the door and gesturing at us. 'Come inside.'

The hallway is enormous, a vaulted ceiling above with a mosaic in the centre. Oak panelling on the walls, a sweeping *Gone with the Wind* staircase.

'The living room's on the top floor, I'm afraid,' Chris says, regaining her composure. 'Are you sure you can both make it?'

Her accent is cobbled together from all over the world: English wrapped in French with a hint of American. She is Luke's mother. I never met her but I can tell: she has the same widow's peak and high cheekbones as the twins. Luke's father died when he and Theo were little and his mother remarried. I remember this now.

Helen and I share a brief glance before following Chris up three flights of stairs.

A vast drawing room with stunning views of the lake afforded by a large bay window. Plush velvet sofas facing each other, crystal chandeliers, gleaming candelabras, an ornate marble fireplace. An oil painting of Luke and Theo on one of the walls draws a faint noise from Helen and a leap of my stomach. There's a huge dollop of the Romantics in the way they're portrayed, their faces wistfully luminous, haughty as fallen angels. Luke is standing with one hand on Theo's shoulder, his face angled upwards as though measuring the triumphs he's yet to scale. Theo sits, hands on his knees as though he's primed to rise and stride off, his face contemplative, turned as though he's observing the commencement of the apocalypse.

'Please, have a seat,' Chris says, gesturing at the sofas. Helen doesn't move. Her hands are clasped, her face drained of colour and anxiety thumping off her in hot waves. I can tell she's thinking of running out of here.

'You know why we're here,' I say.

'Yes,' Chris says after a long moment, visibly rattled and trying to hold herself in one piece. 'Well, why don't we all sit down and . . . talk?'

'I'd prefer to stand,' I say.

'You'll sit, if it's all the same to you,' another voice barks. We both turn to see a man at the other side of the room. Tall, early seventies, navy jumper. A face full of outrage. He is holding a pistol by his side. I hear Helen give a small noise of fright.

'There's no need for this to get nasty,' I say calmly. 'We didn't come here for anything other than to give you what you've been requesting all these years.'

'Alright,' Chris says, and she gives a nod at the man holding the gun. Then, to Helen: 'I apologise for the mess. If I'd known I was receiving guests I'd have cleaned up and made a pot of coffee.' She turns her eyes to the man on the other side of the room. 'Paul, come and talk with us.'

Paul, I don't recognise. No trace of the twins in his lanky form and hook-nosed, heron face. He takes a cautious seat in the velvet armchair opposite, setting the pistol on the armrest without tearing his eyes from mine. 'If we have any nonsense I'll be using it. Understood?'

'Perfectly understood,' Helen whispers.

'Well, this is a long overdue visit,' Chris says. 'And I suppose I'd like to begin with asking the question I've wanted to ask for a very long time.' She turns to me with a grim look. 'What happened on that mountain?'

'It was an accident,' I hear myself say, though the blood is roaring in my ears and I'm there again, on the side of Mont Blanc, looking down at that drop. I see the rope swinging and Luke's body hanging, his arms and legs pulled back by gravity and his head arched back. His hair darkening with blood.

Chris considers my response, waits for more. 'If it was an accident, why run? Why not talk to us, tell us what happened?'

'We were afraid,' Helen says. Her face creases, her eyes brimming with tears. She cups a hand to her mouth and stammers an apology. 'We were afraid of what might happen. How the whole thing would be . . . interpreted.' She wipes her face. 'Hindsight's twenty twenty, isn't it? But I can't turn back time. I was in shock. I was only nineteen. I had lost Luke. I felt like I had nothing to live for.'

Chris studies Helen, taking in the sight of her bruised and swollen face, her wrist brace. I sense she wants to ask what the hell happened, but decides to stay on topic. 'You were Luke's girlfriend, isn't that right?'

Helen nods. 'We were together for about eight months. I never wanted anything bad to happen to him. I never . . . '

'You killed Luke!' Paul erupts. 'Both of you. When we found out you got married we knew you'd planned it from day one. Get Luke out of the way, ride off into the sunset.'

Helen shakes her head, emphatic, a twitch in her gaze. 'That's not how it was.' Then she blurts out the whole story in urgent, slurring whispers: how she fell in love with Luke and couldn't believe it when her feelings were reciprocated. How he talked her into going on the trip despite her lack of training or experience. The weird shift in dynamics, the fight between me and Luke. And then the descent: Luke persuading us to go down when we should just have turned back and found the right path. The rockfall. The moment that we knew Luke was hanging at the bottom of the rope, unconscious, the weight of his body about to pull us all down with him. Helen looks over their faces — Paul is puce, Chris has her palms clasped to her mouth and her eyes squeezed tight against fresh sorrow — and breaks down.

'I'm sorry,' she weeps. 'I'm so, so sorry. I promise I never meant for it to happen . . . '

'How can you say that?' Paul explodes. 'How can you say that you shouted for Luke to be killed and that you didn't mean for it to happen?'

Helen looks wrung out. Her face says she's under siege by a thousand emotions, that there isn't really any answer at all, other than she's sorry. Chris reaches for a tissue on the coffee table and dabs her eyes.

Paul glares at Helen. I can see he wants to go in hard, those big hands of his eager to clamp around her neck and shake the life out of her, as though he can trade it for Luke and Theo's. I bet he's dreamed about doing just that for the last twenty-odd years. I know it well, the terrible urge that has burrowed into him, empowered by grief. Perhaps this is the moment when I should take that gun off him, finish this right now.

Chris takes a weary sigh. 'Enough, Paul. They were all just kids. It was a horrendous position to be in . . . ' She sits closer to Helen and puts an arm across her shoulders, holding her in a deep, stricken look.

Paul's eyebrows jump up at this. 'We don't know it happened as innocently as she makes out,' he cautions her. 'Theo said . . . '

'Theo took his own life,' Chris says firmly, shutting him down. She turns to Helen, confiding. 'Theo blamed himself for not hanging on long enough to save Lukey. We got him counselling, antidepressants, hypnosis. We told him over and over that there was nothing he could have done but that self-blame ran so deep.' She gives a sad shrug. 'He just wanted to be with his brother.'

'Theo blamed himself because there was no conclusive enquiry, no *justice*,' Paul counters. He turns to me, his eyes narrowed and burning with hate. 'We got a phone call from the *gendarme* asking us to come and collect our son's body. The coroner called witnesses. Our most important witnesses were missing. Michael King and Helen

Warren. We tried everything to reach you both. The coroner recorded it as an accidental death. No trial. No justice. No explanation.' His voice breaks, and he waves his hands around, painting the air with his wounds. 'I raised Luke and Theo as though they were my own boys, my own *blood*. We lost both of them in the space of four years. Both of them. Our boys — gone. Because of you.'

'You're right,' I say, and all eyes are suddenly on me. 'I did kill Luke. I was hanging off the cliff, about to die. Luke wasn't answering anyone.' I turn to Helen. 'I looked up and I saw you. I couldn't lose you. So I made the decision. I cut the rope.'

My voice feels like it's detached from my body, like I'm speaking in a dream.

'I cut it. Every day for over twenty years I have thought about what I did. I felt unworthy. I felt I deserved to die. I remembered Luke saying one time that he fancied opening a bookshop when he was older. Not just any bookshop but a really amazing bookshop with special editions of Chaucer. A treasure trove for book geeks. I opened the bookshop for him. I thought that maybe if I fulfilled his dream, the guilt would stop eating me from the inside out.'

I look at Luke's mother, then his stepfather. I can't tell what they're thinking. I feel like I've stepped outside my body. Maybe I'm dead already. Maybe that's what this is.

'Michael didn't kill Luke,' Helen says in a small voice. 'We both ran because we were afraid, in shock at what happened. Michael had a split second to act. Luke was unconscious. He'd been hurt in the rockfall.'

'But you understand why we sent a private investigator searching for you?' Chris asks, emphatic. 'We had questions. And the longer you avoided us, the more urgent those questions became.'

'I'm so sorry,' Helen says. 'But there is *no* justification for what you did to us in Belize. It won't bring Luke back. Or Theo.'

'*Belize?*' Paul says, leaning forward, his face folded in confusion. 'What do you mean, what we did to you? All we did was hire a professional to locate your current address.'

Helen looks from Chris to Paul in a look that's somewhere between confusion and horror. 'But . . . the car crash,' Helen says, her eyes slowly turning to me, as though the pieces are slowly lacing together. 'You tried to kill us all. Our daughter's in a coma.'

'*What?*' Chris gasps.

In a burst of frustration Helen shouts out what happened in Belize, but her voice falters and her eyes steady on me, and I know it's over. She knows. Chris and Paul ask frantic, bewildered questions about the crash, about Saskia, their faces turned to Helen, and so I lunge forward and seize the gun. Paul holds his hands up. Poor guy. He looks like he might wet himself.

'I love you, Helen,' I say. She holds up her hands and shouts something I don't hear. The room is a wintry landscape, a mountain covered in snow.

I put the barrel against my head and squeeze the trigger.

401

52

Helen

9th September 2017

I'm screaming at Michael to stop, my hands reaching out to him, when I hear the *click* of the trigger. My mind lurches, racing ahead to scenes of blood spurting out of his head and barely able to keep up with what's happening. He continues holding the gun to his head and clicking the trigger like it's a toy. Chris and Paul are on their feet, too, all of us with our hands held out. We shout *Stop!* in unison and it seems to reach him. Michael opens his eyes and looks at me blankly, as though I'm not there.

'What's wrong with you people?' Paul shouts, horrified. 'First you burn down your shop and now this . . . I'm calling the police!'

Michael points the gun at him and he jumps back, knocking a table and vase to the ground.

'Michael, *no!*' I shout, taking a step in front of Paul so that the gun is pointed at me. But Michael doesn't lower the gun. He points it hard and firm at Paul, and there is that hard look on his face, the look I saw that night in the attic. As though he's not quite there.

'What does he mean, burned down our shop?'

Michael says. He's speaking to me.

'You did it,' Paul hisses. 'You set fire to that shop and let it burn to the ground. We figured we were dealing with a pair of lunatics! It had nothing to do with us!'

I lock eyes with Michael. The silence clicks a gear, the shadows of truth hardening into shapes. Perhaps we've never been as honest with each other as right now.

'I set fire to the shop,' I say. 'I never meant it to turn into what it was. Please, Michael. Please just put the gun down.'

Finally he lowers the gun and walks to the painting of Luke and Theo. I can see Chris from the corner of my eye shaking from head to toe. Any minute now her legs will buckle beneath her.

'I had to protect our family,' Michael says, barely audible. 'So I did what needed to be done before someone else took it all away. I thought, one final trip together as a family, the holiday of a lifetime, or a lifetime's worth of holidays all in one. We can be together. No separation or divide or loss. They want us dead, and it's my fault. They want to hurt us, pull us apart.'

He turns, staring past us. The room is so charged it feels on the verge of exploding.

'But the letters continued. I had no way of tracing the writer. And besides, the letters had been forwarded from our Cardiff address. They hadn't found us in Northumberland.

'And then I kept seeing this man watching the shop. I thought I was being paranoid until I saw him taking photographs. I approached him and he drove off. I knew they'd caught up with us. Just days later, the fire happened. I knew it was them. I knew that was it. We'd had a lucky escape but it wouldn't end until we were all dead.

'I was never going to let anyone hurt my family. I had to protect them. We would be together.' A shrug. 'The car crash was a means to an end.'

'You . . . you tried to murder your own family?' Paul says.

'It's not like that,' Michael says, flinching at the word 'murdered'. 'We were going to be together for ever, in the best possible place.'

It feels like I've been given a sucker-punch right under the ribs with a force that should launch me to the roof. I drop to my knees, winded, his words pounding all the surfaces of my mind. Michael steps forward and stands over me oddly with his hand held out, as though I've simply tripped over. I am torn between curling into a ball on the floor and leaping up to scratch his eyes out. And there is a third impulse, my body reacting of its own accord. To place my hand in his. As his wife. As his equal.

I do nothing.

His expression is unreadable. I don't recognise it. A new element has grown in him since I saw him, since our time at the beach hut. Crouching down in front of me, he keeps his eyes fixed on mine and says, 'Why did you start the fire?'

I flinch, terror flooding me, primal, over-riding the impulses that stand, confused.

'I think I wanted them to see.'

404

'Who? Who did you want to see? See what?'

He is closer to me now, his hands gripping my upper arms and I can't tell if it's fury or sadness on his face and everything is blurred because I am weeping twenty-two years' worth of tears for the boy I loved and sent to his death. I am crying in harrowing realisation of what Michael has done, that Saskia's life hangs by a thread because of his actions, that our family is over, no more.

'You must stop this,' Paul tells Michael in a thin voice, and when I look over he and Chris look terrified, all trace of grief washed away by horror. I see everything too clearly, the edges of truth so sharp they might slice me to the bone. They were watching us, seeking answers. But they did not try to harm us. The car crash was not their doing.

It was Michael's.

Suddenly he lets go, as though a switch has flipped and he's realised what he's doing. His expression is pained, exhausted. He says, 'I've only ever tried to protect you.'

Downstairs, the doorbell rings, strange in its normality, a shrill call followed by three loud knocks on the front door.

'Who is that?' Michael says. Another loud knock, followed by a voice through the letterbox.

'It's the police,' Paul says, shocked, looking from Chris to us.

Michael turns to me. His eyes are like stone.

'Did you call them?'

'No, I . . . '

He takes my hand, leads me across the room

and picks up the gun.

'Stop!' Paul shouts, but Michael ignores him. He walks with surprising speed out of the room and into the hallway, clasping my hand tightly in his.

'Michael, *please*,' I say. 'You're hurting me.'

He lets go of my hand and I think I'm free, but quickly he snatches my wrist and tugs me towards the large glass apex at the far end of the corridor. I'm stunned by the firmness of his grasp, that he can be so violent. The pistol is held firmly in his other hand and he doesn't let go, not even when he presses down on the handle of the door that swings open on to the balcony. Rich gold sunlight is streaming in, illuminating the brass fittings around the door in a celestial glow.

'I think this was my dream,' he says softly, hesitating in the doorway. He turns to me, his eyes lit with a frightening happiness. It's as though he's returned to his body, though he doesn't loosen his grip on my wrist.

'Will you come with me?'

I look at him. His gaze seems to stretch beyond the balcony into some magical scene in the distance. 'Come with you *where?*'

'Home. The kids will come too, not now but in time. We can be together until then.'

'What?'

He opens the door and pulls me through. He's so strong that there is no give in his step, no resistance.

'Michael, *stop*,' I shout. The balcony is furnished with two wooden sun loungers and several towering conifer trees in concrete pots. He drags me to the railings at the edge of the balcony, searching for a way to climb over, and I realise with horror that he intends to throw us both to our deaths. The drop is forty or fifty feet straight to a stone courtyard. Putting one foot on top he lets go to find his balance, then reaches for me to take his hand again. I back away and shake my head.

'We can be free,' he says, in a tone of confusion. 'Don't you want to be free, Helen?'

With a look of white fury Michael lunges forward, grabbing hold of my T-shirt and tugging me firmly towards him, but not before I've grabbed one of the conifer trees. With all my strength I lift the concrete pot and bring it upwards, smashing against his jaw. He slumps against the railing, almost falling over, and I grab his arm, stopping him just in time. He slides to the balcony floor, unconscious.

Police stream through the door and attend to Michael, who is bleeding from the wound I inflicted. I am crying and gasping for air on the ground beside him. Chris appears, shaken and wild-eyed. She spots the pistol on the ground beside Michael and covers her mouth in horror, the meaning of it all sinking in. The police bark into their handsets. In the distance, an ambulance begins its long wail.

'I thought he was going to kill you,' Chris says, kneeling down beside me. 'Are you alright?'

I nod. 'Yes,' I say. 'Yes, I'm fine.'

PART FOUR

53

Michael

26th November 2017

In the mornings I have breakfast in the main hall with the other service users. In the afternoon there's a range of classes — art therapy, music therapy, sometimes cookery and tai chi — and then it's EMDR, or back in our rooms, which is where I am now. It's brand new, this place. Designed with survival in mind. No glass, no sharp edges, no handles on anything, just gaps in the wood of the drawers and wardrobe. Even the doors come off their hinges if you try to hang yourself on them.

The view from my window is of the Peace Garden, where we've each planted our own tree. Fruit trees. Designed to bear fruit, and thereby remind us rotten inmates that we are still capable of doing good things.

I'm not sure about that. The voices in my head tell me I'm a monster. I see the crash from a distance, as though from overhead or sometimes from the side of the road, and I remember I planned it. I see a man lifting Saskia's broken body into the back of an army truck and I remember I planned it. On those days there is no

411

physical pain to outweigh the kind that happens inside my brain.

Sometimes I dream of Luke. He slips his arm across my shoulders and points at the mountain ahead of us. *That there is the imaginatively monikered Mountain of Penance*, he says. *It's a bit of a trek, ladies. Don't get scared now.*

Sometimes I dream of Helen. She tells me she loves me, that I'm the most amazing person she's ever met. I tell her what I should have told her many years ago: that I would have cut that rope whether she screamed or not. It was the right thing to do, as well as the hardest. I never cut it just because she told me to. In the dream her chest opens and a black oily liquid pours out. She starts to glow as though filled with light. She looks happy.

I dream of Reuben, and in those dreams it's about the way he looks at me. With pride. With a desire to make me proud. And Saskia, the way she cuddled me at bedtime. *Just one more story, Daddy.* I'm writing her stories now. A whole series of stories about ballerina ponies.

One day, I want to read them to her. I want to tell Helen the truth, to see the look of relief on her face.

That is my dream.

54

Helen

20th January 2018

'I want you to know something.'

Jeannie turns off the ignition.

'What?'

'Shane and I are going to buy a house here in Northumberland. Whatever happens, I am here. OK?'

I nod. I attempt a smile, but I'm much too anxious. This is too big a day to pretend I feel anything but terrified.

'I love you, Jeannie.'

'I love you, too.'

★   ★   ★

On 30th August, our family travelled by car following a wonderful holiday on the coast of Belize to catch our flight departing from Mexico City. Several hours into the journey we were struck by a van driven by Jonas Matus, who had been paid by my husband to crash into our car at high speed and ensure we were all dead. I know now that the boots by my face at the scene of the crash were indeed Matus', who was scanning the

413

scene to check his victims were deceased. Small mercies: we were all unconscious and Matus thought the job was done. Or perhaps Matus chickened out of finishing us off.

Either way, Michael was jointly responsible. At Château du Seuil he chose to hand himself over to the police without resistance. He received a sentence of fifteen years in a high security psychiatric unit in County Durham. Matus is serving twenty years in a high security Belize prison.

My own sentencing hearing happened last month. The insurance claim for the bookshop has been dropped, of course — though the insurance company threatened to file a fraud claim against me — and the police prosecuted me for wasting their time. I expected to be locked up for a year, maybe more, but my solicitor had me assessed by a psychologist, Dr Moreno, who probed into the event on Mont Blanc. Complex Post-Traumatic Stress Disorder, she said. Exactly what Michael has been diagnosed with. Some characteristics of complex PTSD are avoidance, dissociation, and self-sabotage. It can take a long time for symptoms to manifest. Setting fire to the bookshop was consistent with these symptoms.

Because the fire didn't endanger any lives and no major structural damage was caused, my sentence was reduced to two hundred hours of community service.

I sent Vanessa Shoman a return ticket to London with three nights at a hotel right beside Harrods. She was over the moon. I suggested she see a show.

As for me, I've started dancing again. Reuben

is doing better, too — his friendship with Josh has helped, and he's developed a group of friends at school who are all hell-bent on saving blue whales.

★ ★ ★

Dr Hamedi greets us both with a kiss on the cheek.

'You feeling OK?' she asks, and I nod. We had a meeting about today's procedure last week. Saskia may not wake. She may wake and be severely brain damaged, requiring round-the-clock care for the rest of her life. The outcome is likely to be indicated by the response she gives in her first moments, if she gives any response at all. She may wake and be paralysed. She may not wake at all. The short version is: no one knows what today will bring.

And that is the only truth I live by.

'Let's get to work.'

She leads Jeannie and me down the corridor to the room where Saskia lies.

★ ★ ★

Guilt can motivate a person in two ways: to try and repair damage caused, or to dodge blame. But what happens when no repair can be made? In Michael's case, I think he believed that the weight of the guilt at causing Luke's death would destroy him. After all, Luke had been one of his closest friends, and he never intended to kill him. He was placed in an unbearable position.

415

But you can't dodge guilt. You can hide from it, ignore it — but it'll always find you. I know this with every fibre of my being. My own guilt at Luke's death all but destroyed me. In Michael's case, his efforts to avoid guilt grew monstrous, controlling. He became someone I don't recognise. He became defined by what happened on the mountain.

I won't let it define me.

I visit Michael often. I visit him on days that he is half-conscious due to the effects of a new medication. I visit him when he relives the night he went online and contacted Jonas Matus. On the days he wants to die because of what he did in Belize. I visit him on days that he is exactly like the man I married: sweet, kind, funny. The man who taught me what love really is.

I miss that Michael.

★　★　★

The machines stop. I wait, turned inside out with anguish, as the doctors retract the tubes, leaning over and calling her name.

Saskia, darling? You alright? Can you hear me?

Her eyes peel open, a hand stretching wide, fingers flexed. Her lips are puckered and dry. She moves them.

'Saskia?' I say gently. 'I'm here, darling. I'm here.' Her fingers curl loosely around mine.

Good girl, there we go. Well done, my lovely. Can you feel your legs? Can you give me a blink of your eyes if you can feel your legs? One for no, two for yes.

She blinks.
And blinks again.
'Oh, sweetheart,' I say, my voice shaking. 'I've missed you so much.'

Acknowledgements

Each book is its own journey, with parts that almost break you and parts that are exhilarating and joyous, with sunshine on your face and the wind at your back. Often these elements are in human form, and with this in mind I'd like to thank my agent Alice Lutyens at Curtis Brown and my editor Kimberley Young at HarperFiction for challenging me to make this book the absolute best it could be and for bringing so much genius to the process. You are both rock stars. My utmost gratitude to all the other legends at HarperCollins, particularly Eloisa Clegg, Felicity Denham, Kate Elton, Martha Ashby, and Louis Patel.

A big thank you again to former DCI Stuart Gibbon for assistance with all matters police-related, and to Graham Bartlett for last-minute queries.

For guidance on coma-related procedures and head trauma, thanks to Professor Karim Brohi at Queen Mary, University of London, and Eliot North, fellow poet, GP, and medical advisor extraordinaire.

For help with climbing matters, my thanks to Andy Fitzpatrick. For help with Minecraft and other gaming matters, thanks to Kelvin MacGregor and Vik Bennett.

Thank you Gemma Davies and Helen Rutherford for advising on legal procedures

— my court scenes ended up on the cutting floor but they made the story all the richer.

All deviations from fact in the pursuit of good storytelling are my fault entirely.

Huge thanks to my fabulous colleagues at the University of Glasgow, especially Colin Herd, Elizabeth Reeder, Zoe Strachan, and Louise Welsh, and to the University for granting me a sabbatical right when I needed it most.

Thank you Max Richter for your beautiful music which provided the emotional stimulus needed to craft the layers of this story.

As always, my deepest love and gratitude to my children, Melody, Phoenix, Summer, and Willow, and to my husband Jared, not only for being an excellent human being but also a school run champ and an ace at remembering packed lunches, for remaining good humoured when I researched Mont Blanc so heavily that I temporarily ceased to function in the real world, and especially for brilliant feedback as I was shaping the plot. I love you so much.

We do hope that you have enjoyed reading this large print book.

Did you know that all of our titles are available for purchase?

We publish a wide range of high quality large print books including:
Romances, Mysteries, Classics
General Fiction
Non Fiction and Westerns

Special interest titles available in large print are:
The Little Oxford Dictionary
Music Book
Song Book
Hymn Book
Service Book

Also available from us courtesy of Oxford University Press:
Young Readers' Dictionary
(large print edition)
Young Readers' Thesaurus
(large print edition)

For further information or a free brochure, please contact us at:
Ulverscroft Large Print Books Ltd.,
The Green, Bradgate Road, Anstey,
Leicester, LE7 7FU, England.
Tel: (00 44) 0116 236 4325
Fax: (00 44) 0116 234 0205

Other titles published by Ulverscroft:

I KNOW MY NAME

C. J. Cooke

Komméno Island, Greece: A woman wakes up without any recollection as to why or how she got there. She has no way of leaving — and soon discovers that the island's handful of inhabitants, who nurse her back to health, each appear to be hiding something . . . Potter's Lane, London: Eloïse, the mother of a newborn and a toddler, vanishes into thin air. Her husband, Lochlan, is desperate to find her — but as the police look into the disappearance, it becomes clear that the marriage was not the perfect union it appeared. As Lochlan races to discover his wife's whereabouts, Eloïse enacts an investigation of her own. What both discover will place lives at risk and upend everything they thought they knew about their marriage, their past, and what lies in store for the future.

THE BANKER'S WIFE

Cristina Alger

Annabel's seemingly perfect expatriate life in Geneva is shattered when her husband Matthew's plane crashes in the Alps. Clues emerge that suggest his death may not have been as accidental as it seems, however, and as Annabel investigates, she puts herself in the crosshairs of formidable enemies, forced to question whether she ever really knew Matthew at all. Meanwhile, journalist Marina is investigating Swiss United, the bank where Matthew worked. She uncovers proof of a shocking financial scandal that implicates some of the world's most rich and powerful, and knows she must expose it — whatever the cost. Possessing evidence so explosive that someone is willing to kill to keep it hidden, the two women find themselves caught up in an international conspiracy. Yet the real threat might just lie closer to home . . .